THE IT GIRL

THE IT GIRL

WITHDRAWN

RUTH WARE

THORNDIKE PRESS
A part of Gale, a Cengage Company

GALE
A Cengage Company

LIBRARY OF CONGRESS CIP DATA ON FILE.
CATALOGUING IN PUBLICATION FOR THIS BOOK
IS AVAILABLE FROM THE LIBRARY OF CONGRESS.

ISBN-13: 978-1-4328-9962-2 (hardcover alk. paper)

Published in 2022 by arrangement with Gallery Books, a Division of Simon & Schuster, Inc.

Printed in Mexico
Print Number: 01   Print Year: 2022

To Meriel, the best kind of best friend

BEFORE

Afterwards, it was the door she would remember. *It was open,* she kept saying to the police. *I should have known something was wrong.*

She could have retraced every step of the walk back from the Hall: the gravel crunching beneath her feet of the path across Old Quad, under the Cherwell Arch, then the illegal shortcut through the darkness of the Fellows' Garden, her feet light on the dew-soaked forbidden lawn. Oxford didn't need KEEP OFF THE GRASS signs; that lawn had been the preserve of dons and fellows for more than two hundred years without needing to remind undergraduates of the fact.

Next, past the Master's lodgings and along the path that skirted round the New Quad (close on four hundred years old, but still a hundred years younger than the Old Quad).

Then up staircase VII, four flights of worn

stone steps, right up to the top, where she and April slept, on the left-hand side of the landing, opposite Dr. Myers's rooms.

Dr. Myers's door was closed, as it always was. But the other door, her door, was open. That was the last thing she remembered. She should have known something was wrong.

But she suspected nothing at all.

She knew what happened next only from what the others told her. Her screams. Hugh following her up the stairs, two at a time. April's limp body sprawled across the hearth rug in front of the fire, almost theatrically, in the photos she was shown afterwards.

But she could not remember it herself. It was as if her brain had blocked it out, shut down, like a memory glitch on a computer: *file corrupted* — and no amount of patient questioning from the police ever brought her closer to that actual moment of recognition.

Only sometimes, in the middle of the night, she wakes up with a picture in front of her eyes, a picture different from the grainy Polaroids of the police photographer, with their careful evidence markers and harsh floodlit lighting. In this picture the lamps are dim, and April's cheeks are still flushed with the last glimpse of life. And she sees herself running across the room, tripping over the rug to fall on her knees beside April's body, and then she hears the screams.

She is never sure if that picture is a memory or a nightmare — or perhaps a mix of both.

But whatever the truth, April is gone.

AFTER

"Seventeen pounds, ninety-eight pence," Hannah says to the woman standing in front of her, who nods without really paying attention and pushes her credit card across the counter. "Contactless okay?"

The woman doesn't answer immediately; she's trying to get her four-year-old to stop playing with the erasers in the stationery display, but when Hannah repeats the question she says, "Oh, sure."

Hannah holds the card against the machine until it beeps, and then hands the books across the counter along with the receipt. *The Gruffalo, The New Baby,* and *There's a House Inside My Mummy.* Baby brother or sister on the way? She catches the eye of the little girl playing with the stationery and gives her a conspiratorial smile. The girl stops in her tracks, and then all of a sudden, she smiles back. Hannah wants to ask her her name, but is aware that might be overstepping the line.

Instead she turns back to the customer.

"Would you like a bag? Or we have these gorgeous totes for two pounds." She gestures behind the counter at the stack of canvas bags, each stenciled with the pretty Tall Tales logo — a teetering stack of books spelling out the shop's name.

"No thanks," the woman says shortly. She stuffs the books into her shoulder bag, and, grabbing her daughter's hand, she pulls her out of the shop. A penguin-shaped eraser tumbles to the floor as they go. "Stop it," Hannah hears her say as they pass through the Victorian glass doors, setting the bell jangling. "I have had just about enough of you today."

Hannah watches them disappear up the street, the little girl wailing now, hanging from her mother's grip, and her hand goes to her belly. Just the shape of it is reassuring — hard and round and strangely alien, like she's swallowed a football.

The books in the parenting section use food metaphors. A peanut. A plum. A lemon. *This is like* The Very Hungry Caterpillar *of parenting,* Will said, mystified, when he read the first trimester chapter. This week's was a mango, if she remembers right. Or maybe a pomegranate. Will brought her an avocado when she got to sixteen weeks, as a kind of jokey present to mark the milestone, bringing it up to her in bed, cut in half with a spoon. Hannah only stared down at it, feeling the morning sickness that was supposed to have stopped, coil and roll in her gut, and then she pushed the plate away and ran to the loo.

"I'm sorry," she told Will when she got back. "It was a lovely thought — it was just —"

She couldn't finish. Even thinking about it made her feel nauseous. It wasn't just the smooth oiliness of it against her tongue, it was something else — something more visceral. The idea of eating her own baby.

"Coffee?" Robyn's voice cuts through her thoughts, and Hannah turns to where her colleague is standing at the other end of the counter.

"Sorry?"

"I said, d'you want a coffee? Or are you still off it?"

"No, no, I'm back on, I'm just trying not to overdo it. Maybe a decaf, if that's okay?"

Robyn nods and disappears up the other end of the shop, into the glorified cupboard they call the "staff room," and almost exactly as she goes out of sight, Hannah's phone vibrates in the back pocket of her jeans.

She keeps it on silent at work. Cathy, the owner of Tall Tales, is nice, and checking phones isn't forbidden, but it's distracting to have it going off during story time or while she's helping a customer.

Now, though, the shop is empty, and she pulls it out to see who's calling.

It's her mother.

Hannah frowns. This isn't usual. Jill isn't one for random calls — they speak about once a week, usually on Sunday mornings after her mother comes back from her swim at the lake. Jill rarely calls midweek, and never during the working day.

Hannah picks up.

"Hannah," her mum says straightaway, without preamble. "Can you talk?"

"Well, I'm at work, so I'll have to go if a customer comes in, but I can chat quickly. Has something happened?"

"Yes. No, I mean —"

Her mother stops. Hannah feels alarm begin to creep over her. Her efficient, prepossessed mother, never lost for words — what can have happened?

"Are you okay? It's not — you're not . . . ill?"

"No!" She hears the short, relieved bark

of laughter that accompanies the word, but there is still that odd tension underneath. "No, nothing like that. It's just that . . . well, I take it you haven't seen the news?"

"What news? I've been at work all day."

"News about . . . John Neville."

Hannah's stomach drops.

The sickness has been slowly getting better for the last few weeks. Now, with a lurch, the nausea is back. She clamps her mouth shut, breathing hard through her nose, holding on to the shop counter with her free hand as if it can anchor her.

"I'm sorry," her mother says into the silence. "I didn't want to ambush you at work, but it just came up on my Google Alerts, and I was worried someone from Pelham would call you, or you'd get doorstepped by the *Mail.* I thought . . ." Hannah hears her swallow. "I thought it would be better having it come from me."

"What?" Hannah's jaw is clenched as if that can stop the sickness, and she swallows back the water suddenly pooling behind her teeth. "Have *what* come from you?"

"He's dead."

"Oh." It's the strangest feeling. A rush of relief, and then a kind of hollowness. "How?"

"Heart attack in prison." Jill's voice is

gentle, as if she is trying to soften the news.

"Oh," Hannah says again. She gropes her way to the stool behind the counter, the one they use for quiet periods, stickering the books. She puts her hand over her stomach, as if protecting herself from a blow that's already landed. The words do not come. The only thing she can do is repeat herself. "Oh."

"Are you okay?"

"Yes. Sure." Hannah's voice sounds flat in her own ears, and as if it's coming from a long way off. "Yes, why wouldn't I be?"

"Well . . ." She can tell her mother is choosing her words carefully. "It's a big thing. A milestone."

A milestone. Maybe it's that word, coming out of her mother's mouth, just after she was recalling her conversation with Will, but suddenly she cannot do this anymore. She fights the urge to sob, to run, to leave the shop in the middle of her shift.

"I'm sorry," she mutters into the phone. "I'm really sorry, Mum, I've got to —"

She can't think what to say.

"I've got a customer," she manages at last.

She hangs up. The silence of the empty shop closes around her.

BEFORE

The parking spaces on Pelham Street were overflowing, so Hannah's mother paused on a double yellow line on the High Street while Hannah scrambled out with the larger of her cases and her mother's promise to come and find her when she'd parked the car. As Hannah stood there, watching the beat-up Mini drive away, she had the strangest feeling — as though, in stepping out of the car, she had sloughed off her old identity like a second skin, leaving a sharper, fresher, less worn version of herself to face the world — a version prickling with newness. As she turned around to gaze up at the crest above the carved stone arch, she felt the cool October wind lift her hair and brush against the back of her neck, and she shivered with a heady mix of nerves and excitement.

This was it. The culmination of all her hopes, dreams, and meticulously plotted revision strategies. One of the oldest and most prestigious of colleges in one of the oldest and most prestigious centers of learning in all the world — Oxford University's famous Pelham College. And now, her new home for the next three years.

The huge oak door in front of her was open, unlike on the day she had come for her interview, when she'd had to knock at the medieval grilled door-within-a-door, waiting for the porter to peer out at her like something out of Monty Python. Now she dragged her case through the arched passage, past the Porters' Lodge, to a table under a gazebo where older students were handing out folders of information and directing freshers.

"Hi," Hannah said as she drew closer, her case grinding on the graveled path. "Hi, my name's Hannah Jones. Can you tell me where I should go?"

"Of course!" the girl behind the table said brightly. She had long, shiny blond hair, and her accent was crisp as cut glass. "Welcome to Pelham! So, you'll need to get your keys and accommodation details from the Porters' Lodge first of all." She pointed back at the arch Hannah had just passed through. "Have you got your Bod card yet? You'll need that for pretty much everything from paying for meals through to checking out library books."

Hannah shook her head.

"No, but I've registered for it."

"So, you pick it up from Cloisters II, but you can do that anytime today. You probably want to drop your case off first. Oh, and don't forget the Freshers' Fair, and the new joiners' Meet and Greet!" She held out a sheaf of flyers, and Hannah took them awkwardly, holding the slippery papers under her free arm.

"Thanks," Hannah said. And then, because there didn't seem to be much else to say, she turned and dragged her case back the way she had come, to the Porters' Lodge.

She hadn't been inside the lodge on the day of her interview — the porter had come out to let her in — and now she saw that it was a little wood-paneled room almost like a post office, with two windows overlooking the quad and the arched entrance passageway, a counter, and rows and rows of pigeonholes neatly marked with names. The thought that one of them was presumably hers gave her a curious feeling. A kind of . . . belonging?

She bumped her case up the steps and waited as the porter dealt with the boy in front of her, or rather, with his parents. The boy's mother had a lot of questions about Wi-Fi access and shower arrangements, but at last they were done, and Hannah found herself standing at the counter, wishing her own mother would hurry up and park the car. She felt she could use the backup.

"Um, hi," she said. Her stomach was fluttering with nerves, but she tried to keep her voice steady. She was an adult now. A Pelham College student. She was here by right with nothing to feel nervous about. "My name is Hannah. Hannah Jones. Can you tell me where I should go?"

"Hannah Jones . . ." The porter was a round, jocular-looking man with a fluffy white beard and the air of an off-duty Father Christmas. He perched a set of spectacles on his nose and began peering down a long, printed list of names. "Hannah Jones . . . Hannah Jones . . . Ah, yes, here we are. You're in New Quad, staircase seven, room five. That's a set, that is. Very nice."

A set? Hannah wasn't sure if she was supposed to know what that meant, but the porter was still talking, and her opportunity for asking had passed.

"Now, you'll want to head through that arch there." He pointed through the mul-

19

lioned window at a tall arch on the other side of the square of velvety grass. "Turn left through the Fellows' Garden — mind you don't tread on the grass — past the Master's lodgings, and staircase seven is the opposite side of New Quad. Here's a map. Free of charge for you, my dear."

He slapped a shiny folded leaflet onto the wooden countertop.

"Thanks," Hannah said. She picked up the plan, put it into her jeans pocket, and then remembered. "Oh, my mother might turn up soon. She had to park the car. Could you tell her where I've gone if she comes in here?"

"Hannah Jones's mum," the man said ruminatively. "That I can do. John," he called over his shoulder to a man sorting post behind him, "if I'm on my lunch, if Hannah Jones's mum comes, she's in seven, five, New Quad."

"Right you are," the man standing behind him said. Then he turned and looked at Hannah. He was a big man, probably six foot, and younger than his colleague, with dark hair and a face that looked both pale and sweaty, even though he wasn't doing anything remotely physical. His voice was oddly out of proportion with the rest of him — high and reedy — and the contrast made

Hannah want to laugh nervously.

"Well, thanks," she said, and turned to go. She was almost at the door when the second man called after her, his voice abrupt and slightly accusatory.

"Hold your horses, young lady!"

Hannah turned back, feeling her heart quicken as if she'd done something wrong.

The man came out from behind the counter, moving ponderously, and then stopped in front of her. There was something in his hand, and now he held it out to her, dangling whatever it was like a trophy.

It was a set of keys.

"Oh." Hannah felt foolish. She gave a short laugh. "Thanks."

She held out her hand, but for a moment, the man didn't let go. He just stood there, the keys dangling above her palm. Then he opened his grip and let them fall, and she shoved them into her pocket and turned away.

VII, said the writing painted above the stairwell, and Hannah, looking down at the plan in her hand, and then up at the stone steps in front of her, had to assume this was the right place. She cast a glance over her shoulder — not so much because she doubted the map, but more for the pleasure

21

of taking it all in: the pristine green square of manicured lawn, the honey-colored stone, the mullioned windows. With the sun shining and puffs of white autumnal clouds in the sky, the view had an almost unreal beauty, and Hannah had the strangest feeling that she had stepped inside the pages of one of the books in her suitcase — *Brideshead Revisited,* maybe. *Gaudy Night. His Dark Materials.* A storybook world.

She was smiling as she pulled her case beneath the archway into staircase 7, but bumping the case up the stairs wasn't easy, and her smile had faded by the first landing. By the time she reached the second she was hot, breathless, and the fairy-tale feeling was wearing off fast.

4 — H. CLAYTON read a neat little notice on the left-hand door, and opposite 3 — P. BURNES-WALLACE. The middle door was ajar, and as Hannah stood there, catching her breath, it opened to reveal a very small kitchen containing two boys, one bent over an electric hob, the other holding a cup of tea and staring at her with an expression that was probably only curious but came across more than a little hostile.

"H-hi," Hannah said, rather diffidently, but the boy only gave her a nod and edged past to the door marked P. BURNES-

WALLACE. What had the porter said? Room 5? One more floor still to go, then.

Gritting her teeth, Hannah yanked her case up the last flight onto the top floor, where two doors stood opposite each other — one ajar. 6 — DR. MYERS said the one to her right, which was shut. The open one was, by process of elimination, presumably her own, and Hannah stepped inside.

"Heeey . . ." The girl sprawled across the sofa barely looked up from her phone as Hannah entered. She was wearing a short broderie-anglaise dress that revealed long tanned legs hooked over the arm of the couch, one sandal hanging from pedicured toes. She appeared to be scrolling through some kind of photo app on her phone. "You must be Hannah."

"I . . . am?" Hannah said uncertainly, her voice rising at the end of the sentence in a way that made her words sound like a question, even though they weren't. She looked around the room. It seemed to be a sitting room, but with piles of the fanciest luggage Hannah had ever seen, stacked up by the doorway. There were hat boxes, hanging bags, a huge Selfridges tote filled with velvet cushions, and what looked like a real Louis Vuitton trunk with a giant brass lock. The pile dwarfed her own modest luggage —

even when you took into account the suit-case her mother would be bringing up from the car. "Who are you?"

"April." The girl put down her phone and stood up. She was middle height and slim, with cropped honey-blond hair that hugged the shape of her skull and finely arched eyebrows that gave her a look somewhere between amusement and disdain. There was something otherworldly about her — some indefinable quality Hannah could not put her finger on. She felt almost as if she had seen her somewhere before . . . or watched her in a film. She had the kind of beauty that hurt your eyes if you looked at her for too long, but made it hard to tear your gaze away. It was, Hannah realized, as if a differ-ent kind of light were shining on her than on the rest of the room.

"April Clarke-Cliveden," the girl added helpfully when Hannah did not immediately reply, as if that name should mean some-thing.

"But I thought —" Hannah said, and then broke off, turning uncertainly back to the door to check the name tag. Sure enough, there it was: 5 — H. JONES. And then, below that, A. CLARKE-CLIVEDEN.

Hannah frowned.

"Are we . . . roommates?"

It seemed unlikely. One of the points stressed in the Pelham College brochure had been the fact that there was virtually no shared accommodation. No double rooms. Not even any flats until the second year. A lot of shared bathrooms, sure, unless you were in the modern wing, but as far as sleeping went, the prospectus had made it sound like everyone had their own space.

"Kinda," April said. She gave a yawn like a cat and stretched luxuriantly. "I mean, not a bedroom — there's no way I'd have accepted that. Just a sitting room." She waved her hand around the modest space, making Hannah feel like she, April, was the gracious hostess, and Hannah the interloper. The thought gave Hannah a prickle of annoyance, but she pushed it down and looked around the room. Aside from April's stack of luggage, the furnishings were sparse and institutional — a rather worn sofa, a coffee table, and a sideboard — but it was clean and bright, with a beautiful stone fireplace. "Nice to have somewhere to hang out, right? Your room's through there." She nodded at a door to the right of the window. "Mine's the door opposite. I'm afraid I picked the bigger one. First come, first served, and all that."

She gave a wink that showed a deep, soft

dimple in one cheek.

"Fair enough," Hannah said. There was no point in arguing the fact. By the looks of it, the girl had already unpacked. Instead she lugged her suitcase across the rug, the wheels rucking it into ridges, towards the door April had indicated.

After April's remarks, she was expecting something small, poky even, but it was larger than her room at home, with another carved stone fireplace and a mullioned window with leaded glass, casting diamond-patterned light onto the polished oak boards.

"Wow, this is pretty cool," she said, and then wanted to kick herself for sounding so transparently impressed in the face of April's sophistication.

Still, she could admit it privately to herself: it *was* pretty cool. How many students had this room seen over the four hundred years since it was built? Had they gone on to be peers and politicians, Nobel Prize winners and authors? It was dizzying, like looking down the wrong end of a telescope, only instead of looking outward, at the end of the line she could see herself, infinitely small.

"Yeah, it's okay, isn't it?" April said. She came and stood in the doorway, one hand against the doorjamb, the other resting on her jutting hip. With the low evening light streaming through the thin material of her white dress, silhouetting her shape and turning her pixie hair into a white halo, she looked like an image off a film poster.

"What's yours like?" Hannah asked, and April shrugged.

"Pretty similar. Want to come and have a look?"

"Sure."

Hannah set down her case and followed April across the living room to the opposite door.

Inside, her first impression was that it was *not* pretty similar at all. Aside from the fact that it was slightly larger, the only things that were the same were the metal bedstead and the fireplace. Every other stick of furniture was different — from the kilim rugs, to the fancy ergonomic desk chair, to the richly upholstered loveseat in the corner.

A tall, burly man in a suit was unpacking clothes into a tall wardrobe. He didn't look up as they entered.

"Hi," Hannah said politely. She put on her best meet-the-parents voice. "You must be April's dad. I'm Hannah."

April gave a shout of laughter at that.

"Ha! You must be kidding. This is Harry.

He works for my parents."

"Pleased to meet you," the man said over his shoulder. Then he slid the last drawer shut and turned around. "I think that's it, April. Anything else I can help with?"

"No, that's fine. Thank you, Harry."

"I'll take the boxes, want me to leave the trunk?"

"No, don't worry. I won't have anywhere to store it."

"Sure," Harry said. "Have fun. There's a little goodbye present from your dad on the windowsill. Nice to meet you, Hannah," he said, then turned, picked up a pile of empty bags and boxes by the door, and left. The door swung shut, and April kicked off her shoes and threw herself onto the newly made bed, sinking deep into the soft feathered duvet.

"So this is it. Real life."

"Real life," Hannah echoed. It wasn't true, though. Sitting here, in a centuries-old center of learning, surrounded by April's rich, beautiful things, breathing in the strange heavy scent of some expensive perfume, she had never felt more unreal. She wondered what her mum — presumably still circling Oxford looking for a parking space — would make of all this.

"Better see what he's left me, I guess,"

April said. "The box isn't Tiffany's, which is a bad start."

She swung her legs off the bed and went to the window, where a tall gift box stood on the stone sill. A card was poking out of a gap at the top of the box.

" 'Start your Oxford life the right way. Love, Daddy.' Well, he signed it himself at least. One up from my birthday card, which was in his secretary's writing."

Digging her nails into the lid, she pried it open and then began to laugh.

"Oh God, just when I think he barely knows my middle name, he proves me wrong." She held up a bottle of champagne and two glasses. "Drink, Hannah Jones?"

"Um, sure," Hannah said. In truth, she didn't really like champagne — the few times she'd had it, at weddings and her mum's fiftieth, it had given her a headache. But there was no way she was going to refuse such a perfect moment. Maybe Dodsworth Hannah didn't like champagne. But Pelham College Hannah was different.

She watched as April popped the cork with a practiced expertise and poured out two foaming glasses.

"Well, it's not chilled, but it's Dom Pérignon at least," April said, handing over a flute. "What shall we drink to? How about . . . to Oxford." She held out her glass.

"To Oxford," Hannah echoed. She clinked her glass against April's and then put it to her lips. The warm, fizzing champagne frothed in her mouth, the bubbles expanding on her tongue and the alcohol tickling at the back of her nose and throat. She began to feel a little light-headed — though whether that was the champagne, or the fact that they had driven through lunch, or just . . . *this,* she could not have said. "And to Pelham."

"And to us," April said. She threw back her head and drained the glass in four long gulps. Then she refilled, looked at Hannah, and smiled, a wide, wicked smile that shot that deep, beguiling dimple into each soft cheek. "Yes, here's to us, Hannah Jones. I think we're going to have a pretty majestic time here, don't you?"

AFTER

As Hannah puts the phone down, she feels the quiet of the shop close around her like a cocoon. She would never tell Cathy, but these times are the reason she came to work at Tall Tales — not the Saturday hustle and bustle of customers, or the August rush of tourists for the festival, but the quiet mid-week lulls when she is — not alone, exactly, for you're never alone in a room filled with a thousand books. But when she is alone with the books.

Christie. The Brontës. Sayers. Mitford. Dickens. These are the people who got her through the years after April's death. She escaped the stares and sympathy of real life, the terrifying unpredictability of the internet, the horrors of a reality where you could be ambushed at any moment by a reporter or a curious stranger, or by the death of your best friend — into a world where everything was ordered. In books, a bad thing might happen on page 207, that was true. But it would *always* happen on page 207, no matter what. And when you reread, you could see it coming, watch out for the signs, prepare yourself.

Now she listens to the gentle spatter of the Edinburgh rain on the bow window at her back, the *tick, tick* of old floorboards creaking as the heating pipes come on. She feels the silent sympathy of the books. For a moment she has a visceral longing to pick up one of them, an old favorite perhaps, a novel she knows practically by heart — and sink into the pile of beanbags in the children's section, shutting out the world.

But she can't. She is on duty. And besides, she's not alone. Not really. She can see Robyn now, edging her way back through the maze of little Victorian rooms that make up Tall Tales, each crowded with display tables and dump bins.

"Beep beep! Robyn Grant, tea lady extraordinaire, coming through!" she says as she enters the front of the bookshop. She plonks the two cups cheerfully down on the counter, slopping hot brown liquid dangerously close to the card display. "The one with the spoon is yours. Are you —" She looks over at Hannah, and then stops, taken aback by something in Hannah's expression. "Hey, are you okay? You look really odd."

Hannah's heart sinks. Is it that obvious?

"I — I'm not sure," she says slowly. "I've had some weird news."

"Oh my God." Robyn's hand goes to her throat, and her eyes flick involuntarily to Hannah's stomach, and then back up to her face. "Not —"

"No!" Hannah says quickly. She tries to smile, though it feels false and stiff. "Nothing like that — it's just — just family stuff."

It's the closest she could come to the truth on the spur of the moment, but she wishes, as soon as the final words leave her mouth, that she had not chosen them. John Neville is *not* family. She doesn't want him or his memory anywhere near her family.

"Do you need to go?" Robyn says. She looks at her watch and then at the empty shop. "It's nearly five. I doubt we'll get a rush now. I can handle anything that comes up."

"No," Hannah says reflexively. She shouldn't need to leave — after all, what's really changed? Nothing. But at the same time, the thought of trying to stand here, smiling at customers like nothing has happened, with the memories boiling and churning inside her . . .

"Go," Robyn says, making up her mind. "Honestly, just go. I'll explain to Cathy if she comes in, but she won't mind."

"Really?" Hannah asks, and Robyn nods firmly. Hannah stands up, picks up her phone, feeling a rush of guilt and gratitude. She finds Robyn irritating sometimes — her relentless Girl Guide–ish cheerfulness, her habit of telling customers "No, *you* have a great day!" over and over again. But now there's something immensely comforting about her solid, unflappable kindness.

"Thank you so much, Robyn. I'll return the favor, I promise."

"Hey, no thanks needed," Robyn says. She smiles, pats Hannah on her arm, but Hannah can see the concern in her eyes beneath the friendly smile, and she feels Robyn's gaze on her as she walks slowly back to the staff room to gather up her things.

When she leaves the shop the rain has stopped, and it's a damp clear autumn afternoon, so like the day she first turned up at Pelham that for an instant the links to the past feel almost sickeningly real. As she stops at the traffic lights, waiting for the green man, she has the strangest sensation — that at any moment she might see April walking casually through the crowd, that lazy mocking smile on her lips and the deep dimples coming and going in her cheeks. For a second Hannah has to steady herself on a lamppost, the past is so real, so close. She feels an unassuageable yearning for it to be true — for that tall blond girl hurrying through the crowd with the light behind her to be April — brilliant, beautiful, *alive*. How would she greet her? Would she hug her? Slap her? Cry?

Hannah does not know. Maybe all of them.

She is heading through the crowds of tourists towards the bus stop for her usual number 24 back to Stockbridge, eager to get home in time to get supper on, put up her increasingly weary feet, watch some trashy TV.

But as she nears the stand and her pace doesn't slow, she realizes that she is not going to stop, that the thought of spending twenty minutes trapped in a stuffy bus in the halting city traffic appalls her. She needs to walk. Only the pavement beneath her feet will help her pace off this sense of unease, order her thoughts before she has to face Will. And besides, what is there for her at home except an empty flat and a waiting laptop, with all the sickly glittering allure of the Google searches she knows she will perform as soon as she's back?

For now, though, she'll allow herself just one — just to make it real, in the same way she didn't quite believe the child in her belly was real until she saw the images on the screen, heard the strange, subterranean whoosh and echo of its heart.

In the shadow of the castle she stops in a doorway and pulls out her phone. Then she opens up an incognito browser tab, and types the words into Google: *John Neville BBC News.* She doesn't need the last part, but she's learned not to put anything as unfettered as just his name into search engines — the sites that come up are full of gross images, wild speculation, defamatory statements about her and Will that she has neither the time nor the resources to fight.

At least the BBC can be relied upon to stick mainly to the facts.

And there it is — the top result.

BREAKING: PELHAM COLLEGE KILLER
JOHN NEVILLE DIES IN PRISON

The shock is like ice water on her skin, but she steels herself and clicks through.

John Neville, better known as the Pelham Strangler, has died in prison aged 63, prison authorities confirmed earlier today.

Neville, who was convicted in 2012 of the killing of college student April Clarke-Cliveden, died in the early hours of this morning. A prison spokesperson said that he had suffered a massive heart attack, and was pronounced dead on arrival at Mersey Hospital.

Neville's lawyer, Clive Merritt, said that his client was in the process of preparing a fresh appeal when he died. "He went to his grave protesting his innocence," Merritt told the BBC. "It's a huge injustice that his chance of overturning his conviction dies with him."

The Clarke-Cliveden family were unavailable for comment.

Hannah's hands are trembling. It's been so long since she voluntarily sought out news of Neville that she'd forgotten how it feels to be confronted with his name, with the memories of April, and worst of all with their pictures. There are only a few shots out there of Neville — the one used most is his college ID, a glowering image like a police mug shot, where he stares uncompromisingly out of the screen at the viewer, his gaze discomfitingly direct. Seeing his face is enough of a jolt, but the pieces Hannah really hates are the ones that focus on April — lissome social media snaps of her sprawled in punts, draped over other students, their faces pixelated to protect a privacy long since ripped away from her.

Worst of all are the shots of her dead body.

Those pictures aren't supposed to be out there, but of course they are. You can find anything on the internet, and before Hannah learned to stop searching, long before she figured out how to use incognito tabs, Google's algorithm identified her as someone with an interest in the Pelham Strangler, offering up clickbait articles on the subject with a sickening regularity.

Is this helpful? her phone would ask, and after she had clicked *Not Interested* enough times, stabbing the screen with such force that her shaking fingers felt the shock of impact long after she had put the phone away, eventually it got the message and stopped showing her the links. But even now, occasionally one will slip through, prompted by some inscrutable inner quirk deep in the workings of Google's news algorithm, and she will open up her phone to see April smiling out at her, with that clear direct gaze that still stabs her to the heart, even ten years on. And every now and again someone will track her down, and an email will ping, unsolicited, into her inbox. *Are you the Hannah Jones who was involved with the April Clarke-Cliveden murder? I'm writing a piece / a college essay / a psychological profile / an article on John Neville's appeal.*

At first she replied, angrily, using words like *morbid* and *vulture.* Then, when she'd learned that only made them keep trying or include her furious emails in their article as attributed quotes, she changed tack. *No. My name is Hannah de Chastaigne. I can't help you.*

But that was a mistake too. It wasn't just that it felt like a betrayal of April. For the researchers to have gotten this far, to have tracked down her email address, they knew. They knew who Will was, and they knew who she was, and the fact that she had taken Will's name on marriage did nothing to obscure her tracks.

"Why don't you just ignore them?" Will asked, baffled, when she told him about them. "That's what I do."

And of course he was right. Now she simply doesn't reply. But still, she can't quite bring herself to delete them. So they sit there, in a special folder buried deep at the bottom of her inbox. It's titled Requests. Just that. And one day, she keeps promising herself, one day when it's all over, she will erase the whole lot.

But somehow that day has never quite come.

Now she's wondering if it ever will.

She is about to shut down the screen when she looks, for the first time, at the photograph accompanying the article. It's not one of April. It's Neville. But it's a shot she's never seen before — not the hatchet-faced ID card she knows so well, nor the snatched paparazzi snap of him sticking two fingers up at reporters outside court. No, this one must have been taken much later, at one of his many appeals, probably quite a recent one. He looks old, and more than that, he looks *frail.* He has lost weight, and although it's not possible that he's lost height, he looks so far removed from the towering figure Hannah remembers that it's hard to believe they are the same person. He's dressed in a prison uniform that seems to hang off his gaunt frame, and he is staring at the camera with a haunted, hunted expression that seems to suck the viewer into his nightmare.

"Excuse me." The terse voice comes from behind her and she jumps, realizing that she has ground to a halt in the middle of King's Stables underpass, and a woman is trying to get past.

"I'm — I'm sorry," she stammers, shutting down the phone with hands that aren't quite steady and shoving it into her pocket as though it has been contaminated by the image on the screen. "Sorry."

The woman pushes past with a shake of her head, and Hannah starts for home. But even as she comes out of the dark underpass, into the autumn sunlight, she can still feel it — still feel his eyes upon her, that dark, hunted gaze, like he is beseeching her for something — she just doesn't know what.

It's quite dark by the time Hannah finally turns into Stockbridge Mews, her feet sore with walking, and she has to search in her handbag for the keys, cursing the fact that no one has replaced the burned-out bulb above the shared front door.

But at last she is inside, up the stairs, and the door of their flat is closed behind her.

For a long time she just stands there, her back against the door, feeling the silence of the flat all around her. She is home before Will, and she's glad — glad of this moment to just stand there in the cool, quiet welcome of their little flat, letting it wash over her.

She should put on the kettle, take off her shoes, turn on the lights. But she does none of these things. Instead she just goes through to the living room, slumps into an armchair, and sits, trying to come to terms with what has just happened.

She is still sitting there when she hears Will's bike draw up outside, its throaty roar reverberating off the other houses in the narrow mews. He kills the engine, and a few moments later she hears his key in the downstairs lock and the noise of him coming up the stairs.

As he opens the front door she knows she should get up, say something, but she can't. She just doesn't have the energy.

She hears him dump his bag in the hallway stand, come down the corridor, hissing some silly pop song between his teeth, flick on the lights — and then stop.

"Hannah?"

He's standing in front of her, blinking, trying to make sense of her being here, alone in the dark.

"Han! What are you — is everything okay?"

Hannah swallows, trying to find the words, but the only one that comes out is a cracked "No."

Will's face changes at that. He falls to his

knees in front of her, his face suddenly frightened, his hands on hers, holding her.

"Han, it's not — it isn't — has something happened? Is it the baby?"

"No!" It comes quickly this time, as she suddenly understands his concern. "Oh my God, no, nothing like that." She swallows, forcing out the words. "Will — it's — it's John Neville. He's dead."

It's unintentionally brutal — harsher even than the way her mother told her — but she's too shaken and broken to figure out a better way of conveying the news.

Will says nothing, but he lets his hands drop, and his face for a second goes unguardedly, heartbreakingly vulnerable — before he closes in on himself. He stands, moves over to the bay window, and leans against the shutters, looking out into the darkness of the mews. She can see his face only in profile, pale against his dark hair and the blackness of the glass behind him.

She's always found him hard to read in moments like this — he's generous with his joys, but when he's in pain or afraid, he holds his emotions close to his chest, as if he can't bear being seen to be hurting — a legacy, she supposes, of a military father and a boarding education at a school where showing emotion was for sissies and crybabies. If it weren't for that split second when he let his defenses drop, she would have thought he hadn't heard what she said. Now she's not sure what's going on underneath his silence, behind the polite, neutral mask of his face.

"Will?" she says at last. "Say something."

He turns and looks at her, as if he has been very far away.

"Good."

It's just that one word, but there's a brutality in his voice that she's never heard before, and it shocks her.

"Now," he says. "What's for supper?"

BEFORE

"Oh. My. God." April's voice was theatrically drawling, more than a touch of Janice from *Friends,* Hannah thought as she followed her down the narrow passage between the long dining tables than ran the length of the hall. It was the first time Hannah had set foot in the Great Hall as an actual Pelham student, and she felt a prickle of wonder as she looked around her at the ancient beams soaring high overhead, and the dark oak-paneled walls, dotted with oil paintings of former Masters. She might have felt overwhelmed by it all, but it was hard to feel intimidated with April beside her, bitching about the limited menu and poor acoustics. Now, April set down her tray on one of the long, crowded refectory tables and put her hands on her hips. "Will de Chastaigne, as I live and breathe."

One of the students sitting at the long oak bench turned, his dark hair falling in his eyes, and Hannah found her heart missing a beat. The glass of water on her dinner tray slid an inch to the left and she hastily righted it.

"April!" He stood up, swinging one long leg easily over the bench, and the two embraced in a sort of part hug, part continental kiss that was so deeply un-Dodsworth that Hannah felt more than ever as if she had landed on another planet. "Good to see you! I had no idea you were coming here."

"Well, that's Liv for you. Doesn't tell people anything! How is she? I haven't seen her since exams."

"Oh . . ." The boy's tanned face suddenly flushed, a streak of color high on his cheekbones. "We, well, we broke up. My fault, if I'm being honest. Sorry."

"Don't apologize," April purred. She ran a hand down the boy's arm, squeezing his biceps in a way that was just the right side of teasing. "Another eligible man on the scene is nothing to be sorry about."

Behind her, Hannah shifted. The tray she was holding was becoming uncomfortably heavy and her arms were starting to ache. April must have heard the movement because she turned and gave a slightly theatrical double take, seeming to remember Hannah's presence for the first time since she'd

46

spoken to Will.

"God, where are my manners? Will, this is Hannah Jones, my roommate. She's studying Eng Lit. We've got a suite, don'tcha know, so I've got a feeling we'll be hosting aaaall the parties this term. Hannah, this is Will de Chastaigne. I went to school with his ex. Our boarding schools were . . . what would you call it?" She turned back to Will. "Twinned?"

"Something like that." A smile crinkled the tanned skin at the side of Will's mouth. Hannah found herself staring up at him. He had clear brown eyes, dark brows, and his nose had clearly been broken, maybe more than once. Hannah's mouth felt dry and she swallowed, trying to think what to say, but Will filled in the silence for her. "I went to Carne — all boys. So they paired us up for socials with April's school to try to ensure we didn't get to uni without having met a real live female."

"No danger of that with you, darling," April said. She took a swig of the chocolate milk on her tray, and then slid onto the bench beside Will without bothering to ask if she could. Will sat back down beside her.

"I was actually saving that seat, you know," he said to April, but conversationally, not as if he expected her to move. Hannah, still standing, hesitated. There was a space opposite — but only one. Maybe Will wanted it for his missing friend? She looked at April, seeking a cue, but April was tapping away on her phone.

Hannah bit her lip, half turned away, and then Will spoke.

"Hey, don't go, we'll make room."

Her heart flipped again. She smiled, trying not to look too pathetically grateful, as Will put his bag on the floor and nudged his neighbor up a few inches, making an extra space.

"Look, sit there." He indicated the space opposite. "Hugh can squeeze in next to me and April."

"Did you say . . . Hugh?" April's head came up from her phone at that. There was an odd expression on her face, surprise, even delight, but mixed with a kind of mischievousness that Hannah couldn't totally figure out. "Not . . . Hugh Bland?"

"The very same. Didn't you know he was applying here?"

"I knew he was trying for Oxford, but I had no idea he'd picked Pelham," April said. She put her phone down, and then a smile curved her lips as a tall, pale boy with heavy Stephen Hawking–style glasses came up to the table. "Well, well, well . . . speak of the devil."

"April!" the boy said, and then, all at once, he stumbled, tripping over his own feet so that his tray lurched out of his hands, the pasta crashing to the floor.

There was a moment's dead silence, every head in the place turned, and then one of the other boys at the table spoke up.

"Ey up, show's over, everyone. Move along now."

Hugh, though clearly mortified, laughed and gave a little self-conscious bow. His face was scarlet as he picked up his can of Coke and scooped up stray tortellini.

"Sorry. Such an ass." His voice was muffled, but plainly what Hannah's classmates would have called classic posh boy. "So sorry. Thank God it landed right way up. Mostly."

He slid into the seat beside Will with the ruined plate of pasta, his cheeks still flaming, and picked up a fork.

"Don't eat that, you idiot," April said a little scornfully. She stood, waving her arm at the counter. "Hey, could we get some help over here? And another plate of the tortellini?"

They all watched in silence as a member of the catering staff came across with a spare plate and a cloth to wipe up the spilled sauce.

"I'm so sorry," Hugh said again, this time to the caterer, who just nodded and walked off. Hugh looked miserable, and Hannah suddenly felt unbearably sorry for him.

"Do you all know each other?" she said to April and Will, more in an attempt to change the subject than because she was in doubt. April nodded, smiling, but it was Will who answered.

"Hugh and I go way back — we were at prep school together, and there's nothing that binds friends like a shit prep school, right, Hugh?"

"Right," Hugh said. The flush was fading from his cheeks, and he had his head down, bent over his food as if he was trying to avoid everyone's gaze. "Hugh Bland," he said to Hannah. "Medicine."

"Hugh and I are *very* good friends," April said with a kind of purr. She reached across and pinched Hugh's cheek, and the scarlet tide rose in his face again, this time reaching to his ears. There was a brittle silence.

"And what about you?" April said, with the air of breaking an awkward moment. She was speaking to the boy sitting next to Hannah, the one who had told everyone the show was over. He was a broad, stocky kid with Mediterranean coloring, wearing a Sheffield Wednesday football shirt.

"This is Ryan Coates," Will said. "He's doing Economics, same as me."

"A'right," Ryan said, grinning. His accent was straight-up Sheffield, and after so many posh southern voices, it sounded almost aggressively northern. Hannah felt a sudden shock of kinship — even though Dodsworth was about as far south as it was possible to get. But here was someone normal like her — someone not from the monied, private-school background that Will and April seemed to take for granted.

"We're all on the same floor in Cloade's," Will said.

Cloade's, Hannah knew from the prospectus, was the big modern wing at the back of the New Quad where most of the first-years had ended up. It was square and made of brutalist concrete, but the rooms were en suite and the heating actually worked. Still, Hannah couldn't help feeling secretly grateful that she and April had been allocated a picturesque old-style room. After all, wasn't this what she had come to Oxford for? She had wanted to walk in the footsteps of four hundred years of scholars — not on the carpet squares of the last few decades.

"Heard him playing the Stone Roses

through the wall." Ryan pointed his fork at Will. "Went over to introduce meself and it turned out we're ont same course. And he introduced me to this bloke." He nodded at Hugh.

"Will and I were at school together," Hugh said, and then flushed again. "Oh wait, duh, Will already told you that. Sorry. Such a thicko."

"Don't listen to him," Will said with an affectionate dig in his friend's ribs. "Hugh was the brainiest chap in our year."

Ryan spoke around a tortellini, his expression rather droll.

"Well, in't that the coincidence. I was the brainiest chap in *my* year. Looks like you and me have summat in common."

"We were *all* the brainiest in our year," said the girl next to Ryan, speaking for the first time. Her voice was deep, and rather brusque and impatient. "Isn't that the point? Isn't that why we're here?"

"And who're you?" Ryan said, looking her up and down. She had long dark hair, a serious, slightly equine face, black rectangular glasses, and she looked Ryan straight back in the eye with none of the diffidence Hannah would have felt at being appraised so baldly.

"Emily Lippman." The girl put a forkful

of pasta in her mouth, chewed deliberately, and then swallowed. "Mathematics. You can call me Emily Lippman."

"I like you, Emily Lippman," Ryan said with a broad grin, and Emily raised a single eyebrow.

"To which I'm supposed to say?"

"Whatever you like," Ryan said. "Nothing if you want." He was still grinning. Emily rolled her eyes.

"Anyway," April said lazily, "it's not true."

"What's not true?" Hugh asked.

"About being the cleverest in our year. I wasn't."

"How did you get in here, then?" Emily said. The remark should have sounded rude, but somehow, coming from her, it didn't. Just preternaturally direct.

"My natural charm, I suppose," April said, and she smiled, the deep, soft dimples showing in her golden cheeks. "Or maybe my dad's money."

There was a long silence, as if no one quite knew how to take this. Then Ryan gave a short, barking laugh as if April had told a joke.

"Well, good for you," Emily said. "On both counts." She shoved the last forkful of pasta into her mouth and stood up, brushing herself down. "Now. What the fuck does a woman have to do to get a drink around here?"

"We could go to that common room place," Ryan said. He stood too. Hannah saw that he was much taller than she had realized. "What did they call it, the JCB?"

"JCR," April said. Her lips curled in a smile that Hannah was beginning to recognize as quintessentially April — beguiling, and at the same time, just a little bit wicked. "Junior Common Room *if* you read the handbook, which you clearly didn't. And there's also a bar next to the Great Hall. But sod that. We're hardly commoners. And who needs a bar when you've got a totally majestic *suite* and a fridge full of champagne?"

She pushed her still-full plate of tortellini away, looked around the group of faces, and then pulled a room key out of her pocket, dangling it from one finger as she raised a fine dark eyebrow.

"Am I right?"

AFTER

The past hangs between them as Will makes supper, chopping aubergine and chorizo in a silence made somehow more oppressive by the chatter of the Radio 4 announcer. Hannah tries and fails to think of what to say, and in the end she retreats to the living room, where she pulls out her laptop and opens her emails.

She deleted the Gmail app from her phone in a panic after her mother's call came through, not wanting to be ambushed by notification pings on her walk home, and now she's more than a little afraid of what will be waiting for her, but she knows that leaving it would be worse. At bedtime, with nothing else to distract her, she will lie there wondering what's lurking in her inbox, until eventually she'll crack and log back in on her phone. And then whatever she finds — whatever new revelation, dangled lead, or fresh attempt to manipulate her into responding — will set her pulse spiking and her adrenaline pumping, driving the possibility of sleep so far away that she will be awake all night, nauseous with apprehension, refreshing and refreshing and googling April's name in a kind of sick terror.

She knows that's how it will go down, because it's what happened before. Daily, *more* than daily messages in the first few months and years after April's death. A constant, numbing flood of beseeching, badgering, beleaguering requests that left her shocked and bruised by the national obsession that April's death had triggered.

As the court case concluded, the requests slowed. First they came weekly, and then, as she and Will managed to slip beneath the surface of everyday life, camouflaging themselves in the reassuringly boring minutiae of accountancy courses, house buying, money worries, and all the other mundane clutter of daily existence, they became more and more sporadic.

Now she is contacted only rarely and almost never by phone, not since they got rid of the landline and Hannah changed her mobile number. It still happens, though — every time John Neville's name rears up in the press — every time there's an appeal by Neville's legal team, or someone publishes a book, or a new podcast is launched. And it's taken this long for her to learn avoidance is not the way to deal with it.

No, it's better to do it now, get it out of the way, allow herself to calm down before bed.

But to her surprise and relief, there are only three unread emails. One is from her mum, sent earlier this afternoon, with the subject line *Call me.* It precedes their phone call, so she deletes it.

The second is just an overdue notice from the library, and she marks it unread.

The third is from an email address she doesn't recognize, with the subject header *A question.*

Her heart rate is already accelerating even before she has clicked it, and the first line confirms her fears.

Dear Hannah, we've never met, but allow me to introduce myself. My name is Geraint Williams, and I'm a reporter with the Daily —

It's enough. She doesn't need to read any more. She takes off her glasses, letting the screen go fuzzy and unreadable, then clicks "Move to Requests" and watches the email disappear.

Afterwards, she sits there holding her glasses in one hand and her phone in the other, staring at the blank screen. Her fingers are suddenly ice-cold, and she pulls her jumper down over her hands to try to warm them. She can feel her pulse running sickeningly fast and shallow, and she wonders, in a kind of detached way, what the stress is doing to the baby. *They're very tough.* She hears her mother's voice in her head, reassuringly robust. *Women give birth in war zones, for goodness' sake.*

"Are you okay?"

The voice comes from behind her and she jumps, even as her conscious brain is registering Will's presence. He squeezes into the armchair beside her, puts his arms around her, and she shifts and settles into his lap.

"I'm sorry," he says quietly. "I didn't mean to go all stiff upper lip on you. I just — I needed to process it a bit."

She leans into his chest, feeling the muscles in his arms flex as he wraps himself around her. There's something about his strength and heft that's inexpressibly reassuring in a kind of unreasoning way. It shouldn't matter that Will is taller and broader and stronger than she is — she had gone far beyond fearing John Neville as a physical threat, even before her mother's call — but somehow it *does* matter, and his physical presence is more comforting than any number of soothing words.

She curls into him, her forehead on his chest, feeling his breath on her parting and the heat of him, warming her still-frozen fingers. As if reading her thoughts, he speaks.

"God, your hands are like ice. Come here."

He takes them in his and puts them firmly up under his shirt, shuddering for a moment as her cold fingers connect with the warm, naked skin over his ribs, but then relaxing into her touch as the first chill subsides.

"How are you always so hot?" she manages with a shaky laugh, and he rests his chin on the top of her head, stroking her hair with one hand.

"I don't know. Years of shit central heating at Carne, maybe. Oh, sweetheart. I'm really sorry this had to come now. I know how hard this is for you."

She nods, pressing her forehead to his collarbone, staring into the warm darkness of the hollow between their bodies.

He knows. Perhaps he is the only person who really does, who understands the complicated maelstrom of feelings Neville's death has stirred up.

Because on the surface, this should be good news. John Neville is gone — forever. And long term, it probably is for the best. But short term, this is going to mean a flurry of interest, a shattering of their hard-won illusion of normalcy, just when she and Will should be concentrating on the new life they are bringing into the world, not thinking about the one they both saw snuffed out. She remembers the days and months after April's death — that searing, relentless searchlight of media obsession — the feeling that something appalling had happened, and all she wanted was to hide in the shadows and rock back and forth as she tried to come to terms with what she had seen, but wherever she ran, whatever she did, that searchlight kept seeking her out. *Ms. Jones, a quick comment, please! Hannah, could we have an interview? Five minutes, I promise.*

For ten long years, ever since the trial, in fact, she's been hiding from that spotlight. For ten years April's death has been the first thing she thinks about when she wakes up, and the last thing at night. And she knows it's been that way for Will too — they have spent the whole of their relationship with the shadow of April's memory looming over them. But these last few months, with the baby and everything else, she has allowed herself . . . not to forget, exactly, because she could never do that. But to feel like April's death was no longer the defining part of her life. And although she and Will have never discussed it in so many words, she's pretty sure it's been the same for him.

Now, with Neville's death and the inevitable media flurry, it will be back to changing their numbers and screening their messages. Hannah will find herself looking twice at customers coming into the bookshop. At Carter and Price, the accountancy firm where Will is a junior partner, the new receptionist will be told what happened, instructed to ask a few more questions before routing calls and setting up appointments.

It's been hard for him too. Harder, in some ways, though he would never say so. But it's no coincidence that he followed her here, to Scotland, a country with its own legal system, its own newspapers, a place almost as far away from Oxford as it was possible to get without leaving the UK altogether. She remembers the gray September day eight years ago when he walked into the bookshop. She was helping a customer choose a birthday present, debating the merits of the new Michael Palin versus the latest Bill Bryson. Something, a noise or a movement behind her, had made Hannah turn, and there he was.

For a moment she had lost the power of speech. She had simply stood there, the customer rattling happily on about Rick Stein — while Hannah's heart beat and beat and beat with a kind of fierce joy.

Three months later they moved in together.

Two years later they were married.

It's strange — Will is the best thing that ever happened to her, and yet they are bound together by the worst events of her life. It shouldn't work. But it does. She would not have survived this without him, she knows that.

Now she lifts her head, looks him in the face, and runs her fingers down his cheek, trying to read his own feelings beneath his concern for her.

"Are you okay?"

"I'm fine," he says reflexively, and then, "I mean — not fine exactly." He's struggling, she can see that. It's been a bone of contention their whole relationship, his tendency to shut himself away from her, to pretend everything is fine just when he's closest to falling apart. The worse things are, the more stressed he is at work, the more worried he is about money, the less he says. *Talk to me!* It's been her cry for almost ten years, and he's still figuring out how to deal with the vulnerability of opening himself up when his entire childhood was about not showing weakness.

"I'm okay," he says at last. "Or I will be. When I've had time to process the news. But I've not had to deal with it in the same way you did. I didn't see —" He stops, begins again. "I haven't had to go through everything you did."

She nods. Because it's true. Yes, Will was there, and yes, April meant just as much to him, maybe even more. But he didn't see what Hannah saw that night. And he didn't have to spend the next weeks, months, even years going over and over and over what happened. First with the police. Then with the prosecution lawyers. And finally in court, in the witness box. But it didn't stop, even after the conviction. Because the fact is that the case against John Neville rested on *her* evidence — and that's something no one has ever allowed her to forget.

Will is speaking again now, his voice sounding softer and deeper than usual, with her head resting on his chest.

"Maybe . . . I mean, maybe in a way this

is for the best?"

Hannah doesn't speak at first. *Why now?* is what she's thinking. Why now, when they should be so happy, so wrapped up in each other and in the baby they have made. She shouldn't have to be dealing with retrospectives and newscast specials at all — but especially not now.

But then she thinks of the years stretching out ahead of them, filled with a never-ending parade of newspaper articles and appeals and requests for comment, and she knows Will is right. And yet . . . why doesn't this *feel* right?

"The BBC said he was preparing another appeal," she says. *Appeal.* The word feels sick with dread in her mouth. "I don't think I could have taken that. I just don't want all the renewed interest, but you're right. When this is over . . ."

She stops, almost too fearful to voice it.

Instead it's Will who says the words, his voice firm as he tightens his arms around her.

"When this is over, it'll really, finally be over."

And for the first time, Hannah allows herself to believe that it might be true.

Before

"Take it off, take it off!" April chanted, flashing a meaningful look around the rest of the group to get them to join in.

Hannah looked down at herself, and then at the cards in her hand.

It had been April's idea to play strip poker, and at first Hannah had felt fairly confident. She was actually a pretty good poker player, and in any case, she was wearing several layers, if you counted accessories. But whether it was bad luck or the amount of champagne she had drunk, she had been losing for several hands now, and she was down to removing either her jeans or her top. She tried to remember whether she had shaved her legs in the shower that morning, and couldn't. It would have to be her top. The thought gave her a weird feeling — halfway between a sickening thrill of nerves and a flutter of excitement. Was she really going to do this? Was she going to strip down to her bra in front of five people she'd only met that day?

"Take it off!" Ryan joined in, and then Emily. Hannah shot a look around the circle at the laughing, drunken faces. Only Hugh looked as uncomfortable as she felt. In fact, he had tried to get out of playing — making an excuse about the time and the fact that he was tired. April had been having none of it, however. *Shut up, Hugh. Nobody cares. You're playing, and that's that,* she had said. And Hugh, to Hannah's surprise, had sat back down, tension and anger emanating from every muscle.

Now he was hunched miserably between Will and Ryan, his arms wrapped self-consciously around his naked, bony ribs — and the only reason he was down to his jeans and not his underpants was because April had graciously allowed him to count each sock as a separate garment. Hannah again cursed the fact that she'd been wearing sandals.

"Hey . . ." Will said. He leaned forward, his black hair falling into his eyes in a way that made something deep inside Hannah twist with desire. He was bare-chested, his torso lean and sculpted in a way so unlike Hugh's that they might have been different species. She became aware that she was star-

66

ing, and forced her gaze up, to his face. He was smiling, but not in a mocking way. "Hey, don't let them bully you."

"Oh, bloody hell," Hannah said, but now she was laughing too, partly at herself, partly out of disbelief that she was really going to do this. But she *was* going to do it. Deep down she knew it. She could storm out, but only back to her own room, right next door to where they were all drinking — she would be able to hear their mocking laughter and the music from April's iPod through the wall. And she couldn't begin her three years at Pelham by establishing herself as a sore loser with no sense of fun.

But it wasn't just that. A part of her *wanted* this. She wanted to be as cool and daring and sexy as April, who sprawled across the circle from her with a wicked glint. She wanted to be brash, sardonic Emily sitting opposite, totally unfazed by the fact that she had lost her jumper, skirt, belt, and shoes, was down to a thigh-skimming shirt and not much else.

She wanted to be one of these people, she *was* one of these people, so she was just going to have to act like it.

"Take it off!" April called again, and with a sick feeling like she was jumping off a cliff, Hannah stood up, pulled off her top, and did an ironic twirl as the others whooped and applauded. Her cheeks were scarlet, her stomach was fluttering, and she wasn't sure whether to laugh or scowl, so she did both, crossing her arms defiantly over her chest as she took her place in the circle. She kept her gaze determinedly away from Will.

Ryan gave a long, piercing wolf whistle and flung his arm around Emily, who was sitting next to him.

"Here you go," he said, holding out the joint they'd been passing around. "You've earned it."

"She doesn't want that soggy disgusting thing," April said. Her eyes were wide and bright with laughter, and her face was as flushed as Hannah's — although not with embarrassment. She herself was down to a pleated satin skirt and her bra — but clearly not one that had been bought in a five-pack from M&S. It was a push-up in turquoise silk, embroidered with tiny scarlet and pink butterflies that made her tanned skin glow. "Have a drink, darling."

She held out the bottle. It was champagne, produced from a seemingly inexhaustible supply in a minifridge that certainly wasn't standard college equipment. The label was jeweled and art deco, and although Hannah knew nothing about champagne, she strongly suspected it must have been expensive. But it had been passed around the group for too long, and now it was warm and acid in her mouth, the flavor not improved by swigging directly from the bottle, as there were not enough glasses. Hannah shuddered, but she took a long gulp, feeling the fuzzy warmth of the alcohol filtering into her blood, and then she grinned and passed the bottle back to April.

"Come on, Hugh," April drawled, "you're up."

Hugh nodded and began to deal.

With the next hand April lost her skirt, taking it off with a shimmying strip-tease panache that revealed long, tanned legs and a very small turquoise thong, Will lost his jeans, but the following round Hannah realized with a sinking feeling that she was about to lose again.

The hand played out with agonizing slowness, but at the end of it, her prediction proved correct and her two fours lost comprehensively. As she scrambled out of her jeans she ran a surreptitious hand over her calves and was relieved to find them fairly smooth. In the dim light no one would be able to see any stubble. Still, when she sat back down, she folded her legs beneath herself just in case. She felt sick with nerves and excitement. She could not afford to lose again. Stripping to underwear was one thing, it wasn't that different from going swimming in the end, but getting actually properly naked . . . could she really do this? From the nervous frisson in the air she could tell she wasn't the only person having doubts. Hugh had his knees to his chest as if trying to hide his skinny frame and was looking frankly mortified. Emily was chewing her lip. And Will . . .

As if pulled by a magnet, her eyes flicked once again to Will. But this time he was already looking at her. Their eyes met with a jolt that sent a little electric prickle running over Hannah's skin, then she tore her gaze away, her cheeks flushed so hot that she was sure someone would notice.

April dealt out the next hand, going around the circle with tantalizing slowness, her eyes wide and dark with excitement. Some people took the cards one at a time. Hannah preferred not to. They were playing straight poker — just a simple five-card deal with no flop, and in that scenario it was hard not to give away what you were hoping for when you were waiting for the cards as they were dealt. Hugh was picking up his cards one by one, and from his body language it was obvious that he didn't have a good hand. Emily was harder to read. She picked up the cards singly, tucking them into her hand with a little double tap on each one. Ryan looked . . . smug. There was no other word for it. And as for Will — but here she was stumped. Will, like her, had left his cards on the floor.

April laid out the fifth card in each hand, and as the last one went down, Hannah scooped up the whole lot and surveyed them.

Almost immediately her stomach dropped, though she tried to keep her face bland and blank.

A pair of threes. Which was about as weak as it got.

"I'm out," Hugh said. He threw in his hand and took off his jeans — the forfeit for folding was one piece of clothing and he clearly didn't want to risk anyone raising the stakes while he still had a garment to lose. When he sat back down his cheeks were scarlet and Hannah shot him a sympathetic look.

April was dealer so was out of the running.

"I bet one garment," Emily said. She was still wearing her top and bra, and she tapped her cards on the floor, looking more than a little smug.

"One garment," Will said, and gave a grin that made Hannah's stomach flutter. He only had one garment to lose, so there was no possibility of him raising the stakes.

"Hannah?"

"One," Hannah said, but her mouth was thick and dry, and she had to take a gulp of champagne before repeating, more clearly. "One garment." There was no point in folding. If she did, she would have to take off her bra. And the rules were that the person with the weakest hand had to strip. Maybe, *maybe* Will was bluffing.

"Ryan?"

"Tw—" Ryan said wickedly, looking at Emily's shirt and his own jeans, and then he laughed. "Just kidding. One garment."

"Okay," April said, "let's see 'em, folks. Emily?"

"Three of a kind," Emily said. She laid them out with a kind of laconic triumph — three fives. It was a good hand. Better than Hannah's. "Beat that," she said to Ryan.

"Well, I hate to disappoint, but . . . flush," Ryan said. He gave Emily a flashing grin and laid out five diamonds.

"You fucker," Emily said equably, but she didn't look too worried. In strip poker it didn't really matter who won. What mattered was who lost. Only the loser would have to strip, and three fives was still a pretty good hand, particularly given she still had her top to lose.

It was down to Hannah and Will.

Hannah looked across the circle at him. He was leaning back against the legs of the armchair, long bare legs stretched out across the circle, his arms folded across his naked chest. He was smiling, and she knew that he must have a good hand, and that he could see the desperation in her eyes. She felt her heart thumping in her chest, so hard that when she looked down at her hand she could actually see the lace trim of her bra trembling. Could she do it? Was she really going to get naked in front of this room of complete strangers?

"Hannah?" April said, with that purring little note in her voice.

Hannah swallowed. She put down one three . . . then another . . .

And then Will let his cards drop, face-down.

"I'm out," he said with a wry smile. "I guess I'll be removing these." He looked down at his boxers, his expression comically dismayed. You could have heard a pin drop.

"Hokay." It was Emily who stood up, breaking the tension. "Well, that's quite enough of that as far as I'm concerned. I have no desire to see anyone's meat and two veg."

She stood up, stretching unselfconsciously so that her shirt rode up, exposing an unexpected flash of Bart Simpson underpants, and then reached for her leather miniskirt.

"What?" April said, sounding aggrieved. "You must be joking! It's barely even midnight."

"It's two a.m.," Emily said, waving her phone. "And I want to be conscious for the Master's induction speech tomorrow."

"Yeah," Ryan stood up too and pulled his football shirt on over his head. "I'm with her. Wanna walk me back to Cloade's?" he asked Emily, who shrugged but followed him to the door.

"Ugh, you're such party poopers," April grumbled. But she seemed to accept defeat and began gathering up the cards as Hugh started hunting around for his socks and phone.

"I guess I'll call it a day too," Hannah said, rather diffidently. She stood up and reached for her top, holding it against herself like a protective shield. "Night, everyone." April didn't respond, she just shrugged, rather sulkily.

It was Will who looked up. "Night, Hannah."

"Yes, good night, Hannah," Hugh said rather awkwardly. "And thank you, April, I had a great time."

April snorted at that.

"Like fuck you did. You looked like I was pulling out your nipple hairs one by one."

Hugh flushed, as if he didn't quite know what to say.

"Are you coming, Will?" he asked, after a short pause.

"In a sec," Will said. He was buckling his jeans. "You head over. I won't be long."

"Night, April," Hannah said. There was a slightly pleading note in her voice which she instantly despised but did not know how to change. She picked up the cards nearest her and held them out.

April took them. "Night," she said, rather crossly, shoving them into the pack, and Hannah turned and walked into her room.

As her bedroom door closed behind her, Hannah allowed herself a shuddering sigh of relief, thankful that she hadn't had to be the one to take a stand and incur April's wrath, and equally grateful that Emily had stepped in before someone lost their last layer.

Now, as she stood there, her head spinning a little from the champagne she had drunk, she had the strangest feeling — almost as if she were surveying herself from a distance, marveling at the fact that she — Hannah Jones — had found herself surrounded by these exotic, clever, glamorous creatures. For a moment she had a piercing flashback to Dodsworth — to the kids who hung around the off-license in the town square, trying to buy cider with fake IDs and smoking Marlboro Lights behind the bus station. Maybe there *were* kids at their school who drank champagne and played strip poker, but if they existed, they weren't part of the crowd Hannah hung around with. She had never been one of the girls who went to parties, applied mascara in the school bathroom, or had their boyfriends pick them up at the end of the day in a car. The closest Hannah had come to breaking the rules was deliberately failing to return a school library book she needed for her exams.

And now here she was. At one of the most sought-after colleges in Oxford. Surrounded by people she would barely have had the courage to say hello to, were it not for her luck in finding April.

As she stood there, peeling off her underwear and shoving her arms into the kimono she used as a makeshift dressing gown, she felt a sudden wash of . . . not gratitude, exactly. But a kind of wonder at the miracle of what had just happened. She was here. At Oxford. Sharing a room with a girl so infinitely cool and glamorous that she might have stepped out of the pages of a magazine.

She, Hannah, could reinvent herself here. Okay, she wasn't as spiky or witty as Emily, or as cheeky and sarcastic as Ryan. But she could be someone else. Someone new. Maybe . . . and here she swallowed, a shiver of longing running across her bare skin beneath the kimono. Maybe she could even be a girl that someone like Will would look twice at.

Will.

Will, who had sat across the circle from her, watching her, with that slow, lazy smile.

Will, who had stayed back at the end of the night, when he could have returned to Cloade's with his friend Hugh.

Will, who — and then Hannah paused, with a sudden, clear picture of the cards she had picked up at the end of the evening. She had turned them faceup at she passed them to April, and now she realized something— the cards weren't her hand. There had been five of them — a single ten, and four queens. Four of a kind.

Not just a good hand, but the winning one.

Not her hand. But Will's.

Hannah took a step towards the door, and stopped, her hand on the knob, trying to figure it out.

Will had saved her. He had taken the hit himself, rather than force her to take off her clothes. But why? Was he just being nice? Was it pity for her obvious desperation? Or was it — she remembered his eyes meeting hers, the little prickle that had passed between them — was it something more?

Whichever it was, it might not be too late to find out.

Will had hung back. And perhaps he had done so for a reason.

Hannah licked her lips, pushed her long hair behind her ears. The mirror on the back of the door showed a girl with a wide, full mouth, huge dark eyes dilated with terror, cheeks flushed with excitement.

Please don't be gone, she whispered under her breath. *Please don't be gone.*

Her stomach was knotting with a mixture of nerves and desire, but she'd had enough champagne to know that she could do this, and that glance across the circle had *meant* something, she knew it. She had felt something travel between them in that moment, the acknowledgment of an attraction so strong it had to be mutual — didn't it?

She tightened the belt of her gown, then turned the handle and counted to three.

Please don't be gone.

The door opened.

He wasn't gone.

He was standing on the far side of the room, still shirtless, but he didn't turn as Hannah's door opened.

He and April were locked in each other's arms.

Neither of them seemed to notice Hannah standing frozen in the doorway. Instead, she watched as April led Will backwards across the little room, her lips against his, one hand in his hair, the other at his belt. At her bedroom door she paused, groped behind her for the handle, twisting it blindly, and then the latch gave, and the pair of them stumbled through the open doorway and into the darkness of April's room.

Then the door closed behind them, and Hannah was left alone.

AFTER

When Hannah wakes up, it's with the feeling that something is different.

It's not the fact that the bed is empty. That happens every Wednesday — Hannah's day off, in lieu of working Saturdays in the shop. On Wednesday Will puts his phone under his pillow so that his alarm doesn't disturb her, and tiptoes out of bed before she wakes.

It's not just the fact that she's pregnant and the strange feelings that go with that — the odd morning stiffness, the heaviness in her body, the feeling of queasiness that she has never quite gotten under control, in spite of what the books say about when it's supposed to end.

No, it's something else. She knows that, even in the dazed aftermath of sleep, before the events of yesterday come rushing back to her. Now she lies there, staring at the ceiling, trying to work out how she feels. Wednesdays are usually a treat — a chance to catch up on errands, call into town, or, increasingly as her pregnancy has progressed, just spend the day lolling around their sunny mews flat, doing nothing, in a kind of lazy trance.

But today the thought of sitting by herself in the empty flat, Will at work, nothing but the news and the yawning Google search bar to distract her, is intolerable.

It's not that there isn't stuff she could be doing — she could be researching prams, or building the flat-pack crib that has been sitting propped in the corner of their bedroom for the last six weeks. But somehow she can't bring herself to slit open the cardboard boxes. It feels like tempting fate, a presumptuous taking for granted of a future she has learned the hard way not to rely on.

But she can't lie there, thinking like that. Instead she gets up, pulls on her dressing gown, and goes through to the kitchen, rubbing the sleep from the corners of her eyes as she makes the one coffee she allows herself these days.

Will has left the radio on, as he often does when running out to catch an early meeting. She hasn't really been paying attention, but now something the newscaster is saying snags at her — and she leans across the counter to turn up the volume.

". . . has died in prison, aged sixty-three. Neville, who was convicted in 2012 of the killing of Oxford University student April Clarke-Cliveden —"

Hannah's hand shoots for the off button, cursing her own stupidity, but it's too late. As the room falls silent, she finds her hand is shaking.

She can't stay here. She has to get out.

It's drizzling in the park, but the rain provides a kind of comforting cocoon as she walks slowly down the leafy avenue in her mac. When she and Will moved into Stockbridge a few years ago it was the hip, artistic district of Edinburgh, still relatively affordable compared to New Town — if anything in central Edinburgh could really be called affordable.

But the area has grown up with them, its village vibe luring in young families alongside the bars and coffee shops, and now the streets are filled with bumps and buggies — or it seems that way to Hannah. Maybe it's just her own bump making her see the world with different eyes.

There are children in the park today, despite the weather, stomping about in wellies or clambering across dripping rope bridges, while their resigned parents and carers huddle under the cover of the trees, doing their supervision from a distance.

Hannah comes to a halt under the shelter of a big yew, watching them, when her phone goes. She pulls it out of her pocket, wipes the mist from her glasses, and glances cautiously at the caller ID. But it's okay.

She picks up.

"Hi, Mum."

"Hello, love, is it your day off? Did I get it right?"

Hannah smiles. Her day off has always been Wednesday, for all of the nine years she's worked at Tall Tales, but for some reason her mother can never seem to remember that.

"Yes, I'm in the park. How are you?"

Her mother ignores the question.

"I'm driving so sorry if I cut out. I'm on hands-free. But are you okay? I felt worried after you rang off yesterday. I shouldn't have ambushed you at work."

"No, it was fine." Hannah watches a little girl evade her father and run gleefully into a huge muddy puddle at the foot of the slide. "You were right, it was better I heard it from you."

"Did you get any trouble?"

She means journalists, doorsteppers, cold callers, Hannah knows. In the early days it was a swarm. When they came back to Dodsworth, in those first few awful weeks after April's death, her mother had wooden shutters installed on the ground floor of their home so people couldn't peer through the curtains, and a brush on the inside of the letter box. Hannah remembers them calling through the door, *Any comment, Mrs. Jones? Is Hannah here? What would you like to say to John Neville if you met him?*

"Not really," she says now. "Just an email. Nothing I couldn't handle."

"And how's Will?"

That's a more complicated question and Hannah pauses. How *is* Will?

"I think he's okay," she says at last. "You know what he's like, he clams up whenever it comes up, but we talked about it a bit last night. I think he's just relieved it's over, mainly."

"He needs counseling," Hannah's mum says severely. "You both do."

Hannah rolls her eyes. This is a discussion they've had before. In fact, she did have a few counseling sessions after the court case, and it helped in some ways — gave her tools to deal with the panic attacks and unhealthy behavioral patterns. It was the counselor who suggested the Requests folder on her phone, so she could mentally put the emails away until she was ready to move on from them. But she got everything useful out of the sessions, and then got out. And Will — she certainly can't imagine Will sitting in some office talking about his feelings.

"I know. We have talked about it. We're just a bit busy right now. You know, work, the baby. Will's working really long hours at the moment — he's barely ever home before seven."

"He should be looking after his pregnant wife!" her mum says, and Hannah feels a rush of annoyance.

"It's not his fault — he's hardly choosing to work twelve-hour days. But there's a partnership position coming up. He needs to be seen to be putting in the hours if he's going to be in with a chance."

And God knows, they need the money before the baby comes, though she doesn't say that to her mother. Cathy is the nicest employer in the world — but the shop barely makes a profit. Hannah will be getting the statutory minimum maternity pay, and that's it. Cathy can't afford any more. And although Will has a reasonable salary, once they've paid their mortgage, there really isn't much left. If Will can make partner before she goes on leave, they will both breathe easier.

"I thought I'd come up in a couple of weeks," her mum is saying. Hannah can hear the *tick-tock* of the indicator over the car speakers. "Help you out. Cook you both a few meals. Faiza at work gave me some absolutely lovely maternity clothes, there's a really good coat. She said take what you want and charity-shop the rest. I'll bring them up when I come."

"That sounds lovely," Hannah says. "I'll try to get a day off, maybe. What date are you thinking?"

She waits for the answer but it doesn't come, and when she looks down at the phone, the call has ended. Great. Presumably her mum has driven through a dead spot.

The rain has stopped, and she leaves the shelter of the yew tree and walks across to the gate to the playground, pulled, as if magnetized, by the little group of kids and their parents. There's a strict limit to how long a lone adult can watch children playing, she's discovered. About five minutes before you start to get glances, maybe ten before someone comes over and asks if you're looking for someone, though her growing belly gives her something of an alibi now. Women are more likely to smile sympathetically than glare suspiciously, and some will even start up a conversation. "Do you know what you're expecting?" or "When's the wee one due?"

Poor Will has no such leeway, though, and if they're out together he pulls her past the park when she stops, lingering, trying to imagine her future here — *Will's* future. Now she watches a father pushing a little girl dutifully on a swing, rain still beading his hood, and she has a sharp, almost painful flash-forward to a possible future — herself, standing at this gate, watching Will, her *husband,* pushing their child in the same swing.

She's standing there, holding her breath, trying to imagine her perfect future in this perfect life, with this perfect man, when her phone rings again.

"Mum?" she says. "We got cut off."

"Is that Hannah Jones?" says a male voice. "You don't know me. I'm a reporter with —"

Hannah almost drops her mobile. Then she stabs the "end call" button with a shaking finger and stands looking down at the phone in her hand.

For the truth is this, and she will never escape it: her perfect life has come at a price. Mostly she thinks of herself as unbelievably lucky to be here, in this beautiful city, with the only man she has ever really loved. But now, with the reporter's voice ringing in her ears, she has a different feeling: that she is living a stolen life. Not just one she never deserved, but one that was never supposed to be hers.

For what would have happened if April had not left the bar alone and gone up to their room to change? What would have happened if Hannah had followed her just five minutes earlier, discovered Neville in the room, interrupted the attack?

Would she have ended up dead too? Or would April have been alive, living with Will, carrying his child?

It starts to rain again as she shoves the phone into her pocket and begins to walk, past the playground, towards the road, with the children's cries following her as she goes. And she wonders. Maybe it wasn't only John Neville who stole April's life. Maybe she has done the same.

BEFORE

"Hannah Jones, I presume." The professor sitting in front of her swung round in his rotating chair and held out a hand. He was younger than Hannah had expected, with dark hair swept casually across his brow in a style that reminded her of someone, though she couldn't quite place who — Byron, perhaps, or a young Dante Gabriel Rossetti. Definitely a minor romantic poet. The white silk scarf tucked into his tweed jacket only added to the look. "Dr. Horatio Myers. I will be taking you for Victorian Literature this term, and then we will be covering some of the early twentieth-century material in Hilary and Trinity terms. Did you receive the reading list I sent through?"

"I did," Hannah said. It had been intimidating, to say the least — with a strong intimation that if she didn't at least start on the reading over the summer break, she was unlikely to keep up during term time.

"Thanks," she added belatedly. "I'm sorry I'm late, I went to the wrong place."

"Ah." Dr. Myers shuffled some papers in front of him and smiled at her. "Stairwell seven, yes? Those are my rooms. And very nice rooms they are too, but rather small, so the college was kind enough to give me a separate office for tutorials. It's a little bit tucked away, I know."

"Just a bit," Hannah said with a laugh. She was still finding her way in the labyrinthine passages and back offices of Pelham. "I actually had to ask a porter for directions."

"I hope he was helpful," Dr. Myers said dryly. "The porters can be a little bit jobsworth about that sort of thing."

"Oh, no, he was very helpful," Hannah said. "He brought me right here. To the door in fact. I'm not sure I would have found it otherwise."

"Good, good," Dr. Myers said, though Hannah had the impression that he had moved on to other things. "Well, as you know, we'll be meeting weekly for these tutorial sessions alongside your lectures, and they will be a chance for us to really drill down into your understanding of the subject. You will normally have a tutorial partner, but I like to begin with a one-to-one, to really allow us to get to *know* each other. Who are you, Hannah Jones? What do you want from Oxford? Tell me about the *real* you."

He leaned forward towards her, steepling his fingers, looking at her seriously over the tops of his horn-rimmed glasses.

Hannah was taken aback.

Who was she? What did that mean? She already felt increasingly that she was a different person here from the one she had been at home. Different from the girl who sang unselfconsciously along with ABBA on the car journey up here with her mother. Different from the geeky student she had been at school in Dodsworth. Different even from the person who had walked through that stone archway on the very first day.

Only deep inside herself was she the same — in the private, inner Hannah that she didn't show to anyone — the Hannah who rolled her eyes at April's excesses and secretly enjoyed films like *Clueless* and *Legally Blonde.* The Hannah who thought D. H. Lawrence was unreadable and pretentious. The Hannah who bit off her split ends and ate peanut butter out of the jar and did all of the myriad other strange and unadmirable things that people did in the privacy of their own company.

"I — I'm not sure what you want to know," she said slowly, and then, as Dr. Myers only looked at her over his glasses, "I . . . I'm an only child. My parents are divorced. But amicably. I don't see my dad much at the moment, he lives in Norfolk with his new wife. My mum teaches A-level physics. I come from a town on the south coast called Dodsworth — you won't know it, it's a —" She gave a deprecating laugh, trying to find the right adjective for Dodsworth. "It's not a hellhole or anything, it's just really boring. It's got nothing going for it, really, no culture; even the library closed down last year." She stopped, trying to think of what else to say. What could she possibly tell him that he would be interested in — about her *bog-standard comprehensive* school with its used textbooks and peeling paint and total lack of any kind of character or history or record of academic excellence? Nothing about Dodsworth or her education there was likely to impress a man who had sat opposite students from the best private schools in the country.

She felt again the crushing sense of imposter syndrome she had experienced when she first walked through the gate at Pelham for her interview — trying not to think of the thousands of other students who were applying for the same place as hers, eighteen-year-olds just like her, but ones who came from storied institutions and famous families, and who walked confidently into Pelham with the air of already belonging here — while she was still trying to convince herself of that fact even as she knocked on the door of the interview room.

But hard on the heels of that came a flicker of something — not anger, exactly, but something close. So what if she went to a state school. So what if Dodsworth had no culture and no history. Didn't that make her leap to Oxford more impressive? She *had* been accepted here after all, when many of those confident, shiny-haired students who had strode past her on the first day had not.

She sat up straighter.

"I was the only person in my year at school to apply for Oxford. I'm the first person in my family to come here too. In fact, my dad doesn't even have a degree — he's a builder who left education when he was sixteen. I didn't volunteer to feed underprivileged kids in my gap year or spend my summer digging wells — I spent my summer working in a supermarket. As you may have guessed, I don't always feel like I fit in here. But I'm determined to prove I belong."

Dr. Myers said nothing for a long moment. But then he sat back in his chair and began clapping, slowly but steadily.

"Bravo, Hannah Jones," he said at last. "Bravo. I think we're going to get along very well, you and I. Very well indeed."

At the end of the hour-long tutorial Hannah felt a strange mixture of drained and elated. Dr. Myers had taken her painstakingly back through her A-level syllabus and then gotten her to itemize the further reading she'd done in her own time, drawing out her opinions on everyone from Jane Austen to Benjamin Zephaniah.

As the tutorial drew to a close, she had the sensation of having undergone a pummeling mental workout as tiring as anything in the school gym.

"Until next week, then," Dr. Myers said with a smile. "And when you come back, I'd like you to give me a thousand words on the role of social anxiety in any of these novels. There's a list of books and essays you may find helpful on the reverse." He handed her a piece of paper, and Hannah glanced down at it, and then turned it over to read the other side. She had read all the novels cited, but none of the critical theory essays listed on the back of the page. She had no idea how she was supposed to find the time to do all of the further reading between now and next week, but she could worry about that later.

"Well, goodbye, Hannah Jones," Dr. Myers said. "Fare thee well, and we shall meet in a sennite."

Hannah nodded and turned for the door. When she let herself out into the corridor, the porter who had helped her find Dr. Myers's room was still there, leaning against a wall. It was the man she had met on her first day — not the grandfatherly one, the other, the one who had given her the keys.

"Got the right room this time?"

Hannah nodded, suppressing her puzzlement. Had he been outside for the whole tutorial?

"Yes, thanks. I don't think I would have found it without your help."

"All in a day's work." His voice was just as off-kilter as it had been before, high and reedy in comparison to his stocky, six-foot frame. It sounded as though it belonged to a much smaller, frailer man. "Where are you off to now, then?"

"Um . . ." Hannah hadn't really thought about it. "I don't know. The library I guess." She glanced at the list of books Dr. Myers had handed her.

The porter nodded.

"This way, then."

"Oh!" Hannah flushed, realizing that he intended to take her. "No, I mean, I know where it is. Honestly. You don't need to walk me."

"Can't have the students getting lost on my watch," the porter said, and Hannah found herself flushing again, her cheeks hot. She felt annoyed — angry at her own stupid embarrassment, but also at this porter for being so weird and patronizing, and for not taking the hint that she didn't need his help. Was he really going to accompany her all the way to the library? Why?

"I don't need you to walk me," she said again, but the words sounded feeble and hollow, particularly as she had no choice but to follow him down the stairs from Dr. Myers's room, there being no other exit.

In the end it seemed easier just to let him tag along however strange she felt, being escorted across the quad and through the cloisters by a fifty-something man in a porter's uniform. When they got to the door of the library she said goodbye with some relief, silently vowing to leave by a different exit. Thank goodness there were several.

"Thank you. Honestly, you didn't have to."

"My pleasure," the porter said. He put out a hand. "John Neville. You need anything at all, you just ask for me."

"Okay," Hannah said. She took his hand in spite of a twinge of reluctance. It was cold and soft and a little damp, like touching raw bread dough. "Thanks."

He held her grip just a little too long. When at last he let go, she tried to walk with dignity into the library, rather than fleeing unceremoniously. But when she got up to the first floor she could not stop herself going to a window overlooking the cloisters to check if he was still there.

To her relief he was not — he was walking away, across the lawns, back to the Porters' Lodge, and Hannah returned to the vaulted reading room with a sigh of relief.

For the next few hours, she was kept busy, tracking down books and navigating the library's unfamiliar shelving system. But something about the encounter had shaken her, and as she sat down at the polished oak desk, the books piled up around her, it came back to her — the sensation of his cold, soft fingers on hers, and the sound of his reedy voice in her ears.

She was being silly. He was probably just

a lonely middle-aged man with no talent for taking a graceful brush-off. But one thing was for sure: she had absolutely no intention of asking John Neville for help, ever again.

AFTER

"Decaf cappuccino and a brownie?" the server calls, and then, when there's no response, "Half-fat *decaf cappuccino* with cinnamon, and a hazelnut brownie?"

"Oh." Hannah shakes herself out of her reverie. "Yes, that's me, thank you. Sorry. I wasn't paying attention."

The boy puts the coffee and brownie down on the table along with the receipt. Hannah picks up the cup and takes a sip. It's good — the coffee at Cafeteria always is — but when she glances at the bill, she puts the cup down. Seven pounds forty. Was Cafeteria always so expensive? Maybe she shouldn't have ordered that brownie. She isn't even hungry.

Her phone rings, vibrating its way across the table with a suddenness that makes her jump. It's probably another bloody reporter, calling from an unregistered number. Picking up the caller that morning was a mistake

— she would never have done it if she'd been paying attention.

But when she digs the phone out of her bag, the caller ID gives her a jolt of surprise.

Emily Lippman.

She picks up.

"Em! This is unexpected."

It is. She hasn't heard from Emily for . . . maybe two years? It's not that they haven't kept in touch, exactly. They've been Facebook friends since uni, so Hannah knows about Emily's flourishing academic career — she and Hugh are the only ones who really lived up to the promise of those early days. She's read the impenetrable academic maths papers that Emily posts with a faux casual *So . . . wrote a thing* that belies the intense ambition Hannah remembers from Pelham. And for her part, Emily responds to Hannah's infrequent posts with what seems like genuine affection. *Let me know next time you're down south!* she wrote, last time Hannah posted a picture from Dodsworth.

But posting on Facebook is a false kind of intimacy, and in real life they haven't seen or spoken to each other for a long time — not since Ryan's wedding. In fact, she wasn't even sure Emily had this number, though she remembers passing it round last time she swapped.

"Well, I saw the news," Emily says now. Her disconcerting directness at least hasn't changed, and that realization gives Hannah a reassuring feeling of familiarity. "You okay?"

"Yes," Hannah says, with more certainty than she feels. "I mean it was a shock — but yes."

"And I heard from Hugh that you're pregnant. Congratulations!"

"Thanks." The news that Emily is still in touch with Hugh is somehow a surprise. She's never thought of them as firm friends. "I didn't know you kept up with Hugh."

"Just occasionally. He came down to an alumni carol service last year. Seems like he visits Oxford quite regularly — he said you and Will never come?"

"No, well, I mean, Edinburgh to Oxford is a long way," Hannah says, though she knows the excuse must sound feeble, particularly since Hugh also lives in Edinburgh. "It's a trek."

"Yeah," Emily says, but not like she's fooled. You don't have to be Sherlock Holmes to figure out why Hannah might not want to return to Pelham.

"Did you go to the Gaudy last year?" Hannah asks, more to divert the conversation than because she really wants to know. Personally she can't think of anything worse than hanging around with their former classmates, reminiscing about the "best years of their lives." What would she say? The truth? That April haunts her like an unquiet ghost? That her short time at Pelham ended in a long nightmare she's spent the rest of her life trying to wake up from?

"No," Emily is saying. "Hugh did, I think, but I'm not really into the whole reunion thing. But I have been back to dine a couple of times. Not often, I find the whole alumni deal unbearably smug most of the time. But I thought since I was back in Oxford I should show willing. You know, work the old network a bit."

"Oh . . ." Memory comes back to Hannah, something Will said last year. "I forgot you weren't in London anymore. You're a fellow at Balliol College, is that right? Is that a step up from Pelham?"

"Yes, practically come full circle." Emily's voice is dry. "As for a step up . . . I don't know. Balliol would probably try to say so, but as far as I can see, the only difference is the wine cellar at Balliol is better."

"What's it like? Being back?"

"Um . . . weird, to be honest. At first, anyway."

She stops. There is a long silence. Hannah is just trying to think what to say when Emily finally speaks, her voice quieter than before.

"Han, are you *really* okay?"

For a moment Hannah can't reply. She closes her eyes, pushes her glasses up her forehead, and digs her fingers into the bony hollows on either side of the bridge of her nose.

"Yes," she says at last. "And no. I mean, no, I'm not okay really. But I'm not *not* okay. Does that make sense?"

"Yes," Emily says. She sounds sad. "Because I feel the same." There is another silence between them, and for a moment Hannah has the strangest impression that no time has passed at all — that the two of them are back at Oxford, phoning room-to-room, and for a sharp, piercing moment she wishes it were true — that she could run down the corridor and tell Emily she's going to the JCR, and does she want a coffee. Then Emily speaks again, her voice stronger this time. "Oh, hey, I meant to ask — has a reporter called Geraint Williams been trying to get in touch with you?"

The name gives Hannah an odd prickle, coming so close on the heels of the email. She nods, forgetting Emily can't see her, and then says, "Yes. I mean — he emailed me. But I didn't reply. I didn't even really read it. How come?"

"I don't know. He's been after me to talk to him. I said no, of course, but . . . I don't know. He's a friend of Ryan's, apparently."

"Of *Ryan's*?" It's a shock. Hannah's not sure why, except that Ryan, out of all of them, is the person she feels most guilty about abandoning after college.

"From his days at the *Herald.* He said it was Ryan who got him interested in the case. Have you seen him?"

"Geraint?"

"No, Ryan." Emily sounds impatient.

"No. Not since his stroke." Hannah bites her lip. "Have you?"

"Only once, when he was first released from hospital. It was so awful I kind of couldn't bear to go back. But from what Geraint said, he's in a better place now."

"Oh. I mean, I'm glad," Hannah says uncertainly. It is what she feared, and part of the reason she never plucked up the courage to visit. Not just the memories it would have stirred up, but the memories it would have erased — the image in her head of the laughing, handsome, mocking boy overwritten by a slurring wreck.

"Geraint said his memory still isn't great,

and he's in a wheelchair — but he's had a lot of physiotherapy and apparently his speech is pretty good now. Plus he's able to feed himself and stuff, which must make a huge difference to someone as independent as him. I could see how much he was hating being dependent on Bella. And he's writing again — I haven't read any of it, but Geraint said he's able to type, and that must be a huge release."

"I'm glad," Hannah says again. And then, because the question is niggling at her, "So, what did he want? Geraint, I mean. Just the usual?"

The usual. Soft focus, syrupy memories of April and her potential. Sad-faced pictures of her friends and family pondering all they've lost. Anecdotes about punting and May balls and bright futures. And then some spicy detail, just to add a prurient kick to the piece — a hint of scandal, maybe. A student rivalry. A sniff of drugs, or promiscuity, or some other act of disreputable behavior, to give the reader a frisson of disapproval and the safe knowledge that this would never have happened to *them.* That they, or their kids, or their grandchildren, are far too responsible ever to get lured in by a predator and strangled in their own room.

She hates them. The journalists. The podcasters. The thought of what it must still be doing to April's parents, after all this time. She hates them all.

"Not the usual . . ." Emily says slowly. "At least . . . not *The April I knew, by Emily Lippman* bullshit, if that's what you mean by the usual. No, he . . ." She stops. Hannah knows that she is trying to find a way to put something potentially upsetting into words, and she sets down her coffee cup, bracing herself for whatever Em might be about to say.

"He thinks Neville was innocent," Emily says at last. "He thinks . . . he thinks they made a mistake."

BEFORE

Four weeks into the first semester (or rather, Michaelmas term, as she had already learned to call it) and Hannah felt like she had been at Oxford forever — but also that she would never get used to this miracle.

It was so strange that it was possible to experience both states at the same time — both the wonder of waking up in a eighteenth-century room, in one of the world's oldest centers of learning, hearing the chapel bells tolling and the high, ethereal voices of the Pelham College choirboys floating up to her windows — and yet at the same time to feel the reassuring rhythm of Meatloaf Mondays in the dining hall, Hugh's regular grumbles about the smell of Pot Noodles stinking up his room from the Cloade kitchen, and the daily visits from the staircase scout, bossy, motherly Sue. The strangest thing of all was that she and April seemed to have become de facto best friends

— in spite of the fact that back in Dodsworth Hannah was fairly sure she would have gone out of her way to avoid someone as intimidatingly beautiful and conspicuously wealthy as April.

Now, thrown together by the simple fact of sharing a room, they seemed to be taken for granted. April and Hannah. Hannah and April. Friends. Roommates. Conspirators.

"She's such a cow," April complained. It was Friday night, and she was sprawled across the sofa eating dry Coco Pops from a bowl, wearing a hand-painted dressing gown in Japanese silk. She was watching *The Breakfast Club* on her laptop and scrolling through the brand-new Instagram app on her iPhone. "I swear she waits until I'm either maximum hungover or got a massive deadline to come and hoover."

"Who?" Hannah adjusted the hood of her gown in the mirror. It was formal hall tonight, which meant if you wanted a cooked dinner, you had to dress the part — academic gown and smart clothes, although in practice "smart" tended to mean "no ripped jeans." She glanced over April's shoulder to check the time on her laptop: 7:25. Emily had promised to call past on her way over to the hall, but they were cutting it fine if they wanted to find seats together.

"I told you — Sue. Were you not listening?"

"She's got to get through the rooms," Hannah said mildly.

"She hates me ever since I pranked her with that bowl of glitter on top of the wardrobe," April said. She put a spoonful of Coco Pops in her mouth and crunched them noisily. "Bitch."

April was, Hannah had discovered, an inveterate practical joker. It was one of the more unnerving things about sharing a room with her — though not sharing a room didn't lessen the risk much. She had gotten Ryan with a fake call summoning him to see the Master — who was not pleased to be interrupted at ten thirty on a Sunday night. Hannah's own "gotcha" had been coming up the stairs one night after dinner to hear panicked screams coming from April's bedroom. She had rushed into the room to see two pale hands scrabbling helplessly at the edge of the open window frame.

It was only when she had raced across the room, her heart in her mouth, and grabbed one of the hands by the wrist that she had looked down to see April standing safely on the projecting bay window below, laughing like a hyena.

Of course, with hindsight it was completely stupid. Why would April be hanging outside her own window? There was no way she could have gotten in such a position by accident. And so Hannah had forced herself to laugh too, and had recounted the incident over breakfast as a joke against herself. In truth, though, she hadn't found it particularly funny. It struck her as pointless and a little unkind — even dangerous, to the extent that April could easily have fallen and broken her neck for real. Climbing out of the window had been fairly easy, according to April, but getting back up proved a lot harder. After Hannah had made two fruitless attempts to pull April back into the room, April had given up and clambered perilously down a very rusty drainpipe, losing a chunk of skin in the process. It would, Hannah reflected bitterly, have been considerably less funny if April had actually fallen to her death. But you weren't allowed to say things like that if you were the butt of a practical joke, or you looked sour and humorless.

"Who's a bitch?" The voice came from the doorway to the hall, and Hannah and April both turned sharply.

"Emily!" April said. She put a hand over her heart. "Jesus, don't do that to me! You gave me a heart attack."

"Sorry. Are you coming, Han? I was calling your mobile, but you weren't picking up."

"Oh, shoot, sorry. It didn't ring. I must have run out of credit again. Are you sure you're not coming?" she said to April, but more to show willing than anything else. April never came to formal hall. She claimed it was because she thought it was stuffy and pretentious — both of which were true, though Hannah had a weakness for the ceremony of it all, the Hogwarts theatricality of the rows of black-gowned students, the polished oak benches, the glimmering little lamps dotted all around, the Latin grace. But Hannah suspected it was something else. Something to do with April's odd relationship with food — the way she would eat six McDonald's cheeseburgers in a row while out in Oxford on a Saturday night, but then skip lunch every day for a week.

In formal hall there was no escape from the full, waiter-serviced three courses of it all. No possibility of taking a side salad, or scooping your still-laden plate into an anonymous pile at the hatch. You had to order a full meal and then sit there, waiting while everyone else finished, until the staff came to clear.

"I'd rather drink bin juice," April said now, but amiably, and Hannah shrugged.

"Okay, suit yourself," she said, and followed Emily from the room.

Ryan was waiting for them at the foot of the stairs, and together they made their way across the quad in the gloaming. It was November already, and the nights were drawing in. All around them were the crisp autumn air and the lights shining out through the chapel's stained glass.

"So who was the bitch?" Emily asked again, and Hannah rolled her eyes.

"Oh, Sue. April thinks she's holding a grudge. You know — over the glitter."

"God, I'm not surprised. If she tries any of that shit with me, I will *end* her," Emily said. She looked surprisingly furious. "It's not funny, it's actually pathetic. I heard about it from my scout, you know. They talk to each other. Sue spent hours hoovering up glitter and getting it out of her hair. If I was her, I'd have reported April to the Master."

"I think she did get a telling-off," Hannah said cautiously. She hitched up her gown, which was sliding off one shoulder. She felt uncomfortable, as if she were bitching about April behind her back. "I'm not sure from who, but someone came to speak to her."

"Yeah, but did anything happen? I'm willing to bet good money the answer is no."

"I wasn't there, but the impression I got was that there would be consequences if it happened again," Hannah said. But she knew it sounded weak.

"I expect Daddy made a few calls and it magically got dropped," Ryan said sarcastically. "Will's a sound bloke, but I don't know what he sees in her, I really don't."

Hannah bit her lip. She couldn't blame Ryan for his annoyance — he was still smarting from the business with the phone call — but April's family wealth had been a bone of contention even before that: the extent of the family holdings, the donation her father had made to the Pelham College gym. And it wasn't just Ryan. *April Clarke-Cliveden?* Hannah had heard someone say as she passed them in the cloisters on her way to a tutorial. *That It Girl? Oh, she's thick as two short planks — she wouldn't be here if it wasn't for her dad's money. He's like, one rung down from Warren Buffett or something.*

The odd thing was that April herself did nothing to dispel the rumors; in fact she seemed to revel in them. Her Instagram feed was a slew of designer clothes, boys in tuxedos, and shots of herself drinking champagne from the bottle and pouting at the camera. She seemed to take a pride in the notion that she did little or no work and yet still got good marks, and Hannah had heard her mention her unconditional offer and poor exam results more than once, as if daring people to put two and two together.

But it wasn't true, that was the thing. April *wasn't* an airhead, not at all. She liked clothes and parties, that much was true, but what her carefully curated Instagram feed failed to show was the hard work behind the scenes. Hannah had lost count of the number of times April had staggered home at midnight, ripped off her heels, and then pulled an all-nighter on some assignment due the next day. Hannah had proofread a few of those essays over breakfast as a favor to April. She had gone in trepidatiously the first time, expecting a load of plagiarized points, ramblingly regurgitated, but to her astonishment the essay was good — even brilliant in parts. Hannah was no historian, but she could recognize good writing — and these papers were much better than anything completed after half a dozen Cosmopolitans had a right to be. They deserved the marks April was getting, maybe even more.

It wasn't just the essays either. A couple of weeks ago Hannah had walked in on

April rehearsing for her part in a play she was supposed to be performing with the drama club before Christmas, and she had stood in the doorway, completely transfixed, goose bumps running up and down her spine. April wasn't just some wannabe starlet. Maybe It Girl was right, though. Whatever *it* was, she had it.

"You know," she began to Ryan — but as she said the words, they passed the Porters' Lodge, and Hannah remembered something. "Oh, I'm really sorry — I'm expecting a letter from my mum. Can you hang on for two ticks while I check?"

"Don't be long!" Emily said, and Hannah nodded and ran up the steps.

Inside it was warm and stuffy, with a strong smell of something that might have been damp cloth or an oddly musty kind of BO. She made her way over to the rows of pigeonholes and peered inside her own. Nothing, apart from a library slip reminding her about an overdue loan. Which was really odd; her mother's letter was a pretty regular Friday occurrence. Had it gotten misfiled? It wouldn't be the first time.

She was just peering into the pigeonholes above and below her own when she heard a reedy voice behind her.

"Looking for something?"

She turned, with a jump, to see the porter standing there — the one she had met on her visit to Dr. Myers's office. He had come out from behind the desk and was standing next to her, just slightly too close for Hannah's comfort. She took a step back.

"No, I mean — I was expecting a letter. My mum writes to me every week. But I don't know if it's here."

"Just arrived. I was about to put it in your pigeonhole." He held it out towards her, between two fingers, and Hannah reached for it, but to her surprise he jerked his hand back, holding the letter just above her head, with what seemed to be meant as a jovial expression.

Hannah frowned, and he held it out to her again; and again, when she reached for it, he pulled his hand back.

This time Hannah folded her arms, looking at him, refusing to reach for the letter. Her heart was quickening in a very uncomfortable way. There was nothing she could put her finger on, but this whole interaction felt so deeply off-balance, so odd and unprofessional, that she just didn't know how to proceed. It reminded her unsettlingly of that moment on the first day, when he had dangled the keys and then held on to them for just a beat too long.

"Can I have my letter?" she said at last, and was irritated to find that her voice wobbled a little on the final word. She glanced out the window. Emily was standing there, glaring at her. As Hannah met her eyes Emily held up her watch, pointing at the dial.

I know, Hannah mouthed through the glass, trying to convey her predicament. She couldn't go out and get Emily or Ryan to back her up, that was too pathetic. But she did wish one of them would come in after her.

"Can I please have my letter?" she repeated, and this time her voice sounded stronger, more annoyed.

"Course," Neville said. He gave a broad smile and held out the letter for a third time, and this time, when Hannah reached for it, her heart pounding, he did not snatch it away, but let her slide it slowly from his fingers. "All you needed to say was the magic word. I like polite little girls."

For a minute Hannah wasn't sure what to say. Polite *little girls*? Was it sexism? Was he coming on to her? Or was this just some weird paternalistic bullshit, like she reminded him of his own daughter?

Neville was grinning at her, as if waiting for a reply, but instead of giving him the satisfaction of a *thank-you,* Hannah turned on her heel, pushing back the door of the Porters' Lodge so hard that it banged against the wall, and stumbled out into the cool night air, her cheeks still blazing with a mixture of anger and discomfort.

Afterwards, talking it over during formal hall with Emily and Ryan, she almost couldn't believe her own memory of the exchange.

"And that's really what he said?" Emily was incredulous. "That he likes *polite little girls*?"

"I mean — I'm pretty sure?" Hannah said. "It's creepy, right? I'm not overreacting here?"

"Too fucking right it's creepy. It's gross! You should report him to someone!"

"Look, he's got to be fifty if he's a day, maybe even sixty," Ryan said. "That's my granddad's age — and that's just what they're like, aren't they? Old blokes. Different generation. You've got to make allowances. He probably didn't mean any harm."

"He probably didn't, but the fact is, it's really fucking patronizing! Please tell me you're going to report this, Han?"

"What, she's going to report him for being a bit old-fashioned? What's next, me suing the scout for calling me *ducky*?"

"It's not the same and you know it!" Emily shot back.

As she and Ryan continued their argument, the conversation drifted away, Emily ranting about sexism and the patriarchy, Ryan goading her by pretending to miss her point, but Hannah found herself preoccupied, thinking over Ryan's words. Because the thing was, he was probably right. John Neville probably *didn't* mean any harm. And she couldn't see herself reporting the incident, as Emily had suggested. What would she say? *He pretended not to give me my letter and I felt uncomfortable?*

Because that was the bottom line. It wasn't anything specific he'd said or done. And although the *little girls* remark was weird, there was not much else she could put her finger on. But he *had* made her feel uncomfortable. He had made her beg for a letter that was rightfully hers, and there was something about the power play underlying the whole exchange that made her skin crawl. She found herself surreptitiously wiping her mother's letter on her knee, even though she knew it was ridiculous.

After dinner, Ryan and Emily disappeared to meet some friends of Emily's from another college, and Hannah finished off the remains of the wine they had ordered with a group of girls from Cloade's, who all knew each other. When they filtered away to the college bar next door, she realized she was more or less alone in the hall, apart from a group of tutors still chatting over coffee at high table and the staff clearing away plates.

At the door she found herself uneasily glancing at the golden light filtering out from the windows of the Porters' Lodge, and wondering when the shifts changed for the night. Would John Neville still be there? Would he see her walking across the Old Quad? There was no other exit from the hall, and no way of getting back to New Quad that didn't involve cutting across the line of sight from the lodge. It had been deliberately positioned to give the porters a clear view of visitors making their way across the college grounds.

She knew she was being slightly ridiculous, but at the same time, there was just something about the thought of him lying in wait, maybe even coming out to ambush her, that set her skin crawling with a mix of fear and revulsion. Had he really been shelving her letter at that exact moment? Surely the post came in the morning? Or had he held on to it, waiting for her to come and look for it so that he could play his strange little game?

She was still standing in the doorway to the hall, hesitating, when she heard a voice from behind her.

"Everything okay?"

Turning, she saw Will's friend Hugh. He was wearing a bow tie and his academic gown, and his glasses were slightly askew in a way that made him look a little comical and perhaps a little drunk too.

"Oh, Hugh!" she said gratefully. "Yes, everything's fine. I was — I was just thinking about turning in. Are you heading back to Cloade's?"

"Actually I'm off to the library." He straightened his glasses, blew his hair off his brow, and gave a slightly rueful grin. "Got to pull a late on an essay I was supposed to hand in today. I've got an extension until tomorrow — I told old Bates that it was written but the printer wasn't working, when the truth is I've not written a word. Do you want me to walk you?"

Hannah hesitated. New Quad wasn't really on the way to the library — at least, not without taking a considerable detour. But the thought of kindly, horn-rimmed Hugh's reassuring company was very tempting.

"Would you mind?" she said at last, and then laughed. "Sorry, that's such a stupid thing to say. You could hardly say no when I put it like that. Honestly, I'm fine either way, I promise."

But maybe Hugh was less drunk than he looked, or more perceptive. Whichever it was, he shook his head.

"It's fine. I'd like the fresh air — probably need sobering up, to be honest." He took her arm. "Come on, old thing. Har fleag, har fleag, har fleag onwards! Toodoo, too-doo!"

He imitated a hunting horn, setting the crows that lived in the trees around the quad crying and wheeling in irritation.

Hannah laughed, and they set out into the night together.

AFTER

They made a mistake.

The words are ringing in Hannah's ears as she shoves a tenner down on the table and shoulders her way blindly out of the cafe.

Outside she leans with her back against the wall, feeling the drizzle on her face, her breath coming quick.

They made a mistake.

Emily chose her words with care, but that "they" is a euphemism and they both know it. Because in spite of the police, and the forensic experts, and the judge, and the jury, and everyone else involved in convicting John Neville of April's murder, there is only one person that "they" really applies to.

Hannah.

Because it was her evidence that sent John Neville down.

She was the one who told first the police and then the courts about his behavior. It was her name on the harassment complaint submitted to the Pelham College authorities, a complaint they brushed under the rug, later issuing fulsome apologies to both Hannah and April's family for their dismissive attitude.

And it was she, Hannah, who saw John Neville that night, hurrying towards her out of the gloom, head down, away from staircase 7.

What "they made a mistake" really means is you *made a mistake. You. Hannah.*

You convicted an innocent man.

And suddenly she cannot do this. She cannot do this anymore — not any of it. Not the memories crowding her head, not the voices in her ears, not the faces in the crowd around her, looking at her curiously as she puts her hands over her face and screams silently, internally, wanting nothing more than for it to *all just stop.*

She becomes aware that she is making a strange sound, like a sobbing moan — and a woman touches her on the shoulder, her face full of concern.

"Are you all right, ducks? Is it the baby?"

"No," she manages, though the word comes out like a wail. "No, I'm fine, leave me alone."

"Maybe you've had a wee bit of a shock?"

the woman asks kindly, but Hannah cannot take it — she cannot take the woman's well-meaning concern, she cannot talk about any of this.

"No, I mean — just leave me alone!" she chokes out. "I'm okay!"

And then she pushes past the woman, stumbling away into the rain.

She is not okay. She is very far from okay.

But it is not because Em's words were a shock.

It is the exact opposite. It is because Emily echoed the voice that has whispered in her sleepless ear every day and every night for ten years.

Did she? Did she make a mistake?

BEFORE

By the time the Michaelmas term drew to a close, just eight weeks after it started, Hannah found it hard to remember a time when she had not been a Pelham College student. The labyrinthine corridors and golden stone cloisters were as familiar to her as her old school halls back in Dodsworth, and outside the high walls of the college, even Oxford, with its off-putting patina of strangeness, was starting to feel like home. She had learned to call exams *collections*, the Thames *the Isis*, and that people studying the classics were taking *Greats*. She knew the difference between rectors, provosts, and wardens, and the place of Pelham's own Master in that subtle pecking order. She had her favorite pubs and curry houses, and was beginning to figure out the shortcuts and winding back ways that students used for slipping between colleges and making their way to the Bodleian, when the college library didn't suffice.

She let Emily drag her around the Saturday morning flea market, and Hugh take her to the History of Science Museum. She went to Oxford Union debates with Ryan, followed by furious political discussions in the pub after, and she adopted the weary tolerance the older students displayed towards the ever-present tourists, with their iPhones and their selfies.

She even got used to April — to her constant Instagram snaps, to her face staring out of the *Tatler* gossip pages, to the half-drunk bottles of Veuve Clicquot crowding the minifridge, and the scent of her strange, heavy perfume. After a few weeks it felt normal to find a Vivienne Westwood coat discarded underneath the sofa, or a Vera Wang camisole crumpled up with the laundry. Her trainers tangled companionably with April's Jimmy Choos in a pile beneath the coffee table.

Only two things she did not get used to.

One was John Neville — who remained a constant, disquieting presence, hovering at the edge of her perception. She found herself taking the long way to the library to avoid passing the Porters' Lodge, going in to collect her letters when she guessed he would be off shift, and entering college by

127

the back gate to avoid passing through the main entrance.

The other was Will.

Somewhat to everyone's surprise, it appeared that April and Will were now an item. It was never spoken, never articulated that April was anything as pedestrian as Will's girlfriend, but from that first night when they had played strip poker together, Will became a semiregular overnight guest in April's half of the set, and it was not uncommon for Hannah to wake to the sound of his deep voice coming through the wall, or to leave her room in the early morning, long before April usually awoke, to find him on their sofa, drinking coffee and looking across the dew-drenched quad.

The first time Hannah had woken to find Will sitting alone in the set, he'd jumped like a guilty person, caught doing something he should be ashamed of.

"I'm sorry," he'd said quickly. He stood up, crossing his arms over his bare chest. He was wearing nothing but jeans, and she had to force her eyes up, away from his lean, muscled body and the fine ribbon of dark hair that arrowed to his belt buckle. "I'm really sorry, I didn't think you'd be up yet — I didn't want to wake April. I'll go —"

"Hey, it's fine," Hannah said. She focused

on a point just past Will's right ear. "You don't need to go. Finish your coffee."

"Are you sure?" He looked at her doubtfully. "I don't want to take the piss — I mean, this is your room. I don't know how I'd feel about a stranger hanging around uninvited."

Hannah found herself laughing at that in spite of herself, and for the first time she found herself able to look Will in the eye, sympathetic to his awkwardness.

"Will, first, you're hardly a stranger. And second, you're not uninvited. April invited you."

"But *you* didn't," he pointed out.

She smiled.

"Okay. I invite you, Will de Chastaigne. Is that better?"

"Okay," he said, and then his face broke into a grin. "Vampire rules, you know. I'm over the threshold now, you can't get me out."

"Don't suck my blood," she said lightly.

There was a moment's charged pause, then Will coughed, breaking the tension.

"Still, I'd better get a shirt on. Pretty sure vampire rules don't entitle me to lounge around half-naked."

"Don't worry," Hannah said. "I was heading out for a run anyway. I like to go in the morning, before the river path gets too busy."

"Sounds nice," Will said. And then he smiled, and Hannah realized that she wasn't having to force her gaze away from his chest, because her eyes were locked on his face, on the way the lines at the corners of his mouth crinkled, on his crooked nose and the shape of his lips. "I'll probably be gone by the time you get back," he added, and she nodded and made herself look away.

"Sure." Her voice sounded croaky in her own ears. "See you later, then. Maybe at breakfast?"

"Maybe at breakfast," he echoed. And she laced up her trainers and left, taking the four flights at a run.

But he wasn't gone when she came back. Not completely at least. He was gone from the living room — an empty coffee cup the only sign of his presence. But as she opened the door to the set, the sound that greeted her from behind April's door was the unmistakable one of two people having sex.

Hannah found herself wincing as she tiptoed across the living room to her own door. Once safely inside her bedroom she shut the door and turned on the radio, a notch louder than necessary.

She had been planning to take a ten-second shower, then work on an essay in her room. Instead she showered, left her towel hanging on a peg in the communal bathroom, and went straight down to breakfast with wet hair and scrubbed face.

But to her surprise, when she walked through the door to the Hall, Will was there, eating a full English.

He saw her as she came in and waved a fork.

"Hannah! Over here!"

He had nearly finished, she saw, and as she moved across to him, frowning and trying to figure out how he had gotten down here so fast, let alone finished the best part of eggs, bacon, sausages, mushrooms, and beans, he swallowed a mouthful and spoke.

"Could I be cheeky and get you to grab me another coffee if you're going up?" He held out his empty cup.

Hannah took it, feeling slightly dazed.

"Um . . . sure."

She had turned half away from the table when she remembered something and turned back.

"Sorry, how do you take it again? I should know but —"

"Black, no sugar. Thanks."

Hannah nodded and moved away to join the queue at the hatch, but she could not shake the feeling of unease as she stood there, Will's still-warm cup in her hand, waiting to be served.

Had she been in the shower longer than she thought? Or . . .

But no. That was ridiculous. Will was . . . well, if not April's boyfriend, at least a significant fixture in her life — and she had seen him going into April's room herself that very morning. She had made a mistake, that was all. Just a silly mistake.

AFTER

In the restaurant, Hannah looks at her phone again, gnawing at a breadstick. Wednesday night is date night — it always has been, virtually since she and Will moved in together, when they realized that between book events for Hannah and accountancy exams for Will, they needed to carve out time for each other. For the first few years it was nothing fancy — fish and chips on summer evenings in Prince's Street Gardens, the castle glowing red-gold in the sunset and the hills shining in the distance. Popcorn and a movie at the Edinburgh Filmhouse, then McDonald's on the way home. Lately, as Will has moved up the ranks at Carter and Price, the restaurants have become nicer — and tonight's is one of their favorites, a cozy little Italian place tucked along one of the winding medieval lanes leading down from the Grassmarket, not far from Tall Tales.

But Will is late, and now, as Hannah stares down at the menu she knows practically by heart, pregnancy hunger growling in her stomach, she notices the prices for perhaps the first time since they started coming here. It's . . . not cheap. In fact, tonight is going to set them back about the same amount as their weekly supermarket shop. They are going to *have* to cut back when the baby comes.

"Can I get you anything to drink or are you still waiting for your companion?" says the waiter, passing her table with his order pad in hand. Hannah is just about to reply when a tall figure appears behind the waiter's shoulder.

"Will!" Relief washes over her.

"Sorry," Will says, half to her and half to the waiter. "I'll order fast, I promise. Can you come back in five?"

The waiter nods and departs, and Will bends to kiss her. As his lips, still cool from the crisp evening air outside, meet hers, she closes her eyes, feeling her body go liquid with it — that need that never goes away, that still unbelieving realization that Will is *her husband.*

"I love you." The words come out in spite of herself, and he smiles, holding on to her hand as he takes his seat, his strong fingers linking with hers as he picks up the menu with his free hand, scanning the specials.

He is her kryptonite, she thinks as she watches him read, one thumb absently stroking the back of her hand. She has never told him this, but she knows how Superman feels when they brandish the green sticks in his face, the way his strength deserts him and his limbs go weak, because she feels exactly the same way when Will touches her. Dazed. Stupid. Meltingly soft. And it has always been so, ever since that first day in the hall at Pelham. He has always had that power over her. Sometimes the realization makes her almost afraid.

After they have ordered, Will runs his hands through his black hair, making it stick up like a hedgehog's spines, and sighs.

"I'm sorry I'm late. Massive cock-up with a client account that needed sorting and I couldn't really run out."

"It's fine," she says, because it is now that he's here. "I get it. Now isn't the time to be coasting, what with the partnership thing."

"I know, but today of all days . . ."

"I'm fine. I didn't sit at home all day moping. I went to the park, then the cafe. I talked to Mum — she's going to come for a visit sometime, bring some maternity clothes. And, well, actually —" She pauses.

For some reason the words don't quite come naturally. "I, um . . . I also talked to Emily."

"Emily?" Will raises an eyebrow. She's not sure if he's surprised or just . . . making conversation.

"Yes. She called me, in fact — she'd seen the news. Did you know she was back in Oxford?"

"Yes, I told *you,* remember? I heard it from Hugh."

Hugh is the one person from college they both still see regularly. He and Will are best friends — have been since they were little prep school boys in short trousers, and perhaps because of that, their bond survived the earthquake of April's death. It helps that Hugh also lives in Edinburgh, in a beautiful bachelor's flat in the elegant Georgian quarter near Charlotte Square. He and Will play cricket for a local team in the summer months, and Hugh comes into the bookshop most Saturdays, buying whatever literary hardback the *Sunday Times* has recommended. The three of them meet up for dinner or brunch every few weeks.

But until today she had no idea that Hugh and Emily were in contact at all. They weren't even particular friends at Oxford — they hung around together because Will was dating April, and Hannah was April's room-mate, and Emily liked Hannah. But beyond that, they had nothing in common. Hugh was shy and bookish, and thirteen years at an all-boys' school had left him awkward around girls. Emily was sharp and spiky with absolutely no time for the kind of old-fashioned courtesies Hugh had been brought up to think were necessary when dealing with women.

"Emily said he'd been down for the Gaudy," Hannah says now. "It's weird, I would never have put them down for the ones to keep in touch."

"I know." Will takes a breadstick and crunches it meditatively. "They were never that close at Pelham. In fact I always got the impression she thought he was a bit of a joke."

"He *is* a bit of a joke," Hannah says, but not unkindly; she doesn't mean it as a put-down. It's just that Hugh is . . . well, he's Hugh. Posh, floppy hair, smudged glasses. He's *Dead Poets Society* crossed with *Four Weddings and a Funeral* — everyone's cari-cature of a public school boy grown up.

"That's just the surface, though," Will says, and she nods, knowing it's not just Will defending his best friend, it's also true. Because although Hugh may come across as slightly effete, the reality is very different. Underneath the self-mocking veneer, Hugh is tough, and driven, and very, very ambitious. It's why he's done as well as he has. Will's family is old money — not that there's much of it left now, apart from some land and a few paintings. April's was new — her father came from nowhere, a brash Essex boy who made his fortune in the city and cashed out at the right time. But Hugh's family were neither, in spite of his schooling. His father was a GP, his mother a housewife, "county" folk who scraped together the money for their only child's education, going without themselves, even as they pinned all their hopes on him.

That sacrifice is something Hugh has been trying to justify ever since he left Pelham — and now, to a large extent, he has succeeded. He followed in his father's footsteps as far as graduation, but then went swiftly and lucratively into private practice — he's now the head of a very successful plastic surgery clinic in Edinburgh. One of his first clients was April's mother. Hannah doesn't know how much he earns, but she can tell from his flat that he must be extremely comfortable — you don't get a place like that in central Edinburgh for small change.

"So, what was she saying?" Will continues,

and Hannah has to drag her mind back to Emily's conversation. The sinking feeling in her stomach returns.

"She was saying . . ."

She breaks off. The waiter has arrived with their starters and there's a moment's respite as they sort out whose is whose, but then Will prompts, "She was saying?"

"She was asking if I was okay and . . ."

"Yes?" Will says. He's looking worried now, and puzzled, and maybe slightly irritated too, it's hard to tell.

"There's this journalist. He's been trying to get in touch with her — and me. He's a friend of Ryan's and he thinks . . ."

Oh God, this is hard.

She puts her knife and fork down, takes a deep breath, forces the words out.

"He thinks there might have been a mistake. He thinks Neville's conviction was a miscarriage of justice."

"Bullshit." Will doesn't even stop to consider her words; his reaction is swift and decisive, and he slams his hand down on the table, making his plate and cutlery clatter and jump. The people at the neighboring table look around in surprise and Hannah winces, but Will doesn't lower his voice. "Utter bollocks. I hope you told Emily not to speak to him?"

"She already has," Hannah says, her voice practically a whisper as if to compensate for Will's, and then, seeing Will's expression, she backtracks. "Not about Neville. They seem to have talked mostly about Ryan. But don't you think —"

She stops.

Don't you think it's at least a possibility? is what she wants to ask. But she can't quite bring herself to say the words. It's been hard enough turning them over and over inside her head without articulating them.

"Sweetheart." Will puts down his cutlery and reaches across the table, holding her hand, forcing her attention. "Hannah, don't do this. Don't start second-guessing yourself. And for what? Just because Neville's dead? His death changes nothing. It doesn't change the evidence — it doesn't change what you *saw*."

And that's the thing. She knows he's right.

Of course he's right.

The fact that Neville went to his grave protesting his innocence proves what exactly? Nothing. There have been plenty of murderers who denied their guilt until their dying day.

But the truth is that Neville could have been heading towards parole by now, if he had played the game — accepted his guilt

— done his time. Instead he spent the years after April's death protesting his innocence and launching futile appeal after appeal after appeal — all of which achieved nothing except to keep his name in the press and public anger high.

Would a guilty man *really* have shot himself in the foot like that?

"Hannah?" Will says. He squeezes her hand, forcing her to meet his eyes. "Hannah, sweetheart, you know that, right? This is *not* your fault."

"I know," she says. She withdraws her hand, shuts her eyes, rubs at the headache that is beginning to build beneath the plastic nose-rest of her glasses. But when she shuts her eyes, it's not Will's face that she sees, full of love and concern — it's Neville's. And not the Neville that has dogged her since university — glowering, full of belligerent defensiveness — it's the one she saw the other day. The haunted, hunted old man, staring out of the screen with a kind of pleading fear.

And she knows, what Will said? It's not true.

This is all her fault — all of it.

BEFORE

"Oh, Hannah," Dr. Myers said, as Hannah closed her folder and stood up, ready to leave at the end of their session. "Could you stay back for a moment? Miles, you're free to go."

Hannah's tutorial partner nodded and left, leaving Hannah standing slightly awkwardly, wondering what Dr. Myers was about to tell her. Had she slipped up? He had seemed pleased with her essay this time, but the same couldn't be said for some of her earlier efforts. It was a moment before she realized Dr. Myers was talking — and she wasn't paying attention.

". . . little drinks party," he was saying. "I always have one at the end of every term. I invite a few particularly promising students along — we make connections — it's rather fun."

Hannah stood, holding her breath, not wanting to make an assumption that might swiftly be shot down. *Particularly promising students.* Was he really talking about her? But surely he wouldn't have mentioned the drinks party if he didn't intend to invite her?

"It's this Friday," he said. "Very informal — just a glass of sherry in my rooms. At least you won't have any trouble finding it!"

Hannah gave a laugh, and then, lacking anything else to say, said, "Thank you. So much. I mean — yes, I'd love to come."

"Wonderful. Eight p.m."

"Can I bring anything?"

"No, just yourself."

Outside, in the corridor, she leaned against the wall, feeling a smile spreading across her face. *Particularly promising.* Could it really be true?

The big question, of course, was what to wear. *Very informal,* Dr. Myers had said, which was the worst kind of invitation. At least with the ones that said "white tie" or "academic gowns," you knew where you stood. *Very informal* could mean anything from party dresses to jeans.

"Jeans," April said decisively when Hannah asked her advice, "and a pleated poplin camisole, very high at the neck, no sleeves, single pearl button fastener behind. Business at the front, party in the back."

"Yes," Hannah said impatiently, "but I

don't *have* a —" What was it? A pleated something something? "A top like that. Friday is two days away. I haven't got the time to go shopping." Or the money, she thought but did not say. Such considerations didn't weigh with April.

"*You* may not have one," April said, "but I have. Come through here."

Hannah had not been into April's bedroom for several weeks — with a joint sitting area, they didn't need to go into each other's rooms to socialize, and since Will was a frequent visitor, Hannah was always half-afraid of what she might find if she knocked.

Now, she was amazed afresh not just at the difference between April's room and her own — a difference which had seeped out into the living room, where the boring, regulation university furniture was slowly being replaced or supplemented by April's own luxuriously expensive taste — but by the mess. There were clothes everywhere: Designer garments piled up in corners. Beaded tops slung over lamps. Jimmy Choos hanging casually by a strap from a desk chair. But not just clothes. Half-drunk cups of coffee languished on the windowsill, sporting an extravagant coating of mold. Books were scattered like splay-winged birds. An open bottle of pills spilled across the nightstand. A half-eaten doughnut leached grease into a pile of essays, and a makeup palette lay burst open on the rug, colored powder ground into the carpet pile.

In one corner a lamp burned, low and golden, and April clutched her head.

"Oh shit, every time I come in here I'm shocked at how awful it is. I wish I could pay Sue to sort it, but she's such a bitch."

"She's not a bitch," Hannah said reflexively, "she's just busy," but she was eyeing the chaos and silently agreeing that it was going to take more than April to sort this out. There were weeks of mess here, and university rules stated that they had to clear their rooms for the Christmas break. "How do you find anything?"

"Well at any rate, I know where the camisole is. I tried it on but it's too big for me so you might as well take it."

She picked her way through the mess to the far corner, near a long gilt-edge mirror that looked like an antique, and began rooting through a pile of clothes there.

"Aha!" Her voice was triumphant as she held up a crisp, starched top in old ivory. "Here it is. It'll be perfect. Try it on. Go on!"

She made no move to turn around or give

Hannah her privacy, so after a slightly awkward pause, Hannah turned her back and stripped off the T-shirt she was wearing, sliding the camisole over her head.

Then she turned around.

"So?"

She could tell at once, even without looking in the mirror, that April was right — the top suited her. April's expression told her that. She clapped her hands together and spun Hannah around so that she could do up the single mother-of-pearl button at the back of Hannah's neck.

"Oh, that is *perfect,*" April breathed, reverentially and seriously. She turned Hannah around again, facing the mirror. "Bend over?"

Hannah bent, obediently, and April tutted.

"Well you can't wear a bra. The whole point of that top is the back; look, when you stand straight it's totally demure." She demonstrated, holding up a hand mirror so that Hannah could see behind herself. "And when you bend or twist . . ." Hannah did so, seeing the sliver of creamy spine that immediately showed between the pleats. It was indeed completely spoiled by her very basic supermarket bra showing through the gap. "But you don't need a bra, oh, you're

146

going to look gorgeous."

"Thank you," Hannah said, rather awkwardly. "And — I mean, should I dry-clean it before I return it? Wash it?"

"I told you." April sounded impatient. "It's yours."

"But April —" Hannah plucked at the tag still dangling from an inner seam. "I can't take this — it's brand-new. If I don't cut the tags you could return it, and —" Her eyes alighted on the price. "Jesus Christ! April, this was *eight hundred quid*!"

"I'm not going to return it," April said carelessly. "So if you don't take it, it's just going to rot in the corner there."

She stood back, appraising Hannah seriously, and then said, "The jeans are fine, but you need proper shoes. Have you got any heels?"

Hannah nodded, and went through to her own room to find the pair of black Dolcis heels her mum had bought her for formal events and interviews just before term started. When she returned wearing them, April made a face of barely concealed disgust.

"Look, I don't mean to be rude, but those shoes are an insult to that top. What size are you?"

"Six," Hannah said. She knew her expression must look mutinous. The shoes were basic, but they looked totally inoffensive to her eye. And so what if she couldn't afford April's designer sandals? Not everyone was the heir to a city fortune.

But April wasn't paying her any attention, she was too busy rooting through a tangle of shoes in the bottom of her wardrobe. Two pairs of Louboutins flew past Hannah's knees, followed by a single Jimmy Choo sandal. And then April straightened, holding a pair of deep green Manolo Blahniks. They were crocodile embossed leather, open-toed, and about three inches higher than Hannah's usual style.

"There. These *are* a loan, by the way, they're one of my favorite pairs. But don't worry about scuffs, I've worn them outside already."

Done protesting, Hannah slipped her feet into the shoes. They were extremely high, and for a moment she teetered, but then she caught her balance and stood, looking at herself in the mirror. Behind her, April pulled Hannah's hair out of its clip and shook it loose over her shoulders. A different person looked back at Hannah from the mirror. Taller. More confident. Rocking her designer top and shoes like she was born to it. The shoes picked out the green in her

148

eyes, and the ivory set off her pale skin and dark hair. She looked like she was beautiful. She looked like she was one of April's friends.

"There," April said, her face so close to Hannah's that Hannah could feel her breath on her ear. "You look majestic."

It was just a couple of days later that Hannah found herself putting the poplin top back on, braless this time, and making up her eyes with smoky eyeshadow and liner. Finally, she put on a swipe of dark red lipstick — but she knew as soon as she'd done it that it was a mistake; it made her mouth look comically huge and with the dramatic eyes, the effect was clownishly overdone. Instead, she wiped it off with a tissue, leaving a faint flush that somehow made her mouth look as if she had just been roughly kissed. That unaccustomed stranger from the other day stared back at her from the little mirror above her desk.

"April," she called, picking her way carefully out into the living room. "What do you think?"

There was the rattle of a door handle, and April appeared in the doorway to her room. She was wearing makeup herself, pale face and scarlet lips, and a devastatingly simple black silk sheath that showed the hollows of her collarbones and the lines of her white throat and made her golden hair glow like it was electrified.

"Perfect," she said, smiling broadly. "You look a million dollars."

"I ought to," Hannah said ruefully. She looked down at the shoes. "I'd better not ask how much these cost or I'll be terrified of snapping a heel. Are you going out?"

"I am," April said, and her smile turned wicked. "But not far. I'm coming with you."

Hannah felt her insides turn over.

"Oh . . . April, I'm so sorry — it's a party for his students. And not all of them — he didn't invite Miles even. I'm sorry, I feel really bad. I should have explained."

"You did," April said. She knelt down beside the minifridge in the corner of the room, where Hannah kept the milk for her morning coffee, and pulled out a bottle of Dom Pérignon. "But I don't care. I'm coming. Oh, don't worry," she added, as Hannah began to protest. "I'll make it clear you didn't invite me. But gatecrashing is my very *favorite* occupation."

She straightened, tucking the bottle under her arm.

"Anyway. Dr. Myers is rather dishy. I'm not letting you have him all to yourself."

For a long moment Hannah just stood, looking at April in helpless exasperation, unsure whether to be angry or push back — and then she caved.

"Fine. I guess I can't stop you. But don't follow me in, or it'll look like I invited you."

"Fine," April shot back. "In fact, you know what, I'll lead the way."

And before Hannah could stop her, she opened the door to the set, stalked across the hallway, and rapped loudly on Dr. Myers's door.

The door opened and the sound of chamber music carried across the hall on a wave of student laughter, followed by Dr. Myers's voice, full of welcome and bonhomie.

"Hello!" And then, slightly puzzled, "I'm sorry, can I help you?"

"Hi." There was no embarrassment in April's voice, and peering through the crack in the door, her face flushed with preemptive mortification, Hannah saw her stick out a hand and lean confidentially in towards Dr. Myers. "I'm your neighbor, April. I heard a rumor that your end-of-term drinks parties were the hottest ticket in Pelham, but my friend . . ." — she paused just long enough to make Hannah nervous — "Joanne told me that I would never get in, because I wasn't clever enough. She bet me a bottle of champagne that I wouldn't get past the door, but I thought perhaps I could persuade you to drink the winnings . . . ?"

She held out the bottle of Dom Pérignon and trailed off, smiling up at Dr. Myers, her expression an intoxicating mix of pleading, adoration, and just a tiny little touch of flirtation.

"Well." Hannah heard Dr. Myers's voice take on an amused quality, and she saw him look April up and down, taking in the willowy limbs, the slim fragile neck, the expensive sheath dress with — Hannah strongly suspected — no underwear beneath. Finally his eyes alighted on the champagne. "Dom Pérignon Oenothèque. Well, well, well. We can't have Joanne furthering the reputation of this college as an elitist establishment, can we?"

The door opened slightly farther and Dr. Myers stood back.

April gave a dazzling smile and stepped forward into his rooms, but as she did she turned, momentarily, and Hannah saw her give the smallest of winks over her bare shoulder. And then she disappeared and the door closed behind her.

AFTER

The meal is delicious and somehow, over the three courses and coffee, Hannah manages to forget Neville and April and all her worries — or at least push them to the back of her mind — and just enjoy being with Will. They may not have that many of these nights left, after all. Once the baby comes, that will be an end to cozy little bistro suppers, at least for a good few months. She needs to make the most of this, make the most of the time they have left with just the two of them.

They talk about Will's boss — about the possible partnership position and what it would mean for Will if he got it. More money, yes. But also longer hours, more responsibility, more pressure to bring in new clients. All of which would be a double-edged sword, with a new baby at the same time. They talk about the birth — the weird mix of emotion and admin that having a baby entails. The deadline is coming up for choosing a hospital, and they haven't even started to look into antenatal classes yet. Hannah talks about work, about the funny customer who comes in every few weeks asking for books he's read about in the paper but can never remember the titles. This week's was *Scots author. Cover's got a wee lad on the front and a funny name.* Will guesses the answer correctly without too many clues — *Shuggie Bain.* Sometimes Hannah wonders if her customer's memory is really as bad as he makes out, or whether it's become like a game between them. And there's another, an elderly lady who comes in every Tuesday and buys a book, and then comes back the following Tuesday and tells Hannah how many marks out of ten she would award it. She has never, ever given ten. *Hamnet* got 8.75. This week *Razorblade Tears* got 9.2. The first Bridgerton novel got 7.7. *Lord of the Flies* got a surprising 4.1. Hannah finds it impossible to predict what will score high — some of her most confident recommendations bomb, but she lives in hope of finding something that will hit the magic jackpot.

At last Will asks for the bill, and then gets up to go to the bathroom. The check arrives while he is away. Normally Hannah would just glance at the total and then shove the printout across the table along with their joint account card, but this time she looks at it — really looks at it. The starters alone were more than a tenner each. And twenty-seven pounds for a bottle of pinot grigio — Will hasn't even drunk all of it, just half. Why on earth did they order a bottle when she's not even drinking? And the bread-sticks! Three pounds for breadsticks. She had no idea they even charged for those.

She pays, and is sitting, chin in her hands, waiting for Will to come back, when she hears a clear, carrying voice from behind her.

"Darling, you call this a Vesper? It tastes more like a gin and tonic, and not a very good one."

All the hairs on the back of Hannah's neck prickle. The voice is coming from the restaurant's bar. It is drawling, confident, and achingly familiar.

Before she can think better of it, Hannah stands up, swings round, sending her chair clattering to the floor. But even as she scans the row of backs at the chrome counter, her heart is sinking, and she knows the truth. It wasn't April. It's *never* April. It was just a well-to-do woman with an English accent. Hannah's own longing did the rest, just as it has a hundred times before.

"Allow me," says a voice at her elbow, and Hannah turns to see a tall, bespectacled figure holding out her handbag.

"Hugh!" She manages a smile as she takes the bag. "This is a nice surprise. And thank you."

It's not a surprise — not exactly. Edinburgh is a small city in a lot of ways, and Hugh's practice isn't far from the restaurant. But it's a big enough place that it's still fairly unlikely to run into friends at random.

"You're most welcome," Hugh says, with that oddly shy formality he's had for as long as she's known him, even after a decade of friendship and more landmark events than she can remember — he was Will's best man at their wedding, for goodness' sake.

They kiss each other on both cheeks, and as she breathes in Hugh's expensive aftershave, Hannah remembers with a laugh at herself how strange and performative that continental kiss first felt to her when she arrived at Oxford. And now look at her — air-kissing without a second thought.

"How are you?" she asks.

"I'm all right," he says thoughtfully, looking at her with a slightly discomfiting air of appraisal, like she is one of his patients.

"More to the point, how are *you*? I thought of you yesterday, when I heard the news."

"I'm . . . I'm okay." It's not a lie, not really. But Hugh is Will's best friend and confidant — not hers. Hannah . . . well, she hasn't really *had* a best friend, if she's being honest, not since April. It's not that she doesn't have friends — she goes for a drink with Robyn every now and again, and there's a handful of people she knows through work, or from her various short-lived hobbies — pottery was the one that lasted longest. But you don't have to be a psychoanalyst to join the dots, and Hannah's not an idiot, she knows the truth — since April died, she hasn't allowed herself to make anyone that important to her. Because she doesn't trust them not to get snatched away. Will is the sole exception — the only person who has penetrated that self-protective armor. And maybe he only managed it because she had let him under her skin before April died.

"Hugh!" The voice comes from over Hannah's shoulder and she turns to see Will weaving his way between tables towards them. "Mate! How are you?"

They hug, a kind of manly back slap, and Hugh says, "I'm good. I was just telling Hannah — my thoughts went to both of you when I heard the news."

"Yeah. It's . . . I mean, it's a lot," Will says with an awkward shrug. His eyes meet Hannah's. He knows how much she hates talking about this, particularly in public. They both live in dread of someone leaning across, tapping their shoulder, *I'm sorry, but I couldn't help but overhear . . .*

Perhaps Hugh senses their discomfort because he straightens, claps Will on the shoulder, and says, "Well, anyway, I won't keep you both. But let's have drinks. It's been too long."

"It has," Will agrees. "I was thinking the other day, I haven't seen you since the cricket season finished and I don't think we've been out as a threesome since . . . God, probably June?"

That was right about when they found out about the baby. Hannah stopped accepting invitations out to the pub because she wasn't ready to tell anyone the news, and it was getting increasingly hard to explain away her tiredness and inability to drink. But it's different now. She's visibly pregnant, and in any case, Hugh was one of the first people Will rang after their twelve-week scan.

"We should do brunch," Hugh is saying now as he buttons up his overcoat. "Soon.

Make the most of your freedom while you still have it!" He gives a laugh, and Hannah and Will echo it.

"Take care of yourself, Hugh," Hannah says, and she means it. She is genuinely fond of Hugh, and this must be hard for him as well. He was there that night, after all. He didn't go through what Hannah did, he wasn't April's best friend, but he was dragged through the courts too, giving evidence on what time they found her, how hard he had fought to revive her. And then, she and Will have each other. Hugh has no one — he lives alone, he doesn't even have a steady girlfriend as far as Hannah knows, though presumably he was dining with someone tonight. He's not like Will — easily gregarious, finding something in common with everyone he meets. He's charming and gentle and courteous, but there's a reserve that can be hard to get past — he's more like Hannah in that respect. Perhaps that's why he followed Will to Edinburgh, and why he's made sure to keep in touch with Emily, even after all these years. Like Hannah, he doesn't make friends lightly, so he can't afford to lose them.

She and Will watch as Hugh tucks his umbrella under his arm and disappears out into the twinkling darkness of a rainy

159

Edinburgh night, the lamps glittering off the steep steps, the honey-colored stone alleyways drenched to dark brown.

For a moment Hannah sees him, silhouetted against a streetlamp. Then he is gone.

BEFORE

As the door closed behind April, Hannah found herself feeling angry in some way she could not quite justify. Wasn't it enough that April had looks and clothes and money and that she had to share a room with her and — and — and —

And Will was what she really meant, but she wouldn't let herself admit that.

Still, though. Did she really have to muscle in on *everything* that was Hannah's?

For a second Hannah was tempted to turn away, go back to her room, wipe off the makeup, and throw the heels into the cesspit of April's wardrobe. But she knew that would be stupid. Dr. Myers was expecting her. She had said she would go. It would be rude to just not turn up — and cutting off her nose to spite her face.

Instead she counted to ten in her head, then teetered unsteadily across the landing to knock on Dr. Myers's door.

"Hello?" It was a tall willowy girl with long dark hair who opened it, looking Hannah up and down with a slightly superior air. A gust of laughter and conversation flooded past her into the corridor. "Can I help you?"

"Hi," Hannah said, a little nervously. "I'm Hannah. Dr. Myers invited me to his drinks party?"

"Hannah Jones!" Dr. Myers's familiar voice came from behind the girl, and he slipped his arm around her shoulders in a gesture that could have been simply an avuncular way of ushering the girl aside to make room for himself in the doorway, but could have been something more possessive. He was wearing a wine-colored velvet jacket, and the same white silk cravat he had worn at Hannah's first tutorial. "Welcome, welcome. Come in, make yourself at home in my humble abode, such as it is. Have a glass of champagne."

The willowy girl stood back and Dr. Myers showed Hannah into a wood-paneled sitting room full of students. Looking around, Hannah saw that they were overwhelmingly female — she could pick out a few boys here and there, but the ratio was maybe five to one in favor of women. Perhaps that wasn't surprising, though, given that Dr. Myers taught English, which was a female-heavy subject.

There was a small table standing by a crackling fire, holding a tray of empty glasses, and Dr. Myers picked up a flute and filled it from a bottle that Hannah recognized as the one April had taken from the fridge.

"Hannah, let me introduce you to a few of my favorite students," Dr. Myers said expansively, waving his hand around the group. "This is Clara Heathcliffe-Vine, a luminary in the Oxford Union." He indicated a small, pixie-faced girl curled up in the window seat, who turned at the sound of her name and nodded briefly before continuing her conversation. "Orion Williams, a particularly brilliant third-year." He indicated a tall, dark-haired boy standing by the fireplace, who nodded a little awkwardly and gave Hannah a shy smile. "Rubye Raye, shining star of my second-year tutorial group." He bowed with mock solemnity to the girl who had opened the door to Hannah. "And . . . oh, this is one of my newest protégées, the — uh — sparkling April Clarke-Cliveden."

He stood back, and Hannah saw April, perched on the arm of a wingback chair, next to a square-shouldered boy wearing a navy blazer that Hannah vaguely recognized as a sporting blue.

"Everybody." Dr. Myers looked vaguely around the room, and then put his arm around Hannah, his palm hot and a little damp against her bare shoulder. "Allow me to introduce the thrillingly gifted Hannah Jones. Who is in the process of proving, once again, that many of Oxford's finest minds come from a state school, single-parent, working-class background."

There was a ripple of approval from round the room. *We're so open-minded. Such a meritocracy.*

Hannah opened her mouth — and then shut it again, unable to think of what to say.

She was still groping for the appropriate response when one of the students behind Dr. Myers touched his arm and whispered something and he gave a little jump.

"Oh, thank you, well remembered, Madeleine. Excuse me, Hannah. I must tend to the canapés."

He gave her shoulder a little squeeze, and then released her and hurried away.

"I didn't realize you were so brave," said a mocking voice in her ear, and Hannah turned to see that April had disentangled herself from the boy in the blazer and was standing behind her. She was laughing.

"Such tenacity, fighting your way up from the mean streets of Dodsworth."

"Oh, piss off," Hannah said crossly. "I don't know where he got all that from. I certainly didn't tell him I was working-class."

"Take the compliment and run, darling. I would."

I know, Hannah almost said, but she bit her lip.

An hour into the party, Hannah was beginning to wish she had never come. Her feet were in agony in April's heels, and she was listening to a long, tedious rowing anecdote from the boy in the navy blazer, the one April had shrugged off earlier in the evening. Far from being the sophisticated soiree she had imagined, the night seemed to have descended into Dr. Myers smoking filthy cigars and holding court with the three prettiest girls in attendance — one of whom was April. He was sitting back in an armchair by the fire, April on one armrest, Rubye on the other, and a beautiful redhead Hannah didn't know sitting on a footstool at his feet. As she watched, April turned and mouthed something over Dr. Myers's head. She wasn't sure what it was, but April's expression was full of wicked laughter. She thought it might have been *So predictable.*

". . . totally gorgeous. Maybe for a drink or something?" the rowing blue said, and then stopped, seeming to expect some kind of answer. Hannah shook herself and looked away from where Dr. Myers had slipped a hand around April's waist, ostensibly to steady her on the chair's narrow arm.

"I'm sorry. What did you say?"

"I said, you're absolutely gorgeous," the boy said. He had flushed a deep red that went from his shirt collar up to his fringe. "I'd love to take you for a drink sometime. Maybe Vincent's? I'm a member. Or somewhere else. You choose."

Hannah felt her color rise in sympathy.

"Oh God . . . that's so kind of you, but . . ."

What could she say? She had a boyfriend? That was a lie, as two minutes' inquiry in the JCR would reveal. That was the problem with living in college — though it had felt so very big on the first day, she was rapidly coming to realize how very small Pelham really was. Part of her wondered if she should say yes — was she really going to spend three years pining after someone who had never looked twice at her, someone, moreover, who was going out with her best friend?

Go out, get drunk, sleep with someone else, and put Will out of her head once and for all. That was what she would have told a friend in her position. But whoever was destined to help her get over Will, her heart knew that this boy was definitely not that person.

"I'm sorry, there — there's someone else," she said at last, hoping that would suffice and he would not inquire any further. The boy flushed an even deeper shade of red, his face pomegranate-colored above his dark blue blazer.

"Oh. Yeah. Sure. Of course. No worries at all. I mean, well, if you change your mind — Jonty Westwell." He held out a hand. "I'm over in Cloisters."

"Thanks," Hannah said. "It's a really kind invitation."

She stood up, casting about for an excuse to end the conversation.

"Um . . . I think . . . I'm just going to pop to the bathroom."

"Yeah, sure. No probs. Nice to meet you."

"Nice to meet you too," Hannah said, and she drained her wine, put down the glass, and hobbled painfully out into the corridor, where she stood for a moment, catching her breath and trying not to groan inwardly at the hash she had made of turning down

Jonty gracefully.

"Sooooo . . ." said a drawling voice from behind her, and she turned to see April, closing the door of Dr. Myers's room. "Someone else, eh? Who's the lucky man?"

Hannah felt her cheeks flush again.

"Oh God, I only said that to get rid of him."

"You should have said yes! I know Jonty. He's thick as pig shit, but he's a sweetie, and more to the point, his dad owns Westwell Pharmaceuticals."

"He can't be that thick," Hannah said irritably, pulling off first one of April's teetering high heels, then the other. She felt as if she had descended a step on an imaginary staircase, suddenly six inches shorter than April. "I mean, he did get into Oxford to study English."

"Oh you," April said affectionately. "You're so naive, Hannah. First, he's a rowing blue. Second, did I mention his dad owns Westwell Pharmaceuticals?"

"So? You still have to pass the entrance exam."

April made a dismissive noise through her nose.

"Oh, that! I had an ex at Carne who made a pretty good living taking people's BMAT for them."

"That's medicine," Hannah retorted, but half-heartedly.

"Well, whatever the equivalent is for English. Just because *you* wouldn't do that, doesn't mean everyone else is as high-minded as you."

"April, you shouldn't talk like that."

"Why not? Because people will think I bought my way in too?" April said, laughing. "So what? They already think that, why not give them the satisfaction of thinking they're right?"

"But they're not!" Hannah exploded. "I know full well they're not. Why do you talk like this? I've read your essays, April. You've got nothing to prove."

"Exactly," April said, and suddenly she was no longer laughing but deadly serious. "I have nothing to prove. So let them say what they want."

There was a silence, then Hannah said, "I'm turning in. What about you?"

"I don't know," April said. She looked out the window at the top of the staircase, across the glittering roofs of the college and away towards the water meadows beyond the Isis, striped black and white in the frosty moonlight. "I'm not sure. Horatio's asked me and a couple of girls to go for a drink in town. I'm not sure if I can be bothered, though."

"Horatio?" Hannah knew the single word dripped disapproval, but it was too late to take it back.

"He's not *my* tutor," April snapped.

"He's *a* tutor, though. Don't you think this is a bit inappropriate?"

"We're not in high school," April said impatiently. Then she turned and opened the door to Dr. Myers's rooms, letting out a gust of cigarette smoke and laughing conversation. "I don't know. I haven't made up my mind. Don't wait up."

"I —" Hannah said, and the door slammed behind April. "Won't," she finished to the empty corridor, and sighed, picked up the borrowed high heels, and crossed the hallway to go to bed.

After

When they get home from the restaurant, Will falls into bed and straight into a deep slumber, but Hannah — though she felt tired in the taxi — finds she can't sleep. She tries hot milk, white noise to drown out Will's snores, but nothing works. Her joints hurt. Her breasts are sore. Everything aches and she can't find a comfortable position in bed.

At last, she pulls out her headphones and does something she hasn't done for months, years, even. She opens up Instagram and navigates to @THEAprilCC. April's account.

April was the first person Hannah had ever met with Instagram, back in the days when filters were strictly for coffee, and plenty of people didn't even have a camera on their phone. But April had been one of an early handful to download the app and she had known, somehow, that this would be big.

Now Hannah scrolls back through ancient selfies, with sun-soaked filters and frames to make them look like Polaroids. There are photos of April draped across punts, pictures from college bars, a snap of some tuxedo-attired boy being led by the tie down St. Aldates. All the drunken, laughing, unselfconscious mementos of student life, a decade ago.

She knows the photos well, and not just because the press mined them for publicity shots. In the early days, when they were all that was left of April and of her own life at Pelham, she had flicked through them obsessively — noting every like, reading every comment, each one testament to April's impact on the world and the gaping hole she had left.

RIP April < 3

OMG still cannot believe you're gone. Luv u.

Wow she fit what a shame lol

It wasn't healthy — she knew that, even at the time. And at last the pain the pictures caused outweighed her need to look, to prove that April had been real, and flesh and blood, and as beautiful and vivacious and happy as Hannah remembered. So finally, as the comments died away and the likes slowed down, she'd forced herself to stop going back.

But now, looking at them again, she is struck anew by April's luminous, unpolished beauty, not just in the photos where she is dressed up to the nines, hip jutting, makeup on point, but even more so in the candid snaps — April lying in bed in a splash of morning sun, makeup-free, smiling sleepily at the camera. *Oh hai there* she had captioned that one, and then a series of hashtags: *#nofilter, #nomakeupselfie, #sunday-morning, #godilookamess.*

I miss you . . . Hannah types out in the comments, and for a moment her finger hovers above the send arrow. But she doesn't post. Instead she deletes the three words and goes back to April's feed, scrolling through the decade-old snaps.

A young, sharp-cheekboned Will laughing at her from the banks of the Isis makes her stop momentarily, ambushed by his vulnerability. And there, halfway down the page, is a photo that always makes her catch her breath, even though she knows it's coming — a picture of herself and April, side by side, each holding up a drink. April has her mouth pursed in a selfie pout, but Hannah looks taken by surprise. She is laughing, uncertain, looking not at the camera but at her friend. *It's a Shirley Temple, Daddy, promise *kiss emoji** reads the caption, and Hannah feels something clench inside her, a mix of grief and anger and . . . oh, she doesn't even know what emotions anymore. For a long moment she stares at the picture — at the two of them, so heartbreakingly young and vulnerable — and happy. Happy in a way that she can't remember being for a very long time.

The urge to reach out through the years and warn the two girls in the photo is almost painfully strong — so strong that, suddenly, Hannah can't bear it anymore. She shuts down the phone and lies there staring into the darkness, thinking of what might have been.

Perhaps it's because of the photos, but the next morning Hannah wakes early, in the predawn, from a dream of April. It was not the usual nightmare — Neville's shadow looming out of the darkness; April's body, golden in the lamplight, her cheeks still flushed.

Instead she was walking up one of the narrow medieval wynds that twist and turn their way up from the gardens all the way to the Lawnmarket in front of Edinburgh

Castle. She was going slowly, her hand over the baby in her belly. And then, as she rounded a corner in the passage, she saw it — a flash of gold, a shimmer of silk. And somehow she knew — it was April.

Hannah sped up, going as fast as she could up the winding passageway, hurrying up the steps, and she could hear April's footsteps in front of her, and see her flitting shape silhouetted against the walls of the alley by the lamps — but she could not catch her.

At the top, where the stairs spit you out suddenly into the bustle of the Lawnmarket, all tourists and bagpipers and souvenir stands, she stopped, catching her breath, casting around to see where April had gone.

And then she saw her — one last glimpse of a mocking face as she disappeared into the crowd, far down the street. And the strangest thing was that it was April — but not April as Hannah knew her, not the April of the Instagram photos, skin dewy fresh, a trace of puppy fat lingering at the curve of her jaw. It was April as she would have been now — a woman on the cusp of her thirties, her features sharpened to show the bones beneath the softness of adolescence.

In her dream, Hannah hurried towards her — pushing her way through the crowd, straining for one last glimpse . . .

And then she woke.

Now she lies there, catching her breath, trying to anchor herself back in the present day. Gray light filters through the cracks in the curtains, and beside her she can hear Will's slow, gentle breathing. Her bladder is complaining — she always needs the loo these days — but she can't quite force herself out of bed yet. She needs a moment to orient herself, remind herself of what's real and what's not.

It's been a long time since she dreamed of April. Longer still since she caught sight of her across a crowded room. There was a time when she would find herself scanning crowds for April's face, her heart skipping a beat at the sound of a certain laugh rising above the hubbub, at the sight of a close-cropped blond head weaving towards the bar. But over the last few years those occurrences have become more and more rare — until tonight, anyway.

Now it's as if the news of John Neville's death has stirred the mud of her memories, and images from the past float up from the depths — not the ones memorialized on April's Instagram, but others, more intimate, more *real*. As she lies there, gazing at the minute cracks and crannies in the ceiling, the faces of the others rise up in front of her — not as they are now, but as they were back then. Hugh, streaking across New Quad on a dare one misty morning, wearing nothing but his glasses, the blackbirds rising all around him, flapping and shrieking their indignation. Emily, bent over her books in the Bodleian, that little frown line etched between her thick black brows. And Ryan. Ryan jumping from the Pelham bridge into the Cherwell, in full white-tie evening dress. Ryan running down Broad Street bare-chested, football shirt flying like a banner above his head, after a Sheffield Wednesday win. Ryan in the Eagle and Child, downing pints of bitter and holding forth about the evils of capitalism, then standing on the table and shouting, "Rise up, my fellow workers, and seize the means of production!" then leaping over the bar and gulping directly from the beer tap before the astonished barmaid could do anything to stop him.

He got thrown out for that, she remembers.

"Next time I'll ban you for life, you fucking layabout student!" the landlord had roared as he slung Ryan out into the street, the others tumbling, giggling after him.

"Fellow workers my arse, you lazy little shit!"

Now she wonders how he is, and feels more ashamed than ever of the way she cut him off after college.

Beside her, Will stirs, and she looks over at him, and feels her love for him clutch at her insides with a force that is almost painful. She has always loved him best when she is watching him unawares. Awake, he is self-possessed, polished, still very much the perfectly mannered private-school boy who offered her a seat in the dining hall at Pelham that first night — and some part of her feels she has never really gotten to know him better than she did that first evening.

But asleep, or in his unguarded moments, he is Will. *Her* Will. And she knows and loves the very bones of him.

He seems to be dreaming, emotions chasing across his face, his eyes moving uneasily behind closed lids. She wonders what he is thinking — as she does so often. Will she ever learn to read him, to see the real depths of feeling that he hides behind his mild, amused manner? But perhaps that is why she loves him so much — the unattainability of him, the rare flashes of vulnerability that he reserves for her alone.

Only once has she seen him cry — and

that was after April's death, as they held each other and wept and wept for what they had both lost, but also what they had found in each other.

BEFORE

When Hannah returned to Oxford after the Christmas break, it was with a sense of coming home.

"Why *is* it called Hilary term?" her mother asked in the car on the way to the station, and Hannah answered, without even thinking, "Because the feast of Saint Hilary of Poitiers falls in the middle," and then wanted to laugh at herself, at who she had become. How did she know this stuff after just one term? It didn't matter. She knew it, just like she knew how one acquired a blue, and what you wore for your collections.

Collections. Even the word gave her a squirmy feeling in her stomach. Three little syllables, not much to feel nervous about, but she did.

"They're not prelims," she had told her puzzled mother. "You take those at the end of the first year. Collections are done at the start of every term, and cover what you learned the term before."

"So they're just tests? They don't mean anything?"

The thing is, her mother was right — but also so, so wrong. Collections didn't count towards your degree class, or really anything as far as Hannah could make out — and yet everyone was in a flat spin about them, even the second-years, who had sat through the ordeal several times already.

What's the point of an 8 week term, Will had texted her on Boxing Day, *when they just make us do the rest of the work in the holidays? Is it just so the tutors get time to write their books? I can't believe all my mates are out getting pissed and I'm stuck here revising.*

Hannah had to admit he had a point.

It wasn't just the collections giving her an uneasy feeling, though. Seeing the text from Will had triggered a sharp rush of pleasure, followed by an equally sharp stab of guilt. It was ridiculous — that just his name coming up on her phone should make her grin like an idiot. He was *April's boyfriend.* Completely off-limits. But the problem was that while her head knew that, her heart didn't seem to be able to remember it.

Before the holidays she had half hoped that her crush on Will was wearing off —

and surely six weeks' absence would give her plenty of time to forget his wry grin, the shape of his long, slim hands, and the way he looked at her across the crowded JCR with a smile that made her heart light up. But that one single text had shown that was not true. She still liked him. A lot. Which made her officially the worst best friend in the world.

Instead of replying to Will, she'd typed out a text to April, trying to assuage her guilt.

How are you? Merry Christmas! Hope you had a lovely day.

thanks, April texted back. *it was fucking awful tho i did get a balenciaga tote so every cloud*

Pause.

how was urs?

Pretty okay, Hannah typed back, *though no balenciaga tote so every silver lining.*

ha ha! April texted, with a picture of a laughing frog.

Now, as the train drew into Oxford station, Hannah had a rush not of homesickness, but of whatever the opposite was. Homecoming, maybe. The thought of Pelham, and April, and their little room high in the rafters made her smile with a happiness that even the prospect of collections couldn't dim.

She was getting off the train when she saw Ryan up ahead of her on the platform and half ran, shoving her way ruthlessly through the crowd of students, to try to catch up with him. It wasn't easy — she was wearing a rucksack and dragging a suitcase, but she caught him at the ticket barrier, where he was rummaging in his wallet.

"Ryan! How was your holiday?"

"Ey up, Hannah Jones!" Ryan said with a broad grin, and he turned and gave her a bear hug. "How're you, pet?"

"I'm good. How are you?"

"Pretty sweet, yeah. Had a good holiday, but I'm chuffed to be back."

"I bet you missed Emily?"

"Missed the sex anyway," Ryan said, with a grin that dared her to react. Hannah rolled her eyes.

"You know full well if you actually were the sexist pig you pretend to be, Emily wouldn't touch you with a barge pole."

"She's like all clever women," Ryan said, yanking his bag through the turnstile. "Secretly wants a caveman to throw her over his shoulder."

Hannah shook her head, refusing to rise to the bait.

They shared a taxi back to Pelham, swapping gossip and catching up as it wound its way slowly through the crowded streets.

"Fucking collections," Ryan groaned when she asked him about his revision. "Yeah, I've revised. I'd like to pretend I didn't, but we can't all have a rich daddy to donate a library wing if we flunk out."

"It's all an act," Hannah said, a little nettled on April's behalf. "You know that, right? All that *party girl, I don't care* schtick. She actually works pretty hard, and she's bloody clever."

"It in't just her, though, is it? It's all of them. All them private-school types getting the shock of their lives as they realize we can't *all* be top of the class. I mean, look at me and Will, we're mates, sure. But only one of us is going to come out at the head of the list. And we both want it to be us. Everyone at Pelham does. And for some of them it'll be the first time they don't."

Hannah nodded soberly. It was true — Pelham wasn't the most rabidly academic of the Oxford colleges, but it certainly leaned that way, rather than towards the sporting, drinking culture of some of the others. On a scale from work hard to play hard, Pelham definitely prized the first more. But nor was it the most meritocratic of the colleges. As Ryan had pointed out, it had a high intake of private-school students, higher than the already high Oxford average. Taken together, the two made for a weirdly febrile atmosphere that combined academic privilege with a panicked realization that no one here was getting a leg up — there were no kindly teachers to help with cramming or hint at which papers to revise. Here there were no extra classes, no mummy or daddy to organize after-school tutors and emergency summer school. You were on your own — sink or swim. And Hannah had no idea which camp she would be in.

"Hannaaaaah!"

The shriek set Hannah's ears ringing as she opened the door to the set, and someone barreled across the living room to fling her arms around her, almost knocking her off-balance with her heavy rucksack.

"April!" Hannah set down her case, laughing, and hugged April back. "How are you? Sorry your Christmas was a bit pants."

"Pants is not the word. It was a big steaming pile of crap," April said, throwing herself back on the sofa. "If it wasn't for my sister, I'm not sure I'd bother to go back next vac."

"You have a sister?" Hannah was surprised. She wasn't sure why — April had never explicitly said she was an only child, but somehow Hannah had just assumed that was the case.

"Yeah, she's eleven and a little brat, but I wouldn't leave a dog alone with my parents at Christmas. Oh, by the way" — she threw out a hand at a small gift bag sitting on the table in front of the sofa — "I got you something."

"For me? April, you shouldn't have."

"Well, I did, so suck it up."

Surprised, Hannah wriggled her rucksack off each shoulder and made her way over to the armchair in front of the fireplace. The bag was small, white, and made of stiff card with handles of thick black grosgrain ribbon, and inside was a miniature parcel done up in holly-green paper. Carefully she took it out, unpicked the tape, and drew out the little jewel-bright box inside.

"Chantecaille," Hannah read out. It wasn't a brand she knew, but she could tell from the packaging and the feel of it in her hand that that was probably because it was far too expensive for the makeup counter at Superdrug. "Is it nail varnish?"

"Lipstick," April said. "I'm so fed up of seeing you use that horrible axle grease you call makeup." She took the box from Hannah, pried open the top, and said, "Mouth open, please."

Hannah did so, parting her lips in that strange frozen smile that little girls learned from watching their mothers in the mirror and closing her eyes as April stroked her mouth in a gesture so intimate a shiver ran down her spine. When she opened her eyes again, April was looking smug.

"I knew it. Go and look in the mirror."

Hannah did.

The girl that stared back at her was herself, but not herself. It was Hannah, but her lips were soft, full, and a deep rose pink that begged to be kissed. The color was dramatic without looking clownlike, the way her dark red lipstick had. It was, somehow, perfect.

"Thank you," she said to April, and then, without really meaning to, Hannah found she was hugging her friend, feeling her fine, bird-thin bones, her face in April's cloud of platinum-blond hair, smelling that strange dark scent that April always wore. "I love you, April. I really missed you over Christmas."

Hannah felt, rather than heard, April swallow against her shoulder. An intake of breath, a catch in her throat. She felt April's fingers tighten on her spine as though she almost didn't want to let go.

Then she was pushed away, and it was the same insouciant April rolling her eyes and laughing at her.

"Yeah right, you sentimental cow. Now come on. Let's go down to the bar. I've got some drinking to do."

AFTER

Rainy days have always been Hannah's favorite in the shop. It's not good for business — the regulars stay home, and the tourists get taxis to the museums instead of browsing up and down Victoria Street and the lanes surrounding the castle. But the truth is that although Hannah likes the customers, they are not why she came to work at Tall Tales.

She has always felt safest surrounded by books. The library back in Dodsworth, happily browsing the early readers while her mum graded papers in the reference section. Blackwell's in Oxford, a cornucopia of culture, everything from Aeschylus to X-Men comics. The Bodleian — an actual living temple to literature and learning. The quiet of the library at Pelham, with the low shaded lamps glowing off the dark wooden desks. Hannah has never understood people who get married at their college chapel —

she has no religion, she feels no connection to that remote, austere place with its psalms and hymns and Latin lessons. She and Will got married at Edinburgh's town hall, in a civil ceremony that lasted only a few minutes. But the library . . . yes. If she could have married Will in the Pelham library, that she could imagine — in the deep, reverential quiet, surrounded by all that humankind has ever known about love — every novel, every poem, every word.

So when she came to Edinburgh, all those years ago, running away from the unanswered letters from Pelham, filled with questions about her future that she couldn't answer, perhaps it was natural that she looked for bookshop posts. A professional librarian position was out of the question, without a degree. So was work at a publisher. Once, Hannah had dreamed of being an editor, stacks of manuscripts on her desk and a wall of books she had edited in her living room. But the adverts all specified a BA at minimum, some of them asked for a master's, or specialist qualifications. Bookshops, though . . . bookshops were not so prescriptive. Cathy didn't even mind about her lack of retail experience. "As long as you love books," she'd said, "it'll all work out."

And it had. At first she and Cathy had worked side by side, Cathy teaching her how to work the till, how to keep track of stock, who to help and who to leave alone.

Now, nine years on, Cathy is semi-retired and it's Hannah, as much as anyone, who runs the shop — she and Robyn between them. It's Hannah who speaks to the reps, checks the stock, decides how many of the new Paula Hawkins they will want, whether to put Haruki Murakami in the window, and when to ask Ian Rankin for an event. Robyn is their children's specialist, and takes care of the shop's Facebook page and Twitter feed.

Today, it's been raining hard since twelve, and they've had only one customer in that time — a young man who has been browsing in the back room of the shop for a while. Cathy doesn't like them to harass the customers with offers of assistance unless they look actually lost; *Nothing worse than feeling jumped on,* she always says. But customers who lurk out of sight in the back room are a bit of a red flag for shoplifting, particularly students with a rucksack, and it's the nonfiction section, housing some of the most expensive books in the shop — academic reference volumes, and the fifty-pound Taschen art books. If you *were* going to steal stuff that's where you'd start.

"He needs to shit or get off the pot," Robyn whispers to Hannah when she comes back from the staff room to find him still there, and Hannah laughs.

"I'll go and see what he wants."

She coughs as she enters the nonfiction section, not wanting to be seen to sneak up on customers. The man straightens and turns around and Hannah sees that he's not as young as she thought. From the other side of the shop there was something about his sandy hair and flushed cheeks that made him look like a teenager with a schoolbag, but up close she can see he's quite a long way past that, and as he stands, she catches a pink flash of scalp through the thinning hair at the back of his head. He's probably in his mid-twenties, a little younger than her. Not a student, then. And probably not a shoplifter either.

"Can I help with anything?" she asks.

"Oh, h-hi," he says. "Yes, actually." His voice is tentative, and there's a slight lilt in his accent. Not Scottish. Welsh, maybe? "I'm looking for a biography of Ted Bundy."

Ted Bundy.

Hannah feels her lips thin. She tries not to be judgmental about reading — *No such thing as a guilty pleasure* is Cathy's motto, and it's one Hannah largely subscribes to. Jeffrey Archer to Geoffrey Chaucer, *Outlander* to *The Outsider* — they all keep the wheels of publishing turning and money coming into the tills, and if they give someone a happy few hours, that's good enough for her. But still, she doesn't really understand why anyone wants to buy true crime. Why would they voluntarily soak themselves in the misery of people like her?

"I'm not sure," she says, trying to keep the tightness out of her voice. "You're in the right place — it'll be in this section if we have one. If not, I could order one in for you."

They stand, side by side with their heads tipped, looking down the stack of true-crime biography, and at last Hannah shakes her head.

"No, sorry, it doesn't look like we do. Was it specifically Bundy you were after, or can I recommend something else? *I'll Be Gone in the Dark* is supposedly very good." She taps the spine. "I haven't actually read it, but my colleague Robyn liked it a lot, and it had great reviews. It's about the hunt for the Golden State Killer. It's not exactly a biography — more about the investigative side of things, I think."

"Okay," he says, somewhat to her surprise.

He pulls it out of the bookshelf — a hefty hardback retailing at north of twenty pounds. "Thanks, I'll take it."

"Great, was there anything else?" Hannah asks.

She's turning away for the till, expecting him to say no, but something in his face catches at her. He's looking oddly . . . nervous. Expectant.

"Actually, yes," he says. His voice flutes up half an octave, like a teenage boy's. "Are you Hannah J-Jones?"

She stops in her tracks.

Her whole body goes instantly stiff, and then her cheeks flame with heat. For a long moment she just stares at him, frozen, trying to figure out what to say. Should she lie? Walk away? Refuse to answer?

It doesn't matter what she says. Her stricken silence is an answer in itself, and she can see from the man's face that he knows it, in spite of the subtle ways she's changed her appearance since the trial — the glasses she started wearing full-time instead of just for watching TV; the long hair she sacrificed to anonymity. The difference is enough to fool the casual observer. But this guy is clearly far from that. He's trying not to look pleased, but he is. He has hit the bullseye.

"Who are you?" she manages at last, and her voice surprises her. It is a hiss of anger. "Who *are* you?"

The young man's pink-and-white face falls a little, and he looks slightly hurt.

"I'm a writer. My name's Geraint."

Of course.

"I'm sorry," he's saying. "I emailed asking if it would be okay if I p-popped past to introduce myself, but I didn't hear back so I thought —"

Fuck.

Fuck.

The man is still speaking, something about an article, a podcast, an interview, but the words make no sense above the ringing in her head.

"I can't do this," she says, interrupting him. Her voice is still harsh and strange in her own ears. "Not here. You can't come here again, do you understand?"

"I'm really sorry," he says, and now he looks it. His face is crestfallen. "I should have thought. It never occurred —"

"Just — go," she breaks in desperately, and he nods and sets the book gently back on the shelf.

"I am *really* sorry," he repeats, with more emphasis this time, but she's walking away from him now, unable to look him in the face, unable to think of anything except getting away from him. "Ryan said —"

It's that one word that breaks the spell.

Ryan.

She stops, turns around.

"You spoke to Ryan?"

"Yes, he's a good friend. It was Ryan who suggested coming to see you."

"How — how is he?"

"He's . . . I mean, he's all right. He's better than he was."

She swallows, unable to admit that she wouldn't know — because she hasn't seen him for more than five years. What kind of friend does that make her?

"I really *am* sorry," the man — Geraint — says again, miserably this time. "I really apologize for springing this on you like that. I should have realized this wasn't the right time and place."

"It's okay," she says, though it's not, and it never was, and she wants to kick herself for saying it. "Look, email me, okay? I'll reply, I promise. But you can't come here. This is my work — they don't know anything about — that time."

"I understand," he says, dropping his voice to a whisper, as though they are conspirators. "I'll email. Thanks, Hannah."

And then he's gone.

After the shop door swings shut behind him, Hannah finds her legs are trembling and she gropes her way to the story corner beanbag and sits, her face in her hands, trying to stop shaking.

Why, *why* did she say that about the email? Now she will have to read it — and reply. *Why?*

Because it was the only way to get rid of him, she realizes. Or it felt like the only way. And because part of her, at heart, is still the nice polite girl from Dodsworth who wants people to like her, and who doesn't want to disappoint anyone, or cross anyone, or let anyone down.

For a brief flashing moment she tries to imagine how April would have handled the young man.

Fuck you, probably, in her most bored, drawling tone. And then laughed after he'd gone, and poked fun at his prematurely balding hair.

But then she pushes the thought out of her mind. She can't think about April. Not now. Least of all now.

She is heaving herself to her feet when her phone starts vibrating. Her first thought is *What now?* And her second is an instinct to silence it, send it to answerphone. She can't be dealing with her mother — not now. But when she looks at the screen, it's not Jill. It's not even Will.

It's the hospital.

She presses answer.

"Hello?"

"Oh, yes, hello." The woman on the other end sounds brisk and a little bit pissed off. "Is that Hannah de Chast—" She stumbles over the surname, as people always do. "De Chasti-gan?"

"Yes." Hannah doesn't bother to correct the pronunciation. "Is everything okay?"

"Well, yes and no, it's Ellie here from the midwifery team. We had you down for an appointment at two. Had you forgotten?"

For the second time that day, the blood drains from Hannah's face and then comes rushing back.

"I'm so sorry." She stumbles over the words, even while she is heading to the staff room, picking her way through the teetering displays with all the haste she can safely muster. "I totally forgot — something happened — family stuff —" Ugh, *no,* that word again — but it's too late to take it back. "I'm so sorry, am I too late?"

"Well, you're lucky, my next two ladies have arrived early so I can put you back to two twenty, if you can get here in time? Where are you?"

"Just around the corner. I am *so* sorry." Hannah has reached the staff room. She grabs her coat off the back of the door, shrugging her arms into it as she speaks. "I'll be there in five minutes, I promise."

As she hangs up she sees Robyn staring at her over the kettle.

"Everything all right?"

"Yes. No. I mean, I forgot my midwife appointment. I'm *so* sorry, can you hold the fort?"

"Sure!" Robyn says cheerfully. "But calm down. You'll do yourself a mischief!"

"You're a star," Hannah says breathlessly, and then she snatches up her bag and runs from the shop.

BEFORE

"So, drink then?" Hannah said, coming into the living room, where April was scrolling through her phone. Hannah had finished putting away the last of her belongings, and the set finally looked like home again.

"Sure," April said. She stretched, catlike, spreading out all her toes and fingers. "Pelham bar? I don't think I can be arsed to go into town."

"Sure. But can we go via Cloade's? I met Ryan on the way over and he said to knock on if we were going for a drink." She said the last part with a slight flush, knowing that she was giving herself an alibi for calling past Cloade's that had nothing to do with Will, but knowing too that of course April would collect Will while they were over there, so it would come to the same thing. By picking up Ryan, she was ensuring Will's company.

"No probs," April said. She grabbed her

phone, keys, and purse, glanced at herself in the mirror, and followed Hannah down the staircase and across the quad to Cloade's.

As they crossed the courtyard in front of the big, blocky modern building, Hannah found herself glancing automatically up at Will's window, as she always did — second from the right, sandwiched between Hugh's and Ryan's. It was dark, but next door Ryan's was bright, and the window was open, in spite of the cold air.

"Bet they're smoking," April said with a slightly wicked look that made Hannah's stomach shift a little uneasily. She had come to know that look of April's, and it usually foretold some kind of mischief. The only question was how far she would go.

When they reached Ryan's room Hannah raised her hand to knock, but April put her finger to her lips. Her eyes were full of laughter.

"Can you smell it?" she whispered. Hannah nodded. The smell of weed was filtering under the door, in spite of the dense municipal carpet, along with the sound of Bellowhead's "New York Girls."

"Don't say anything," April whispered, and then she raised her hand and knocked, a sharp peremptory rat-a-tat, quite unlike her usual single thump.

"Er, who is it?" Ryan's voice came from inside. April winked at Hannah and then, to Hannah's enormous surprise, she spoke, but in a voice quite unlike her own — plummy and rather prim.

"Mr. Coates, this is Professor Armitage. We have received a complaint that the scent of the marijuana weed known as skunk has been detected emanating from your room. Could you please open the door?"

"Shit," Hannah heard, very muffled from within, and the sound of people scrambling to their feet. The music was abruptly silenced. Then, still Ryan, but more loudly, "Um, just a minute, Professor — I'm — I'm just on the bog. Hang on a sec."

More flurried noises came from behind the door — the sound of the bathroom door opening and then a toilet flushing.

"Open the window," she heard, whispered urgently from within, and then, in reply to some remark she couldn't hear, "Well open it wider, you dickhead."

April meanwhile was creasing up with silent laughter. She recovered herself enough to say, "Mr. Coates, Mr. Coates, I must ask you to kindly open this door immediately!" though there was a suspicious wobble in her voice at the last word as the toilet flushed again.

"One sec!" came Ryan's voice, this time with a note of desperation, and then the door opened and Ryan, face red and hair tousled, his clothes giving off a strong smell of weed, was standing in the doorway. For a second he just looked at them both, puzzled, trying to make sense of the situation, but as April burst into an irrepressible guffaw, realization dawned, and his whole face flushed purple with barely suppressed rage.

"You little fucking bitch," he said, grabbing April's arm and dragging her inside the room. April was still howling with laughter, but she was also trying to pull herself out of Ryan's grip.

"Get off me, you bastard! That hurts!"

"It fucking should hurt." He shoved her, and she sprawled backwards into an armchair, looking up at him with a mixture of annoyance and defiance, rubbing her arm. "I just flushed a perfectly good eighth down the bog because of you, you stupid little cow!"

"Hey, hey, Ryan, calm down," Will said. He came across to stand between Ryan and April. He looked torn between relief and irritation. "Come on, it was just a joke. April didn't know we'd flush it."

"Yeah, I had no idea you'd be that stupid,"

April retorted. "Why didn't you just drop it out the window like a normal person?"

"Because I thought I was about to get sent fucking down," Ryan said through gritted teeth. He was standing over April as though he would have liked to hit her, and Hannah wasn't certain whether he would have done so, if it hadn't been for Will. "I daresay this is all very funny to posh birds like you, in't it? But those of us without a rich daddy to pay people off have to live with the consequences of our actions. If I get expelled, that's it. Kaput. I am royally fucked. And you know what, I understand why you wouldn't get that — but you." He rounded on Hannah. "I didn't think you were such a silly little bitch. Maybe living with her, it's rubbed off."

"Hey, leave her out of it," April said, standing up and facing Ryan. "She had nothing to do with it so pick on someone your own size."

"That'd be you, would it?" Ryan said, with a kind of snarling laugh. He gestured at the disparity between them — April probably no more than five foot four, and eight stone soaking wet, Ryan over six foot and built like the rugby player he was. "Well, you've got balls, at least."

"Two more than you have," April retorted.

They stood for a moment, glaring at each other, a kind of palpable tension crackling in the air between them so strong that Hannah felt the hairs on the back of her neck stand up. "Wanker."

"Bitch."

"Hey, hey," said a voice from the corridor, and they both swung round to see Emily standing in the doorway, hands on hips. "What's with the rampant misogyny, Coates?"

"Rampant misogyny my arse," Ryan snapped. "She just made me flush an eighth of weed."

"Yeah, I *made* him," April said sarcastically. "With the power of my miiind, woooh!" She made wavy ghost fingers in front of Ryan's face, and he slapped her hand away irritably. "I knocked on the door while he was having a spliff and the idiot was so scared he flushed his entire stash."

"Nice move, Coates." Emily raised one eyebrow. "With cool like that, maybe better not take up drug smuggling."

"Both of you can go shove something painful where the sun don't shine," Ryan growled. "And you" — he stabbed a finger at Will — "don't stand there like you don't know she isn't a complete pain in the arse. That's the best part of fifty quid I'm down.

And some of us actually have to work for our cash instead of milking the stock market for unearned money off the backs of the workers."

"Oh, well *now* we're getting down it, Mr. Capitalism Is Robbery," April said. "Fifty quid, is that the real problem? It's all the same with you socialist types, isn't it — money's a construct and debt is a tool to subjugate the proletariat, until someone owes *you* a tenner, at which point you never stop harping on about it. Look, here we go." She pulled out her purse and began riffling through the notes. "Twenty, forty, sixty — here you are — fifty quid for the stupid weed plus a little extra for your trouble. Buy yourself something pretty, sweetheart."

She held out the cash. Ryan stood there glaring, a vein visibly pulsing in his temple and the muscles in his jaw working. His expression flickered between fury and something else — something Hannah couldn't quite pin down. Not humiliation, he didn't look humiliated. More like a strong desire to slap April's face.

But then he seemed to make up his mind. He reached out and took the money, with a little comedic bow and a mocking tug of his forelock.

"Why thank you, milady. Your 'umble

servant, I'm sure, and a pleasure to be rogered by you any day of the week."

Hannah let out a breath and exchanged a glance with Emily. It felt like a crisis had been averted, though she wasn't completely sure what or how. Would Ryan really have punched April in front of all of them, including Will? It didn't seem likely, but there had been *something* in the air between them, something electric and powerful and very dangerous.

"I say," said another voice from behind her, this one mild and hesitant. "What's been happening here? Smells like a bonfire."

Hannah turned to see Hugh standing in the doorway, blinking owlishly through his glasses. As she watched, he blew his fringe up out of his eyes and gave a rather fatuous grin.

"Been indulging in a spot of the old Mary Jane?"

"Jesus Christ," Ryan muttered under his breath. "Where the fuck have I ended up, some kind of P. G. Wodehouse novel?"

"Hello, Hugh," April said. She stalked across the room to kiss Hugh on either cheek. "Thank you for the Christmas present."

Christmas present? Hannah was disconcerted somehow. She hadn't thought Hugh and April were close enough for that. She flicked a look at Will to see what he made of the odd remark, but he was picking up tobacco from where it had spilled across the desk, and didn't seem to have heard. Hugh said something to April in return, his voice sounding a little uncomfortable, but too low for Hannah to make out, and April laughed, not entirely kindly.

"Look, why *did* you come up here?" Ryan said now. "It wasn't just to make me flush my stash like a fucking dickhead, was it?"

"No," April said coolly. "Hannah and I are going to the bar. Are you coming?"

Hannah had expected Ryan to give April the brush-off, but instead, somewhat to her surprise, he nodded.

"All right. I need a pint. And you —" He pointed a finger at April. "Fifty quid or no fifty quid, you're buying. Got it?"

"Got it," April said. She linked arms with Ryan and gave him a little squeeze, and then said in her plummy fake professor voice, "You love me really, Mr. Coates, you know you do."

"I do fucking not," Ryan said. But the edge was gone from his voice, and when April dug him in the ribs, he tickled her back, making her laugh and squeal and writhe away, and then chased her all the way down the stairs and across the quad, the rest of them following in their wake.

"Assault!" April shrieked as they rounded the corner of the library. "Bad touch!"

"Oh my God," Will groaned as the two disappeared through the dark shapes of the rose garden. "I swear, she'll be the death of me. She'll kill me, Hannah. She really will."

"But you love her," Hannah said lightly. "Don't you?"

Afterwards she wondered if it was her imagination, the way Will paused and then looked away before answering, not meeting her eyes.

"I do," he said at last, and then gave a laugh. "Of course I do. You know what they say — can't live with her, can't live without her. Right?"

"Right," Hannah echoed. Hugh and Emily had outpaced them, and she and Will were alone in the winter-clipped rose garden, and the college was silent and empty in the way only a sprawling building full of several hundred students and dons could sometimes inexplicably be. "Of course you do."

AFTER

It's closer to fifteen minutes later that Hannah climbs the stairs, sweating profusely, to the waiting room at the midwifery clinic, clutching her maternity notes in one hand and her bag in the other. Her face is scarlet and her heart is hammering. How could she have forgotten the appointment?

As she enters, a doorway on the far side of the waiting room opens and a woman's head pops out.

"Are you Hannah de Chasting?"

"Yes! I'm so sorry." She is trying not to pant too obviously.

"It's fine, come on through."

Hannah follows her into the little office and sits on the hard plastic chair, shrugging off her coat for what she already knows is coming. She feels a bead of sweat run down the hollow of her spine and squirms against the chair back to stop the tickle.

"Got your notes?" the midwife asks.

Hannah nods and passes over the folder.

"And your sample?"

"Oh God." Hannah puts her hand to her forehead. "I'm so sorry — in all the kerfuffle I totally forgot —"

"It's okay, you can do one after. So we are . . ." She looks at a calendar by her desk. "Twenty-two plus four, is that right? Okay. Let's get you up on the couch and we'll measure the bump."

Nodding again, Hannah moves across to the couch and lies down, trying not to ruck up the giant roll of toilet paper stretched across the slippery cover. Her dress is stretchy jersey, and lying like this she can see the still faintly surprising bulge of her stomach, smooth and round beneath the fabric. The midwife takes out a tape measure and measures from her ribs to her pubic bone, then she slips a stethoscope up under Hannah's dress with a deft movement and listens for a moment before nodding and writing some figures down on Hannah's notes.

"All good. You're measuring right on track for twenty-two weeks, and baby's heartbeat is nice and strong too. Right, sit up." She helps Hannah upright with a strong, pale arm, and waits while Hannah swings her legs round and off the couch. "Let's do your blood pressure now."

She wraps the plastic cuff around Hannah's arm, chilly against Hannah's still hot skin, and pumps it up. She presses the stethoscope against Hannah's inner arm and deflates . . . counting. Then a little frown creases her brow.

"Hmm, give that a minute and we'll have another go. Why don't you try for that sample while we're waiting. There's a loo in the hall."

She hands Hannah a clear vial and nods towards the door, and Hannah obediently slides off the couch and makes her way across the corridor, feeling a little disquieted. In the loo she shuts her eyes, trying to drive out all thoughts of April and Ryan and Geraint, but she can't seem to banish them and they crowd round her, intruding on her thoughts, pushing into this time that should be about her and her baby.

At last, though, the sample pot is close enough to full and she reenters the little office and passes the vial across, with the faint sense of embarrassment that never seems to leave the act of handing over a still-warm container of your own urine, no matter how many times she does it. The midwife dips a stick into the pot, reads something off, and nods.

"Very good. Nothing to worry about there. Now, let's do that BP again and then we're all done."

Hannah sticks out her arm and the midwife slides on the cuff and inflates it again, this time much tighter, or maybe it's just that it's for the second time, Hannah's not sure, all she knows is that it's no longer just faintly uncomfortable but actually verging on painful.

There is silence. Hannah can feel the blood rushing in her arm, trying to get past the constriction, and hear the midwife breathing heavily through her mouth. It sounds like she has a cold and her nose is blocked.

Then the woman straightens and undoes the cuff.

"Okay, well it's probably nothing to worry about, but it is still quite high."

"I did run here," Hannah points out, rolling her sleeve back down. She says nothing about the shock she had with Geraint before the midwife called, but she's uncomfortably aware that it probably didn't help.

"Let's get you back next week for a check, and I'm sure it'll all be back to normal."

"Next week?" Hannah is dismayed. The normal routine is monthly. The fact that this is considered worrying enough to upgrade her to a weekly visit has unsettled her. "Are you sure?"

"So that takes us to the twenty-first . . . I can't do two o'clock," the midwife is saying, running her finger down her appointment book, "in fact the afternoon is completely blocked out, but I could see you at nine forty a.m. Does that work?"

Hannah sighs. She nods and takes out her phone to input the appointment.

"Sure. But I'm certain it was just because I was running late."

"I'm sure you're right. But better safe than sorry, eh? Now, go home and relax."

Hannah nods, but as she leaves, the thought of Geraint's email pops into her head like an unwanted intruder, and she finds herself thinking wistfully, *If only it was that simple.*

Before

"I can't do it." Hannah stood in the center of the set living room, twisting her fingers together, nausea and dread mingling in the pit of her stomach. "I can't. I can't go down there and find out in front of everyone."

"Fine. I'll go." April stood up and stretched luxuriantly. "I'll text you. Castanets for a first, thumbs-up for a second, or skull and crossbones for a third."

"Dickhead," Hannah said, but she couldn't help laughing. Somehow April's attitude was exactly what she needed — a reminder not to take this *too* seriously. It wasn't the end of the world, even if it felt like it. What made it worse was the unfairness of it all: April hadn't even done collections — it turned out her professor didn't believe in setting them in the first year. Will and Ryan had just done some kind of extended essay and got the marks back the same week. Hugh, on the other hand, had gone off white and trembling in his academic gown to sit a proper exam paper, and had been checking his pigeonhole every morning to see if the results had come through yet.

Hannah wasn't sure how she had been expecting to get her results — a slip of paper in her pigeonhole, or an email from Dr. Myers. Instead, without warning, she'd had a group text from Rubye, one of the girls at Dr. Myers's drinks party. *Marks are up on Dr. M's office door. Rx* And that was it. No photo. No hint of how anyone had done. And everyone doing English seemed to have received it — which meant there was a very good chance they were all down there now peering at her name, while she was up here too scared to go and look.

"No," she said now, making up her mind. "No, I have to go. It's better to know."

"You know it's bullshit, right?" April said. She put her hand on Hannah's arm. "You do know that? It doesn't count for anything."

Hannah nodded. But it wasn't true. Right in that second, that list was everything.

Some ten minutes later Hannah was walking down the corridor towards Dr. Myers's office door, her palms sweating against her jeans. Even from this distance, she could see there were three pieces of paper tacked against the wood, and a girl Hannah recognized as third-year English was bending down, reading the rightmost one. As Hannah neared she stood and turned, a satisfied smile on her lips.

"Good luck," she said to Hannah. "Hope you get what you wanted."

"Thanks," Hannah said, "you too. I mean — I hope it was. What you wanted, I mean."

The girl smiled again, a little patronizingly this time with a slight *calm down, dear* air, and then moved past Hannah, leaving her alone to study the short lists of names.

The left-hand one was first-years, and she looked automatically halfway down, where *J* normally sat in the alphabet, before realizing that it wasn't in alphabetical order but some other, confusingly randomized system. Her tutorial partner, Miles Walsh, was roughly where she would have expected her own name. Beside each name was a list of symbols — $\beta\alpha$, $\beta+$ Hannah read beside Miles's name. And $\gamma++$, $\beta-$ beside another's. A lump rose in her throat. What did it mean? Was this some kind of particularly cruel Oxford trick, dangling her marks in front of her in some kind of impenetrable code?

"Oh, hi," said a voice behind her, and Hannah whirled around to see Jonty Westwell, the boy from Dr. Myers's party, standing in the hallway. "Checking out your mark? Same here. Wish he wouldn't put them up publicly. Most tutors only do that for prelims. What did I get?"

"I have no idea," Hannah said, her voice stiff with a rage she could only half contain, "because they're in some kind of fucking foreign script. What does that even mean? What's a bloody y plus when it's at home?"

"Oh!" Jonty began to laugh. "God, yeah, sorry. They used Greek grading at my school so you forget how weird it must be to people who're used to percentages. That's not a y, it's a gamma — you know, like . . . alpha, alpha minus, beta, gamma plus, all that. Oh look, here I am." He ran his finger down the second-year list to a position about halfway down. "Beta alpha, gamma plus plus. Could have been worse. I knew I fluffed the second essay. Where are you?" He looked over at the first-year list curiously, and then laughed. "Well, you don't need me to translate that."

Hannah looked at where he was pointing — to her name at the top of the list, with α, α written beside it.

"What do you mean?" she asked uncertainly, and Jonty grinned.

"Myers writes them out in order of class position. So from the fact that you're first, you can probably guess you're home and dry. But in case you hadn't worked it out, that's alpha, alpha." And then, when she didn't answer but only stared at him, waiting for the translation, he clarified. "There *is* no alpha plus. Alpha is the best mark. You got it for both papers. I'd say you did okay."

"Cham-fucking-pagne," April crowed, when Hannah came back, blushing and unable to hide her huge grin.

"I can't," Hannah said. "I really can't. It's —" She looked at her phone. "It's nearly six, I've got an essay I've got to get done for tomorrow, and besides, I'm broke."

"Hannah." April was severe. "It's not every day you come out top of your class in your first exams. I am taking you out for a drink, whether you like it or not."

"Okay," Hannah said, a little reluctant, but laughing. "But just *one,* okay? Seriously just one. I have to get back for supper and I *have* to get this essay done. It's due in first thing tomorrow."

"Just one," April said seriously. "Pinkie

swear. And I know the *perfect* place to take you."

Some forty-five minutes later, Hannah found herself wearing her new Chantecaille lipstick and a pair of borrowed heels, balanced on a stool in a private members' bar that she had never even noticed, with a Bellini in her hand that she didn't remember ordering. As April chatted away about Valentine's Day balls and the dress she was ordering from London, Hannah took a gulp of the cocktail and felt the alcohol filtering through her blood, giving everything a distant, unreal quality, as if she were looking down on herself from a great height. It wasn't just the drink, though, she knew. Every day she spent with April she felt increasingly dissociated from her old self, the gulf between this gilded existence and humdrum Dodsworth gaping wider and wider until it seemed that no train could bridge it.

"Smile," April instructed, and held up her iPhone high above the bar, angling her head towards Hannah's with a provocative little pout that made her lips look like two plump red cherries. Hannah smiled — and the camera clicked, and then April was uploading the picture to an app on her phone, with the caption *It's a Shirley Temple, Daddy, promise *kiss emoji**

"*That* is definitely not a Shirley Temple," Hannah said, pointing at the Bellini in April's left hand. "It doesn't even look like one."

"No, but my father doesn't look at my Instagram, so it all cancels out," April said, rather sourly. Hannah looked at her curiously as she sat there, swinging one leg and scrolling down her feed, a frown between her finely plucked brows. She was never quite sure how much April's poor-little-rich-girl act was just that — an act. On the one hand, she hadn't witnessed any evidence of April's parents at all — the closest thing she had seen to a parental figure was Harry, the minder/bodyguard who had accompanied April to Pelham that very first day. On the other, that was true of lots of people at college. Some parents had done a swift drop and run. Others had hung around for a few hours, making indulgent conversation, before being shooed away. And many students, particularly the international ones, had arrived without any parental escort at all. April wasn't alone in that.

"What about your mother?" Hannah asked now, with the sensation of treading on rather thin ice, unsure how deep the water was beneath her feet. She knew that April *had* a mother, because she had referred to her in passing once or twice — but there was something about the tone April used in discussing the topic that warned Hannah that there were complicated emotions beneath the surface, quite different from Hannah's own mix of affectionate exasperation with Jill.

"Oh, she's a professional fuckup," April said. She took a swizzle stick off the bar and stirred her Bellini thoughtfully. "You know, Prozac before lunch, Stoli after. Little Vicodin chaser before bed."

"Stoli?" Hannah echoed, puzzled, and April rolled her eyes.

"Vodka, darling. You're such a little provincial."

Hannah said nothing. April probably meant it as a dig, albeit an affectionate one, but it was true, she *was* provincial, and she wasn't ashamed of that. That wasn't the reason for her silence. It was more that she didn't know what to say, faced with this unexpected slew of information. Did April want sympathy? Or just a breezy agreement?

"Can I get you two ladies another cocktail?" The bartender broke the silence, pushing a little dish of olives towards them. He was dressed in a crisp white shirt and black waistcoat, and his accent was Spanish, or perhaps Portuguese, Hannah wasn't sure. He was extremely handsome, and she was not surprised when April put away her phone and rested both elbows on the bar, giving the man a good view of her cleavage in a sheer white silk top.

"What are you offering?" she asked, a hint of a purr in her voice.

"What do you like?" the bartender countered, a smile tugging at the corners of his lips. "For you ladies, I could make something special."

"What do you think, Hannah?" April asked, turning to her, and Hannah suppressed a guilty thought of her essay waiting unwritten at home, and the effect of not just one but *two* cocktails on an empty stomach.

"Well . . . I did *say* just one, but . . . I guess I could stay for one more. But then I *have* to get back."

"Just one, then," April said with a slightly theatrical sigh. "So we'd better make it count. Make us . . ." She skewered an olive on a cocktail stick and put it to her lips, twirling it gently against her teeth with mesmerizing slowness as she thought. "Make us . . . Oh, I know, make us a Vesper. You know, like in *Casino Royale.*"

"Excellent choice," the bartender said, and he turned, pulling three bottles off the rack behind the bar with a theatrical flourish, spinning one in the air before pouring a long stream of clear alcohol into the shaker.

When the drinks were finally mixed, the bartender strained the cold liquid into two tall brimming martini glasses, and picked up a sliver of lemon zest. Very, very carefully he pinched it over the left-hand glass, spritzing the oil from the zest across the surface of the drink in a little iridescent cloud. Then he dropped in the rind and repeated the action with the right. Finally, he slid the glasses slowly across the bar, the cloudy white liquid trembling at the meniscus.

"Aquí tenéis," he said, and gave April a little bow. "A drink named after a beautiful woman, for two beautiful women."

"You flirt," April said. She picked up her glass and took a long, luxurious swallow that drained it almost halfway. "Oh my God, that's delicious. What do you think, Hannah?"

Hannah picked up her own glass, put it to her lips, and took a gulp to match April's. She nearly choked. It was pretty much pure alcohol, from what she could tell. In fact, it tasted like almost neat gin.

"Jesus," she spluttered, setting down the glass. Her eyes were stinging. The Chantecaille lipstick had left a deep rose imprint on the glass. "What's *in* this?"

"Six parts of gin, two parts of vodka, one part of Lillet Blanc," the barman said laconically. April laughed and raised her glass to him across the bar.

"I'll drink to that."

"And how many units of alcohol is that?" Hannah said. She knew she sounded prim and censorious, but she couldn't seem to help it.

"Does it matter?" April said. Her voice was a little stiff, like she was trying to hide her irritation. "It's not like you're planning on driving home. Jesus, you sound like my dad." She took another swallow of the cocktail.

"This is like —" Hannah eyed her own glass, trying to estimate the contents. It had to be close to a quarter of a pint of liquid. "I mean what, the equivalent of four, maybe five gin and tonics? Right?" She turned to the barman, who simply shrugged and smiled at April as if they shared a private joke. "And how much does one of these *cost*?"

"Who cares?" April said, and now the annoyance in her voice was plain, and she wasn't trying to hide it. "Stop being so petty, Hannah. I'm putting all of this on Daddy's account. He won't notice." She picked up the glass and tossed back the remaining inch of her Vesper with something like defiance. "The same again," she said to the bartender, thrusting the empty glass towards him. "For *both* of us. And what's your name?"

"Raoul," said the bartender. He smiled at April, showing very white, very even teeth. "Two more Vespers coming up, it will be my pleasure."

"One, please, Raoul," Hannah said firmly. She swallowed the remains of her Vesper, then stood up, feeling the rush of alcohol to her head. "April, I'm sorry, it's not just the money, I *have* to get back. I've got that essay to hand in tomorrow. I did say."

"Fuck the essay! I never do them until the last minute anyway."

"I *have* left it until the last minute. I told you, it's due in tomorrow morning."

"Tomorrow!" April scoffed. "Tomorrow is hours and hours away! I do my best work at three a.m."

"Well — then — great," Hannah said. Her arguments were slipping away along with her temper. "Good for you. But I don't. In fact I'm pretty useless after midnight, and my tutorial with Dr. Myers is at nine a.m., so —"

"Oh, Dr. *Myers*," April interrupted, mocking. She made a face to the barman that Hannah couldn't read, but it was droll, as if she had secrets she could tell if she wanted.

"Yes, Dr. Myers," Hannah said. She was getting cross. She could feel her cheeks becoming flushed. Why was April always like this? She was the perfect friend — until she wasn't. Funny, generous, totally inspired on occasion. When she was in the mood, there was no one Hannah would rather spend time with. But then with the flip of a switch she would turn and become mean. "What of it?"

"I wouldn't worry about *him*."

"What's that supposed to mean? I have to worry about him, April, he's my tutor."

"Well, good" — April reached out and tweaked Hannah's nose — "for" — she pinched it again — "you."

"Will you stop that!" Hannah said irritably, pushing April's hand away, perhaps harder than she had meant, but there was something extraordinarily annoying about the action, the patronizing element to it, the physical invasion of her space. "For God's sake, April, I'm going back, and that's an end to it."

"Fine," April said. She crossed her legs, wrapping her arms around herself, looking for all the world like some kind of Siamese cat curling up to lick her fur. The candles on the bar winked off the huge rings on her fingers and she leaned confidentially across the bar. "Raoul and I will be fine, won't we, Raoul?"

"I will take good care of your friend," the barman said, and he smiled again at Hannah. "Don't worry, I will make sure Miss Clarke-Cliveden gets home safely."

"You" — April leaned still farther over the bar so that her top slipped lower and Hannah saw a flash of rose-colored brassiere — "can call me April. And I *don't* say that to all the staff."

"Okay," Hannah said. It was that last word that did it, that little reminder of the world April inhabited and she didn't. "Okay, that's it. I'm out, thank you for a lovely evening, April, I'm going to go home and get some food and I suggest that you do the same."

But April said nothing. Instead she pointedly turned her back to Hannah and began watching Raoul carve off a long coil of lemon zest.

Hannah hesitated for a moment, wondering if she was doing the right thing but unsure what her other options were, and then picked up her bag, turned, and made her way down to the street entrance.

A porter was standing at the door, and opened it as she came near.

"Can I get you a taxi, miss?"

"No, no thank you," Hannah said. "I'll be fine walking, but —" She paused in the doorway, uncertain of what to say, how to put it.

"Yes, miss?" The porter was kindly, in his seventies perhaps. He looked like a grandfather.

"My friend, she's still upstairs — will you make sure she gets home okay? She's had a bit to drink . . ."

"Say no more, miss." The porter tapped the side of his nose and winked, but not in the way the barman had, with a hint of suggestion. This was purely avuncular. "I'll see to it myself. Where's home?"

"Pelham College. She's a student."

"You leave it with me. She'll be grand." He nodded at the rain, which was just starting outside, turning the stone flags of the pavement to dark mirrors and the lamps to splashes of gold. "Are you sure you don't want that taxi now? I can put it on Mr. Clarke's account."

Hannah smiled, knowing that he had sized up her clothes, and April's, and had a very good idea of how much cash she had in her account, and shook her head.

"No, that's very kind, thank you. I'll be fine. I've got my mac."

"All right, then. Good night, miss. You take care."

"Good night," Hannah said.

And pulling her hood up, she headed out, into the rainy winter night.

AFTER

Hannah arrives home at the same time as Will. She's looking through her handbag for her key when she hears the low growl of a motorbike coming up the mews, and turns to see him, blindingly bright, driving towards her. He comes to a halt, kicks out the stand, and unbuckles his helmet.

"How was your day?" he asks. She's still trying to think of what to say, how even to begin, when he turns aside, pulls his work bag out of the bike's rear pannier, and heads towards the front door.

Upstairs, she sinks into an armchair with a sigh, watching as Will peels off his leathers and shakes his folded suit jacket out of its creases.

"Let's get takeaway," she says, ignoring the brief twinge provoked by the thought of the cost. "I can't face cooking."

"Bad day?" Will asks, looking up, and Hannah nods, and then regrets doing so.

She doesn't want to talk about it, but now she'll have to. She's always going on at Will for buttoning things up; she can't very well do the same. Plus she has to tell him about the midwife appointment. It's his baby — it wouldn't be fair to keep that stuff from him.

"I had high blood pressure at the midwife appointment," she says at last. "My own fault. I ran there."

"Okay . . ." Will says slowly. He sits down on the arm of the sofa next to her, his face puzzled. "Is that a big deal?"

"It can be, apparently. It can be a sign of this thing called pre-eclampsia, which is pretty serious, though they don't seem to think it's that. But they want me to come back next week for another check."

"Next week?" Will's face doesn't betray much emotion, but Hannah knows him well enough to read the flicker of alarm beneath the surface. "Well, that's annoying for you. Seems pretty stupid they didn't just wait for it to go down and try again."

"They did," Hannah says reluctantly. "But it was still high. I think I'm just stressed — oh God, I don't know. She told me to go home and relax, so that's what I'm doing."

"Stressed?" Will says. He has picked up on the word immediately, and Hannah wants to kick herself. "Stressed about what?

Is this still about Neville?"

Hannah says nothing.

"Han, love, we've discussed this. It's *over.* Neville is gone. It's time to move on."

It isn't over, Hannah wants to say through gritted teeth, *if I made a mistake. It isn't over if Geraint Williams is correct and my evidence left the wrong person to rot in jail. If all that's true, it's very, very far from over.* But she doesn't say that. She can't. She can't bring herself to say those words aloud, to make the possibility real.

"I really need a cup of tea," she says at last, and Will nods, jumping up, glad to have something to do, a way to be a good husband in all of this.

As the sounds of the kettle boiling and Will moving cups and containers in the kitchen filter down the corridor, it comes to her like a reluctant realization — she has to tell him the truth about the encounter in the bookshop. Anything else would be a betrayal. It's just a question of how.

"Will," she says at last, when they're both settled, him on the sofa with the takeaway menus, her curled up beneath a fluffy blanket with a mug of peppermint tea warming both hands.

He looks up.

"Yes? I was thinking pizza — what do you

reckon?"

"Pizza's fine, but listen, there was something else. Something happened today."

"At the clinic?"

"No, at work. This — this guy came into the shop. The journalist I told you about, the one who emailed —"

"He came into the *shop*?" Will puts down the menus and turns to face her. His expression takes her aback — this is exactly why she didn't want to tell him, out of a fear that he would overreact. But his face has a fury in it that's even more out of proportion than she was expecting. Will knows what she's been through with the press over the years; he's watched her change her number and her appearance and even her name. He gets angry on her behalf, angry enough to swear at reporters who call the house, even threaten them sometimes, but that doesn't begin to touch what she sees in his reaction now.

His face is still, almost unnaturally still, but there is a contained rage in it that frightens her, and a vein beating in his temple that she knows is a sign that he's very close to losing his temper. Will doesn't lose it very often — she can remember only once or twice in their whole relationship. But when he does, he *really* loses it. She can remember him hitting a man once, late at night, on their way home from the pub. The guy had been catcalling a woman in a headscarf with horrible racist innuendo, and when Will called him out, the man refused to apologize and then took a swing at Will.

He missed. But Will hit him back, and his punch connected. And he didn't just hit him once, he pounded him and pounded him, while Hannah watched in a kind of mute, frozen terror, unable even to protest, she was so shocked. Will came very close to being arrested for assault that night. He was saved only because two witnesses attested to the racist abuse and that the other man had swung first — that and the fact that the man had turned out to have a long record of racially aggravated offenses, which perhaps made the police more willing to overlook Will's actions.

But Hannah has never forgotten that moment of watching her gentle, loving boyfriend snap. That moment when his mood turned in an instant, and he became someone capable of inflicting severe injury on another human being. Seeing his face now, she is reminded of that night, and a shiver runs down her spine.

"Hannah?" Will says, his voice very level, but there's a sound in it like a warning, and

Hannah swallows, and forces herself to answer.

"Yes. Apparently he said in his email that he might pop in." She finds herself trying to make excuses, downplay her own shock and indignation at the invasion, in order to preempt his fury. "And when I didn't reply, he thought that was a green light. Anyway, I told him — I told him work wasn't the place for it and he's going to email —"

"He's *what*?" Will breaks in, his voice rising.

"Will, please calm down." Hannah's voice is pleading, and she hates herself for it. "He's a friend of Ryan. I can't just tell him to go away."

"You can and you will!"

It's that *will* that does it. If he'd said *should*, Hannah would probably have nodded. But that *will*, there's an autocratic snap to it, like she's not his wife but his employee, his *servant*. And it makes all her hackles rise.

Will's parents didn't want them to marry — *too soon, too young* was what they said, with a vague implication that Will was still traumatized by losing April, but to Hannah it had sounded very much like an unspoken *too common* formed part of their objections. Mostly she and Will don't talk about that

— they don't discuss the fact that neither his parents nor his sister came to their wedding, and have never really welcomed Hannah into the family. They skirt round the fact that Hannah's mum visits regularly and helps out, the fact that Hannah's dad contributed most of the furniture when they moved in together and guaranteed the rent on their first flat, while Will's family basically pretend Hannah doesn't exist.

All of that Hannah can put up with, because it's Will's family, not him.

But that haughty *you will* is a bridge too far.

"I'm sorry?" she says now, putting down the cup and folding her arms. "I *will*? Is that an order?"

"I didn't mean it like that," Will says, and she can see him struggling to overcome his anger. He takes a long breath and says, more quietly, "I just meant — you're really bad at putting yourself first, Hannah. I don't see why you should feel beholden to some friend of Ryan's you've never met, just because you feel guilty about what happened to him after college."

"That's not why," Hannah snaps, but it's not true, and Will knows it. They *both* feel terrible about Ryan; they were together when Hugh phoned, and Hannah remembers Will's absolute devastation. *Ryan? A stroke? But he's so young.*

Was it what happened at Pelham that caused it? The stress, the sleepless nights, six years of PTSD . . . If it hadn't been for Neville, would Ryan be okay?

They will never know. But what they do know — both of them — is what utter shits they have been for not visiting. It's been four years since Ryan's stroke. Four years. Oh, they've sent cards, and Christmas presents, texted their congratulations when Ryan's little girls were born, but it's basically the absolute minimum. So Hannah's denial rings hollow, and they both know it.

"Okay," she says at last, "that's part of it, but all I said was that he could send me an email. What harm can it do?"

"Well, the harm is this." Will waves an arm at her, wrapped up in the armchair. "I don't want you getting stressed out by this — stressed out by some wannabe hack's conspiracy theories. So what if Neville never admitted his guilt. Plenty of people don't. There doesn't need to be some great undiscovered reason for that. And Hannah, you're —"

He stops, and she knows why. What he wants to say is, *You're pregnant with my child, I want you to take care of yourself,* but he's holding himself back. He doesn't want to make their baby into a stick to beat her with.

It's the fact that he doesn't say it that makes her capitulate.

She stands, goes over to where he's sitting on the sofa, and putting the takeaway menus aside, she kisses him.

"I know. And I promise I'll take care of myself. He's only emailing — I'll answer his questions and then make it clear that's it. Okay?"

"Okay," Will says. He smooths her hair back from her forehead, smiles up at her. "I love you, Hannah Jones."

"I love you too, Will de Chastaigne. How did we get so lucky to find each other?"

"Right place at the right time?" Will says. But it's only half-true, and Hannah knows it.

Later, after supper, when they're sitting curled up watching a film on Netflix, Hannah's phone buzzes with an email, and when she looks down, her stomach lurches. She glances at Will. He's absorbed in the film.

"Just going to the loo," she says lightly, tucking her phone into her pocket. Will looks up.

"Want me to pause?"

"No, it's fine. I know this scene." It's

Amélie, and she's seen it half a dozen times. Will nods and turns back to the screen, and she slips out of the room and into the bathroom, where she sits on the loo and reads the email.

Hi Hannah, Geraint here. Really sorry again for ambushing you at the bookshop. Listen, I would love to meet for a coffee or a phone conversation — or whatever you feel happy with. I've spent the last five years investigating what happened the night April Clarke-Cliveden was killed and talking to John Neville, and, as I assume you know, he was absolutely resolute from the trial onward that he had nothing to do with her death — that he went to her room to deliver a package and she was absolutely fine when he left.

I totally understand that this opens up a can of worms for you that you probably don't want to deal with, but I feel like he gave me a task — and that his death puts a responsibility on me to complete that task. Not to prove his innocence — I've got an open mind on that score. But to find out the truth and tie up some of the loose ends. Because there's certain things that don't add up. Why wasn't any of Neville's DNA found on April's body? Why didn't anyone hear a struggle? The two boys in the room below said they heard her walking around, but nothing like anyone fighting for their life.

I would love just a few minutes of your time to ask you some questions that have always puzzled me about that evening and the sequence of events. Obviously if you don't feel able to help with that, I understand. You don't owe me anything. But I feel like I owe John Neville something, and more importantly, I feel that I owe April something too. Because if it's true that John Neville didn't kill April, someone out there got away with murder. And I want to see that person brought to justice. I hope you feel the same way.

I'm up in Edinburgh for the next week and I'd be available any time for a coffee, or for a phone call at any point if this week is not convenient. My number is below.

Warmest wishes, and thanks again for your time,
Geraint Williams

P.S. Please do say hi from me to Ryan if you speak to him!

Slowly, Hannah puts down her phone and sits, elbows on her knees, staring at the shower cubicle opposite. She knows what Will would say. He would say *Leave it alone.* He would tell her not to open the can of worms Geraint referred to in his email. But that's the problem — that metaphor is a little too close to the truth, and it reveals something she has refused to admit to herself for a long time. For there *are* messy, wriggling, unfinished ends putrefying beneath the surface of what happened that night — things that she has refused to think about and look at for a long time. And there should not be.

She cannot just leave this. However much she should. Because if she doesn't find out the truth, Neville's ghost is going to haunt her forever.

Will believes that Neville's death has freed them — but Hannah is only just starting to realize that that's not true. In fact, if what Emily said is right, if she *has* made a mistake, then it's the exact opposite. Because while Neville was alive, he could fight to clear his own name. But now that he's dead, that responsibility has passed to others. To her.

But she's getting ahead of herself. Maybe what Geraint has to say isn't new evidence at all. Maybe it's just some conspiracy theory he's spun out of thin air. If that's the case, the best thing she can do is put it to rest — destroying his illusions and her own fears in the process.

She picks up her phone again, and presses the reply button on his email.

Dear Geraint, I have a day off next Wednesday. If you are available at 10 a.m., I would be happy to meet at Cafeteria, just off —

She stops, thinks, then deletes the last seven words. She isn't happy to do anything, and she doesn't want Geraint at the cafe she goes to every weekend with Will. No. Better to choose somewhere else. Somewhere she won't be bothered about avoiding in the future if the meeting goes sour.

able to meet at the Bonnie Bagel in the New Town for a coffee and to answer any questions you might have. I can't promise to give you the answers that you want — everything I said at the trial was true. John Neville engaged in persistent stalkerish behaviour for months before that night, and I saw him coming away from our staircase just moments after April was killed. He never denied being in our room, and he never explained what he was doing there — porters weren't supposed to deliver parcels, so that part of his story was shaky from the start. The bottom line is this — I believe John Neville was guilty. I hope I can set your mind to rest on that point when we meet.

Hannah

Then she closes down her email, shuts off her phone, flushes the toilet, and goes back to join Will in the living room.

BEFORE

Hannah was cold and wet by the time she got back to Pelham. It was also gone nine — she had heard the clocks striking as she turned onto the High Street — and the porters began locking up the back entrances at 9:00 p.m. She had been planning to slip through the Cloade gate on Pelham Street, in order to avoid going past the Porters' Lodge at the main entrance. Now she might have no other option. Still, it took them a while to get round, sometimes. It was worth a try.

As she turned into Pelham Street she heard the quarter past chime from the chapel bell tower, and she quickened her step. She could see the dark arch of the gate in the long wall just a few meters ahead. *"Don't be locked,"* she found herself whispering under her breath. *"Don't be locked."*

And, amazingly, it wasn't. The wooden door was still open. Inside there was nothing but a metal grille with a card reader cutting off the general public from the quad.

Hannah's fingers were cold and numb as she fumbled in her pocket for her Bod card, wondering all the time if she would see the figure of John Neville lumbering across the courtyard to lock up, but at last she found it. She swiped the card, held her breath, and when the lock clicked back, she pushed open the heavy metal gate and slipped inside.

The rain-soaked quad was crisscrossed black and gold, with light from the warm bright windows of the rooms in Cloade's reflecting back off the rain-soaked flags, and as she passed in front of the building, Hannah couldn't help turning to look up at the third floor, where Will's room was.

His curtains were open, his window a glowing amber square, and even through the rain Hannah could see him, hunched over his desk, writing. As she watched he raised a hand to rub his eyes tiredly, and she turned away, feeling like an intruder, and ducked beneath the cloisters.

Why? she asked herself as she walked away, forcing herself not to glance back over her shoulder. Why did she torture herself like this? Watching Will unawares, finding her gaze tracing the line of his jaw over breakfast, or the shape of his broken nose as he stared up at high table during formal hall. He was April's boyfriend, completely off-limits, even if they broke up. You couldn't date your best friend's ex. It just wasn't the done thing.

And in spite of everything, that's what she and April were. Best friends. In spite of the differences in their backgrounds and personalities, in spite of the fact that right now this second April was drinking Vespers in a private members' bar, while Hannah trudged home in the rain. They had been thrown together by the simple expedient of being roommates, and out of that had grown an improbable but genuine affection.

She couldn't betray that. Not now, not ever.

New Quad was quiet, no sound apart from the pattering rain as she stepped out from under the shelter of the cloisters. The gravel path crunched beneath her feet as she crossed the quad. Under the arch of staircase 7 she folded her umbrella, shook off the worst of the water, and made her way slowly up the stairs. Behind each door was a different sound. The silence of study; the laughter of friends congregating; the quiet thump of someone's music, the volume just slightly too low for Hannah to recognize the song.

When she turned the corner of the last landing, she stopped. Dr. Myers's door was closed. But the one opposite — the door to their set — stood ajar. Had April beaten her back? Taken a taxi, maybe?

Frowning, Hannah put her hand to the wood and pushed.

And then there was the sound of her umbrella falling to the wooden boards with a clatter and a flap of wet fabric, and her own shocked gasp.

"What are you doing here?" The words that came out of her throat were oddly low and guttural, uttered in a voice that didn't sound like her own.

"And a good evening to you too." John Neville straightened from where he was bending over the coffee table in the middle of the room. She could smell him — that faint musty scent of BO that made all her nerves shudder.

"What are you *doing* in my *room*?" she demanded again, her voice rising in spite of herself.

"Well I like that," Neville said. He was fully upright now, a foot taller than her, his head almost touching the delicate ceramic chandelier April had fitted over the regulation light fitting. His shape threw a long shadow over the room. His broad face was a picture of injured innocence, and he held up something wrapped in brown paper. "You had a parcel, wouldn't fit in your pigeonhole so I thought I'd do you a favor and bring it up. If this is the thanks I get, I won't bother next time."

"Thank you," Hannah said in a strangled voice. She held out her hand for the parcel. She was shaking, but she hoped the fact wasn't perceptible to Neville. She had only one thought. Get him *out* of her room. "Now if you'll excuse me, I'm very tired."

"Where've you been anyway?" Neville said conversationally. "You look like a drowned rat. Catch your death in that little raincoat." He was making no move to leave, or to hand over the parcel, and Hannah had a sudden panicked thought. What if he didn't go? What if he just — *stayed*? She couldn't physically make him leave.

Suddenly, she couldn't do this anymore. She pushed past him to her bedroom, opened the door, and walked inside, locking it behind her, and then she stood with her back to the solid oak, feeling a strange lightheaded sickness.

She was shivering with a mix of shock and cold, and now as she looked down at herself she saw herself as Neville must have seen her — her sodden jeans, her thin top clinging to her skin where the rain had soaked through her coat and dripped from her hair, the wet cotton cleaving to every rib and every seam of her bra. She felt impossibly, unbearably exposed.

Her handbag was still clutched in her left hand, and she pulled out her phone, staring at it as her teeth chattered, wondering who she could call. The Porters' Lodge *was* the de facto security for the college. Even if there was another porter on duty tonight — which she doubted, evenings were usually quiet — she could hardly ask one porter to bounce another.

April? Not the way they had left things — and anyway, she was in a bar halfway across town, and probably drunk by now.

Dr. Myers? He was the closest — and the nearest thing to authority. In fact, if she was going to tell anyone about Neville's behavior, it would probably be him — as her tutor, he was supposed to be her first port of call for pastoral matters. But Hannah felt a strange compunction about dobbing Neville in to the college authorities. What could she say? *He brought me up a parcel.* It didn't sound exactly convincing. And besides, she didn't know Dr. Myers's number.

She was still standing, paralyzed, trying to

figure out what to do, when there was a knock from outside, making her jump, her heart skittering uncomfortably in her chest. Her first thought was Neville, trying to gain entry to her bedroom, but it sounded too faint for that — the knock had not been on her door, but somewhere farther away.

She held her breath, trying to stop her teeth from chattering as she pressed her ear to the door, trying to hear whether Neville was still out there.

There was no sound at all, not even the creak of a floorboard, and then the knock came again, shockingly loud in the silence. It must be someone trying to get into the set. Did that mean Neville had gone?

Slowly, trying not to make a sound, Hannah turned the latch and opened the door to the sitting room. The overhead light had been turned off, but a lamp burned in the alcove by the fireplace, illuminating the room just enough to show that it was empty. The door to the corridor was closed.

Then the knock came again, one final loud thump, and with it a voice.

"April? Hannah? Are you in?"

Will.

Hannah almost flew across the living room to the door, her numb fingers fumbling with the lock. When she finally got it open, Will was standing there.

"Your light was —" he began, but something in her face must have told him everything was not right, because his expression changed almost immediately. "Hannah? Are you okay? Where's April? Did something happen?"

Hannah couldn't speak. She could only shake her head, *No, I'm not okay, no, nothing happened.* Both were true, after all. Will shut the door behind himself and led her across to the sofa. Then he sat her gently down.

"Hannah, you're shaking. What happened? Do you need me to get someone?"

"No," she managed, "I'm okay. I'm sorry, I —"

And then she burst into tears.

Before she really realized what had happened, Will's arms were around her, and she was sobbing into his shoulder, feeling the warmth of him, the softness of the skin at the crook of his neck, breathing in his scent of laundry detergent and body wash and warm skin.

"You're okay," she heard his voice, strangely intimate and close, felt the heat of his breath on her ear as he said it over and over, "You're okay. I've got you. You're okay. It's okay. There, there. I've got you."

She could feel the shaking subsiding, feel her breathing getting calmer, and she did not want to move. She wanted to stay here, in the circle of Will's arms, feeling his warmth and protection. Her lips were pressed into his T-shirt, in the hollow below his collarbone. It was not a kiss — but it so nearly could have been. And suddenly she knew that if she did not pull away, she was going to do something very, very stupid.

"I'm sorry," she managed at last. She sat up straighter. Will let her go, although — was it her imagination? — there seemed to be something a little reluctant in the way he released her, and he kept his arm along the back of the sofa in a gesture that was close to an embrace, even though they weren't actually touching.

Hannah coughed, pushed her hair back, and wiped her eyes, thankful that the lights in the sitting room were low. Her red eyes and puffy face would not look as bad as they really were.

"Do you want to tell me what that was about?" Will asked. His voice was quiet. Hannah swallowed. *Not really* was the honest answer. The truth was that now that Neville had left, she wanted nothing more than to pretend the whole thing never happened, but that was impossible with Will here. There was a long silence as Hannah tried to think up the right words, part of her hoping that Will would fill in the blanks, or else maybe just stand up and say, *Right, I've got to go.* But he did neither. Only sat there in a charged silence. She was painfully aware of his arm along the spine of the sofa, of the fact that if she leaned against the cushions, his bare forearm would be touching the back of her neck.

"It was nothing," she said at last. It was a lie, and a transparent one at that. But she had the sensation of teetering on the edge of a precipice — and that to tell Will the truth would be to jump, setting in motion events she might not be able to stop. "I was being stupid. It's this porter, Neville, he's been really weird with me ever since I arrived. Nothing I can put my finger on but just — and then I came back and found him *in* my room. He didn't do anything —" she said, hurriedly, seeing Will's face. "It was just a shock, that's all."

"He was *in* your room?" Will said, ignoring the last part. He seemed not so much angry as incredibly confused. "I'm sorry, but what? Since when do porters hang around female students' rooms? *Any* students' rooms, for that matter?"

"He brought up a parcel." Hannah felt

like she was making excuses, but it was the truth after all. He *had* brought up a parcel. It was there on the coffee table in front of them. "It was too big for the pigeonhole."

"Okay, but —" Will seemed momentarily lost for words. "But, that makes *no* sense. I mean, since when do porters do that? Surely the normal thing is to keep it behind the counter? They don't take stuff up to students' rooms, but even if they *did,* they shouldn't be letting themselves into people's rooms at" — he looked at his watch — "nearly ten o'clock at night, for God's sake. You could have been asleep. And how did he even get in? Did you leave it unlocked?"

"I — I don't know." Hannah was taken aback by the question. She hadn't considered how Neville had gotten in. Now the idea began to creep her out. Did the porters have keys? Or was it possible she and April had left the door ajar? They had been in a hurry, and April had gone back to get her gloves. "It's possible," she said slowly, "but . . . I don't think we did."

"This isn't right, Hannah," Will said. He was shaking his head, and now he ran his hand over his face, like he was trying to rub something away, some kind of clinging dirt.

"It's nothing," Hannah said, almost pleadingly. A sense of panic was beginning to take over, as if events were spiraling out of her control. She had wanted Will to make her feel better about this — not worse. "Nothing happened."

"It's not nothing, it's *weird.* Is he the one who told you he liked little girls?"

"What?" Hannah was taken aback. "Jesus, no. He said he liked polite little girls. But how did you even — you weren't there that night."

"Ryan told me. And does it really make a difference? Little girls? Polite little girls? It's fucking creepy."

"It's creepy, but it's not creepy like that." Hannah found she was getting heated. "I mean, he didn't say it like that. He meant he liked polite — oh God, this is stupid."

"Yes, this *is* stupid, why are you defending him?" Will looked bewildered now, and angry. Out of the corner of her eye, Hannah saw the muscles in his forearms tense and relax as he clenched his fist against the sofa back and then forced himself to let go.

"I'm not, I just —" She felt her throat close with a mix of frustration and impotent anger. How dare Neville do this — come into her room, soiling everything he touched. And why was Will acting like this was *her* problem?

She felt the blood rush into her cheeks

256

and stood up.

"I'm okay," she said. She walked to the window, deliberately not looking at Will, unable to meet his eyes. Over in the window bay she swiped at the condensation on the panes, sending little runnels of water trickling down into the leaded grooves, and stared out into the night. Across the top of the cloisters she could see the stained glass windows of the chapel glowing bright, and the steeple rising into the night. The rain had stopped and the sky was clear and speckled with stars. She shivered, feeling the chill strike through the gappy old glass, and through her still-damp clothes.

"I'm not defending him," she said at last. "I just — I think maybe I overreacted. I was shocked to find him in the room, but — but that was all."

"Okay," Will said. His voice was quiet, and she heard the rustle of fabric as he stood and cleared his throat. "Are — do you want me to stay? I could take April's room . . . or the couch."

Hannah closed her eyes. She wanted more than anything to say yes. She couldn't bolt the set door — April would not be able to use her key to get in — and the thought of lying in her room waiting for Neville to return, however unlikely that was, was almost more than she could stand. But the other option, the thought of Will lying just feet away, no April between them . . . that was unendurable in a very different way.

"I'm fine," she said, but her voice was so low that she wasn't sure if she was really talking to herself. She heard Will's footsteps creaking on the old boards as he crossed the room and stood behind her.

"Sorry," he said, "I didn't catch —"

As he spoke, he put his hand tentatively on her shoulder, his skin shockingly warm through the thin, damp cotton of her shirt. Hannah shivered uncontrollably, in spite of herself, and Will took his hand away as if he had been stung.

"Sorry, sorry," he said again, and she realized that he thought it was a shudder of revulsion.

"No," she said, swinging around, "it's —"

And then somehow, and afterwards Hannah was never sure how it happened — whether she had leaned into Will, or he had pressed himself to her, or whether their bodies had just met in one of those stupid clumsy clashes when two people move in the same direction while trying to avoid each other — she never knew.

She only knew that somehow she was crushed against him, hip to breast, and he against her, and that she would not, could not move. And then their mouths were touching, lips and tongues, in a way that made something deep inside her melt into a liquid puddle of desire.

A sound escaped her, a kind of soft moan, and Will's lips were on her throat, and his hands under her shirt, and she was pressing herself into him, feeling him against her, and she *knew,* she could *feel* that he wanted this just as much as she did.

And then something happened — a sound from the corridor — and they both broke apart at the same time, panting and horrified, staring at each other with wild dilated pupils and mouths still soft and wet from kissing.

"Fuck," Will said. His face was white in the moonlight streaming through the window, and he looked suddenly much older than nineteen. He turned away, frantically tucking his shirt back in, shaking his head like he was trying to shake away the memory of her touch, the memory of what had just happened. "*Fuck.* God, what — I'm sorry — I'm so, so sorry —"

"Will," Hannah managed. "Will, it wasn't just you — we both —"

"*Fuck,*" he groaned again, and somehow she knew that it wasn't only what he had just done, what they'd both done, but what it meant — the impossibility of them ever being together now, because their joint betrayal of April would surely destroy her.

She stood, watching him helplessly as he crossed the room, snatched up his jacket from the back of the sofa, and then stood for a moment in the doorway, looking back at her.

"Hannah, please —" he said, and then stopped. She wasn't sure what he was going to say. *Please don't tell April? Please don't hate me? Please don't come near me again?*

She waited. Her heart was pounding in her throat.

But he only shook his head.

"Take care of yourself," he said at last. And then he left, closing the set door very gently behind himself, as though he was frightened to make a sound.

AFTER

The bell above the Bonnie Bagel's old-fashioned door gives a tinkling chime as Hannah pushes it open. Inside she stands for a moment, catching her breath and waiting for her glasses to unfog. As the lenses clear she glances around the little cafe; there's no one here, even though she's ten minutes late.

For a second her heart lightens. Maybe he's given up, gone home? She won't hang around to find out. She'll send him an email — *I'm here, but I must have missed you.* She's about to turn on her heel, breathing more easily with a palpable sense of having discharged her duty to the young man, when a woman hurries out from the kitchen, wiping her hands on her apron.

"Hello love, sorry I didnae hear you come in. Where would you be wanting to sit?"

"Well . . ." Hannah hesitates. "Actually I was here to meet a friend, but I think I've missed him. I should probably —"

She's turning towards the door when the woman interrupts, cheerful and happy to be of help.

"Young man with sandy hair? No, no, you havenae missed him, he's just in the back room, there. Said you'd be wanting to talk so could he have a quiet table. Mind, they're all that way today! I don't know what's making the tourists so shy, it cannae be the rain for we've had none to speak of." She gives a comfortable laugh. Hannah feels her face fall, and then tries to rearrange it into something more appropriate for someone who's just avoided a wasted journey.

"Oh, good. Thank you," she says weakly.

"Will I bring you up a cup of something? Tea? Coffee? Or a scone maybe?"

"I'll . . . um . . . I'll just have a bottle of mineral water, please," Hannah says. "Flat."

The woman nods. "I'll bring it up, love. It's just through there, up the stairs."

Hannah nods back, then hitches her bag up over her shoulder and makes her way through the arch the woman indicated and up a half flight of stairs.

Geraint is sitting at a table by the window, though he stands as she comes in.

"H-Hannah, hi." The sun is shining through the window and it turns the tips of his ears pink, making it look as though he's blushing, though she's not sure if he is.

"Hi," she says awkwardly. He pulls out a chair and makes a little gesture and she sits, feeling like an idiot and beginning to wonder if this was a huge mistake. She's grateful for the privacy, but she hadn't bargained on being tucked away at the back of the cafe like this — it's going to be very difficult to make a quick getaway if the conversation takes a turn she doesn't like. There's a brief pause.

"Do you want to see the menu?" Geraint asks.

Hannah shakes her head. "No, it's fine, thank you. I already ordered downstairs. How are you?"

It's a stupid question, meaningless really, but she doesn't know what else to say, and apparently neither does Geraint because he seizes on it gratefully.

"Yeah, good, I mean, really happy that you agreed to come and meet with me. I just wanted to say that — I know it was, well I mean, I wasn't expecting —"

You didn't really give me any choice, she thinks resentfully, but she's finding it hard to resent him now that they're face-to-face. He looks so anxious and unthreatening. So . . . *nice.*

"You said you're a friend of Ryan's?" she says at last when he runs out of steam, and Geraint nods.

"Yeah, he was working at the *Herald* when I started there after uni, and he was — well, I guess, you'd call him my mentor." He looks down at his hands, his face suddenly seeming years older. "He's such a good bloke. I felt terrible about what happened."

"Yeah, me too," Hannah says softly. "How" — she swallows — "how is he?"

"I mean, good, I think? It was pretty awful at first, I used to go and visit him in that horrible convalescent place, you know the one that smelled of cabbage."

Hannah nods, but it's a kind of lie. She doesn't know the place Geraint is talking about. She is painfully aware of the way she and Will let Ryan down — although that's not completely fair on Will. Left to his own devices, Will, she is fairly sure, would have kept in touch with the others, the way he's kept up with Hugh. It was she who fled England, she who dropped ties with everyone from Pelham, refusing to go back, to dredge up memories. Will had wanted to invite Ryan and Emily to their wedding, make it a proper catch-up with save-the-date cards and a hotel in the Borders — it was Hannah who pushed for the registry office, just Hugh as best man, and her father to give her away. And Will, as he always does, agreed — not wanting to cause her pain.

But now, listening to Geraint chatting on about Ryan's grueling journey back from his stroke, she realizes what they did, what *she* did, and she feels a sharp stab of something halfway between grief and guilt.

"But he's really enjoying being back home with Bella," Geraint finishes. "I know that's made a huge difference. That and the fact that he can talk and type again. I think he was going up the wall not being able to speak *or* write, for someone like him, I mean he's never exactly held back from giving his opinion, has he?"

Hannah laughs at that, a shaky laugh but a real one. Because it's true. And because, black as it is, she can see the humor in poor Ryan, the person who always talked longest and loudest at any party, the person who would pin you against the wall in the kitchen to harangue you about late-stage capitalism and Engels and Marx, being silent against his own will — having to listen to all the nurses chattering on without a single *I think you'll find,* or *Look, love, if you haven't read David Graeber . . .*

"No," she says now. "That's true."

There's a long silence. Geraint stirs his coffee, staring down into the depths as though he can find a conversation starter in there if he swirls the murky liquid hard enough. He looks for a moment as if he might be about to speak, but then there are footsteps on the stairs, and they both turn to see the cafe owner coming through the doorway with a bottle of mineral water and a glass of ice balanced slightly precariously on a tray. She puts it down on the little table and then smiles at them both.

"There you are, loves. Anything else, you just give me a shout, I'm only downstairs. I'll hear you. I'll leave you be now."

And then she departs.

Hannah opens the water and pours it, more to have something to do than because she is really thirsty. And then, because she has the increasing feeling that if she doesn't bring it up they will never get to the point, she says, "So. What did you want to ask me?"

Geraint flushes, and for a moment there is a flicker of almost absurd relief on his face, as though she has absolved him of something. He swallows his coffee with determination and speaks.

"So. Yes. First of all, thanks for agreeing to talk about this. I can't imagine how difficult it must be to revisit all this so many years on."

Amen, Hannah thinks, but she says nothing, only waits for him to continue.

"So a bit of background about me — I first heard about the case when I was a teenager and I guess . . . well, I guess I was just fascinated really. I was a bit of a morbid kid and there was something about it, something about April . . ." He trails off.

I bet there was, Hannah thinks, but again, she does not say it. She knows, though, exactly what that *something* was that Geraint is talking about — the shots of April's lovely, high-cheekboned face, the photographs of her lounging on the banks of the Isis, one shoulder bare as the strap of her top slipped down her arm. April was every spotty young teenager's fantasy girlfriend, and the fact that she had been murdered probably only made her more unattainable and therefore safer to desire.

"So anyway," Geraint is saying, "I kept reading accounts of the case, and earlier this year I did this long-form article about it — it was called 'Death of an It Girl — Ten Years On, Ten Unanswered Questions.' Maybe you read it?"

Hannah shakes her head. She's unsure whether to be honest, whether to tell

Geraint that she hasn't read any press about April's murder for years, but Geraint is still talking.

"The piece went kind of viral and, well, long story short, I've been commissioned to do a ten-part podcast on the case."

"Okay," Hannah says slowly. She's not sure why, but a podcast makes her feel even more uneasy than an article. Then something occurs to her. "You're not recording this conversation, are you?"

"Um, I mean, no," Geraint says, a little awkwardly. "Not yet. That's to say, I usually do record stuff just for my own records, but I wouldn't broadcast anything from today. I'm still in the research stage. Would you rather I didn't? I can just take notes if it makes you feel more comfortable."

"I would prefer that," Hannah says a little stiffly. She knows she's being irrational — what's the difference between a quote on paper versus recorded on a phone? And yet the idea of Geraint capturing her trembling voice talking about that night — it feels unbearable.

"Okay, sure," Geraint says. He puts his phone away and takes out a pen and a notebook. "Look, I want to be really clear, I don't want this to be a whitewash. I'm not out to prove Neville's innocence if he really did it. In fact that's *why* I wanted to talk to you, make sure I did justice to the case against him. I just — I just want to understand what happened. There's gaps I've never been able to fill in."

Hannah says nothing at that. She is holding the water glass so tight her fingers are white.

"Could you — would you mind just . . . going over what happened that night?" Geraint asks now. His expression is diffident, and he is twisting his fingers together, playing with his pen.

Hannah takes a deep breath. This is not new, it's all stuff she has gone over a thousand times before; you would think the pain would have dulled, but it hasn't, or not completely. Still, it's better if she just gives Geraint chapter and verse, and then he can go away and get rid of whatever little conspiracy theory he's dreamed up.

"It was late. I'd been in the college bar. Hugh was there, and so was Ryan. Emily was working on some problems in the library. Will wasn't in college, he'd gone home for the weekend. It was the last night of April's play, *Medea,* and we'd arranged this celebration — special cocktails and everything. And about three-quarters of the way through the evening, April went up to our room to change . . . and she never came back. So I went to find her."

She closes her eyes, remembering. Remembering the feel of the grass beneath her feet as she and Hugh ran lightly across the Fellows' Garden. The glow coming from April's bedroom window as they crossed the quad.

And then, Neville. Slipping out of the opening to the number 7 staircase, his steps surprisingly quiet for such a big man. She had stopped, frozen, half expecting him to see her — but if he did he gave no sign of it. He just turned and hurried off into the night, and she had continued to the foot of the stairwell.

And then — and then — and then —

"I climbed the stairs up to our landing. And the door was open." Her voice sounds strange in her own ears. "Just like before — just like that night when I came back and found Neville there, waiting. I should have known something was wrong. But I didn't. I didn't suspect anything, even though he'd been on the stairs. I should have known."

The pictures come now, seared into her memory like images seen in flashes of lightning. Her hand on the door. A fan of dark hair, April's Medea wig, splayed across the rug. And then —

But that's where it cuts out. *The mind protects itself from what is too painful to face,* a psychologist told her once, which made the fury rise up inside her, because that sounds like she *wants* to forget, like it's an act of supreme selfishness.

"I don't remember much after that," she says now. She puts the glass to her lips and takes a long swallow, feeling the iced water numbing her throat and shooting needles of pain through her teeth.

"So it's never come back?" Geraint says, scribbling, and she shakes her head.

"Flashes, sometimes, in dreams. But I'm never sure how much of that is memory and how much of it's just my mind reconstructing what it thinks I saw. Nothing I can rely on. I definitely saw Neville, though, coming down the stairs from our room. That, I'm absolutely certain of."

"The thing is, John Neville came from my town," Geraint says now. Hannah looks up from her water.

"He did?"

"Yes, his mum lived round the corner from my aunt, and obviously that doesn't make him innocent, but I suppose it gave me a different kind of perspective on him. I heard all about his defense case, and the holes in the prosecution. It's not just the

271

crime scene stuff, although that's odd enough. The fact that they never found any traces of Neville's DNA on April is something no one ever really explained. Okay, the killer could have used gloves, but it doesn't seem credible that Neville could have strangled April without her clawing at him or fighting back. For that matter, no one heard a struggle at all, even though there were people in the room below. But it's not just that — there were loads of other angles the defense never brought up. For example, did you know that April was supposedly pregnant when she died?"

There is a clatter. Hannah has knocked over the glass bottle of water. Fortunately it's empty, or near enough, and now she scrambles to pick it up before it rolls off the table, her cheeks flaming, trying to figure out what she's going to say to this extraordinary assertion.

"Sorry," Geraint is saying, as though it were he who knocked over the bottle. He moves his notebook, mops at the small puddle of water with his napkin. "Sorry, sorry. I take it you didn't know?"

"No," Hannah says thinly. She goes to put her hand over her own stomach, and then stops herself. She is still at the stage where her pregnancy isn't completely obvious to strangers. People who know her can tell she's changed shape, but to Geraint she might be just carrying a bit of extra weight, and for some reason she doesn't want him to know, though she can't put her finger on why.

She feels a strange flutter inside her and the sensation stops her in her tracks. Is it the baby? She hasn't felt it kick yet — the books say anytime between twenty and twenty-four weeks is normal for a first pregnancy. She is just over twenty-three weeks now, and has been waiting, bated breath, trying to figure out if every little flicker is her child, or just a muscle ticcing. Now she is completely distracted, and Geraint has to say, "Hannah? Are you okay?"

"I'm fine," she says, dragging her mind back to the present. "I'm — no, I didn't know. But to be honest —"

She stops. She doesn't want to call this a lie to Geraint's face. It will make her look prejudiced, set in her opinion. But his words have angered her. April, pregnant? It's ridiculous.

"Look, I don't want to be rude, but I'm —" She stops, corrects her tense, as she has so many times before. "I *was* her roommate, her best friend. I find it really unlikely that she wouldn't have told me something like that. And if it were true, why wouldn't Neville's lawyers have brought it up at the trial? It just — it doesn't ring true to me. I'm sorry."

"Oh, I agree," Geraint says urgently. "I dismissed it too when I first heard it. But when I asked Ryan, he confirmed it."

Hannah goes completely still. She has no idea what to say, and she finds she is gaping at Geraint, her mouth open. She closes it, but the words still don't come and the silence hangs between them, oppressive. Inside her head, though, it's the opposite problem. There are too many words — words buzzing and whining like bees in a jar. Ryan. April. *Pregnant.*

Why on earth would she have told Ryan, of all people? Unless . . .

But Geraint is speaking, cutting across her spiraling thoughts.

"Ryan's theory was the defense didn't bring it up because they thought it would look like victim blaming," he says. "You know, smearing someone's sexual past to distract from what's happened to them. They believed it would go down very badly with the jury, and they thought they could get Neville off by pointing out other flaws in the evidence. Only . . . it didn't work."

"And Ryan told you this? He confirmed it?"

Geraint nods.

"Did he say why April told him?"

Geraint shakes his head.

Hannah sits back, trying to make sense of this. But she can't. It makes no sense at all. Can it really be true? Or is this another one of April's pranks?

"The thing is . . ." she says now, the words coming slowly. "The thing that you have to remember is that April was . . . well, she made stuff up."

"What do you mean?" Geraint looks puzzled.

"She was . . . I suppose you'd call it a practical joker, though it doesn't seem very funny in hindsight. She used to do stuff to get a rise out of people. Elaborate stuff sometimes. Like she sent Hugh this whole thing about how his mobile phone had a possible safety recall on it, and persuaded him to ring up Nokia and go through this diagnostic test. Only of course the number wasn't Nokia, it was April. She put on this funny accent and talked him through the supposed test, and I can't remember the whole thing, but the punch line involved typing out what was supposed to be a diagnostic numerical command code — it was back when some of the older phones still had a number pad. Only when you typed out the numbers in a text message it came out as *I am a knob.*"

"Ha!" Geraint says, and then looks slightly ashamed of his own levity, as if he forgot, for a moment, the gravity of why they are here and how the topic came up. "So . . . um . . ." he says, more diffidently. "Do you think this was a practical joke against Ryan?"

"Maybe," Hannah says, but it sounds weak in her own ears, and she knows it. Her heart is still thumping and her mind is whirling, trying to figure things out.

Why would April have chosen *Ryan,* out of all the possibilities, to confide in? And why would Ryan believe her?

She thinks of April's closed door, early in the morning, of the unmistakable sound of two people having sex, filtering through the wood.

She thinks of the way she walked into breakfast to find Will already there, cheerful and unsuspecting. *Could I be cheeky and get you to grab me another coffee if you're going up?*

"I'm sorry," she says now. She pushes away her glass and stands up. "I'm really sorry, I have to get back. I've got an appointment. I hope this was helpful."

But she knows it wasn't. She doesn't know what Geraint wants from her, but whatever it is, was, she's fairly sure he didn't get it. She's told him nothing he didn't already know. She, on the other hand, has a whole mess of unwanted information and thoughts in return that she is going to have to sift, sort, and eventually live with. *Why did I come here?* she wants to cry as she turns for the door. *Why did I agree to this?*

"Yeah, thanks," Geraint says. He's standing too, and now he follows her to the door, though she desperately wants to tell him not to. "I really appreciate it. Listen, could I call you sometime, if I dig anything else up?"

She stops at that, turns, trying to keep her face neutral so that it doesn't reveal to him all the horror that's roiling underneath. Dig something up? Why? Why would he do this?

"What do you mean?" she says, her voice level. "What kind of thing?"

"Well, you know, I'm talking to people — Neville's lawyers, some of April's family. If there's something I think you might want to know —"

No, is what she wants to say. In fact she wants to scream it. *No, there is nothing about that case I could possibly want to know. I want to forget it — move on — pretend none of it*

277

ever happened. Leave me alone!

But she can't forget it. She can't pretend it never happened. Not if it's really true that she made a mistake. Because Geraint's right — she's spent over a decade trying to strangle those doubts, push them down, hide them away. But they've always been there, gnawing at her. Why *would* Neville protest his innocence, year after year, sabotaging his own chance at release, if he was really guilty? Why *didn't* anyone hear a struggle, why *wasn't* there any DNA at the scene? These are all questions that have floated to the top of her mind in the long hours between midnight and dawn, questions she's pushed back down, drowned in sleeping pills and therapy and the reassuring monotony of everyday life.

And now this — the news that April may have been pregnant . . . it feels like the last straw. Something she can't ignore, can't push away.

She shuts her eyes. The image of Neville, the gaunt, frail old man in the BBC news clip, floats up before her eyes, with his hunted, pleading expression . . .

She opens them again.

"Fine." The word that comes out of her lips is short, clipped, almost strangled, spoken in spite of herself.

Then she turns, clatters down the stairs, shoves a fiver onto the payment desk, and leaves without waiting for change, with the nice owner looking after her in surprise.

"Are you okay, pet?" she hears as the door slams shut after her, and she wants to say yes. She wants to say, *I'm fine, it's nothing, everything's going to be okay.*

But none of it's true.

BEFORE

"You're coming? You're definitely coming?"

It was the opening night of April's play, and for the first time since they had met, almost eight months earlier, Hannah was seeing what April looked like when she was really and truly nervous. She was pacing around the room, vibrating with a tense energy and muttering lines under her breath, cursing when she missed her own cues.

"Hannah!" she barked now, when Hannah didn't answer immediately. "I *said,* do you promise you're coming?"

"Yes!" Hannah said, exasperated, and then she felt mean, and added, more gently, "Yes, April, I promise. I said so, didn't I?"

"I know, but everyone's so wrapped up in bloody prelims. I'm worried they'll all be revising. I practically had to force Hugh to say he'd come. I can't think of anything worse than looking out over an empty auditorium on the first night."

"It won't be empty. I'll be there — and Emily said she's definitely coming too." Was Will? She didn't know, and couldn't quite think how to ask. Something had not been right with April and Will for a while, but it had become increasingly impossible for Hannah to find out what. She was too afraid of what April might tell her — or of giving something away herself. "I'm sure the other cast members will bring friends. Someone even put a flyer up in the bar — I'm sure you'll have loads of people. What time are you supposed to be there?"

"Six," April said, and then looked at her phone. "Shit. I need to leave now. The makeup takes ages. *Swear* you'll be there, yes?"

"Yes, I'll be there. Front row. I swear. Now go!"

After April had left, Hannah rang Emily.

"Em? I hope you've remembered about tonight. She's having kittens."

"Tonight?" Hannah could feel Emily struggling to remember.

"Yes, tonight. April's play, remember? At the Burton Taylor."

"Shit." There was a pause. Hannah could hear Emily clicking stuff on her computer diary. "I've got an exam tomorrow."

It was the last fortnight of term, and they were deep into end-of-year exams, the first ones that really counted.

"Em, you *have* to come. She'll lose it. She's already incredibly nervous about playing to an empty house. If we're not there —"

"I told her I'd come, and I'll come. But I'll have to leave on time."

"No worries, I'll have to get back too. I've got to revise."

It went without saying at this point. Only the lucky few whose prelims were already over weren't burning the midnight oil and cursing their carefree, Michaelmas-term selves for not taking better notes.

"How does April do it?" Emily said. "I mean, I know she doesn't go to the lectures, and I haven't seen her in the dining hall for about three weeks. She's been rehearsing nonstop and now they're playing every evening this week, aren't they? Is she doing *any* work?"

"I honestly don't know," Hannah said. She had wondered the same thing, as April came in night after night at 11 p.m., wired and full of nervous jubilation. "I think she's barely sleeping. I got up to go to the loo at four a.m. the other night and she was still there, typing away at something."

"Fucking hell," Emily said. "Well, whatever she's on, I want some. At this point I can hardly remember my own name."

"Me too. I've only got one paper left, but it's the worst." Hannah thought of the Anglo-Saxon translations lying on her desk, scored over and over with her attempts at remembering the complicated grammatical declensions. She could barely do a passable translation with a copy of *A Guide to Old English* sitting in her lap. How she was going to manage in a closed-book exam was anyone's guess.

"Well, hokay . . ." Emily said now, with the air of someone ending the conversation. "Better get back to the grind. What time are you leaving?"

"The play starts at eight and I should think it's probably a fifteen-minute walk . . . so maybe say half seven? Are . . ." She paused, trying to think how to phrase her question. "Do you know if anyone else is coming?"

"Will must be. I don't suppose April would let him off the hook. And I assume Hugh, given he always does whatever April tells him to. Ryan tried to get out of it, said he had some rugby thing, but I said if I was suffering through it, the least he could do was support me. I'd better text him and check he's remembered. He's going straight there."

"So . . . we'll walk over together?"

"Sure. Half seven at the main gate?"

"Actually —" Hannah began, and then stopped. She didn't want to tell Emily the truth — that she almost never used the main gate now, unless she couldn't avoid it. Neville never seemed to leave the Porters' Lodge, and every time she came through the arched entrance he would appear out of the little back office and stand in the doorway of the lodge, arms folded, his eyes fixed on her all across the Old Quad, until she passed out of sight to the Fellows' Garden. Hannah never looked back, never acknowledged his presence, but walking across Old Quad with his eyes fixed on her retreating back made her skin crawl, and each time she found herself fighting the urge to run.

The problem was, there was so little she could put her finger on. Since the night in her room he hadn't said anything directly to her, but his silent surveillance was almost worse. And it wasn't just the lodge. The other night, as she had been getting ready for bed, she had heard something outside. When she went to the window, there was a figure standing in the center of the quad, staring up at her. It was impossible to make out a face in the darkness, but it was hard to mistake that tall, broad slab of an outline for anyone else, and Hannah was sure in her heart that it was Neville, watching her as she got ready for bed.

She had torn the curtain across with shaking hands, making the curtain rings screech and rattle against the pole, wishing that April were home instead of out rehearsing. Since then she had kept her curtains closed, even in daylight. *It's like a tomb in here!* motherly Sue, the scout, had said the following day when she came in to clean, but Hannah had just shaken her head and switched on the overhead light.

"Yes? No?" Em prompted now, breaking into her thoughts.

"Actually . . . let's go out via the Cloade gate. It's a bit closer." That was more or less a lie, but if Emily thought so she didn't call Hannah on it. "I'll come and pick you up, shall I?"

"Okay," Emily said. "Seven thirty. See you then."

When they arrived at the theater, Hannah saw that April's fears about playing to an empty room had been unfounded. With a quarter of an hour to go, the little auditorium was already almost full, and her promise to April to sit in the front row was going to be impossible to keep.

She was scanning the rows, looking for two seats together, when Emily nudged her and pointed to the far side of the room.

Hannah turned and saw Ryan standing up, waving an arm to and fro, pointing with his free hand to a couple of empty seats. Beside him was Hugh, bent over a textbook, presumably squeezing in a few extra minutes' revision, and beside *him* — but here her stomach flipped.

Since the kiss last term, she had avoided Will's company as much as possible. It hadn't been easy, making sure she didn't eat in the dining hall at the same time as him, or swerving away from an empty desk in the library when she saw him, head down, at the adjacent table. But this term it had become easier. Everyone was revising hard for prelims, and April's rehearsals had meant she was almost never in their shared rooms, and so neither was Will.

Even when they were forced together — at formal hall, or for celebrations she couldn't get out of — she had made sure they were never in close proximity, and she'd had the sense that Will was doing the same. Now, with Emily pushing past rows of people to the seats Ryan was saving for them, it seemed that there was no escape.

"Hey," Ryan said as they made their way through the throng. "About bloody time. It's been murder keeping these seats free."

"Sorry," Emily said, though she didn't sound apologetic. "You know how it is, Coates. Places to go, people to see."

She squeezed past Will and Hugh into the free space next to Ryan, and with a sinking feeling Hannah realized that the final free space, the only one left for her, was next to Will.

They looked at each other, and she could tell that he was having the same misgivings as she — and coming to the same realization: that there was no plausible reason to rearrange the seating, at least not without raising eyebrows. The free seat was one in from the aisle, between Will and Hugh. Even if Hannah pretended that she had forgotten something or needed the loo, the only logical rearrangement would be for Will to move up one next to Hugh and leave her with the aisle. There was no possible excuse she could find to move herself farther down the row.

Will gave a small resigned smile, and she knew that he had just gone through exactly the same mental calculation, and was trying to signal that it was okay. That they could still sit next to each other. The theater wouldn't burn down around them if they sat a few inches apart for a couple of hours.

Still, it was with a sense that she was doing something very stupid that Hannah slid into the seat between Hugh and Will. She sat there mutely, listening to Ryan and Emily bickering good-naturedly farther up the row, and Hugh muttering his revision notes under his breath. And all the time she was horribly conscious of her cardigan-clad arm just millimeters away from Will's shoulder. He had his hands pressed between his knees, as if to make his body as small as possible and keep his hands as far away from her as he could, but the seats were narrow, and Hugh was unselfconsciously manspreading on her other side. It was all Hannah could do to keep her arm from touching Will's, her knee from grazing his, and as the lights went down and the auditorium fell into silence, the sense of intimacy only increased.

She had never been so conscious of her body, of the heat of someone else's skin, of the sound of their breathing and of every minute movement they each made. As the hush descended and the darkness enveloped them both, Hannah found that she was holding her breath in an effort to keep every muscle strained away from Will, and she was forced to let it out with a shaky rush.

"Are you okay?" Hugh whispered beside her, and she nodded.

"Yes, sorry. Just a — a sneeze that didn't go anywhere."

It was a stupid excuse, but Hugh seemed to accept it for what it was. Still, Hannah wanted to kick herself.

A single spotlight came up on the stage, and as it did so, she felt something — the lightest, gentlest touch on her knee, the knee closest to Will. It was only for a moment — and so softly that under other circumstances she would have thought she'd imagined it — but with every muscle attuned to his presence, she knew she had not, and it was all she could do to stop herself from jumping.

She knew what it meant, though. What Will was trying to convey.

It's okay.

She shut her eyes, pressed her fists against them. *It's okay. It's okay. It will all be okay.*

And then she opened them — and a girl was there, standing in the narrow pool of light. It wasn't April — it was someone Hannah didn't know — but she leaned forward, glad of the distraction from her own thoughts.

"I wish to God that ship had never sailed." The girl's voice rang clear from the stage, and the production had begun.

"Bloody hell," Ryan's voice, raised over the hubbub of the intermission bar, was grudgingly impressed. "She's pretty amazing. Did you know she was this good?" He turned to Will, who shook his head.

"No, I mean — I knew she was good. She was in a couple of plays at school, I didn't see them but my girlfriend at the time was in them and she always said April was a good actress, but I had no idea she was *this* good."

Good did not begin to cover it, Hannah thought. April was not good. She was electrifying. Hannah could not even have said why — it wasn't her looks. The director had gone with the strange choice of making the cast up to look like characters on a Greek urn, with jet-black wigs, terra-cotta skin, and heavy kohl eyeliner, so physically it was actually pretty hard to tell the actors apart onstage. It wasn't her technique, although that was fine. There were people in the cast who delivered the lines better, and more accurately, with more expression and animation.

It was something else. When she was onstage it was impossible to tear your eyes from her, even when someone else was speaking. When she left, she left behind a hole that made you unable to forget her absence, and Hannah found herself looking eagerly at the wings, wondering when she would next come on.

Most of all, it was that April *was* Medea. She radiated Medea's anguish, betrayal, and rage. Every line simmered with it, and she made what could have been a stiff, classical portrayal into something utterly human and believable.

They were finishing up their intermission drinks when a voice from behind them made Hannah swing round.

"What's up, maddafakkas?"

"April!" Emily threw her arms around April with an uncharacteristic lack of reserve. "What are you doing out here? Shouldn't you be backstage?"

"Ah, rules, schmules," April said with a wave of her hand. "But never mind all that, I came out to hear what you think of the performance."

"April, you don't need me to massage your ego," Emily said with a grin. "But if you want to hear me say it — you're a bloody revelation, woman!"

"Why thank you," April said smugly. She

didn't quite say *I know,* but the inference was there. "How's it hanging, my dudes?" She gave Ryan a punch in the ribs and he grinned and edged away a little awkwardly.

"A'right. You did okay, Cliveden."

"Thanks. What do all you think of the wig?" She patted her hair. "I quite like it. Haven't had long hair for years but I'm tempted to nick it after the run's over. Hugh? What d'you reckon?"

"It — it looks charming," Hugh said, blushing. Even after almost eight months eating, drinking, and socializing together, it was plain that April still made him nervous. "Very classical."

"And?" April said. She was fishing, but Hannah couldn't blame her.

"You're absolutely superb, April." Hugh took the hint obediently. These kind of old-fashioned courtesies were his comfort zone. "We should have brought flowers."

"Sod flowers. You should have brought something stronger than that," April said. "Just what the doctor ordered, am I right?" She winked at Hugh and tucked her arm possessively through his. Hugh blushed again, more violently this time, and Hannah had the strong impression he was forcing himself not to pull away.

"S-so what, then?" he countered. "Champagne?"

"I doubt they run to vintage here, but a double G and T would be a good start," April said. Hugh nodded, unlinked his arm with an ill-concealed air of relief, and began threading his way through the crowd to the bar. April turned to Will.

"So? No congratulations from you, Will de Chastaigne?"

"You were very good, April," Will said, but there was an edge in his voice that made Hannah look up. Apparently whatever it was, April heard it too, for she frowned.

"*Very good?* That's it? That's all I get?"

"Okay, you were great. Is that better?"

"What I want," April said through gritted teeth, "is something a bit more effusive than *great.* If Hugh can come up with *absolutely superb* I think my actual bloody boyfriend could manage more than a one-line review. How about a congratulatory kiss?"

There was a charged silence, and then Will leaned down and kissed April dutifully on the lips.

Hannah knew she should turn away. She *wanted* to turn away, but instead she stood, hypnotized, as April threaded her hands through Will's hair, pulling his head down to hers, forcing his mouth open into a long, wet-tongued kiss that seemed to go on, and

293

on, until with a desperate kind of wrench Will pulled himself away.

He stood, his chest rising and falling, staring down at April without saying a word. There was copper-colored makeup smeared across his chest and face, and the black of April's lipstick was on his mouth like a bruise. April stared back with something like triumph.

Then, without another word, she turned on her heel.

"Must go," she shot back over her shoulder. "I'm straight on after the second act."

And then she was gone, disappearing into the crowd, just a small black head bobbing through the sea of students.

"What the fuck was that all about?" Emily said with astonishment. Will shook his head. He touched his fingertips to his face and looked down at the makeup there.

"Has anyone got a tissue?"

"There's paper napkins at the bar," Emily said. She raised her voice to where Hugh was standing by the counter. "Hugh! Grab us a few paper towels, would you?"

"Everything all right between you two, mate?" Ryan said. His voice was uneasy and he rocked on his heels, his hands shoved in his back pockets as if he didn't trust them not to betray something about his mood.

"Fine." Will's voice was short. Hugh had come back from the bar with a plastic cup of gin and tonic and a handful of cocktail napkins, and now Will took them and wiped his mouth and chin. "How do I look?"

"Hang on," Emily said. She took the cleaner of the two serviettes and dabbed at the streaks of orange still on Will's cheekbone and jaw. "There you go. There's not much I can do about your T-shirt, though."

"It's fine," Will said again, his voice tight as a snare.

It's not fine, Hannah wanted to say. She stared at him, trying to understand what was going on. Had April found something out? Had Will told her?

She was opening her mouth, groping for what to say, when the interval bell rang, and they turned and began filtering back into the auditorium.

It was only as they took their seats that Hannah noticed something — or rather, someone. Someone she was sure had not been there in the first half. It was a man sitting about two rows back from the front, very tall and broad.

It was John Neville.

AFTER

After she leaves the Bonnie Bagel, Hannah finds herself wandering, aimlessly, through the drizzly streets of New Town, her mind buzzing with thoughts of April and Neville. She's walking the cramped aisles of a Tesco Express, more to get out of the rain than because they really need anything, when her phone goes.

"Hey!" It's Will. "Have you booked anywhere, or should I?"

Shit. Date night. She had completely forgotten, and now the thought of sitting opposite Will for two hours in a restaurant, no phones or TV or work emails to distract them or fill the gaps in conversation . . . she's not sure if she can face it.

"I thought maybe Mono," Will is saying now. He's clearly on his lunch break; she can hear the hubbub of a sandwich bar in the background. "But do you reckon we'd get a reservation at such short notice? Or there's always Contini's, but we go there so often. I don't know. What do you think?"

What does she think? She has no idea. She only knows that the question of which restaurant to go to seems painfully insignificant in the aftermath of Geraint's bombshell — and that she can't have that conversation here, in the supermarket. She swallows.

"Look, would you mind if we didn't go out tonight? I'm just — I feel like we ought to be saving money."

There's a short silence.

"Sure," Will says. His voice is crackly on the other end of the line, but she can still hear the faint puzzlement. "But, you know, we don't have to go fancy, we could just get fish and chips."

"I know," Hannah says. She picks up a bag of organic rice, looks at the price, and then swaps it for normal. "But it's not just that — I've got the midwife again tomorrow, and I feel like I should be putting my feet up."

"Of course," Will says, and now the puzzlement has been replaced by concern. "Are you not feeling great?"

"I'm feeling fine, honestly. I just want a quiet one in front of the TV. Is that okay?"

"Of course," Will says again. "Quiet one it is, then. Love you."

"I love you too," she says, and then Will hangs up, and she is left standing there, staring at the pasta, Geraint's words ringing in her head.

April was pregnant. April was *pregnant*? If it's true, it changes everything. It opens up a whole mess of motives and possibilities that have nothing to do with Neville. There's Ryan, of course — the supposed source of this information. If it's true — if April really did tell him that she was pregnant, and Ryan really did believe her — Hannah can think of only one plausible explanation, unlikely though it is on the surface: Ryan must have been sleeping with April. Why else would she tell him first, out of everyone in their group? April didn't even particularly *like* Ryan, so the prospect of her picking him as a confidant is totally outlandish. But apparently she did choose him. And when she really considers it, Hannah *can* imagine April sleeping with Ryan. Or sleeping with *someone,* at least.

Because it wasn't just that one morning, when she found Will in the dining hall when he should have been in bed with April; there were other times. Nights when she heard footsteps padding across the sitting room followed by hushed whispers and giggles floating across the hallway. Afternoons when she caught a scent of cigarettes that Will didn't smoke coming from April's room. Mornings when she found shoes that weren't his by the front door as she headed out to early lectures.

And there was always something between April and Ryan. Not friendship, definitely not. But it is all too easy for that prickly antagonism to mask a very different kind of attraction. Hannah remembers the strange electrical charge that crackled between them the night April pranked Ryan, and the weird energy the first night of April's play, and she does not find it hard to believe that Ryan was sleeping with April. Not at all.

But if that's the case, it's not just Ryan who is implicated — and this, this is why she is distracted and why her answers to Will are short and strained. Because if it's true . . . if it's true it gives someone else a motive too.

Will.

It's absurd, of course — she knows Will like she knows her own heart. But if this comes out — and if Geraint is digging, it still might — it would destroy Will. She has caught glimpses of them — the articles on the internet making snide references to *De Chastaigne — who is now married to April's college roommate —* as though their happiness were somehow bought at the cost of April's death. *It's always the boyfriend* is a cliché, but clichés are clichés for a reason. With this new information, the internet gossip boards would go wild. Her and Will's life would once again become a misery of paparazzi doorsteppers and newspaper speculation.

How can she keep this from him? It feels impossible — but then, asking him whether he knew and concealed something so momentous feels equally impossible. It would be like asking him whether he has lied to her all their relationship — and admitting to him that she thinks he may have done so. How do you ask someone something like that? And what if he tells her —

Her phone pings and she looks down, realizing that she is still frozen in the middle of the aisle, holding it out like a compass. It's a text from Will.

Han, I'm sorry I hadn't remembered about the antenatal appointment. I'm a horrible husband. Please don't stress — I'm sure it's all fine. Our baby is fine. I love you x

A wave of guilt washes over her as she realizes what she has just done — she has used this appointment, used their *baby,* as an alibi for her own stress over Geraint.

She is just trying to think what to reply

when her phone buzzes again.

Why don't you take a day off so you're properly rested? Really put your feet up xx

You're a LOVELY husband. And good idea, Hannah texts back. *Love you x*

She puts the phone away, picks up the rice, and goes across to the queue for the checkout, but the sinking feeling in her stomach tells her that this isn't over. She has to find out if Geraint is telling the truth, if April really *was* pregnant, or she will spend the next ten years stressing about it. And only one person knows for sure.

She will take the day off tomorrow, as Will suggested. But not to put her feet up.

She will go to the appointment. And then she will go and see Ryan. And she will ask him about the rumors. But that means . . . that means she *has* to tell Will.

It's late — or what passes for late for Hannah these days. They are in bed. Will is scrolling through his phone, and Hannah is reading a dog-eared copy of *Tinker Tailor Soldier Spy.* She picked it up because she wanted a familiar comfort read, but she knows the clock is ticking and that she cannot put this conversation off any longer. She owes to it Will.

She puts the book down on the bedside table.

"Will . . ."

"Mm?" He barely looks up. She can see he's on Twitter. He doesn't tweet under his own name — they've both learned the hard way that's not a good idea — but he has an anonymous account under the name Two Wheels Good where he retweets indignant blogs about poorly designed road junctions and articles about vintage motorbikes.

"Will . . . did you . . ." She swallows. Stops. Tries again. "Did you . . . did you ever hear a rumor that April was . . . pregnant?"

"What?" Will sits up straight, turns to look at her. The lazy postsupper, two-beer contentment is suddenly gone from his face, and his expression is wary and watchful. "I'm sorry, *what* did you say?"

"I . . . I heard a rumor . . . something on the internet —" Oh God, there it is, the actual lie she was trying not to tell, but now she's said it she can't take it back. "Someone said that April was pregnant when she died."

"Ugh, what absolute bullshit," Will says, and his face twists into something so shocked and unhappy that she wishes she had never brought it up, even though there's a kind of comfort in seeing his surprise. "Of course she wasn't. Where do people get this poisonous shit? More to the point, why are you reading it?"

"I don't know — I wasn't trawling conspiracy forums, it just cropped up," she says, and that's true in a way. Geraint did just crop up, out of the blue, like an unwanted Google Alert. "So you think it's crap?"

"Of course it's crap. Are they saying it came up at the autopsy but the coroner just — what — decided not to mention it to anyone?"

"No," Hannah says, but Will's words have cleared her head, blowing away some of the fog of stress and worry, because of course he's completely right. If it were true, then of *course* it would have come up at the autopsy. "No, it wasn't anything to do with the autopsy it was just this rumor, something about, she took a pregnancy test right before she died — but you're right — that's so unlikely." She should have talked to Will about this earlier. She is feeling better already. She rolls over and puts her arm over his middle. "I mean, she would have told one of us for sure, wouldn't she?"

"Of course she would. And anyway, it makes no sense. The idea that April would ever have touched John Neville with a barge pole, let alone had *sex* with him, God,

303

people are fucking imbeciles. They'll believe anything, however unlikely, if it makes a good conspiracy theory."

Hannah says nothing. She only squeezes him tighter, and he hugs her back, and now *he* is the one who is tense, but not with stress and fear. As her arms tighten around him she can feel his anger, feel the sinews in his arms and shoulders as he strives to simmer down so as not to upset her. In a strange way, though, his fury is comforting. Because he has missed the point completely. He has failed to understand what Geraint was saying, the narrative of guilt and revenge that the pregnancy theory implies, and *that* somehow is more reassuring than almost anything else.

"Well . . . it's still a bit high." The midwife unstraps the band from Hannah's arm, and Hannah feels a sharp pang of disbelief. She had been so sure that it would be fine. She had gotten the bus, arrived ten minutes early, sat there taking deep breaths in the waiting room trying to calm herself down. And now this? It feels like her body has betrayed her.

"How high?" she says in an odd, strangled voice.

"It's hovering around the one-forty over

ninety mark. Which . . . isn't ideal. Have you noticed any swelling in your ankles? Any unusual headaches?"

"No, and no." Hannah feels her cheeks flush with annoyance. "But hang on, one-forty over ninety, that's not *that* high, is it? I thought anything below that was normal."

"Clinically, yes, but pregnant women are a bit different." The midwife's voice is gentle, but there's a slightly patronizing note that makes Hannah's hackles rise. *I'm not stupid,* she wants to say. *I know I'm pregnant.* But she knows that she won't be the first person to have had this back-and-forth with the midwife, trying to argue away figures that are right there on the dial in front of her, and that her anger isn't really at the woman sitting opposite, it's at herself.

"There's no protein in your urine," the midwife continues, "so I'm not too concerned, but any rise needs keeping an eye on, that's all. What was it when you booked in?" She flicks back through Hannah's notes, but Hannah already knows what the answer is. She can't remember the exact figures, but it was normal to low. "One-fifteen over eighty, yes, that is a bit of a jump. Well, let's not worry about it now, but we'll have you back next week for a quick check. And in the meantime, if you get any sudden swelling, any headaches or flashing lights, then call the maternity unit urgently." She's running her finger down her appointment diary. "I have a slot at ten a.m. next Thursday if that suits? And try not to worry, it may be just one of those things."

But Hannah's not listening. She's too focused on what the midwife said before that. *We'll have you back next week.*

"I can't," she says without thinking. "I can't take another morning off." Even though that's not true. Maternity checks are a legal right, and besides, Cathy is far too nice to make a fuss about something like that. She would be the first to tell Hannah to take the whole day off, no leave required, if she knew about this.

"If you need a note for your employer I'll be happy to give you one," the midwife is saying. "They're legally required to let you —"

But Hannah is shaking her head. She doesn't need a note. She just doesn't *want* to be in this situation.

It's only when she's out in the street, her notes under her arm, the wind cooling her hot cheeks, that she realizes how true that is. It's not just her blood pressure. She doesn't want any of it — she doesn't want to be here, now, still dealing with the fallout

306

from a tragedy that dropped into her life like a bomb more than ten years ago. *Why me?* she wants to wail. But that is too selfish even to say in her own head, let alone out loud. Because, if it comes to that, why any of them? Why Will, questioned for hours by police, hounded on social media, forever trying to shake off the reputation of being the boyfriend of a murdered girl? Why Ryan, struck down by a stroke in his twenties, a bolt of bad luck so unfair it seems impossible that it could happen to anyone on top of what they suffered in college? Why Emily? Why Hugh? Why Pelham? And most of all, why *April*? Why beautiful, glittering April — someone with the whole of life stretched out at her feet? Why, why, *why* did she deserve to have that taken away from her?

But the answer was, of course, that she did not. That she never had. It was just one of those things.

The train to York takes two and a half hours, and Hannah has forgotten her book, so she buys one at the station, a Louise Candlish that Robyn recommended as particularly gripping, in the hopes that it will keep her from obsessing over the coming conversation with Ryan. It works for a while, but as the train draws closer to York she finds her nerves are taking over, and that she's turning the pages without properly concentrating. Is she really going to do this? She hasn't seen Ryan for more than five years, and since his stroke, she hasn't spoken to him either — first because he couldn't talk on the phone, and then . . . well . . . after that there was no excuse, really, apart from her own selfishness.

Now she wonders if she's mad to do this — turn up out of the blue unannounced. What if he sends her away? He's hardly going to be out, she supposes. She should have called. She should have made an appointment, cleared it with Bella, checked he was up to seeing people. But it's too late for that. She's on the train. She quite literally can't turn back. No. She's going to have to see this through — even if that's only as far as Ryan telling her to her face that she's four years too late, rather than by text.

When she gets to York she catches a taxi, carefully reading out Ryan's address from the contact list on her phone. And then at last she's there — standing outside a neat suburban house with a garage to one side and a little square of lawn in front.

Her heart is beating in her throat, and she can't help thinking of her blood pressure, of what it's doing to the baby, but she forces herself to cross the drive, step up to the blond wood front door, and ring the bell.

She's not sure what she's expecting. Bella, most likely, or perhaps a carer of some kind in a uniform. Whatever she thought, it's not the person who opens the door, awkwardly wheeling his chair out of the way as he pulls it back.

"Ryan!" His name comes out without her even meaning it — a jolt of surprise. For a minute his face is blank and puzzled as he stares up at her, a frown between his brows. He looks older than she remembers, older than the years of water under the bridge would warrant. He looks far more gaunt and drawn than Will, who is his exact contemporary. But it's not just that — there is something slack about the muscles of his face, a kind of lopsided stiffness beneath the dense, dark beard he has grown since college days. Then his expression clears and he smiles, one side of his mouth lifting more than the other.

"Well fook me, if it ain't Hannah bloody Jones. What in God's name are you doing here, woman?"

And it's still him. It's still the same Ryan. His voice is slightly slurred, his smile is slightly tilted, but it's the same old Ryan.

Hannah just stands there, smiling nervously. She finds she doesn't know what to say. Ryan is grinning up at her, enjoying her awkwardness just a little — he's still got that knack for discomfiting people — but he's pleased to see her, and that wasn't a given.

"What took you so long?" is all he says.

Before

"Where is she?" Emily was tapping her foot irritably. "I've got to get back, I have an absolute mountain of revision to get done before tomorrow."

Hannah looked at her phone. It was gone 10 p.m. The gates would have shut long ago. They were hanging around in the foyer, waiting for April to finish up and come out, but they'd been there for almost half an hour and she still hadn't showed.

"Should we go backstage?" Hugh asked, looking rather nervously at Will.

Will shrugged. He had said very little since his altercation with April, and now he was just standing stone-faced in the foyer, the streaks of makeup still smeared across his T-shirt. Hannah found herself wondering what he was thinking.

"Well, I'm going," Emily said, making up her mind. "Coming, Han?"

Hannah was torn. Part of her desperately

needed to get back and revise for her last exam. The other part felt like a disloyal friend for leaving April on her opening night. But if Emily was leaving, then Ryan would probably join her, and maybe Hugh too.

"I don't know." She glanced at Hugh, then Ryan. "What do you think? Are you staying?"

"I'm leaving," Ryan said. "I'm bloody starving. I came straight from rugby practice and all I've had is a couple of beers. I'm not hanging around here when I could be getting meself a large kebab outside."

"I have to get back," Hugh said. His voice was slightly reluctant and now he looked at Will. "I've got an exam tomorrow. You'll be okay, Will?"

Will said nothing, but he gave a tight nod.

"Fine," Emily said, as if that settled matters. "In that case, we're offski. See you back at the ranch, Will."

Outside the theater, Hannah found herself looking up and down the street, half expecting to see Neville lurking in the shadows, but to her relief, he was gone.

"Are you okay?" Hugh said, rather curiously.

Hannah let out a nervous laugh.

"Yes, sorry. I just thought I saw . . ."

"Saw what?"

Hannah bit her lip. She hadn't said much about Neville's behavior to the others, not since that day when he'd talked about *little girls* in the Porters' Lodge. Since then there had been nothing she could put her finger on, and she had begun to feel almost ashamed of her antipathy to him. Well, nothing, right up until the night he had come up to her room with the parcel — but that was weeks ago, and besides, it was so bound up with what had happened afterwards, her kiss with Will, that she had found it almost impossible to talk about. The whole night was so bound up with her feelings for Will and her shame over her own actions that she was afraid that if she unpicked one edge of the tangle, the whole mass would come unraveled — and risk betraying Will in the process.

"I thought I saw one of the college porters," she said at last. Hugh looked puzzled, but Emily, a couple of paces ahead, swung round.

"Oh my God. Not that weird Neville guy? The *little girls* creep?"

"Yes," Hannah said. She felt a deep unhappiness take hold of her, somewhere inside. "I thought — I thought I saw him

313

near the front, in the second half. But I don't know if it was him."

"It was him," Ryan said, somewhat unexpectedly. "I clocked him in the queue for the gents. Is he still bothering you?"

"N— I don't know," Hannah said. She felt like someone was pulling slowly at a bandage over a cut, exposing something very raw and tender underneath. "He's just — he's always there, always hanging around. He came up to our room one time — I don't want to talk about it," she finished hurriedly, seeing that Emily was about to open her mouth to interject something horrified and furious. "I told him to go away and he did, but I just — I find him really creepy and I don't know what to do about it."

"You have to go to the college authorities!" Emily burst out. "This isn't okay!"

"And say what? He came to see my friend's play? He made me feel a bit weird?"

"She's got a point," Ryan threw over his shoulder. "It in't exactly a smoking gun, is it?"

Emily was opening her mouth to reply when Ryan stopped, pointing up a side street at a kebab van parked at the intersection, a line of people snaking across the pavement.

"Ey up, I spy supper. Hold up. I'll be back in a tick."

"Have you seen that queue?" Emily said explosively. "And did you not hear me about the revision?"

"So don't wait," Ryan called. He was already halfway down the side road towards the van. "Keep the bed warm!"

"You should be so lucky!" Emily yelled back, then let out an exasperated sigh. "Knob. Well I'm off, he'll be half an hour in that queue *if* he's lucky, and then he'll want to eat it. Hannah?"

"I'll come with you," Hannah said. She looked at her watch, trying to figure out the likelihood that Neville would be back at Pelham by now. Did he live in college? It dawned on her she had no idea about the lives of the porters outside their jobs. "Hugh?"

"Well, I am pretty hungry. I might . . . I might join Ryan?" Hugh said, as if seeking their approval. He looked a little uncertain. Hannah had the impression that he and Ryan had never really been the best of friends — that they were linked by default, through Will, rather than via any real connection of their own. But maybe Hugh was trying to change that.

"Knock yourself out," Emily said. "Laters,

Coates!" she bellowed down the alleyway after Ryan, and then turned on her heel and left.

It was almost eleven when they got back to Pelham, and Hannah found her footsteps slowing as they approached the front gate, wondering if Neville would be there.

"Come on," Emily said impatiently as they crossed Pelham Street.

"You go on," Hannah said. "I just want to check if the Cloade gate is still open."

"It won't be," Emily said. She stopped, looking harder at Hannah. "Is this about Neville? Do you want me to see if he's in the lodge?"

"No, it's fine," Hannah said, rather wearily. "You'll have to knock at this time of night, and then how will you explain going back for me? I'll just brave it out. I mean, so what if he's there. He can't eat me."

"Okay, well, first of all, let me reiterate once again how extremely fucked up it is that you're rearranging your life to avoid this man without going to the college authorities, and second, you know you can climb the wall behind Cloade's?"

"What?" Hannah wrapped her arms around herself, trying not to shiver in the draft coming down Pelham Street. It was

June, but the night air was cool in spite of her cardigan. "No, I had no idea. Where? All the walls are eight foot and covered in spikes."

"There's a bit where you can get a foot-hold. Ryan showed me — he used it one time when he'd forgotten his Bod card and couldn't be arsed to go round the front. Want me to show you?"

"Yes!" Hannah said, more eagerly than she had meant, and then felt ridiculous. "I mean, not that it's that much of an issue. I don't mind going past the lodge. It just might be — you know. Useful. One day."

Emily shot her a look like she was in absolutely no doubt of how much Hannah did not want to face Neville, but said nothing, only turned up Pelham Street. They passed the Cloade gate without stopping, and then rounded the corner and ducked into a small lane that led between houses to the Meadow, a large field that backed onto Pelham and was used for cricket in the summer and lazing out on sunny days. Here, the high wall that bounded the college on four sides was covered in ivy and creepers, and Emily walked slowly through the scrubby trees, picking her way by the light of her mobile, before stopping at last at a place where the ivy grew particularly thick.

"There," she said, pointing. "Can you see? The ivy makes a kind of mattress over the spikes, and you can get a foot onto that sticking-out stone halfway up, and pull yourself up."

"That one?" Hannah said, disbelievingly pointing to a stone at least four feet off the ground. "Maybe Ryan can, but I definitely can't. It's much too high."

"Yeah, that one. Ryan had to give me a leg up, but maybe we can find a log," Emily said. She was searching around in the undergrowth, using her phone as a torch, but then seemed to realize that was a nonstarter. There was nothing solid enough around. "Okay, scratch that. New plan. I'll boost you, and you pull me up if you can. If you can't, I'll go round by the main entrance."

Hannah nodded. Emily made a platform of her hands and braced herself, and Hannah put her weight onto the living, yielding flesh of Emily's linked fingers and felt Emily shove with all her might.

Hannah's hands caught on the top of the wall, but for a second she wasn't sure if she would make it. The stone was old and crumbling, and the creepers began to peel away under her fingers. But then her kicking left foot caught on something, the sticking-out stone Emily had pointed out, and it gave her just enough purchase to haul herself up, panting and scrabbling, and swing her right leg over the top of the wall.

"Ow!" The yelp of pain came out louder than she had meant.

"Are you okay?" Emily whisper-shouted from below.

"I'm fine," Hannah said, though it wasn't completely true. She had grated her thigh over one of the unprotected spikes on top of the wall, and now as she pulled herself up to sit astride, she could feel a spreading wetness that she was pretty sure was blood. She poked herself gently, feeling the broken threads of denim and an ominous dampness. "Think I just stabbed myself on a spike. I'll live, but RIP my new jeans." She gave a shaky laugh. "Okay, your turn. I'll pull, you jump." She braced herself, holding her hand down for Emily, now nothing but a dark shape and a glimmer of phone screen in the darkness below.

"You know what," Emily's voice said, with a new reluctance, "on second thought, I think I'm going to take a pass on that. Can you get down?"

Hannah looked at the drop on the other side. It was not quite as high and there was a convenient buttress that she could lower herself onto to break her fall.

"I think I'll be all right. Are you sure?"

"Yeah, I think this shortcut is probably fine if you're a six-foot rugby player, but not so great if you're a fragile five-foot-nothing bluestocking like moi, not to mention these sandals are my favorite. If you're sure you're okay getting down, I'll go round by the lodge."

"I'm sure," Hannah said. "Good luck with the revision."

"Cheers, see you at breakfast, then."

Hannah sat, listening, as Emily's footsteps crunched off into the darkness of the wood, and then she swung her other leg over the wall and sat, contemplating the drop.

It would be easiest, she thought, if she rolled round to lie on her stomach; then she could hold on to the wall with her hands and lower herself feet-first onto the buttress. Painfully, she began to roll over, feeling the thick twisting ropes of ivy digging into her hip, and the protest from her inner thigh as the material of her jeans chafed against the cut.

At last, though, she was lying on her front, her legs dangling roughly over where she thought the buttress should be, and she began to lower herself cautiously down. She was almost at full stretch, her arms quivering with the unaccustomed strain, when she felt something, some*one,* grab her ankle.

Hannah kicked out instinctively. The hand let go, and she heard a male voice cry out in pain, and someone stagger back. And then her arms gave way and she slid to the ground in a slither of grazed ribs and jarred ankles

She landed heavily, but picked herself up almost at once and began to run around the side of Cloade's, in spite of the pain in her knees and thigh. She wasn't sure who had grabbed her, but she knew that she didn't want to wait and find out. What she had done was strictly against the rules, and if a tutor or a member of college staff found out, she would be in trouble.

"Oi!" she heard from behind her, as whoever she had kicked recovered himself. It was a man's voice, but oddly high, almost falsetto. "Oi, you, stop!"

Hannah pushed herself to run faster and rounded the corner into the passage that led into New Quad.

And then whoever it was behind her tackled her.

She felt a whiplash jolt as the pursuer grabbed at her collar, jerking her back, and then her feet were hooked out from under her. She went down in a rush, elbows and knees onto the graveled path, all the wind knocked out of her. She felt a man's body land heavily on top of her, covering her almost completely, his hips pressing into her backside, his chest crushing hers against the ground. There was an arm across the back of her neck. She couldn't breathe — but she could smell something — something horribly familiar — that sickening musty smell of body odor and damp.

Panic engulfed her.

"Get off me!" she choked, but the words came out so smothered they were barely audible; he was grinding her face into the path, she could hardly get any air in. Her hands were wet with sweat, her whole body shaking with fear, her lungs screaming for oxygen. She felt his hips grinding hers into the ground — and she felt something else too, something hard and thick and urgent, pressing against her. "Ge—" she tried again, but the words dissolved into a sobbing gasp. Stars were beginning to explode against the inside of her skull, obscuring her vision. "G-ge—"

And then another voice, a deeper one, unfamiliar.

"What on earth is going on here, Mr. Neville?"

"I found this person climbing over the

wall —" Neville panted. He got to his knees, putting his weight painfully on Hannah's arm as he did. She lay there, gasping and trembling as he lumbered slowly to his feet, feeling the crushing sensation in her chest slowly lifting.

"Well still, but I'm not sure —"

Hannah didn't wait around to hear any more. She had only one instinct — to get away.

As the last of Neville's weight came off her she twisted like an animal in a trap and wrenched herself out from underneath him — and then she was gone, stumbling around the corner of the quad, into staircase 7, up the stairs, three at a time, until at last she was in the sanctuary of the set, the good, solid wooden door of her bedroom hard against her back — and then she sank down to the floor and burst into tears.

AFTER

"So," Ryan says, with another of his lopsided smiles.

They are sitting in his living room, nursing cups of tea that Hannah has made under his direction.

"What brings you here, then?" He puts on a plummy accent quite at odds with his normal one and intones, "Rumors of my death have been much exaggerated."

Hannah laughs at that, she can't help it. He's still Ryan, still stupid, piss-taking, sarcastic Ryan, even after everything he's been through.

"I can't believe how well you look," she says, and he grins.

"Aye, well, you should have seen me a few years ago. Adult nappies, surgical hoists, the whole shebang. Pretty sexy it were."

"And how's Bella?"

"She's grand. She's been my lifeline, her and the girls."

The girls. Of course. She had almost forgotten that Ryan has two little girls now.

"How old are they?"

"Mabel's almost four and Lulu's two. Mabel was born right after I had the stroke. Bella always said I couldn't stand to share the" — he pauses, frowns infinitesimally as though searching for a word, and then his brow clears and he finishes — "limelight. Had to make it all about me."

"Will and I are expecting," Hannah says. She pats her stomach, feeling like a performative fool, but she still can't quite get over it — the fact that it's *there*, their baby, a melting pot of her and Will growing inside her. "Did you know?"

"Aye, Hugh said. Congratulations. They'll pull your life apart and stick it back together with vomit and shit, but it'll still be more beautiful than you ever thought possible."

Hannah smiles at that, and Ryan smiles back, a little sadly this time. Maybe he's thinking of how their own lives were ripped into little pieces after April's death.

"I didn't know you kept up with Hugh," she says, as much to change the subject as anything.

"Yeah, it's funny, I wouldn't have put us down for pen pals neither, and I never heard from him much after college. But he got in

325

touch after my stroke. He's been a good mate."

Better than you and Will. The words hang in the air between them. Ryan doesn't say it — he wouldn't reproach them like that, and Hannah knows it — but it doesn't stop it from being true.

Hannah swallows. She needs to bring it up — she can't stand the way they're both dancing around her betrayal, not mentioning the years of silence, the lack of visits.

"I'm sorry," she says. "Ryan, I'm *really* sorry we never came to see you. And I know Will feels bad about it too. It was just — I don't know. I was running from everything about Pelham for so long. It's why I ended up in Edinburgh. And I don't want you to think Will and Hugh and I formed this cozy little clique up there, it wasn't like that. Will came to find *me.* I don't think I would ever have sought him out off my own bat — it was all just too painful. And Hugh . . ." She stops. She has never thought about why Hugh ended up in Scotland. "I guess Hugh followed Will," she says finally. "Or I think he had some kind of surgical residency there at one point — maybe he just liked it there. But I never meant to drop you the way I did — or Em. It was more like . . ." She stops again, groping for the words. "More like I was just trying to survive."

"It's okay," Ryan says softly. He puts out his good hand, touches hers, very gently. "We've all been a bit rubbish. I mean, how often did I call you before my stroke? Once, maybe twice? And that was only to tell you about the wedding — way to make it all about me, huh. And yeah, I'm not gonna lie, things have been a bit shit here. But it's not like you were having a great time either. It's not just you — I've barely spoken to Em since uni. We let each other down. We all did."

Hannah nods. There are tears pricking at the backs of her eyes. She wants to tell him how much she's missed him, how often she's thought of him and Em, but she can't find the words.

"Do you think it was because of April?" she manages at last. "The stroke, I mean? I've always wondered."

"What, the . . ." Ryan pauses as if he's searching for a word. "The stress, you mean?"

Hannah nods. Ryan shrugs lopsidedly, one shoulder rising more than the other.

"Maybe that contributed, but only in terms of my own behavior. Bottom line, I was drinking too much, smoking too much, eating shit — my blood pressure was bad . . .

all of that was my choice. Well, not the blood pressure." He laughs. "That's genetic. But I should have got it treated instead of burying me head."

Hannah bites her lip. She doesn't want to think about that.

"So what brings you down here?" Ryan asks again, this time with the air of changing the conversation. Hannah takes a gulp of tea — remembering how much she hates PG Tips — and then a deep breath.

"Do you know a reporter called Geraint Williams?"

"Ger?" His face is a little surprised. "Yes, course I do. He's a good bloke. We worked together at the *Herald*. How come?"

"He came to see me, at the bookshop. You probably heard John Neville died?"

"I did. Hard to miss it, to be honest. It was all over the news."

Hannah nods.

"Well, Geraint came to see me afterwards. He'd been working on a podcast, with Neville's cooperation, or at least that's what he said. And he wanted my side of things."

"Right," Ryan says. He's frowning slightly, but not like he's contradicting her, just like he's trying to see where this is going.

"We had coffee, and he . . . well, he thinks Neville is —" She swallows a gulp of scalding tea, trying to force herself to say the words. "He thinks Neville might have been innocent."

To her surprise, Ryan doesn't recoil. He only nods slowly.

"Aye, well, he's not the only one. With a defense like that, there's bound to be questions."

"What do you mean?" Hannah asks, and now it's her turn to frown.

Ryan gives a sigh and lifts himself slightly in his chair, as if the pressure of the seat hurts him. He can only really use one hand, Hannah's noticed. He picks up his cup with that hand, operates his chair, now he lifts himself sideways on one arm, and then slumps back down with a squeak from the wheelchair's brakes.

"Look, you're not part of that circuit, you wouldn't have known. But journalists — we talk to lawyers a fair bit and, well, there's a fairly widespread — a fairly —" He stops, his expression frustrated.

"A what?"

"A — oh shit, what do you call it." His face is twisted in annoyance. "When everyone agrees on the same thing. An acceptance, that's the word I was looking for. Sorry — since the stroke, it's like things have fallen through the gaps. Words, names, faces. It's getting better, but it comes back when I'm tired. What was I saying?"

"A widespread acceptance," Hannah prods, and Ryan nods.

"That's it. An acceptance that his defense didn't do a very good job. I mean basically what did it boil down to? You saw him coming down the stairs. That was it. Not much to lock a bloke up for life."

"But the stalking," Hannah says. She feels suddenly nettled, as if Ryan is accusing her of something. "All the stuff that came out at the trial about the other girls he'd spied on. It was part of a pattern of escalating behavior, isn't that what the judge said?"

"He did, and there's an argument that half of that shouldn't have been ad —" He stops, pounds his hand down on his knee in frustration. "Fuck it, it's gone as well."

"Admissible?" Hannah ventures, unsure of the etiquette of filling in for him, but Ryan nods in relief.

"Yes! *Thank* you. Admissible. It prejudiced the jury and none of it spoke to him being a murderer, did it?"

"Ryan, he attacked me!"

"*Or* he did his job and stopped someone he'd seen breaking into college," Ryan says, and then holds up his hand as he sees her begin to protest. "Look, I'm not saying you were in the wrong — you said what happened, and the rest was down to the jury. It wasn't up to you to make Neville's defense. I'm just telling you why some people have a problem with the verdict. But it's too late now."

She nods, thinking. It *is* too late now, that's true. She can't bring Neville back. But at the same time, she knows that she can't let this rest either. Not if there's even the slightest chance that Geraint is right.

"There . . . was something else . . ." she says, very slowly, and then stops. She's not sure how to say this. It's not the same as asking Will, the man she loves, the man she's married to, *April's boyfriend.* But it is still an accusation of a sort.

"Spit it out, pet," Ryan says, but kindly, as if he knows this is hard for her. Hannah takes a deep breath.

"Geraint said . . . he claims that April told you —" She stops again, swallows, feeling the blood pounding in her throat. This *can't* be good for the baby. "He said that April was pregnant," she finishes in a rush.

Whatever Ryan was expecting, it wasn't that. His face goes white beneath the dark beard. But he's not surprised, or not as surprised as he should be, if the accusation were news to him.

There's a long silence. Ryan raises his cup to his lips, takes a slow, painful swallow, and then sets it down and gives a shaky nod.

"It's true?" Hannah asks. Ryan shrugs, one shoulder lifting higher than the other.

"Who knows. You know what April was like."

"You think it was a prank?"

"I still have no idea. We . . ." His face twitches and he looks away from her, not meeting her eyes. "We were sleeping together; you probably knew that already."

Hannah exhales. She's not sure what to say. It's weird to have her suspicions confirmed.

"I — I didn't know for sure," she says at last. "Not then. But looking back . . . I'm not completely surprised. How long?"

"Most of that year," Ryan says. His mouth twists unhappily. "The first time was before I knew she and Will were an item — I wouldn't have done if I'd known they were official; least, that's what I tried to tell myself. When I found out, I felt like a complete prick. But I'd already done it once, so . . ." He shrugs again.

"What about Emily?" Hannah says. Her throat is tight, thinking of Em and this serial betrayal. April was never Em's friend in the way that she was Hannah's friend. There was always something a bit antagonistic there, a little mistrustful. But they *were* friends, in the meaning of the act. They hung out together.

"Yeah, I felt like a prick to her too. More than a prick. But that was the problem — once I'd done it the first time, April had me over a barrel."

"What, you mean she was forcing you into it?" Hannah doesn't try to keep the skepticism out of her voice. This is all a little bit too convenient for Ryan — and April didn't need to emotionally blackmail people into sleeping with her. She would have had candidates queuing up around the block if that was what she'd wanted.

Ryan's face is unhappy.

"I know. I know what you're thinking. And yeah, a' course the truth is that I could have stopped it anytime I wanted. I had a choice — every time she called or texted or sidled up to me at chucking-out time saying *Will's busy,* I could've turned her down. I know that. I'm just saying, it's fucking hard to say no to someone who's got your girlfriend on speed dial. I knew I was being a shit, but . . . yeah, I'm not going to lie. I wanted to shag April. So I did. I knew she din't want to get found out any more than I did."

His mouth twists, and Hannah can see the

self-hatred still in his eyes, but there's another kind of loathing there too, and now she understands . . . or she thinks she does. Ryan's antipathy to April was real — but it wasn't because April was rich and beautiful and had life handed to her on a plate. At least, it wasn't *just* that. Ryan had hated her because of what they were doing together.

"What about the pregnancy, then?" she asks. Her throat is dry, and she takes another sip of tea. It's cooler now. "When did that happen?"

"I'm not sure. I didn't see her those last couple of weeks, she was so busy with rehearsals and everything. But she texted me the morning after the first night of the play. The text just said, *Look in your pigeon-hole.* So I looked. And there was a Jiffy bag containing a pregnancy test — two lines. I texted back saying, *Is this a joke?* And she replied back, *Positively not.*"

"Shit." Hannah doesn't know what to think. It's the kind of prank April would pull — but at the same time . . . "Did it look real?"

"How the fuck should I know?" Ryan says bluntly. "I'd never seen a pregnancy test. She could have drawn those lines on with a . . . a —" He screws up his face, searching for the missing word, and Hannah bites her

334

lip, trying to stop herself jumping in. "With a *biro* for all I knew. But . . . yeah, if I'm being honest, it looked real. Enough to send me into a tailspin, anyway. I spent the rest of the week panicking and alternately crapping myself and telling myself that it probably wasn't mine — and then — and then —"

He breaks off. Hannah sees there are tears in his eyes. *And then April was killed.*

"Why didn't you say anything?" she says gently.

Ryan gives a short, barking laugh and runs his good hand through his hair, making it stick up like a porcupine's spines. "Why do you think? Because she'd been strangled and I knew that if I told them about the test it would be me *and* Will in the firing line. And because I didn't *know.* I had no idea if it was just one of her stupid fucking pranks. I thought if it *was* true then they would find out at the — the medical thing, autopsy, that's it, and it would all come out without me having to admit I knew anything. I waited and waited for days and then weeks — but the call never came. And then they arrested Neville and I thought —" He stops. His eyes are filled with tears and there's a muscle ticing in his cheek. Hannah can see he is tired, exhausted in fact.

She feels a stab of remorse.

"I was so fucking thankful, you know?" he says. His voice breaks on the last word. "It was just April's sick joke. But later . . . later on I started to wonder."

"I'm sorry," Hannah says. She stands up. "I'm really sorry, Ryan, I shouldn't have dug all this up. Listen, I should go, I've kept you talking too long, and I have to get back to Edinburgh be —" She stops, stumbling over the last words. *Before Will gets home* is what she had been going to say, but she doesn't want to admit to Ryan that she's here without Will's knowledge. "Before rush hour," she finishes uncomfortably.

Ryan nods.

"Fair enough. Look, take care of yourself, okay? And if you want any baby clothes —"

He waves a hand at the living room, which is strewn with the plastic detritus left by two small girls.

"As you can see we're due a clear-out. And I don't think Bella's up for any more kids."

"Thanks," Hannah says. She smiles. It's a relief doing so after the seriousness of the last half hour. "I'd like that. And you take care of yourself too."

"I will," he says. He wheels with her to the door and unlatches it. Then, on the doorstep, he beckons her to lean over, and somewhat to Hannah's surprise, he plants a kiss on her cheek. His lips are soft, and his beard even softer, much gentler than Will's occasional three-day stubble when he forgets to shave. "You didn't deserve this, Hannah Jones. Remember that, a'right?"

"I'll remember," Hannah says. She swallows, finding her eyes suddenly hot with unshed tears. "Thank you, Ryan. You —"

She doesn't know what she wants to say.

You're a good man.

You're a better friend than either Will or I had any right to expect.

You didn't deserve this either.

But she doesn't find the words. Instead she just kisses him back, his beard soft beneath her lips, and then she picks up her bag and heads off towards the train.

BEFORE

When Hannah awoke the next day it was slowly, painfully, crawling up from dark dreams of being chased and hunted down and beaten. As she came back to consciousness, she became aware that the aching muscles and bruised bones were not part of the dream but real. She was still fully clothed under the covers, and she could feel the crusted blood on the inside of her thigh, and the pull of the denim where it had dried into the cut. There were grazes on her cheekbones and chin where her face had been ground into the gravel, and every joint seemed to have seized up overnight.

For a long time she simply lay there, blinking and trying to come to terms with what had happened and what she could do about it, but then she became aware of something else: the unmistakable sounds of sex coming from April's room.

All of a sudden Hannah knew that she

couldn't stay there, listening, wondering if it was going to be Will, bruised lips in a sheepish grin, sidling out of Hannah's doorway, or someone completely different slipping out unseen. She didn't want to know. Either possibility was unbearable.

Instead, she grabbed her towel and a change of clothes and headed out of the flat down to the landing where the bathroom was.

Beneath the hot water, the cuts and abrasions were even more painful, the bruises on her skin even more clearly delineated. She had to do something. She had to *say* something. It didn't matter, surely, that she had been climbing a wall. She wasn't trespassing — she was a member of the college, who didn't deserve to be assaulted.

But who could she tell? Obviously not the other porters — though they were supposed to be the first resort for immediate security threats. And not the Master. Hannah had never met him, but she had seen him at the top table at formal dinners and attended his address at the beginning of term, and she couldn't imagine going to such an austere, remote figure with a problem like this.

Which left . . . Dr. Myers . . . ? She couldn't think who else she could approach.

For a while, she stood under the stream of

hot water considering the problem, trying to imagine bringing it up with Dr. Myers, trying out the words in her head. *He assaulted me?* No, that wasn't quite right. That sounded more . . . sexual than she wanted it to, though the memory of Neville's crotch pressing into her backside was still uneasily vivid in her mind.

He tackled me. That was closer to the mark. But did it sum up the seriousness of what had happened? Did it convey the real fear she had experienced, feeling Neville's crushing weight on hers, his arm on the back of her neck, his body pinning her to the gravel as he ground her face into the dirt?

He hurt me.

No. That had the pathetic ring of a child in a playground scrap, even though it was true.

At last, Hannah gave up and turned off the tap, toweling herself gingerly, trying not to open up the partially healed scrapes and grazes from last night. She got dressed and then stood, uncertainly, her towel and pajamas in one hand, her wash bag in the other.

What she should do — the logical thing to do — was go back up to her room and drop off her things before heading to breakfast. But she couldn't face it. April's visitor might still be there and Hannah wasn't sure which would be more awkward, confronting April in a potential betrayal of Will, or bursting in on their makeup sex and having to deal with Will's concern and pity over her bruised face.

Neither appealed — at least not before coffee.

Instead, Hannah rolled her pajamas up inside her damp towel, tucked it under her arm, and headed down the stairs to the hall, and breakfast.

"Hannah! Over here!"

She heard Emily's voice before she saw her, waving an arm from the other side of the hall and pointing to an empty place on the bench beside her. Taking a deep breath, Hannah waved a hand back, and then began to edge her tray of coffee and cheese on toast through the breakfasting students.

When she got to the table she was half fearing Emily's reaction, but Emily was busy talking to Hugh, sitting opposite, and didn't seem to clock the bruises on Hannah's face. Feeling an odd sense of relief, Hannah slid into the free space with her head down and said nothing as she began to eat.

"Well," Hugh said at last, pushing away

an untouched slice of toast and standing up, "I'd better get going. I've got my first exam at two and I haven't done nearly enough prep." He looked almost sick with nerves, and Hannah found herself wondering, vaguely, why he had allowed himself to be talked into attending April's play the night before his prelims when he was clearly so worried. "Wish me luck."

"Good luck," Hannah said, and smiled encouragingly at him. As she did so, her face caught the light filtering through the high leaded windows, and Hugh stopped. He put his tray back on the table and adjusted his glasses with a frown.

"Hannah, what happened to your cheek?"

"What . . . oh." She touched her fingers to the graze on her cheekbone and gave a self-conscious laugh. "Is it that bad?"

"Hannah?" Emily said. She leaned forward, drawing back the curtain of Hannah's hair with one finger, and then her expression changed. "Whoa, did you fall off that wall?"

"No," Hannah said. She felt a sudden wash of self-consciousness and something else . . . something closer to guilt, though she could not have said why. She twitched her hair out of Emily's hand, letting it fall back over her cheek. "Not exactly. I got . . .

well, someone caught me."

"Someone caught you?" Hugh was frowning. "Doing what?"

"I climbed over the wall and, well —" She stopped, glancing over her shoulder to see if anyone else was listening. Why did she feel so ashamed of what had happened? "One of the porters . . . kind of . . . tackled me." She gave a shaky laugh, trying to lighten the atmosphere. "I'm quite sore this morning. Makes me feel like maybe the rugby players earn those stupid blues after all."

"One of the porters?" Emily said in a hard voice, ignoring Hannah's attempts at diversion. "Hannah, which porter are we talking about? Not — ?"

Hannah said nothing, but she nodded, and Emily's face changed.

"Jesus Christ. What did he say? Have you reported this?"

"Not yet," Hannah said. She kept her voice low, horribly conscious of Emily's ringing indignation. "He didn't say anything — I didn't wait around to talk. Someone turned up and I ran off."

"Oh my God." Emily stood up, as if her anger was too much to be contained while still seated. "Hannah — this is. I don't know what to say. Why didn't you call me?"

"I felt —" Hannah stopped, she swallowed. "I felt — I didn't —"

But Emily was shaking her head, and Hannah knew that she didn't have to finish the sentence, that somehow Emily, like all women who'd ever been alone and afraid at night, understood the strange mix of guilt, disgust, and self-hatred she was experiencing, and knew exactly how she was feeling.

Hugh's face, by contrast, was a mixture of alarmed and bewildered, and he looked first at Emily, then Hannah, then back at Emily as if seeking guidance.

"What — I mean, gosh. Do you — can we do something?" he forced out at last. His cheeks were flushed, though Hannah was not sure if it was with anger or embarrassment.

"Don't worry, Hugh," Emily said grimly. "I've got this. You get to your exam. Hannah, we're going to report this."

"I will," Hannah said firmly, trying to claw back some control over the situation. But Emily shook her head.

"Not *I will;* do it now, while you've still got the bruises, while they can't shake this off. We'll go to the Master."

"*No.*" Hannah's voice was sharp, and now people really were looking. She lowered it, forcing herself to speak more calmly. "No, honestly, I think that's too drastic. I was

344

thinking about it in the shower this morning. I want to take it to Dr. Myers. He's my professor and it says in the handbook that he's first port of call for any pastoral issues."

"Dr. Myers?" Emily looked doubtful. "Isn't he that creepy one? The guy who's always inviting students up to his room?"

"He's had a couple of parties," Hannah said wearily. "April and I went to one. It wasn't exactly Sodom and Gomorrah."

"Okay. So we'll go to him. Ready?"

Hannah opened her mouth, and then stopped.

She wasn't ready. She probably wouldn't ever be ready. But she could see that Emily wasn't going to let her off the hook.

Some fifteen minutes later they were standing outside Dr. Myers's office door, listening to noises from within.

"He's with someone," Hannah whispered. "We should come back."

But before Emily could answer, the door opened, and a girl Hannah recognized from Dr. Myers's party came out, swishing her long dark hair over one shoulder as she passed them in the hall.

"Have a good break, Dr. M," she said over her shoulder.

"Au revoir, Rubye," Dr. Myers called after

her. "Until next year. Ah, Hannah," he said in slight surprise. "We don't have a tutorial this week due to exams — had you forgotten?"

"No," Hannah said reluctantly. "I hadn't forgotten. And if now isn't a good time —"

"Hannah wanted to speak to you about something," Emily cut in. "Something important. Do you have ten minutes, Dr. Myers?"

"Ten minutes?" Dr. Myers looked at his watch, and then nodded. "Yes, ten minutes I can do. Come in."

He stood back, and Hannah and Emily edged past him into the little office. The blinds were drawn against the summer sun, casting the room into pools of light and shadow. Hannah perched, rather nervously, on the edge of the chair she used in tutorials, letting her hair fall around her face, while Emily took the armchair in the corner and folded her arms with a grim expression.

"What can I help you with, Hannah?" Dr. Myers said pleasantly. Hannah felt a flutter in her gut at the thought of what she might be about to set in motion, but then steeled herself. John Neville had gone too far this time. She *had* to say something.

"It's about one of the porters," she said.

Her throat was dry and she swallowed, wishing she'd had something to drink at breakfast other than strong coffee. "John Neville. He's the very tall one."

"Yes, I know Mr. Neville," Dr. Myers said, frowning, as if he didn't understand quite where all this was leading.

"He caught me last night climbing over the wall behind Cloade's," Hannah said. Her heart was beating fast. "And he — well, he rugby-tackled me. To the ground. He —" She swallowed again. It felt like something was blocking her throat, making it hard to breathe. "He threw himself on top of me. I couldn't move. It was —" She stopped, unable to think how to go on. "It was —" she managed again, and then shut her eyes.

"Hannah's hurt, Dr. Myers," Emily broke in furiously. "Look at her face. It was totally disproportionate. And it's part of a pattern of really threatening behavior towards Hannah and —"

"Ladies, hold up, hold up," Dr. Myers said, raising a hand. "What's this about your face, Hannah?"

Reluctantly, Hannah pulled back the curtain of hair shielding her bruised cheek and leaned forward, into the pool of sunlight. Dr. Myers looked at the marks in silence for a few moments and then folded his arms.

"I see. Run me through what happened step-by-step, Hannah. You were climbing over the wall? Why were you climbing over the wall?"

"I didn't —" Hannah started, and then stopped. She had been going to say, *I didn't want Neville to see me going through the lodge,* but now she was worried that would sound like she had a preexisting grudge against Neville. "It was a shortcut," she finished, rather lamely. "The Cloade gate was shut."

"Very well, so you climbed the wall, and what happened next?"

"I was climbing down the other side, and I felt someone grab my ankle."

"Someone? You didn't know it was Neville at first?"

"No, I didn't know it was him at first — it was dark — and I was scared, so I kicked out, and ran away."

"And he ran after you?"

"Yes, he called out something like *stop,* or *stop, trespasser.* I can't remember."

"Very well, and then what happened?"

"He caught up with me by the cloisters," Hannah said. The words felt thick in her mouth. She heard again Neville's pounding footsteps behind her, the whiplash sensation as he grabbed her collar, jerking her back. "He grabbed my coat and then tripped me and I fell, and he threw himself on top of me. He had his arm across the back of my neck. I couldn't —" Her breath was coming fast, her heart was knocking in her ears. "I couldn't breathe. I started to see stars."

"And then?"

"And then someone else came along and said something like, *what's going on,* and he stood up, and I — I just ran. I was so scared."

"But you saw it was him?"

"When he tripped me, yes. I knew it was him." Her voice was shaking now. She felt tears prick at the corners of her eyes. "I'm *absolutely* certain it was him, I recognized his voice and his —" She stopped. She couldn't bring herself to say *his smell.* It implied a level of intimacy she wished she didn't have. "And th-there was someone else there," she said instead, stumbling over the words. "A man. I think it was a member of college staff. Whoever it was spoke to Neville — he'll corroborate my story, confirm it definitely was Neville who tackled me. And it's not just my face, look." She stood up, yanking at the hem of her shirt, pulling it up to show her torso, the scarlet scrapes, fast darkening into blotched purple bruises. "Look, I'm *not* making this up."

Behind her Hannah heard Emily suck in her breath at the sight of her battered ribs, and she let the T-shirt drop and sat back down, her cheeks flaming.

"Well look, let me say first and foremost I'm absolutely *not* trying to cast doubt on what you experienced," Dr. Myers said slowly. He stood up too, pacing to the window as if trying to give himself time to consider his response. "It sounds . . . well, deeply unpleasant and I'm not at all surprised you're shaken up by it. But I'm just trying to understand the sequence of events from Neville's perspective — you say yourself that you didn't realize it was Neville until he tackled you?"

"And?" Hannah said angrily. She took a shaky breath, realizing that her voice had become shriller and more accusatory than she meant it to be. "No," she said, more evenly. "No, that's correct, I didn't."

"So it's very likely that Neville didn't recognize you either. He simply saw someone breaking into the college and — quite properly — asked them to stop, and then pursued them when they didn't."

"Dr. Myers, did you see those bruises?" Emily said, standing up in her turn. Her voice was calm, but dangerously so, and Hannah could tell she was only just keeping her temper in check. "And have you seen Hannah's face? He didn't just pursue her, he leaped on top of a defenseless female student and ground her face into the dirt until she couldn't speak, and more to the point this isn't the first time that he's targeted Hannah, in fact —"

"Well, that's just it," Dr. Myers broke in. "That's what I'm trying to understand here. Because obviously if you're saying, Ms. . . . ?"

"Emily Lippman," Emily said shortly.

"Ms. Lippman, that this is part of a pattern of inappropriate behavior, that's quite a serious allegation, but I can't see how this fits with that. From Hannah's own admission it was a very dark night and she didn't recognize Neville until he was actually tackling her. I'm not sure, under those circumstances, how Neville was supposed to have been targeting Hannah specifically. As far as I can see he just tackled a supposed intruder — maybe a little harder than necessary, but . . ."

"He broke into my room," Hannah said. Her heart was thumping. "He came into my room while I was out —"

"And did anything inappropriate happen

while he was there?"

"Fuck inappropriate, he shouldn't have been in a goddamn student's room in the first place!" Emily shouted.

Dr. Myers's face changed at that. He held up a hand.

"Ms. Lippman, I'm sorry, I'm going to have to request that you lower your voice and if you swear at me again, I will be asking you to leave this office. It's Hannah's account I would like to hear. Hannah, did anything happen? When he came to your room?"

"He said he had a parcel," Hannah said. Her throat was dry and she looked away from Dr. Myers now, out of the window. Her eyes were prickling again and she blinked hard, trying to squeeze back the tears that were threatening to fall. She would not, she would *not* cry in front of Dr. Myers. "He wouldn't give it to me when I asked."

"And did he have a parcel?"

Hannah said nothing. She shut her eyes and nodded.

"Well," Dr. Myers said, in a slightly brisker, *I'm sympathetic but this interview is coming to a close* tone. "I'm very sorry you've had what was clearly a very unpleasant experience, but can I suggest that in the meantime you refrain from climbing over college walls and enter in the appropriate way like everyone else. Now, I'll speak to Mr. Neville about this —"

"What?" Hannah broke in, horrified. "No! Please, no, don't tell him I told you all this."

"Well, I can't address these — these *allegations,* without hearing Mr. Neville's account of what happened," Dr. Myers said. His expression was exasperated now, the sympathy receding further, and he paced to the window, turning his back on them both, before returning to the desk to perch on the corner, one thigh hooked over the edge, smiling with what was clearly an effort at being conspicuously understanding.

"Look, Hannah, the bottom line is, I can take this further *if* you would like me to. But not without talking to Mr. Neville to hear his version of events. Which is it to be?"

Hannah looked at Emily. She had her arms folded across her chest, plainly only just containing her fury, but didn't speak, only raised her shoulders in a tight *this is your decision* kind of way.

Shit.

Dr. Myers consulted his watch. He did not make a pretense of hiding it.

"Can I think about it?" Hannah asked. Her voice sounded small and uncertain in her own ears. It did not sound like the voice of someone making a credible accusation.

"Certainly." Dr. Myers stood up again, all warmth and bonhomie now. "Take your time." He moved to the door, plainly signaling that the interview was over. "Now, if you'll forgive me, I have to prepare for my ten o'clock. I'll look forward to seeing you for our final tutorial next week, Hannah? Pleasure to make your acquaintance, Ms. Lippman."

But as they filed out into the corridor Hannah knew, with a depressing certainty, that one thing was sure. She would not be back to Dr. Myers's tutorial next week. In fact, she wasn't sure if she could ever face him again.

AFTER

On the train back to Edinburgh she sits and stares out the window, replaying Ryan's words over and over. *Is this a joke?*

A pregnancy test. A positive pregnancy test.

It's nothing she didn't know from her conversation with Geraint, but somehow, hearing it from Ryan's mouth . . .

Was it real?

She could have drawn it on with a . . . with a biro *for all I knew.*

Fuck. *Fuck.* She rubs her face. Part of her wants to scrub away the memory of the conversation and all the poisonous suspicions it's stirred up, but she knows she can't. Not just because she can't think of anything else, but because even if she were given the choice of magically erasing Ryan's words from her memory, she wouldn't do it. She can't let this go. Because whether or not it's true, whether or not even April, inveterate practical joker, would have been cruel enough to play this unforgivably harrowing hoax on Ryan, it is a missing piece of the puzzle which has finally turned up, out of the blue, throwing the whole existing pattern out of alignment.

A positive pregnancy test — real or not — is exactly what was missing from the case against Neville. It is a motive. And not just for Ryan. It's a motive for Will, and for anyone else who was sleeping with April.

Hannah remembers again the noises coming from behind that closed bedroom door, the morning after the premiere of April's play. And, more than ever, she wishes that she had stopped, pulled back that door, and put a face to whoever was in there.

Because it *wasn't* Ryan, that much she is sure of, or at least as sure as she can be without asking him outright. Not just because of the way he reacted on the first night of the play, pulling away from April as if reluctant to touch her, but because of what he said in their conversation just now. *She texted me the morning after that first night.* If April were in bed with Ryan, why would she text him with the news just an hour or so later? It wouldn't be plausible — to go from carefree noisy sex to a pregnancy test in a single morning. Ryan wouldn't have been taken in, he would have wondered why she hadn't raised her worries just an hour or so earlier.

But if it wasn't Ryan, then who?

Will is the next most obvious candidate. But Hannah isn't sure about him either. There was something wrong, that night at the play. Some kind of reserve or antagonism between him and April that didn't seem to mesh with the loud, performative sounds coming through the wall the following morning. And, though it makes her flush to think of it, Hannah knows what Will sounded like — *sounds* like — during sex, both now and then. She watches the countryside rippling hynotically past the window, thinking about her husband — thinking about the way he holds himself over her, bracing his weight on his forearms, staring into her eyes, silent, concentrated, attentive. He doesn't whimper and grunt and thrash about like someone in a blue movie.

Why. *Why* didn't she stay behind that morning? Why didn't she curl up and wait in the living room armchair to see who exactly came out of April's bedroom?

Why didn't she confide in April what had happened?

Because she was traumatized, and in denial. Because she was recovering from —

and now ten years on, she can say the words, without feeling they are too strong — an assault. And because she didn't *know*. She had no idea how important that question would become. She didn't know that many years later, so much would end up hanging on it. Her happiness. Her future. Her marriage.

It is at that moment that the train goes into a tunnel and momentarily loses power. The lights in the carriage go out — just for a second — and it's then that Hannah feels it. Something just below her belly. A flutter, like a bubble popping, or an elastic band snapping, or something small and slippery and feathered rippling inside her.

She goes utterly still. She doesn't even breathe.

And then the train comes out of the tunnel and the carriage is flooded with light again and she is left, sitting perfectly still, her hand over her stomach, iridescent with happiness. And for the first time since John Neville died, she isn't thinking about April, or the past, or the fact that she may have condemned an innocent man to die in prison.

She is thinking about her baby, and the new life inside her. And her happiness is so intense that it hurts.

BEFORE

"Well fuck you."

"Well fuck *you.*"

The voices came clear through the door of April's room, making Hannah wince, wondering if they knew she was sitting just on the other side of the wall, working on her final essay of the term.

She thought about calling out, *Hey, some of us are trying to study* as a jokey way of alerting them to her presence, but before she could do so the door to April's bedroom opened and Will walked out, slamming it bad-temperedly behind him.

"Oh." He had the grace to blush when he saw her sitting there. "Sorry, I didn't realize —"

"No, gosh, I mean — it's fine," Hannah said. She put down *The Faerie Queene* and stood awkwardly, twisting her fingers together. "You weren't disturbing me." The lie makes her cheeks color. "I mean, I could —

should — have moved. Are you —"

Are you okay was what she wanted to ask, but she wasn't sure if it sounded patronizing, or disloyal. She was supposed to be April's friend — April, who was probably listening from the other side of the doorway right now. She couldn't be seen to be taking Will's side.

But Will was frowning, and now he came across the room to stand closer, looking at her with an unsettling intensity.

"Hannah, what happened to your face?"

Hannah felt a sinking feeling inside her. Was this how it was going to be for the next few days? Having to tell the story over and over?

"Does it show?" She knew she was evading the question, but she still hadn't made up her mind what to do about Neville. Could she really face taking it further?

Will nodded.

"I mean, it doesn't look *terrible,* but it does look like you had an argument with a door and lost."

"That's pretty much it," Hannah said with a shaky laugh. It was another lie — or as near to one as made no odds — but she couldn't bear to tell Will the truth. His reaction would be worse than Emily's — she would probably get frog-marched down to see the Master, and have to face that exquisitely polite skepticism all over again.

"Are you coming to April's closing night on Saturday?" she asked at last, more as a way of changing the subject than because she really wanted to know.

Will's mouth twisted, and his eyes met hers.

"No, it's my mother's birthday weekend and she's not — well, never mind, that doesn't matter. The point is, I'm going home to Somerset. I'll be back Sunday. That's what we were — well. You heard."

For a minute they stood in silence, holding each other's gaze with an intensity that was almost painful. His eyes were a clear brown, like peat water. She could see a muscle move in the side of his jaw as he swallowed. He took a step towards her, one hand outstretched, and something shivered down her spine — a prickle of desire so strong it felt like water running over her skin.

For a moment she thought he was going to touch her. But then, involuntarily, she glanced at April's closed bedroom door — and somehow that one simple thing broke the spell between them. Will dropped his eyes and took a step back as if he had only just remembered why he was here.

"Well, see you around," he said. And then he was gone.

There was a long pause, and then April's bedroom door opened. She was scowling, and Hannah had the strong impression that she had been listening and waiting for Will to leave.

"Are you okay?" Hannah asked. "What happened?"

"My so-called boyfriend's bloody mother is what happened," April said. She was tapping her foot, radiating a furious wired energy. "How dare he. Saturday is the final night — he knows what that means to me, but no, Mummy's not well, Mummy's turning fifty, Mummy must come first." She put on a whining babyish voice for the last phrases that sounded so extremely un-Will that Hannah felt she ought to protest. One look at April's thunderous face made her reconsider.

"He did come to the opening night," she ventured, but April rounded on her.

"So? He's my bloody boyfriend! Or *was.* I'm seriously reconsidering, given he apparently doesn't give a wet fart about my feelings. The opening night is about the lowest possible bar — I mean, *everyone* came to the opening night, even Hugh! Even sodding *Emily*! This is the most important thing

I've ever done, Han. Is it too much to hope Will would come and support me instead of his hypochondriac mother?"

His mother's ill? was what Hannah was thinking, but she could see, instantly, that there was no point in saying that to April. It would only fan her indignation.

"Forget about him," she found herself saying instead. "I'll come on Saturday. And you know what — we'll do something afterwards. An after-party. A proper one. We'll have all the cast back here to the bar, we'll organize themed cocktails. The Medea. What should it be? Something bloody — cranberry juice with vodka and grenadine!"

"Isn't that a sex on the beach?" April said, but Hannah could see she was softening, that the idea of an after-party was reeling her in. Her taut fury was relaxing a little, and she came around the side of the armchair and flung herself back into it, the springs squeaking. "An after-party would be pretty cool, though. You'd really do that for me?"

"Of course," Hannah said. She gave April a friendly punch on the arm. "You're my best friend."

There was a moment's pause, and then April's face broke into a wide, beaming smile — that smile that felt like a megawatt spotlight had been turned on you.

"You, Hannah Jones, are the bloody best, that's what you are." She stood, brushing down her skirt. "Right. Coming down for supper?"

"I can't," Hannah said bitterly. "I've got to finish this essay. I spent all week revising for prelims, and now I'm just so bloody knackered, I can't think straight."

April paused, looking at her, and then she said, a little smile flickering at the corner of her lips so that her dimple came and went, "I could help with that, if you want."

"Help with my essay?" Hannah looked up at her, frowning. "Have you read Spenser?"

"No, I mean, help with the concentration." She turned and went back into her room, and Hannah heard her rummaging in the mess of her bedside table. Then she came out, two pills in the palm of her hand, holding them out towards Hannah.

Hannah stared down at them. They were little capsules, half-colored, half-clear, filled with what looked like dozens of tiny little balls inside.

"What are they — like, NoDoz or something?"

"NoDoz for grown-ups," April said. She gave that little half smile again, the dimple coming and going in one cheek. "Go on, take them. There's plenty more where those came from."

"I — I mean, look, thanks, but honestly I'm nearly there. I just need to nail this last paragraph and then I can turn it in."

"Okay," April said lightly. "Suit yourself." She put the pills carelessly in her pocket and then picked up her coat. "Oh, and vodka, cranberry, champagne, and crème de cassis."

"What?"

"For the Medea. Vodka, cranberry, champagne, and crème de cassis. In a champagne coupe. With a maraschino cherry on top."

"You're on," Hannah said, and April smiled.

AFTER

On the walk back from the train station, Hannah calls Will.

"The baby moved!"

He's in the street, she can hear the background noises, the sound of a fire engine passing.

"What did you say?" He raises his voice above the siren. "Who's moving? Sorry, it's really loud."

"Not who! The baby. I felt it, Will, I felt our baby move."

There is a split-second silence and then she hears his incredulous, joyous laugh.

"It moved? You really felt it?"

"Yes! Twice! I was on the way home and I felt it, Will, it was the strangest thing, like bubbles popping or something. It was *so* weird. Like, I've had things before where I wasn't sure, but this — it was so alien. I just knew. I *knew* it was him."

"Him?"

They haven't found out the sex. It was Hannah's decision more than Will's — a kind of superstition, although she can't put her finger on why she doesn't want to know.

"Or her." She blushes. "It just feels weird to keep saying *it* when he's becoming a real person."

"I really want to feel it," he says, and she can hear the delighted grin in his voice. "Do you think I'll be able to yet?"

"I don't know." She puts her hand over her belly now, as if to test, but of course it's not moving. "I'm not sure. Are you on your way home?"

"Yeah, I knocked off early," he says. His voice changes and he sounds suddenly weary and pissed off. "Work was a bitch. Do you think it's normal to hate your boss?"

Hannah bites her lip. Poor Will. He never wanted to be an accountant. He wanted to change the world — but he fell into this when he moved to Edinburgh, and now he can't afford to quit.

"I mean . . . I don't hate Cathy," she says, a little lamely.

"There aren't many Cathys around, though," Will says. "Not in accounting, anyway. And like my dad always used to say, if work was meant to be fun, people wouldn't pay you to do it."

Hannah laughs at that, but when they have talked about supper and said their good-byes, she puts her phone away with a sinking feeling. Will has always been the main wage earner — accountancy just pays better than bookshop work, that's all there is to it. But now it feels like the pressure of her impending maternity leave is getting to him. She just doesn't know what to do about it.

"Can I feel it? Is it moving now?" Will has taken the stairs two at a time, and now he pulls Hannah into a big bear hug, his leathers cool against her cheek. Hannah shakes her head.

"I don't think so. I can't feel him at the moment, but even if I could, I don't think you'd be able to tell anything from the outside. It's too soon. I think the books said it's normally about six months before the dad can feel any movement."

"He moved," Will says, as if trying out the words. He stands there, the huge foolish grin spreading across his face, like he doesn't know what to do with himself, and then he kisses her, as if he cannot contain himself, his hands on either side of her face, his lips cool against her warm ones. "Our baby moved. Oh my God, Hannah, this is real. It's really happening."

I know, she wants to tell him, but she doesn't, she just stands there, smiling back, feeling their shared happiness balloon between them, huge and fragile.

"What's that smell?" he says now, breaking their reverie.

"Oh shit, the onions!" Hannah had forgotten in the excitement of hearing Will's feet on the stairs. "I'm making Bolognese."

They go through to the kitchen, where Hannah peers into the pan, scraping the sticking onions off the bottom.

"I think they'll be okay. Just a bit caramelized, maybe."

"They'll be delicious," Will says reassuringly. "Hey, how was the appointment, by the way?"

God, the appointment. It feels like a million years ago, and for a moment Hannah has to struggle to remember what happened.

"Oh . . . fine . . . I mean, not totally fine. I was still a bit up. But it's no big deal. They don't think it's pre-eclampsia or anything serious, I just probably need to destress a bit. The midwife wants me back next week, just to check." She pauses. This is the moment she has to say something. About her visit to see Ryan. Because she *can't* keep this from Will. It concerns him too.

"I had a free day after the appointment," she says carefully, tipping the mince into the pan so that she doesn't have to look at him as she says the words. "So I . . . well, I called in to see Ryan."

"Sorry?" Will cups his ear. The meat is spitting and hissing, making it hard to hear above the noise of frying. "Who did you see? I didn't catch what you said."

"I went to see Ryan," she says, more loudly. She puts down the spoon and turns around. "Our Ryan. Ryan Coates."

"Wait a second." Will is frowning. She can't quite read the expression on his face — it looks like disbelief mixed with a kind of controlled annoyance he is trying not to show. A flush is climbing up from the collar of his biker jacket, staining his tanned cheeks. "You went all the way to York to see Ryan Coates? And you didn't tell me?"

"It wasn't premeditated," she says quickly, though that's only half-true. "I didn't even call ahead to warn Ryan. I got halfway there and realized he might be out." That part at least is right. "But I *had* to, Will, I couldn't get what Geraint said out of my head, and I wanted to hear it from Ryan, and find out whether Geraint was some kind of delusional stalker or if he really is a mate of Ryan's. If he was making all this up I

370

needed to know — maybe even get the police involved."

Will looks a little less blindsided, as if he can see the sense in this last part at least, but he's still shaking his head in bewilderment.

"And you couldn't call? I mean — York! It's not exactly down the road, is it?"

"It's not that far, it was actually really nice just relaxing on the train, and I felt — I don't know, Will. I felt like I owed it to him to make the trip. To see him face-to-face, rather than just ringing him up to pick his brains. I don't exactly feel proud of the amount of support we gave him after the stroke. Do you?"

Will has the grace to look slightly ashamed at this. He gives a very slight gesture with his head, halfway between a nod and a shake, not quite either, but she knows what he means. Yes, he can see her point. No, he isn't proud of his actions either. Ryan was a friend — one of their best friends. They owed him more.

"How was he?" he says at last. He turns away and begins to shrug off his jacket, more for something to do, Hannah has the impression. The back of his neck is still flushed and red.

"I mean . . . surprisingly good, actually,"

Hannah says. She looks at Will's back, at the shape of his shoulders beneath his shirt, trying to imagine him struck down overnight the way Ryan was. The idea gives her a sharp pain beneath her heart. "He's still in a wheelchair but his speech is amazing — just a very slight slur, and he misses the odd word, but nothing major. I didn't see his kids, but they sound adorable. And Bella's clearly a keeper."

"Yeah . . ." Will says slowly. "Yeah, he hit the jackpot with Bella all right. So what did he say? About that reporter bloke? And I take it you talked about" — he swallows — "about April?"

"Yeah," Hannah says. She sits down on a stool by the counter, rubbing her sore feet. "Yeah, we did. He really does know Geraint. Says he's a good bloke, and that he shares some of Geraint's concerns. And he said . . ." Oh God, can she really say this? But she has to. She can't keep the conversation from Will, not when so much of it concerns him. It wouldn't be fair. "He said he was sleeping with April. Did you know that?"

"I had a pretty good idea," Will says, very shortly. He moves across to the stove, taking over where she has left off. She can see that the muscles of his shoulders are tense beneath his shirt.

"And he . . . he confirmed that rumor I told you about last night. About the —"

She stops. This is so much harder than she thought it would be. How is telling the truth to the man she loves so difficult?

"About the pregnancy test. Will, she told Ryan she was pregnant. She said, at least, she *implied* it was his baby."

Very slowly the flush drains out of the back of Will's neck. For a long moment he just stands there, motionless, his shoulders sagging.

"Jesus."

"I know." There is a knot in her stomach. "He doesn't know if she was telling the truth about the pregnancy but . . . she did say it."

"Why?" Will says, and his voice is like a groan.

"Why would she lie to Ryan?"

"No, I mean, why *you*, Hannah?" He puts down the spoon and turns to face her and she sees that his face is pale and set. "Why are you doing this? Why now?"

"Why am I doing what?" she cries. "Trying to find out the truth? Because Neville is dead, Will. *Dead*. And I have to know if I condemned an innocent man to die in prison! Don't you understand that?"

"No, I understand," he says. He has himself under control now, the anguished note in his voice is gone, and when he speaks again, his words are almost unnaturally level, as if he's spelling something out to a small child. "In fact I think it's *you* who doesn't understand, Hannah. Don't you see what you're doing? If Neville didn't do this, *someone else did.* Yes, Neville's dead, and you can't change that. So why can't you leave this alone?"

She's staring at him now, as if a stranger is standing in the corner of her kitchen.

"Will, are you seriously saying that if April's murderer is still out there you don't care?"

"I'm saying that April's murderer — as tried and convicted *in law* — died in prison and that was the best thing for everyone! What good are you going to do by digging all this up — finding motives where there were none, and unearthing decade-old dirt? I mean, so what if April sent Ryan a pregnancy test — are you really going to the police with that? For what? So that a bloke in a wheelchair with two little girls and a wife who adores him can rot in prison instead of John Neville?"

"I'm not saying Ryan did it —" Hannah says hotly, but Will interrupts her.

"Then who? Hugh? Emily? *Me?*"

"Don't be stupid, you weren't even in college that night," Hannah snaps. "But there were hundreds of other students and staff members who *were,* and who weren't investigated because of *my* evidence against Neville. I can't let that go, even if you don't give a toss about what happened to April!"

She shuts her mouth at that and stands there, panting, horrified at her own words. She knows she went too far with that. Will is not stupid, anything but. And he certainly cares about April, just as she does.

She waits, expecting him to call her out on it — on the unfairness of what she just said, on her irresponsibility in pursuing this. She's waiting for him to call her selfish, or obsessive, or to point out that she had no problem in letting Neville rot for ten years so why *now,* what does his death change?

And she wouldn't be able to answer any of it. Because if he said any of those things, he would be right.

But he doesn't. He doesn't say anything at all. He just turns away from her, puts the pan back on the heat, and goes on stirring.

Before

"She's coming," Hannah said to Ryan, looking up from her mobile phone. As promised, Hugh, stationed in a room above the Porters' Lodge, had texted her when the group of actors came in through the main gate. "They'll be here in five. Someone turn off the music."

Where are you???? she texted to Emily as the lights dimmed.

There was a kerfuffle behind the bar and, in the nick of time, the sound of Beck's *Odelay* got muted and everyone went silent, or as close to silent as a room of fairly drunk students could pass for. "Turn the bloody lights back on!" someone grumbled from the far side, but the barman shook his head good-naturedly.

"Ah, give 'em a break, it's only five minutes, mate."

They crouched there in a greenish darkness, lit only by the illumination from the fridges behind the bar and the glow from the emergency exit signs. There was a momentary squeak of excitement as the main door creaked open, but it was swiftly quelled by Hugh's voice whispering, "It's only me, they're right behind me," as he slipped in beside Hannah, behind a table.

The silence was thick with tension, and when Hannah's phone beeped, there was a gust of nervy laughter. Getting it out of her pocket was awkward, given her crouched position, but she knew it was probably Emily, hopefully on her way but running late.

It was Emily. But she wasn't running late. *Sorry. Work.*

Hannah stared down at it, half-shocked, half-furious. *Sorry. Work.* was all Emily could manage? The exams were over. April was supposed to be her friend. But there was no time to compose a response. The door to the bar was swinging open once again, wide this time, letting in a gust of summer night air, and Hannah heard April's distinctively carrying tones.

". . . and I said to him, that's a bloody joke and a half, and I'm not having it. Hey, what's happened to the lights?"

"Surprise!" The shouts rang out across the room, and the lights came up. The little group of cast members were standing just inside the door in full costume, looking appropriately stunned. April was squealing and putting her hands to her face in a very good impression of someone who had no idea this was happening, even though, as Hannah knew full well, she had helped direct everything from the guest list down to the exact proportions of the signature Medea cocktail.

"Oh my God!" she was saying, hugging person after person, wiping away what Hannah was pretty sure were nonexistent tears. "You guys! You didn't! I can't believe you did all this."

"Congratulations, April," Hannah said. "You were amazing, all of you." She walked across and gave April a hug, feeling the unfamiliar roughness of April's wig against her cheek, and very much hoping that the terra-cotta makeup wasn't coming off on her top. "But especially you," she whispered.

"Bloody well done you, putting all this together," April whispered back. Then she pulled away and did a twirl, her toga fanning out as she did. "Like the getup?"

"Very much! I wasn't expecting you to be in full costume, though. What brought this on?"

"Well, it was already half nine when the curtain came down. I thought no point in wasting more time when we could be drinking. Luis and Clem brought a change of clothes in a bag. I don't know about Rollie or Jo."

"Do you want to go up and change?" Hannah asked. "We can hold off on the speeches until you get back."

"There are speeches?" April said in mock horror, and Hannah grinned.

"I'm joking."

"No, bring it on! I want *all* the glory. But no, don't worry, I'll go up in a sec. I want a *drink* before I do anything else. Where is my cocktail?"

"Come over here, I'll treat you and the other players to the first round."

"No," April said firmly. "I'm going to treat *you.* Oy, gang!" she hollered over the rising babble of voices and music, waving an arm at the little gaggle of actors. "Come over to the bar, I want to buy you all a drink!"

It was almost an hour later when April stood up from her seat at the head of the big table in the center of the bar, swaying slightly. She was holding her phone in one hand and a champagne coupe in the other, and for a moment Hannah thought she was going to get up on the table, but she didn't, she only raised her voice above the sound of the hub-bub.

"Attention, maddafakkas," she called, pointing round as the table of amused, slightly drunken faces turned towards her. "I would like to propose a toast. This year is almost over, and it's been a hell of a start to the rest of our lives — am I right?"

"Hear, hear!" called someone, and others raised their glasses.

"That old fart the Master would probably tell you that coming to Pelham is about work or learning or some academic bullshit like that. But I'm here to tell you that's a lie — it isn't about work. It's about . . . friend-ship."

Here she raised her glass to Hannah, and Hannah felt a flush rise up her cheeks.

"Because friends, *good* friends, are fuck-ing hard to find," April said. She was clearly very drunk, swaying slightly, even, but she was holding it together. "Friends who've got your back, friends who would never betray you. So when you find one, you have to hold on to that person. Am I right?"

"Yes!" someone called from the other side of the table.

"Okay then, so that's my toast. To friends. To *true* friends!" April said, and she held up her glass, spilling red juice down her arm.

380

"To true friends" came back the roar from around the table.

"To you, April," Hannah said, holding her own glass high, and April did a slightly theatrical bow, her wig slipping over one eye, and grinned back.

"And now, if you will forgive me, I am retiring to my boudoir to change," she announced.

"Isn't it rather late?" Hannah said doubtfully. "It's getting on for eleven. They'll be chucking us out soon."

"Not a bit of it," April said grandly. "And as for *you*" — she stabbed a finger at Hannah — "none of your slipping off to bed while my back is turned, young lady. I'm coming back down to party on until I'm thrown out, and I'm expecting you *all* to be here. That goes for the rest of you too," she said, swinging her gaze accusingly round the little crowd huddled around the table. "It's Saturday, and it's almost the end of term. You swots can afford to let your hair down for once."

With that, and a dramatic swirl of her toga, she disappeared out the door. Hugh raised one eyebrow at Hannah, who laughed, feeling a little disloyal.

"I know, I know. But you know what she's like. It is her big night. And she was *so* disappointed about Will not coming."

"I don't blame him for scarpering," Ryan muttered. "She's treated him like shit all this week."

"Yeah, I gotta say, she may be a great actress but she's a royal pain in the butt," one of the actors from the play said. Hannah wasn't sure of his name, but thought he might be the one April had referred to as Luis. "A week was about all I could take of her. Respect to the dude who's put up with that drama queen for the best part of a year."

"Maybe they've broken up?" Clem put in. Hannah had the impression that she was trying to steer the conversation away from April's failings. "I mean, that speech — all that stuff about friendship. It felt a bit *sisters before misters* to me. It's the kind of thing you say when you've just been dumped."

"Does that mean April's back on the market?" asked Rollie. "Should I join the queue? I mean she's a pain, yeah, but she's still hot."

"What d'you mean *back on*? The way I hear, she was never off it," his friend said, pulling a drolly lecherous expression. They both burst out into guffaws of laughter, but Hannah wasn't laughing. Nor, she saw, was Ryan. In fact, his face looked like thunder.

Across the room, the first bell rang out, and Hannah stood up.

"I'm going to the bar for last orders. Anyone want anything?"

"I'll have a pint," Ryan said rather shortly.

"Anyone else?"

"I'll have a Guinness, ta," Luis said. Clem shook her head.

"I'll have a bottle of something," said Rollie. He spoke like he was addressing a barmaid. "What have they got here? Sol? Estrella?"

"I'll find out," Hannah said curtly.

"I'll have a lager," Hugh said, "but let me come with you, you'll need a hand carrying."

Hannah nodded, waited as Hugh extricated himself from the narrow bench, then turned and threaded her way through the crowded room to the bar. It was three minutes to eleven, according to the clock over the counter. April had been gone for nearly twenty minutes, and the bar would be closing soon. It didn't take more than a couple of minutes to walk to New Quad and back. Add on a generous ten to remove her wig and makeup — had she changed her mind? Invited someone back to the room instead?

"What can I get you?" the barman shouted

across. Hannah raised her hand.

"Hi, yes, I'm next," said a big bloke in a rugby shirt, shoving into the gap beside her. The second bell went, and Hannah made up her mind.

"I think we've missed the boat," she said to Hugh.

"Agreed. What are you going to do? Turn in?"

Hannah nodded, and she and Hugh made their way back to the table where Ryan and the others were still sitting.

"I'm really sorry, I couldn't get near the bar."

"Should have sent a bloke!" said Luis's friend. "You need a bit of muscle to make last orders."

Hannah felt her smile thin.

"I think I might turn in, actually, I'm really knackered. Sorry to be a party pooper. It was really nice to meet you guys," she said to the little group of actors.

"Huh?" Ryan looked up from where he was deep in conversation with a guy Hannah vaguely recognized from Cloade. "Sorry, what did you say?"

"Well, that just makes you a fucking Marxist, then, doesn't it!" the other man crowed, ignoring the interjection.

"I'm heading back," Hannah said, raising

her voice. "Sorry I didn't get your pint, I couldn't get served."

"No worries," Ryan said. "Look, Rich, if you want to call basic redistributive fiscal policy Marxism —"

"I'll, um, come with you," Hugh said to Hannah, rather diffidently. "Walk you over and all that."

Hannah smiled at him gratefully. Since her encounter with Neville in the cloisters, she had found herself glancing over her shoulder more and more at night. Running footsteps behind her set her heart racing and her adrenaline spiking, and since Dr. Myers had announced his intention of speaking to Neville about the "allegations," she had lived in real fear that he might have done so, with or without her permission. The possibility that Neville might seek her out to ask her what the hell she was playing at, accusing him of assault, was all too real. The idea of having someone to walk her was immensely comforting.

"If you're sure then, yes, please, Hugh," she said. Hugh picked up his jacket from the bench and together they forged their way towards the exit.

They got there at the same time as a group of girls, and Hugh immediately stood back, opening the door for the first with a little bow.

"Yeah, all right, mate," the girl said as she passed through. "I do have arms, you know. Christ, this isn't the 1920s anymore."

They pushed past Hugh, laughing, and disappeared across the quad.

"Thank you, Hugh," Hannah said apologetically as Hugh held the door open for her. The air outside was pleasantly cool and clear after the fug of the bar.

"You're welcome," Hugh said a little sadly, and Hannah felt a sudden wave of protective anger wash over her. Hugh was so *nice.* He had been the only person to notice she didn't want to walk back alone, and the only person who had been any real support in organizing tonight, in spite of the fact that April certainly wasn't *his* best friend. In fact, she had always treated him with a kind of amused disdain, bossing him around, making him fetch and carry and generally do her bidding. And Hugh — Hugh just put up with it, with that good-natured smile. And so what if his courtesies were old-fashioned — it was his way of trying to relate to girls. Not everyone could have Will's easy charm, or pull off Ryan's goading banter. Holding a door open was hardly the crime of the century.

She laced her arm through his, squeezing it affectionately as they began to trace the familiar route back along the graveled path of Old Quad. It was hard to tell in the dim light from the moon and the lamps dotted around the quad, but she thought Hugh looked tired and drawn.

"How are you doing? Are you okay?"

"Oh, you know. All right," Hugh said. He gave a little deprecating shrug. "I have to be honest, I'm pretty stressed about the prelim results. I'm fairly sure I fluffed the paper I took after April's first night."

"You are?" Hannah was surprised. She thought of Will saying *Hugh was the brainiest chap in our year.* "But — look, I'm sure you're worrying over nothing. Everyone always thinks they flunked until they get the results. It'll be *fine.*"

"Will it?" Hugh's face twisted. He looked, Hannah thought with shock, as if he was trying to keep back tears. "You know they don't let you fail medicine. If you don't keep up, you're politely asked to leave. This year . . . well, it's been a bit of a shock, to be honest. Carne wasn't exactly tolerant of slackers, but it felt like the masters were on your side, helping you to keep up. Pelham . . . it just feels like you're struggling alone, afraid of letting everyone down. Do you know what I mean?"

Hannah said nothing. She wasn't sure what she *could* say. The truth was, she didn't feel that way, and she hadn't found the jump nearly as hard as she had feared. She had never felt particularly like anyone at Dodsworth was on her side. Sure, they wanted her to do well, but she was just one out of hundreds of students in her year. And she certainly didn't feel scared of letting anyone down. They were just delighted she had gotten this far.

Of all the group, Hannah thought as they rounded the corner, she probably knew Hugh the least. Brash, witty Ryan; dry, sarcastic Emily — she had known them for less than a year, and yet it felt like a lifetime. She had heard their worn anecdotes, she knew their catch-phrases, she had heard about their friends from home and their first times and their nightmare exes. With April she shared the easy intimacy only room-mates can, the person who sees you first thing in the morning, who hears you groaning over your essay, who knows when you've got period pains, who sees you swigging milk from the carton.

Even Will, who was emotionally reserved in a way that the others were not, she knew about his time at boarding school, his militarily minded father, his softhearted mum, his acrimonious breakup with April's friend Olivia. She knew which tutors he hated and what he planned to specialize in next year.

But Hugh — Hugh she had known none of what was going through his head, until he told her. Now she felt a rush of sympathy for him, dealing with his academic worries by himself. Sure, he had Will, but Will had dozens of friends — and April, of course. Hugh had just one, and for the first time she realized how lonely it must be for him when Will was away, or wrapped up with April.

"You should have said something," she said now. "I had no idea you were so worried. And why did you come to April's first night? You should have told her to piss off."

"Oh well." Hugh's face twisted. "I just . . . she was so worked up, you know? And April . . . she's not very easy to say no to."

Hannah said nothing. *That* she could understand.

"I can't afford to cock this up," Hugh said as they passed underneath the Cherwell Arch, which separated Old Quad from the Fellows' Garden. "My parents aren't well off, you know. Not like Will's. My father's just a GP, my mother's a stay-at-home mum. They really scrimped and saved to send me to private school, and Pelham — well, it's all they've ever wanted. My dad went here, and he was so proud when I got in after him. I'm an only child so I'm really — I'm all they've got. I can't let them down. I just *can't*."

"You won't," Hannah said, surprised by the desperation in his voice. She squeezed his arm, feeling his thin muscles tense beneath his jacket. "And you know what, even if you *have* failed, which I don't think you have, so what? They'll still love you, won't they?"

Hugh only shrugged again, and then, as if trying to change the subject, he cleared his throat and said, "I can feel your goose bumps. Do you want my jacket?"

It was folded over his arm and Hannah stopped, facing him, and touched his face for a moment.

"Hugh, why are you so *kind*?" she asked, and Hugh gave a little shrug.

"I don't know. Just that kind of ass, I suppose."

"You're a lovely ass," Hannah said, and smiled. "And thank you."

She took the jacket, slung it over her shoulders, and turned to face the Fellows' Garden, the grass silvered with dew. An idea occurred to her.

"Do you . . . fancy breaking the rules? It's the last week of term. They can hardly send us down."

For a moment Hugh didn't seem to understand what she was saying. Then his worried face broke into a smile.

"You're on."

They unlinked arms and ran across the pristine, untouched expanse, the dew-soaked grass soft beneath their feet. When they got to the other side, they were both breathless and Hannah looked back and saw the imprints of their footsteps, a dark guilty green against the pale jeweled tips of the untouched blades, and stifled a sudden desire to laugh.

As they passed through the wrought iron gate into New Quad, she was grinning, and she opened her mouth to say something — later she could never remember what — and then stopped. A figure was coming out of one of the staircases. A figure that looked very like . . . it couldn't be.

She stopped short.

Hugh continued for a couple of paces and then realized that she had ground to a halt, and turned to see what was wrong.

"Hannah?"

"Shh!" she hissed peremptorily, and then

pointed to the other side of the quad. They were standing in the shadow of a tall yew, and she was fairly sure that they were not visible to the man opposite as he plodded slowly down the far side, making his way towards the cloisters.

"Hugh," she whispered urgently, trying to keep her voice low but loud enough for him to hear. "Hugh, is that, is that — Neville?"

Hugh peered after the departing figure, then took off his glasses, wiped them on his shirt, and put them back on, squinting at the shape as it disappeared towards the cloister side of the quad.

"Um . . . could be? He's about the right build. Why?"

"Because I'm fairly sure he was coming out of staircase seven. Out of *my* staircase," she spelled out, as Hugh looked at her blankly.

"Do you think he was looking for you?" Hugh asked, after a long moment's pause. Hannah wrapped her arms around herself. Suddenly she was shivering, in spite of the balmy summer night.

"I don't know."

"I mean, he might have just been doing his rounds," Hugh said, rather lamely.

"What rounds?" Hannah said. "What could he be doing prowling around the staircases at this hour?"

"Someone could have called him," Hugh said, but there was no conviction in his voice. Hannah's hands were trembling now and she clamped them under her arms, trying to quell her rising unease. Suddenly she just wanted to get home — back to her room, where April would probably be slumped on the couch in full makeup, snoring her head off, and Hannah could lock the door and curl up under her duvet with the hottest hot water bottle she could manage.

John Neville had passed out of sight now, at the far side of the quad, beneath the cloisters, and without speaking, Hannah set off again, her pace quickening. Hugh, after a moment's hesitation, followed her at a jog.

They skirted the quad in silence until they got to the foot of staircase 7.

"Are you *sure* he came out of here?" Hugh asked at last, as Hannah stopped in the lighted shelter of the staircase, looking up at the darkness above.

She shrugged.

"I can't be certain. But I think so. You really didn't see him coming out?"

Hugh shook his head.

"I'm quite nearsighted. I didn't see anything until after you pointed him out. Look,

I'll wait until you're inside."

"You don't have to, he's gone —" Hannah began, but Hugh was shaking his head firmly.

"No, I want to. Just send me a text when you're safely in, and then I'll go, but I'd rather know you're okay."

He looked tense and worried, Hannah saw, the light from the staircase lamp casting ridged shadows onto a brow that looked too anxious and furrowed for a nineteen-year-old.

"Okay," she said at last.

The first step into the shadows was always the worst. It was like a leap of faith — stepping into the darkness of the stairwell, before the sensor at the turn of the stairs caught your movement and the lights above flickered on.

But as she climbed, Hannah found herself relaxing. There was something so familiar, so comforting about the smells and sounds of staircase 7. She could hear Henry Clayton's booming voice coming out from behind door 4; he and his neighbor Philip were obviously having one of their long-running political debates, which Hannah knew from experience would probably last until 3 a.m. On the landing below, someone was having a late-night shower, the smell of

Dove body wash filtering up the stairwell along with the sound of splashing water.

Dr. Myers's room was silent, but there was a glimmer of light showing under his door. He must be awake, and probably marking papers. For some reason the sight made Hannah feel better. So what if John Neville had been up here with another one of his lame excuses. April had probably told him to fuck off and sent him away with his tail between his legs.

Her own door, though, was open, just very slightly. As if April had come back in a hurry and hadn't closed it firmly enough. It wasn't the first time she had left it ajar — it was something people did quite often, if a roommate had forgotten a key, or just to signify that they were home and open for visitors. Not usually this late at night, though.

Hannah put her hand to the door and stepped inside.

And then —

AFTER

Hannah can't sleep.

She lies there with her hand over her bump, listening to Will's steady breathing beside her, wondering if he too is awake, but she can't bring herself to ask.

Instead she runs over and over in her head the conversations of the day. Her exchange with Ryan. The new spin he has put on the days running up to April's death. And her argument with Will before dinner.

The thing is, she understands his point of view — his need to move on, put the past behind them. It's what she has wanted herself . . . until now. But if her evidence put an innocent man in jail and led to a murderer walking free — well. She can't just accept that, no matter how much Will wants her to. She can't spend the rest of her life wondering if she got something so devastatingly wrong. She *has* to know.

Now she lies there, straining her mind

back to Pelham, trying, trying, trying to remember. If only she could recall the end of that night as clearly as the beginning. But it feels as if the shock did something to her brain — made it shut down, refuse to remember what was in front of her eyes.

Then it comes to her. Hugh.

Hugh was there too. He saw as much as she did — almost — and perhaps he remembers even more.

She was the first one in that room with April, falling to her knees beside April's body, her screams tearing at her throat, but Hugh was the second. It was Hugh who tried mouth-to-mouth, not Hannah, pumping desperately at April's dead heart long after it was clear that she was gone.

Perhaps Hugh remembers what she cannot.

It is with that thought in her mind that Hannah rolls over and finally closes her eyes.

She doesn't care what Will says. Tomorrow, she will go to see Hugh.

"I'm going to see Hugh." She tries to drop it into conversation the next morning while cutting a bagel, as if it's no big deal, but of course Will knows what she's saying. This isn't a social call she's suggesting. "Do you want to come?"

"No."

"Will —"

"Look, you asked." He puts down his cup. "And that's my answer. I don't want you digging into this. It's pointless and it's upsetting for everyone. I can't stop you — but I'm not going to be part of it."

"So what will I tell Hugh when he wants to know why you're not there?"

"Tell him what you like," Will says. He picks up his bag. "It's your business, not mine."

"Fine." She struggles to keep a note of defiance out of her voice. "But I'm still going."

"Fine."

And then he turns and leaves, the front door banging behind him with a sound that sets the baby jumping in her belly.

She hates it when they argue — and she knows that later she will text him an apology, try to make things right. But when she gets her phone out, it's Hugh's profile she clicks on WhatsApp.

Hey Hugh, she types. *Fancy a coffee?*

She stops, reading the message back. Does it sound natural? It's not that it's odd for her to be meeting up with Hugh exactly, but normally it's Will who does the running. For her to make the first contact, without involving Will . . . well, it's unusual. And her message needs to acknowledge that without making a big deal out of it.

I talked to Ryan yesterday, she adds, *and he was asking how you were. Made me realize it's ages since we caught up. Hx*

Hannah's finger is hovering over the send button when her phone beeps, the *leave for work* reminder, and with a sudden burst of decision, she presses send, shoves her phone in her pocket, and switches off the coffee machine.

She's halfway down the stairs to the front door, mentally running over her to-do list for the day, when her phone buzzes, and she takes it out of her pocket. It's a reply from Hugh.

Sure. What about a quick one after work? I should be free by 6.

Her face breaks into a smile of relief.

6 is great, she taps out. *Shall I call past your office?*

Typing . . . reads the header, and then Hugh's reply comes through.

Great. See you at 6. Hx

The day is blessedly busy — more like a Saturday than a Friday — to the point where at 3 p.m. Hannah realizes that she hasn't taken a lunch break and is feeling light-headed with hunger. She gulps down a sandwich from the deli next door, and then hurries back to help Robyn with the queue. At four thirty she's wondering if she is really going to be able to get away. It's still heaving and she can't leave Robyn to deal with so many customers, it's not fair. One person can't manage both the till and a stream of inquiries, let alone if you need the loo or something.

But at five thirty the shop empties out as if the customers are obeying a magic command, and Robyn looks up from where she's ringing up a lone woman's wrapping paper and sees Hannah surreptitiously checking the time on her phone.

"You off?"

"Well . . . it's five thirty, but . . . are you sure?" Hannah asks. "It's been so crazy today."

"I'll be fine, look, everyone's gone home. Fifteen pounds, ninety-seven, thank you so much," she adds to the woman at the desk, who nods and gets out her debit card.

"Well . . . if you're sure," Hannah says. "I'll be here a bit longer, so if there's a last-minute rush, I can still help."

In the staff room she puts on her coat. The face looking back at her from the mirror is pale and worried, and she wishes she had planned ahead, thought to bring makeup. She needs something to make her feel like she's ready to face Hugh.

The only thing in her bag is an ancient lipstick, but it's better than nothing. Now, standing there, applying it in the cracked mirror over the sink, she thinks of April, doing her makeup at the crowded chest of drawers in her bedroom.

Seriously, the only lipstick I would wear is Chantecaille, Han. Or Nars at a pinch. Number Seven just doesn't cut it — I mean, what's it made out of? Engine oil? And barely any pigment.

Hannah looks down at the lipstick she's holding, the worn stub of the deep rose Chantecaille that April gave her for Christmas so long ago, and for a moment the stabbing pain of the past feels very close and very real. She closes her eyes, takes a deep breath.

Then, she snaps the cap back on the lipstick, shoulders her bag, and shuts the door of the staff room behind her.

"Big night out?" Robyn says in surprise as she passes the till. Hannah smiles and shrugs.

"Not really, just a quick drink with an old friend. But he's very smart, I always feel dowdy whenever we meet up. He's a cosmetic surgeon."

"Probably earns a packet?" Robyn raises an eyebrow, and Hannah grins and nods. "Well, if he's single . . ."

"He's single," Hannah says, but she can't imagine Hugh and Robyn together. Truth to tell, she can't really imagine Hugh with anyone — he's just . . . Hugh.

"Well, have a good one," Robyn says as Hannah moves towards the door. "Don't do anything I wouldn't do."

"What does that rule out?"

"Not much," Robyn says, and grins, and Hannah laughs and opens the shop door, setting the bell jangling, and makes her way out into the chilly night air.

It's been raining while she was in the shop, and now the pavement is dark and slick, reflecting the jeweled shop lights back at her, and the glitter of the streetlamps, and the moving car headlights.

At the end of the road she crosses, then turns right, and then left, feeling her breath frost in the night air. At the junction she stops, waiting for the Walk signal. There is a limousine idling at the lights on the opposite side of the road, two cars back, blacked-out rear windows, and Hannah is just wondering whether it's a celebrity or a hen party when the rear window opens a crack and someone peers out, wiping condensation from the glass. And Hannah's heart almost stops.

The woman inside — the woman inside . . . it's *April.*

For a moment Hannah just stands, frozen, staring, and then she realizes that the lights have changed and the green man is blinking in her face, telling her it's her last chance to cross.

April. *April.* It can't be. But it is — surely it is?

"April!" she calls, but the woman has wound the window back up. Her heart racing, Hannah almost runs across the pedestrian crossing. She reaches the pavement and instead of turning right, to Hugh's practice, she turns left, hurrying up the line of cars to where the limousine is waiting. But before she reaches it, before she can knock on the glass, demand to speak to the occupant in the back seat, there is a revving of engines and the line begins to move.

Damn. *Damn.*

"April!" she calls helplessly as the limousine shifts into second gear and picks up speed, but it's too late. The car is gone. As it disappears around the corner, though, she knows. It wasn't April. It never is. For this is not the first time this has happened

— not the first time she's seen a cropped blond head through a crowd and hurried towards it, her heart pounding, to find a teenage boy or a forty-something woman looking at her in surprise.

It is never April, she reflects as she turns slowly on her heel and retraces her steps back to the junction, back in the direction of Hugh's practice. It never will be. But she will never stop looking.

It's exactly six as she rounds the corner and finds herself in front of Hugh's practice — a discreetly shiny black front door that could be just a residential address, were it not for the small brass sign that says THE PRACTICE, and underneath it the names of Hugh and his two partners in engraved Garamond font.

She pushes the bell and when a receptionist answers says, into the grille, "Hannah de Chastaigne, here to see Hugh Bland."

"I'm afraid he's finished for the day." The woman's voice crackles back through the intercom. "Did you have an appointment?"

"Oh, I'm not here for a consultation. This is personal. He's expecting me."

"Just one moment," the voice says, and then the line goes dead. Hannah stands there, waiting, for a surprisingly long time.

Just as she is wondering if she should try the front door, or ring again, there is the noise of feet on the stairs inside and the gleaming black door swings open.

It's Hugh, tall and immaculate in a long camel-hair trench coat, tweed waistcoat, and perfectly tailored herringbone suit. He is smiling, and when he sees Hannah he opens his arms.

"Hannah!"

They hug. Hannah inhales Hugh's expensive cologne and feels the umbrella he's holding digging into her back. Her bump presses between them in a slightly disconcerting way. She is still getting used to the baby asserting itself in these situations. She can't imagine how it's going to be when she's eight months. Then Hugh releases her, and they step back, surveying each other in the golden glow filtering through the fan light above the door.

"Well," Hugh says at last, "no need to ask how you are, I can see you're blooming."

Hannah blushes at that, although she can't put her finger on why exactly.

"Thank you. You look very well yourself."

"I can't complain," Hugh says. He hooks his umbrella over his arm and tosses his fringe out of his eyes. "Where shall we go? I know a nice little bar around the corner, the Jolie Beaujolais. It'll probably be a bit noisy at this time, but the owner knows me, so he'll be able to get you a seat."

"I can still stand for an hour, Hugh," she says, half-offended, half-touched by his solicitude. "I'm pregnant, not ill."

"I know you, Hannah Jones," Hugh says, waving a finger. "You'll have been standing all day in that bookshop; the least I can do is get you a chair now."

"Well, thank you," she says, smiling. "And honestly, the Jolie whatever it was sounds great, I really don't mind where we go."

Hugh links his arm with hers and they walk companionably down the street, Hugh matching his stride to hers. Glancing sideways at him, Hannah can't help but smile. He looks like such a caricature of the English civil servant, straight out of Central Casting for a John le Carré film with his camel-hair coat, suit, hooked umbrella, and horn-rimmed glasses. He's even wearing his old school tie with the Carne crest. Only a bowler hat could finish the ensemble. But Hugh has always been good at playing a part — in a different way from April, of course, but even at Oxford, he always had the air of someone who was playing at being the quintessential student he had seen in films like *Brideshead Revisited* or *Chariots of Fire.*

"How's work?" she asks, as they round the corner. It is beginning to drizzle, and Hugh opens up the umbrella and holds it above them both with his free hand.

"Good," he says, smiling down at her. "Profitable. No one's suing me this year."

Hannah laughs. Last year a disgruntled client sued Hugh's practice over her new nose not being sufficiently different from her old one, but she lost, after Hugh was able to produce a recording of their preop discussion where she requested that any changes be "very, very subtle . . . almost indistinguishable from my current nose." Apparently she got what she asked for.

"How was Ryan?" he asks in return, and Hannah bites her lip. She should have known this was coming. In some ways she had been hoping for it — it's the natural way to segue into the subject she really wants to discuss, but this feels too soon. She had imagined bringing up April when Hugh had a drink in his hand.

"He was . . . good," she says, after a pause. "Surprisingly good. I hadn't seen him for a while, I felt really bad when I realized how much time had passed. He said you'd kept in touch?"

"Just every now and again," Hugh says. His voice is kind; Hannah knows he's trying not to add to her guilt. "I think perhaps it was easier for him to talk to me, you know, being a medical man and all that."

Hannah nods, grateful that he's letting her off the hook, and then Hugh turns abruptly down a little alleyway between two tall stone buildings, where a lighted sign flickers above a stairwell. LE JOLIE BEAUJOLAIS, Hannah reads as they descend a short flight of stairs and find themselves in an almost aggressively French-themed bar, complete with Toulouse-Lautrec drawings on the wall, Gauloises drinks coasters, and row upon row of shining wineglasses and bottles. LE BEAUJOLAIS NOUVEAU EST ARRIVÉ! says a sign above the bar.

It's hot and very, very full, but after a shouted conversation with the man behind the bar, true to Hugh's promise, a tiny table is found for them in the corner. Hannah is ushered onto a velvet-covered banquette, and Hugh hitches his pressed suit trousers and sits opposite on a stool. The barman wipes their table with a theatrical flourish, puts a fresh candle in the wax-spattered bottle between them, and then hands them two menus.

"Thank you so much!" Hannah says to

the barman above the noise of the crowd. He gives a little Gallic bow.

"De rien, mademoiselle! For Monsieur Hugh, nothing is too much trouble. What can I get you?"

"Just something soft, thanks."

"Perrier? Evian? Orangina? Coca? Jus d'orange?"

"Um . . . Orangina would be great, thanks," Hannah says.

"Monsieur?" The barman turns to Hugh.

"Well, I have to have a jolie Beaujolais really, don't I?"

"A glass of the nouveau? It's very good this year."

"That would be great, thanks. And maybe something to nibble — an assiette de fromage, perhaps? And some bread?"

The barman gives a grin and another little bow, and then turns and weaves his way back through the crowd to the bar.

"It wasn't just auld lang syne that made me go and see Ryan, though," Hannah says, as if there had been no interruption to their conversation. She feels as if she's taking her courage in her hands. Hugh raises an eyebrow.

"No?"

"No, I had a visit. From an old friend of his."

She begins to explain, about Geraint, about the meeting in the coffee shop, about the pregnancy test and Will's reaction . . . everything. By the time she is winding up the account, Hugh's expression is mild as ever, but his right eyebrow is nearly up to his hairline.

"And so, well, I thought . . . I would come and see you," Hannah finishes. "You're the only other person who really knows what happened that night. Who really remembers."

"I see," Hugh says. He takes off his glasses and polishes them on his pocket square as if buying himself time. Without them his face looks different, less finished, somehow, his eyes smaller and less defined. Before he has finished polishing, the barman comes up with a tray bearing Hugh's wine, Hannah's Orangina, and a plate of mixed cheeses and charcuterie. At the sight of it Hannah realizes suddenly how very hungry she is, but also that she can't eat 90 percent of what's on there.

When the glasses and plates are laid out, the barman retreats and leaves Hannah and Hugh in silence. Hannah waits. Is Hugh going to speak? Should she? She's not sure what exactly she wants to ask.

"Will — Will isn't completely on board,"

she adds at last, more as a way of breaking the painfully stretching silence than because she thinks she really needs to tell Hugh this. "That's why he isn't here. He's not — I don't think he understands why I'm pursuing this. As far as he's concerned Neville's dead and that's it. But for me . . . it was *my* evidence, Hugh. And if I got it wrong, and Neville died in prison because of me . . ."

"I see," Hugh says again. He settles his glasses back on his nose and sighs. He looks very tired, as if Hannah's story has put a huge weight on his shoulders that wasn't there at the start of the evening.

"Hugh, listen," Hannah says impulsively. "Look, if you'd rather forget all this, just say, I can go. We don't need to talk about this. If you feel the same as Will, I wouldn't blame you, but —"

"No, I understand," Hugh says. He rubs his face with his hand, his palm rasping against his stubbled cheek. "I wish — I mean, I wish this Geraint chap hadn't opened this can of worms, I'm not going to pretend otherwise. But I understand your feelings. What do you want to know?"

"Just what you remember from that night, something, *anything* that I might have missed or forgotten. I don't care if it's something to reassure me or something to make me doubt the verdict even more, I just feel like I have to know."

"I don't know if I can tell you very much more than what you already know," Hugh says. He takes a long gulp of his wine as if gearing himself up for something painful. "But I'll try. I mean, the first part of the evening you know — I was up in that room above the Lodge, acting as lookout, and she came in with those friends of hers from the play. They were all dressed up, do you remember? All in their wigs and makeup."

"Yes, but the two girls changed halfway through the evening, didn't they," Hannah remembers. "Clem and whatever the other one was called. Sinead, or something like that? Only April and the boys stayed in costume."

"We were all in the bar all evening," Hugh continues. "None of us left, I'd swear to that." Hannah nods. That chimes with her recollection too. "And then it was almost last orders and April decided to go up and change."

"It was so late," Hannah remembers. "It was utterly stupid, the bar was never going to let her back in. I suppose she thought we'd all carry on drinking in our room or something."

"But she didn't return," Hugh says. "So

you said you were going up to find her, and I said I'd come too. We walked across the quad, and just as we were about to get to your stairs, you saw Neville coming out."

"You didn't see him?"

"I saw someone who looked a lot like Neville, but I didn't see him coming out of *your* staircase," Hugh says. "But you did — and you saw it before you knew there was anything going on. And besides, he admitted being up there, didn't he? Don't start second-guessing yourself now."

"I'm not," Hannah says. "I mean — I am — but not like that. I don't want you to think I'm looking for holes in my own memories, not exactly, I just want . . . I just want to be sure — do you know what I mean? I want to see it from another perspective, see something that I might have missed. Does that make sense?"

Hugh nods.

"Well, then, what happened next?" Hannah asks.

"Well . . ." Hugh says slowly. He takes another sip of his wine. She has the impression he is steadying himself, steeling himself to answer. "After that . . . you went up the stairs. And I waited. I was just about to walk away when I heard you cry out. I knew it couldn't be Neville, we'd seen him leave, or at least you had, but you sounded . . . you sounded really scared. I *knew* something was wrong, I can't explain it. I ran up the stairs, the door was open, and you were inside, on your knees, leaning over —" He swallows. His face in the candlelight looks suddenly much older. "Over April's body."

"You knew she was dead?" Hannah whispers. Her throat feels dry, but she doesn't raise the Orangina to her lips. She doesn't think she would be able to swallow it. Hugh shakes his head.

"Not at first. I mean — I wasn't sure. She looked an odd color, but that could have just been the remains of the makeup. She was —" He chokes suddenly. "She was still wearing her wig." He puts a hand to his face, over his eyes, as if he can't bear to look all of a sudden. "I always wondered —" and again, he swallows, and then stops.

"What?" Hannah says. She is puzzled. She has heard Hugh's story before, but not this detail. What has he wondered?

"I always wondered," Hugh says softly, "if he thought she was you."

Hannah feels suddenly cold.

"What do you mean?"

"April had short blond hair. Back then you had long dark hair. And the lights were very dim, it was just that one lamp in the corner burning."

Hannah nods. She knows the lamp Hugh means, it was the one with the rose-colored shade, the one they always left on when they left the set, so that they didn't have to come back to a dark room.

"I always wondered if Neville walked in, saw a girl with dark hair and thought . . . and thought . . ."

"You mean, he meant to kill *me*?" Hannah says. Her lips are dry and her hands feel suddenly cold, as if all the blood has drained out of them.

"You had just reported him to the college authorities," Hugh says miserably. "Hadn't you? I've always wondered . . ."

"Oh my God," Hannah says. She picks up her glass and takes a sip of her drink, trying to cover her shaking hands. "You mean . . . you mean she might have died because of what I did?"

"No," Hugh says forcefully. He leans across the table, takes Hannah's free hand in his. His hands are large, capable, and bony, and very strong. They are surgeon's hands. "That's not what I'm saying. Whoever killed April, it was *their* fault, Hannah, not yours. Don't let yourself get sucked into that narrative. But I've always wondered, if you had gone up first . . ."

"Oh my God," Hannah says again. She feels sick.

"That's what I meant. Don't let yourself get caught up in what-ifs. That way madness lies."

"I just want to know," Hannah says. She swallows against the dryness in her throat. "I just want to know what happened. I don't remember what happened after that. I remember you doing mouth-to-mouth —"

She puts her hand to her head, as if she can press the memories back into place, remembering the sound of Hugh's feet on the stairs, Hugh dropping to his knees beside April.

Hugh lets his hand drop and he brushes his fringe away from his forehead. His face is profoundly unhappy.

"I went over to her. You were kneeling over the — her body. You kept saying *Oh April, oh my God, April,* over and over again. I tried her pulse and I think in my heart I knew she was gone, but I couldn't quite bear to admit it. I began pumping her heart, just kind of hoping against hope, and you were standing there, looking so awful, your face was just white and drained and you were kind of swaying, and I thought you were going to faint — and I said, Hannah, for God's sake go and find someone, go back to the bar and get help. It was partly for April but partly because I thought I had to get you out of there before you passed out. I wanted someone to look after you as much as anything. And you gave this kind of gasping sob and you stumbled out into the hallway and I heard you kind of staggering down the stairs gasping *Oh God, oh someone help, please help.* I carried on giving April mouth-to-mouth and heart compressions for . . . oh God, I don't know how long." He stops and takes a long, shuddering swig of his wine. "I carried on until the police came. It felt like forever. But they did come. They did come in the end. They said I'd done all I could. But it wasn't enough. I don't think — I don't know if I'll ever forgive myself for that. It wasn't enough."

"Thank you, Hugh," Hannah says. Her voice is husky and her eyes are prickling. This is the first time they have ever discussed this, the first time she has ever heard Hugh's version of events. Before the trial they were told strictly not to discuss the case, for fear of prejudicing each other's evidence. And afterwards — afterwards the last thing she wanted was to wallow in the pain and horror of that night. Now she is ashamed to realize that what Hugh went through was just as bad, maybe even worse.

He has lived all these years with the memory of April's dead lips on his, of his failure to save her. "Hugh, it wasn't your fault, you know that, right? April was already dead — she was strangled. You couldn't have saved her."

Hugh says nothing. He only shakes his head. His eyes, behind the horn-rimmed glasses, are squeezed tight shut, as though holding back tears. When he speaks it's with a catch in his throat and a little grating laugh.

"I'm sorry, I — I wasn't expecting this. I would have bought a larger glass of wine if I'd known."

"I'm sorry too," Hannah says, and she means it. "I should have warned you. It wasn't fair to spring this on you."

"It's all right," Hugh says. He tries for the suave, urbane smile he probably uses on his patients, though it's not completely convincing, not to someone who knows him as well as Hannah does. "God knows, I should be over all this by now. These days we'd probably all be offered free therapy. Back then it was, *Oh well, chin up, and we'll go easy on you in the exams,* you know?"

Hannah nods, though the truth is that she doesn't know. She never went back to Pelham. Hugh, Will, Emily, and Ryan, they all returned — shaken and traumatized, but they returned — and eventually they all graduated. But not Hannah.

Instead she moved back to her mother's house. She would return to Pelham eventually, she told herself. Take a year out, perhaps. But then a year turned into two. Going back to Pelham became moving on to the University of Manchester. Or Durham. Anywhere else.

And then gradually that goal disappeared too, fading into the distance, along with the memories of her friends, her essays, and the girl she used to be. Only Will remained. Will, whose letters kept arriving, regular as clockwork, in his distinctive spiky handwriting, telling her about May balls and end-of-term parties, about rowing on the river and fluffing exams, about essays and tutors and rags and, eventually, about graduation ceremonies and MAs and postgraduate training.

She had thought at the time that nothing could survive April's death, that she had been burned out by it, left a shell of the girl who had gone up to Pelham so hopefully that bright October day. And for a while that had been true — or almost true. Because one thing had survived. Her love for Will. It was the only thing that had endured.

"So . . . do you think it was Neville, then?" she forces herself to ask. She picks up her glass and takes a sip.

Hugh shrugs.

"I don't know. I thought so at the time but now you're making me wonder. I mean it's not like —"

He stops.

"It's not like?" Hannah prompts. Hugh, unexpectedly, flushes, a splotch of bright color appearing high on his cheekbones. He tosses his hair out of his eyes with that nervous tic she remembers so well from the very first time they met. He looks embarrassed.

"What were you going to say?" Hannah says, frowning.

"Oh, I feel like a shit," Hugh says. He looks really pained now, but Hannah shakes her head.

"Go on, just say it. We're in a safe 'no judgment' space here." She puts air quotes around "no judgment" and Hugh laughs shakily, as she had intended, breaking the tension a little.

"Oh . . . if you must. Well, look, all I was going to say was . . . it's not like she didn't have her enemies."

"Enemies?" Whatever Hannah had expected Hugh to say, it wasn't this, and she looks up at him, surprised. "What do you mean, enemies?"

"Well, I mean. You know. Her constant pranking. It . . . it pissed people off, you know?"

"They were just jokes —" Hannah says, but Hugh raises an eyebrow, cutting her off.

"Jokes to her, maybe, but not always very funny to the person being pranked. Remember how annoyed Ryan was when she made him flush his weed? And the call to the Master? I don't think he found that very amusing. I got off pretty lightly in comparison. That stupid mobile phone thing, and a blow-up sex doll in my bed one night — God, I had a job smuggling that out without everyone seeing. It's amazing we all let her get away with it."

There's an edge to his voice that surprises Hannah. When they were at university he was always so meek and pliable, passing everything off as a joke with a good-natured laugh. She never thought of Hugh as really minding anything. But now she remembers — a thousand tiny moments, a thousand small cuts, the way April bossed him around, took the piss out of him. She remembers even that very first night, Hugh trying to excuse himself gracefully from playing poker, and April's flat *Shut up,*

Hugh. Nobody cares. She remembers Hugh's expression as he sat back down, a kind of tense, mutinous fury.

"Hugh . . ." she says slowly. "Hugh, did you actually . . . *like* April?"

There is a long silence. Then Hugh sighs, as if he is releasing something long pent up.

"Truthfully, I didn't. I would never say that to anyone else but you. But I didn't think she was a particularly nice person, and she certainly wasn't good for Will — she made him absolutely miserable that last term. I do get why everyone else fell for her. She was so funny, and she could be incredibly sweet when she wanted to. But some of her antics were pretty cruel. Think about what she did to Emily."

"What she did to Emily?" Hannah echoes, puzzled. "I don't think she did anything to Emily, did she?"

"Didn't you know?" Hugh frowns, and then his expression changes. "Ah, no, it would have been right before . . . well. Right before."

He doesn't need to spell it out. Hannah knows what he means.

"What did she do?" she asks.

"It was another letter one," Hugh says, a little reluctantly. "Similar to the Nokia one she pulled on me. Only this time she pretended . . ." He takes a breath. "She pretended that Emily's A-level results had been called into question. She wrote this letter — it was very convincing, Emily showed it to me. It was on headed paper and everything, I have no idea how April made it look so good. These days it would be a cinch, of course, with scanner apps on everyone's phone, but back then, she must have worked quite hard to make it look official. It said it was from the exam board and that Emily's answers had been found to correspond very closely with another girl's at her school. It basically accused Emily of either cheating or feeding another student the answers."

"Wow." Hannah is taken aback. That really *is* cruel. She can see what Hugh means. It's not even funny. Most of April's jokes had at least a slight twist of humor to them, even if it didn't seem that way to the recipient. But this . . . this just seems horrible. "How did Emily react?"

"Well, I only found out about it afterwards, so I'm not sure. But . . . I mean, you know Emily."

Hannah nods slowly. She does indeed know Emily. And all of a sudden it comes to her, a memory as sharp and clear as a voice hissing in her ear — Emily, walking past the chapel on a frosty November evening, her voice ringing out as cold as the night air: *If she tries any of that shit with me, I will* end *her.*

"How did Emily find out?" Hannah says. "That it was a hoax, I mean?"

"The letter asked her to call a number at the exam board and talk to one of their examiners. So Emily rang up and from what she said, she was completely taken in at first, but then something tipped her off — I think she heard something on April's end that made her twig that the caller was at the college, a bell chiming or something. And she realized. She said April didn't even apologize, just laughed idiotically and said it was Emily's fault for being so stuck up and pleased with her own intellect. And then she hung up."

"Oh, Jesus." Hannah puts her hand to her face. Suddenly so many things make sense. *Sorry. Work.* Of course Emily didn't come to April's after-party. She must have been sitting in her room fuming and trying to figure out what to do. What *would* she have done?

I will end *her.*

Go to the college authorities? Complain to a tutor?

Whatever it was, she didn't have time to act. Unless . . .

The thought comes unbidden, rushing in like chill sea water racing up a beach to soak you unexpectedly.

Unless she did.

But Hannah pushes that away. It's ridiculous. Emily might have had a grudge against April, but she wouldn't *kill* her, would she?

"Why would April do that?" she says, now looking up at Hugh, almost pleading with him for answers. "Why would she do something so horrible to Emily?"

"Well . . ." Hugh says slowly. "I might be wrong but I've always wondered . . . I think perhaps April had given Ryan an ultimatum, and it didn't go the way she thought it would."

"You mean . . ."

"I don't know," Hugh says, very gently. He puts out his hand and takes Hannah's. "But . . . the way you and Will felt about each other, towards the end it was . . . well, it wasn't obvious exactly, but I don't think you had to be Freud to see it. And April was nothing if not good at reading people."

Hannah goes hot, and then cold.

"You mean you knew? April knew?"

"I don't think she *knew* anything. But I think there was a hell of a lot of tension that last week. And I think maybe April had already decided to cut her losses with Will

425

and move on. But Ryan . . ."

"But Ryan wouldn't play ball," Hannah says slowly. "Because although he'd been messing around with April, he loved Emily."

"It's the only reason I can think of," Hugh says with a shrug. "Why she would have been so frankly horrible to Emily. I mean, there wasn't a lot of love lost between them, but there wasn't much actual animosity. But that last prank — that smacked of real hate."

Hannah says nothing. She is sitting there, chewing on her lip, trying to count back. As far as she can recall, Emily was perfectly civil to April in the week running up to the party. Which means she probably didn't get the letter until Saturday morning. If it was in her pigeonhole on the morning of the party, then April must have posted it the day before, and she must have taken a few days before that to write it and mock up the headed paper. Which means that on Monday, when they were all at the theater, supporting April for her first night, raising glasses and smiling and telling each other how awesome April was, April herself was probably already planning this.

Hannah is remembering. Remembering the tension between Ryan and April, the polite smiles, the teeth-gritted argument with Will. Had April known she was going to do this to Emily all along, even while she was smiling and sharing drinks and inviting her over for coffee? She must have done. There's no other explanation.

For a moment Hannah feels quite sick.

Then something occurs to her. If April was angry at Emily, who had after all done nothing apart from being Ryan's girlfriend, how furious must April have been with Ryan for rejecting her? Furious enough to fake a pregnancy test?

In which case, maybe April *wasn't* pregnant when she died?

But then if she *was* pregnant, and she had just been rejected by the father of her unborn baby, then perhaps that would explain her vicious overreaction to Emily.

Oh God. She has to stop going back and forth like this, guessing and then second-guessing. She has to find someone who actually *knows* what April was thinking that week. She's just not sure who that could be.

For the next hour they talk about other topics, as if by unspoken agreement. The baby. How Will is doing at work. Hugh tells her some funny anecdotes about his patients, and she counters with some of her more eccentric customers. It's only later, when they're leaving, paying their bill, and Hugh is helping her into her coat, that something else occurs to her about Hugh's revelation. Something that makes her stomach twist with a strange mix of anxiety and guilt, and makes her stop, coat half-on, half-off, so that Hugh has to gently cough and remind her where she is.

If April was that angry with Emily — poor Emily, who had done nothing wrong at all — how angry must she have been with the girl Will was, maybe, falling for? How angry was she with Hannah?

AFTER

The next few days and weeks had the cadence of a waking nightmare, and afterwards Hannah could only remember that time in jolting, disordered snatches.

First the running feet, the porters and the college staff pushing her aside to climb to the stairs, Hugh standing in the hallway, saying in a cracked and desperate voice, "No one should touch her until the police get here, please, no one should touch anything in the room."

Then the sound of sirens, uniformed police taping off the landing, the blue lights of the massed squad cars reflecting back from the building opposite on Pelham Street and flickering off the still, black waters of the river.

Hannah was interviewed by the police until the small hours, when she was given a parcel of her own belongings and allowed to go to bed in a strange room in Old Quad.

The next day she was interviewed again, and then moved to a different room in Cloisters with better sound insulation, because her sobs the night before had kept her neighbors awake. Her parents arrived, and she cried in her mother's arms, and moved rooms again, this time to sleep on a pull-out sofa in her mother's hotel room. The college closed for the summer break, but Hannah was not allowed to leave Oxford, and neither was Hugh.

Emily, Ryan, and Will were interviewed but then told they were free to return home. None of them were suspects. Ryan had spent the whole night in the bar, with multiple witnesses including Hannah and Hugh. Will had been away from the college, at home in Somerset until Sunday morning. Emily had been in the college library all evening, and examination of her swipe card showed she hadn't left until after 11 p.m., when she, along with the few other students still studying, had come out to see what was going on, why the police were hurrying across the forbidden lawns to New Quad.

Hannah and Hugh were different. They weren't suspects — but they were witnesses. They had discovered April's body, and Hannah had reported the prime suspect to the college authorities just days before April's death.

Lying awake at night beside her sleeping mother, trying to reconstruct what had happened, what she could have done differently, what she might have missed, Hannah came to think of her existence as divided into two sharp halves — before and after.

Before, everything was fine. After, everything was broken.

Hannah saw April's parents only once. She was leaving the police station after giving yet another statement, and a tall blond woman with enormous sunglasses accompanied by a man in a gray suit straining across his gut walked past her, their faces stony and grim. She was never quite sure what made her do it, perhaps something about the shape of the woman's mouth and chin, but she pulled out her phone and googled "April Clarke-Cliveden parents" and there they were. April's mother, Jade Rider-Cliveden and her father, Arnold Clarke, former city banker turned private equity investor.

There were older shots, pictures of Mr. Clarke climbing into taxis, waving with a broad self-satisfied smile, or shaking hands after a successful business deal; photos of

Mrs. Clarke-Cliveden entering a spa, or leaving Harrods, shooting daggers at the photographer. But the one that held Hannah's attention was the most recent — one plainly taken after news of April's death had been broken. Their faces stared out at her from the search page, snapped by some opportunistic paparazzo as they hurried into a waiting car. They looked like people in a waking nightmare — and she knew how they felt, for she was trapped in the same bad dream.

Part of her wanted to hurry after them, tell them how sorry she was, ask if they were okay — though that was clearly stupid, for how could they be okay? Their child had died, the worst thing that could happen to any parent.

But she could not do it. She stood, paralyzed, watching them until the doors of the police station closed after them and they disappeared.

Now, more than a decade later, Hannah wonders.

She wonders what happened to Mr. and Mrs. Clarke-Cliveden. She wonders how April's mother, that fragile fuckup April talked about so dismissively, had coped with the death of her child. She wonders if April's father was as strong and as self-centered as April had believed. Had he picked himself up and carried on, making money, running his businesses? Or had his world fallen apart?

As Hugh walks her to the bus stop, waves her goodbye, and she turns her head to watch him, standing there under the streetlight with the rain pattering around him, she wonders.

AFTER

Hannah is still wondering when she wakes the next day. She lies there under the warm covers next to Will, thinking about April, about her parents, and about the conversation with Hugh last night.

It is Saturday — Will's day off, but not hers — and she is getting quietly out of bed, trying not to wake him, when he rolls over.

"Morning."

She stops, turns back, hugging her dressing gown around herself. It is cold outside the covers, the first snap of winter in the air.

"Morning." She feels a little uncertain, their recent row still hanging in the air. "Sorry, I was trying to be quiet."

"It's okay." He sits up, rubbing the sleep out of his eyes. "What time did you get home last night?"

"Not that late. About ten. But you were asleep — I didn't want to wake you."

There's a minute's silence and then he says, "I'm sorry I was such a dick," at the same time that she says, "Do you — do you want to know, what Hugh and I talked about?"

They both laugh, a little shakily, and Will gives a little rueful smile.

"Honestly? Not really."

She nods. He doesn't want to dig up painful memories, and she understands that, it's how she's felt for more than ten years. But the fact is that Neville's death has jolted her into feeling differently — even if she can't fully explain why.

"Look, I have to get up," she says now, glancing at her phone. "But let's make a plan for tomorrow. Something fun. A walk maybe — Arthur's Seat?"

"Sure," Will says. He smiles, and she understands that he's trying to make it up, repair the hurt they caused each other. "I love you."

"I love you too."

On the bus to work she checks her emails. There's one confirming delivery of a maternity bra and some leggings she bought online. Another from her and Will's favorite restaurant offering them a coupon valid throughout November.

Then there's an email from her mum, subject line *Weekend of the 12/13?*

Han, lovely to talk to you the other day. Quick question — how would the weekend of the 12–13th be for a flying visit? I've got those clothes I was talking to you about and you might as well have them before you have to buy new. Reduce, reuse, recycle! Mum x

Hannah suppresses a smile and is about to tap back a quick response when a new email alert flashes up on her phone, and the sender ID makes her stomach flip. It's from Geraint Williams, and the subject line says *Update.*

Ignoring her mother's message, she opens up Geraint's, feeling the baby inside her give a little shuddering jolt as she does. Her nerves are affecting them both.

Dear Hannah, hope you are well and that our conversation the other day didn't stir up too many difficult memories.

I'm sorry to email again, but you did ask me to let you know if I found out anything I felt you should know and — well, I've found something. Someone, in fact — November Rain. I think you should meet

436

her as she has some information about the autopsy results that could be important. I'm nervous about putting too much in writing — and I think it would be better for you to hear it from the horse's mouth anyway as you may have questions.

I know this is short notice, but I wondered if you could make today? The reason is, November is London-based, but happens to be in Edinburgh at the moment for work, however she is flying back this evening. So this is probably your last chance to meet face-to-face for a few weeks.

Please let me know. I am also in Edinburgh all day today and could make any time. November is working, but tells me she could make space for a meeting anytime before 5 p.m., when she leaves for her flight.

Please let me know.

Geraint

Fuck. Hannah closes down the phone and stares off into the middle distance, chewing her nail furiously. *Fuck.* Geraint probably doesn't know what he's asking — he would assume she has Saturdays off like everyone else. And yet — a chance to find out what happened at the inquest, a chance to discover whether April really was pregnant, maybe even who the father was — who is this November? Is she a pathologist? Hannah certainly can't google. The name sounds completely improbable — more like a drag queen than a forensic expert, although she supposes even pathologists can have Axl Rose fans for parents. Even so, *Dr. Rain* would seem more appropriate for a professional contact. *November* sounds like a friend — or a colleague. Maybe it's another journalist. The thought makes her uneasy. Is she being lured into an interview she doesn't want to give?

Hi Geraint, she writes back, and then stops, pondering her next move. *I am actually working today, could you tell me a little bit more about this? Is there a reason you can't explain over the phone? Hannah.*

There's a pause, and she's just about to return to her mother's email when a reply pops into her inbox.

Sorry, Hannah, I totally understand but I don't actually have all the info myself, it's sort of sensitive. Plus I think November really wants to meet you and explain in person. Understandably.

Hannah shuts her eyes, feeling a mix of frustration and annoyance, but there's not much she can do short of refuse to meet this person, and there's no denying it, she *does* want to find out about the autopsy results. If April really was pregnant, this could change everything. At last she opens her eyes again and presses reply, trying to quash her irritation. No point in antagonizing Geraint before she has even met this mysterious person.

Okay. It's a bit tricky to get away, but I could come and meet you and November late morning. It would have to be fairly brief, though — I can't leave my colleague alone in the shop for too long. Where would suit? Somewhere close to the bookshop if possible. Hannah.

There. If things unfold in a way that she doesn't like, she has a cast-iron excuse for cutting and running. She will have to clear it with Robyn, but late morning is when she usually takes her lunch hour on Saturdays — the shop doesn't get busy until around twelve, and they have a Saturday girl called Ailis who comes in at eleven and can handle the till.

The reply pings back almost before the email has left her outbox.

Great. 11.30 okay? November is staying at the Grand Caledonia Hotel just off the Royal Mile so perhaps we could meet there. They have a coffee shop in the foyer. Do you know it?

Hannah raises an eyebrow. She does indeed know the Grand Caledonia. It's easily the most expensive hotel in Edinburgh. Not quite what she had imagined a journalist would choose for work. Geraint, for example, looks more like a Holiday Inn type of chap. Still, it's only a ten-minute walk and the coffee is certain to be good.

Sure, she types back. *I'll see you there.*

When she arrives at the shop Robyn is already there — she opens up on Saturdays, as it's Hannah's night to stay late — and when Hannah explains that she'd like to take an early lunch to have coffee with a friend, she nods, breezily unconcerned.

"Yeah, sure, no probs at all. Ailis will be in by then so we can easily hold the fort. Take your time."

It's raining hard, a miserable day in fact, so trade is slow and at 11:20 Hannah grabs her coat and her umbrella from the staff room and tells Robyn and Ailis she won't be long. The rain increases as she hurries

440

towards the Lawnmarket, and she arrives at the Grand Caledonia looking like a drowned rat.

Under the gilt-edged canopy she stands, shivering for a moment and shaking off her umbrella as the doorman holds the huge shiny black door open for her, and for an instant she has a sharp flashback to the night at the private members' club in Oxford, the kindly old doorman offering to call her a taxi on April's father's dime. She shuts her eyes. She can't think about this right now. She's already regretting turning up for this without probing Geraint further. If she walks in with her head full of Oxford memories and grief . . .

"Can I take your umbrella, ma'am?" the doorman asks, and Hannah shakes her head, knowing she'll end up leaving it.

"No, thank you, I'd rather hang on to it. Is that okay?"

"Of course." He hands her a plastic sleeve and she slides the umbrella inside, reflecting that even if the umbrella doesn't drip, she certainly will, and enters the hotel.

The foyer is vast and marble and gold, like a banking hall, with an enormous chandelier in the center. A huge staircase winds up to the right, and glancing up, Hannah sees that some kind of photo shoot is taking place — a giant gold umbrella is reflecting light up the stairs, where someone is clearly having their picture taken against the sweep of the staircase.

"That's great," she hears. "Now lean back against the banister. Tilt the chin?"

The coffee shop is tucked away behind the curve of the staircase, and she makes her way across the expanse of marble, painfully conscious of her dripping mac and rat's-tail hair.

As she rounds the edge of the stairs, she sees Geraint sitting at a little bistro table, tapping at his phone. He stands, his face lighting up as he sees her.

"Hannah! Thanks for coming. Can I get you a coffee?"

Hannah pauses. Her instinct is to accept nothing from Geraint, but on the other hand, he's the one who invited her here, and more importantly, if he pays, she won't be held up waiting for the bill if she wants to make a quick getaway.

"Sure," she says at last. "A — um . . . a decaf cappuccino and . . . maybe a biscotti if they have any."

She's feeling a little light-headed. Low blood sugar, probably — the midwife at her last appointment told her it could happen, and advised small, frequent snacks.

"November's just texted," Geraint says, "she'll only be five. They're just wrapping up. Right — let me get the drinks. I'll be back in a sec."

He walks up to the counter and Hannah sits there chewing her nail and wondering why she did this.

Geraint is just returning from the counter with an enormous green juice and a biscotti when he turns and looks at someone over Hannah's shoulder.

"Ah! Perfect. We're all here," he says happily. "Hannah, this is November Rain. November, this is Hannah de Chastaigne — Hannah Jones, you would have known her as."

Hannah stands, turns, and then her stomach seems to fall away from her.

Standing in front of her, willowy, inexpressibly beautiful, and most undeniably, unbelievably *alive,* is April.

For a moment Hannah thinks she's going to faint. Everything goes very far away, and there is a roaring sound in her ears. She holds on to the edge of the table with both hands, trying to steady herself, trying to tell herself this cannot be true.

"Hannah?" she hears Geraint saying, worriedly. "Hannah? Are you okay?"

"Hi," the girl says. She comes towards them, shoving her mobile into the pocket of her silk harem pants. Her Louboutins click as she walks across the marble. She holds out a hand towards Hannah. "Hi. I'm November, really pleased to meet you."

And then — something snaps into place. Hannah isn't sure whether it's the sound of the girl's voice, which is very like April's, but *not* April's, or something in her eyes. There is no mistaking that expression; the girl coming towards her does not recognize Hannah and even April, superb actress

444

though she was, could not have faked that.

"Who — who *are* you?" Hannah says, and her voice is harsher than she intended; it comes out as a kind of hoarse accusation.

"Oh God," Geraint says, as if he understands only now what he has done. "I'm so sorry, I should have said — I thought you knew. November is April's sister."

Hannah blinks. And then, very slowly, she sits down. The girl — November — sits opposite her, and she smiles, a soft, sad smile that's so like April's it catches at Hannah's heart, but she doesn't have April's dimple, and for some reason Hannah finds that obscurely comforting; concrete evidence that these are not the same people. Up close she can see that the girl is also much too young to be April. She is closer to the April Hannah remembers than April as she would be now — if she had lived. This girl can't be more than twenty-two or twenty-three.

"I'm sorry we never met," November is saying. "I heard about you, of course, from April. I kept begging to come and stay in Oxford, but I was just her little snot-nosed baby sister at the time. And then afterwards, I think my parents wanted to protect me from all the coverage. I was never allowed in court or anything. I can understand why, to be honest — I was only eleven or twelve at the time."

"I — I'm sorry too," Hannah says. She is still trying to make sense of this. April's sister — after all these years. And what was it Geraint had called her in his introduction? November Rain? "I'm sorry, did Geraint say your surname was Rain? Did you change it?"

"Oh . . ." November gives a slightly self-conscious laugh and brushes her short white-blond hair out of her eyes. She is wearing long feathered earrings, Hannah sees, the tips brushing her tanned bare shoulders. "Sort of. Rain is my professional name, I suppose you'd call it. I'm an Instagram influencer, but Clarke-Cliveden as a surname . . . aside from sounding a bit posh, it's got all that . . . history. Rain . . . I suppose it was just a bit of a joke. The song, you know. And somehow it seemed to make the November part stand out less."

Of course. Suddenly Hannah understands the photo shoot, the hotel, November's effortlessly made-up beauty. Out of context the name hadn't clicked, but even Hannah, who rarely goes on Instagram except to torture herself with memories of April, has heard of beauty influencer November Rain.

"I've been in Edinburgh all week doing a shoot for D and G, and, well, it just seemed like serendipity. When Geraint messaged me on Insta and said you lived here, and would I have time to meet . . ."

She shrugs. A waiter arrives with Geraint's Americano and Hannah's cappuccino and there is a brief pause as they sort out the drinks and Hannah refuses sugar.

When the waiter is gone Hannah takes a deep breath. There is so much she wants to ask November, so much she wants to discuss, but she has to cut to the chase here, she doesn't have much time.

"November, I'm sorry to ask this so abruptly, but I've only got a short lunch hour. I have to get back to work pretty soon. Geraint said . . . he said that you knew something . . . about the autopsy?"

November nods.

"Yes. I mean — not everything. Obviously no one was going to tell a twelve-year-old girl the grisly details, but they couldn't stop me listening at doors and so on. There was a lot of stuff that didn't come out in court — the drugs, the pregnancy —"

Hannah catches her breath at that. So it's true?

"How — um — oh my God." She lets out a shaking breath. "I'm sorry, this is a lot. So, she definitely was pregnant?"

"Or had been very recently," November

says. "I was never quite sure which. Whichever it was, there were enough hormones for them to trip a blood test. And I think they tried to do DNA matches to determine a father, but I'm not sure if they ever pinned it down. I don't know if they just didn't swab enough people or if they couldn't get enough DNA from April to get a good profile."

Hannah shuts her eyes. Suddenly it all makes sense. She remembers the police coming around, swabbing her, Will, Ryan, and all the others. "Elimination DNA," they called it, along with the fingerprints. At the time Hannah had assumed it was simply to rule out all the people who had been in April's room for innocent reasons. Now she wonders if there was more to it than that, with the boys at least.

"So it wasn't —" Her voice is croaky, and she is not sure she can bear to say it, but she has to. "It — it wasn't . . . Will's?"

November shakes her head sympathetically, but her eyes are sad.

"I'm sorry, I don't know. I don't think so, or I think we would have heard. But I just don't know for certain. You could probably go to the police and ask — I don't know if they would tell you, though."

But now it's Hannah's turn to shake her

head. She knows she won't do that. Not just because the police are unlikely to hand out confidential information on a closed case. Not just because of what it might unleash if she admitted her fears, admitted that all these years later she is becoming more and more uncertain of whether she pointed the finger at the right man. But because she is afraid of what she might find out.

"Wh-what about your parents?" she asks now. "Would they know?"

"I doubt it," November says. "My father died — did you know that?"

"I didn't," Hannah says. She bites her lip. "I'm so sorry."

"Massive heart attack two years ago. He was never really right after April's death, to be honest. She was his firstborn, his golden girl, you know? I don't think he ever got over what happened. And my mother . . . well, perhaps April told you. She has . . . problems. Even before April died. Her memory isn't reliable at the best of times and she's done her best to block all this out. I don't think she would agree to talk about it, and even if she did, I don't think you could trust anything she told you."

"Oh God, November, I'm so sorry," Hannah says. "That's so difficult."

November gives a little shrug as if to say,

What can you do?

"And . . . drugs?" Hannah asks. "You said the autopsy showed up drugs in her system? Did that have something to do with her death?"

"No, I don't think so," November says. She sighs. "From what I could tell it was mostly that stuff, what's it called — they give it to kids with ADHD . . . dex something."

"Dextroamphetamine," Geraint says quietly, and November nods.

"That's it. They found a stash of it in her room at home, as well as at college. I don't think there was any suggestion that someone gave it to her covertly, or she overdosed. She was taking it deliberately, methodically, and for quite a long time. I'd say she was well aware of the toxicity."

"An ADHD medication?" Hannah is puzzled. "But that makes no sense. Why would April be taking that? She didn't have ADHD."

"It's sometimes used as a study aid," Geraint says. "They gave it to air force pilots in the war, to help them concentrate and stay awake. Kids use it to pull all-nighters, study for exams and so on. But it's not easy to get hold of — you have to have a prescription because it can be extremely addictive if you're using it recreationally. It's highly controlled."

"Oh God." Suddenly so many things click into focus. April's frequent red-eye essays, her seemingly superhuman ability to act all week and then study all night. Hannah remembers her own complaints about her essay, April holding out her hand, two pills in her palm, Hannah's puzzled *What are they — like, NoDoz or something?* And the way April laughed, and said dryly, *NoDoz for grown-ups.*

"What do they look like?" she asks Geraint, and he googles for a moment and then holds out his phone. Hannah's heart sinks. It's them. It's the capsules filled with little beads that April offered her so long ago.

"I knew she was taking those," she says. "I just didn't know what they were. But — that doesn't have anything to do with her death, does it?"

November shakes her head.

"I don't think so. I assume that's why it never came out at the trial. The pregnancy stuff, though . . . I mean, I'm surprised Neville's defense lawyer never brought it up."

"I think they thought it was too risky," Geraint says. "I mean, they had a good shot with reasonable doubt — there wasn't anything concrete to tie him to April's death apart from having been seen coming out of the building around the time she was killed. But he did badly in the witness box."

Hannah nods. She remembers hearing about this. First, Neville had denied being in the room at all — had claimed that he had simply been checking something in the building. But halfway through cross-examination he'd become flustered and changed his story — confronted with fingerprints on the inside doorknob, he had abruptly admitted that he had been in the room. But he said that he had simply been bringing up the weekly parcel from Hannah's mum, and that April had let him in. He claimed they'd had a pleasant chat, which Hannah found implausible in itself, and that he had left her alive and well just a few minutes later.

That had sealed his fate. By John Neville's account, he had seen April alive at 11:00 p.m. Hannah and Hugh had discovered her dead body just a few minutes later — and they'd had a clear view of the entrance for the whole time. There had been absolutely no opportunity for anyone else to enter staircase 7. It was Neville, or no one.

Or . . . was it?

Hannah is frowning, trying to puzzle something out, when she realizes Geraint is speaking again.

"The thing is, being devil's advocate for a moment," he is saying, "even if April *was* pregnant, it's hard to see what that's got to do with the case. It's not Victorian England. No one was going to force anyone into a shotgun marriage. There's the sexual jealousy angle" — he shoots Hannah an apologetic look, knowing that he is tacitly pointing the finger at Will here — "strangulation typically points to a domestic murder, usually a crime of passion — but April's boyfriend was never in the picture, he was away from college the night of the murder. Pregnancy just isn't much of a motive."

"Well, you say that," November puts in. "But there's pregnancy and there's pregnancy. What if it was someone who couldn't afford to be found sleeping with a student? Someone whose job or marriage might be at stake?"

"You mean a member of staff?" Geraint asks. November shrugs and Geraint looks intrigued. "It's certainly a possibility," he says.

"Oh my God," Hannah says. Her hands have gone suddenly cold. "Oh my *God*."

"What?" Geraint asks, and then frowns.

"Are you all right, Hannah?"

Hannah shakes her head, but she's not sure if she means *I'm not all right,* or *That doesn't matter right now.* She knows her face has gone pale, and from Geraint's expression she can tell that she must look as stricken as she feels.

"Dr. Myers," she whispers, more to herself than to them.

"Who?" November says. Geraint is frowning.

"That tutor who lived on your stairwell?"

"Yes." Hannah's heart has started pounding, sickeningly hard. She feels unutterably stupid. She cannot believe this never occurred to her before. "Yes. Oh my God, he's the one person who could have accessed April's room between Neville leaving and me and Hugh arriving. He wouldn't have needed to enter the building, he was *already there.*"

"But are you saying —" Geraint frowns, and then starts again. "He couldn't have got April pregnant, surely? He wasn't even her tutor."

"No, he was mine — but April knew him. She went to a party he threw. He had this reputation." Hannah feels sick. There is a buzzing in her ears. "He used to invite students — female students — out for drinks. They were all April's type, very beautiful, very —"

Suddenly she cannot go on. The ringing in her ears is growing louder. The room is taking on a strange, distant quality.

"Are you saying he could have been sleeping with her?" Geraint asks. He looks skeptical but also strangely hopeful. Hannah feels anything but.

"I don't know —" Hannah manages. Her tongue feels strange and thick in her mouth. Her fingers are freezing. She feels numb all over. "Did I get it wrong all along? I don't — I don't —"

The words are not coming. Suddenly her body feels as if it doesn't belong to her, like her limbs are made of Plasticine.

"I don't —" she says. Her voice sounds like it's coming from very far away.

"Hannah?" she hears. "Hannah, are you okay?"

"I —"

Everything disintegrates, and she slides into the dark.

AFTER

When Hannah wakes it's to a confusion of noise, people crowding around, Geraint saying "Give her some air!" over and over, and November kneeling beside her, concern all over her face. There is a coat under her head and someone has removed her glasses. It makes her feel strangely vulnerable, even more than she already did.

"Someone call an ambulance," she hears, and she struggles up onto her elbows.

"No, no, please, I don't need an ambulance." Her voice is shaky, but she tries to put conviction into it. "I'm pregnant — that's all."

"You're pregnant?" The words don't seem to calm Geraint down. If anything he looks more alarmed, like she is a ticking bomb that might explode at any moment.

"We need to get you checked over. Is there a doctor here?" November calls over her shoulder to one of the hovering hotel staff

She stands up. "Anyone? Do you guys have a house doctor for the hotel?"

"I'm a doctor." The voice comes from the far side of the foyer, a man's voice, his accent English, not Scottish, getting louder as the footsteps approach. "Can I help?"

Hannah tries to sit up. Without her glasses all she can see is a blur of faces.

"This lady — she's fainted," Geraint is saying in a worried voice. "She's pregnant. Should we be calling an ambulance?"

"I really don't think I need an ambulance," Hannah says. She feels on the verge of tears. This can't be happening. She looks at the doctor, pleading with him to say it's nothing serious. "People do faint when they're pregnant, don't they? I didn't eat breakfast."

The doctor is opening his bag. Inside is a stethoscope and a blood pressure monitor. He smiles kindly.

"Well, it's not uncommon for low blood pressure to cause faintness in early pregnancy, but getting as far as actually passing out, that's a bit less standard . . . Do you mind?"

He holds out the blood pressure cuff, and Hannah gives a shaky nod of assent. He straps the cuff around Hannah's arm, inflates it, and puts the stethoscope to the curve of her elbow, listening as the cuff deflates. Then he sits back and smiles reassuringly.

"Probably nothing to worry about, but I think we should get you along to the maternity department for a spot of monitoring. How far gone are you?"

"Twenty-three — no, almost twenty-four weeks. Twenty-four tomorrow. Could someone call my husband?"

"I've got your phone," November says, holding it up, and then turns to the doctor. "Thank you for checking her over. She should be in hospital, right?" She jerks her head at Hannah, her huge earrings swaying.

The doctor nods reluctantly.

"I'm afraid so. It's a long time since I've done any obstetrics, but actually passing out does warrant a check. Your BP is a little bit up; they may want to take some bloods and do a trace."

"I've got a driver round the corner," November says. She picks up a leather jacket from the back of the chair. "Give me five minutes, I'll get him to pull up at the front."

"I can manage," Hannah says. She feels almost tearful at the idea of being ushered out of the foyer into a waiting car like an invalid being carted off. "I don't need a lift, I can call Will, get the bus."

"By all means call your husband, but I'm not putting you on a bloody bus. It's my car or an ambulance," November says. She folds her arms, and her expression is pure April, at her most haughtily inarguable. "Which is it to be?"

Hannah shuts her eyes. She knows when she is beaten.

Some forty-five minutes later Hannah is sitting in a padded chair in the maternity unit of the Royal Infirmary, a monitor strapped to her stomach, a blood pressure cuff around her arm, and November, slightly uncomfortable with all this, perched on the edge of a plastic stool beside her. She's had a pee test and given what felt like about a pint of blood in little vials, and now part of her wants to be left alone with her thoughts, but a larger part of her wants anything but.

Mostly she wants Will, but his phone is ringing out. Where *is* he?

"Do you want me to try him again?" November asks, as if reading her mind. She has been allowed to stay as Hannah's "companion," which feels a little strange given Hannah has known her all of ninety minutes. But there is something about her, something so close to April that she feels as if it's been much longer.

"No, I'll do it," Hannah says, knowing that Will shouldn't hear this from November. She rubs her arm where the bruise from the needle is beginning to bloom, and then dials his number for what her phone says is the ninth time. It rings . . . and rings. She hangs up. *Call me,* she texts. *It's kind of urgent.*

She puts the phone down in her lap, fighting the tears. It's not just the fact that Will is unreachable — it's everything. The idea that she has somehow *caused* this with her own actions, put her baby at risk by investigating April's death. But the alternative feels equally unbearable — for how can she spend the next sixteen weeks in this state of agonizing uncertainty, obsessing over what she saw and thought and said? She just wants to *know,* to prove Geraint's fears wrong and move on with her life. The baby flutters inside her stomach, and the monitor whooshes, speeding up with her heart.

"Is there anyone else?" November asks now. "Anyone else you can call, I mean?"

Hannah shakes her head. "Not really. My mum lives miles away. But if you need to go . . ."

"I'm not going," November says firmly. "Not until you're discharged. But I'm happy to wait in the car if you don't want me here.

I get that this is weird — I mean, we hardly know each other."

"No, I'm happy for you to stay. It's nice to — to talk."

"Okay then," November says. She folds her arms. "I'll stay."

There is a silence, punctuated only by the whoosh and click of machines and the faint conversation of the women in the next bay.

"It could have been Dr. Myers," Hannah says. It's what's been preying on her mind ever since that moment in the hotel, and now it's a relief to say the words out loud, but there's also a different quality — it is as if saying them makes the possibility real. "He was already on the staircase. He could have got access to the room between Neville leaving and Hugh and me arriving. Geraint's right — if he was sleeping with April, if he had got a *student* pregnant — well, that would give him motive *and* opportunity. Neville was convicted because he was the only person who had the opportunity to kill April. He never had a motive. But Myers — he's the one person who could have slipped in there without anyone noticing."

"I wonder if he was ever interviewed," November says. Her expression is sober. "I mean, the police must have asked him whether he heard anything. But was he ever seriously a suspect?"

"I don't know," Hannah says. "I never saw him in court, but I wasn't allowed to see the other —"

She breaks off. Her phone is buzzing in her lap. She turned the ringer off, in semi-deference to the hospital's NO MOBILE PHONES sign, but now it's vibrating with an incoming call. It's Will. Thank God.

"Will!"

"Hannah." He sounds out of breath. "I just got your message — I was swimming. What happened? Are you okay?"

She swallows. Will is not going to like this.

"I — I fainted," she says at last. "I've gone into the maternity unit for some monitoring."

There is a long pause. Hannah can tell he is trying to keep himself in check, not overreact, make her more upset, particularly after their recent argument. She hears him swallow on the other end of the phone.

"How — is everything all right?" he says carefully. "Is the baby okay?"

"I think so," she says. "I haven't been signed off yet, but they keep coming in and looking at the baby's heartbeat chart and they don't seem too worried."

"Good," Will says. "Look, I can be there in . . ." His voice goes faint and she can tell he's looking at his phone screen, figuring out how long the journey will take. Then he comes back on. "Twenty, twenty-five minutes?"

"I don't know if I'll still be here." Hannah looks up at the clock on the wall. "When they hooked me up they said they'd monitor me for half an hour — it's been nearly that now. Shall I call you when I know what's happening?"

"Okay," Will says. He sounds worried, but also like he's trying to keep his concerns from her. "I love you, and Han—"

"Yes?"

"I'm — I'm *really* sorry about . . . you know."

"It's okay," she says. For anyone else, his words might be hard to decode, but Hannah knows he means their fight. She bites her lip. She wishes Will were here. "This isn't your fault, I promise."

"Okay," he says, though he doesn't sound completely convinced. "Love you."

"Love you too."

She hangs up. November has moved away, trying to give at least the illusion of privacy, but now she turns around, looking over her shoulder.

"Everything okay?"

"I think so."

There is a rattle at the door and a tall, smiling obstetrician comes in, holding a clipboard.

"Hannah de Chastaigne?"

"Yes," Hannah says. She struggles to sit up straighter in the padded chair, the plastic creaking. "Yes, that's me."

"Excellent. Could we have a moment?" She looks at November, though it's not clear whether she's inviting her to leave or stay.

"I'll be in the corridor, Hannah," November says tactfully. She picks up her bag and slips out.

The doctor takes November's stool and begins to look through Hannah's notes and at the readout on the monitor.

"Well," she says at last. "I hear you had a little fainting spell."

Hannah nods. "I think I just — I don't know, I'd had a bit of a shock, low blood pressure probably. I feel fine now."

"Well, the good news is you *look* fine, and so does baby, all the vitals are really good, and your urine is clear, but . . . we do want to keep an eye on your blood pressure."

"How do you mean?"

"Well, it's been creeping up a bit over the last few appointments, and I'm afraid it's a bit higher than we'd like."

"What? But I don't understand — the

doctor at the hotel said *low* blood pressure was what makes people faint."

"It can be, but yours isn't very low, I'm afraid. I understand it's been up at the last couple of checks?"

"Yes — but — but there were reasons —" Hannah feels tears rising in her throat, forces them down. If only Will were here. "I ran there. You don't understand."

"Have you had any headaches? Flashing lights? Dizzy spells?"

"No! I mean — other than today, obviously, but the rest, no, absolutely not. I feel completely fine."

"Well, I think we'd like to get it down regardless. I'm going to give you a prescription for methyldopa — it's a very safe drug, we've been using it for years with pregnant women —"

"You're kidding." Hannah heart is sinking, a hollow feeling of guilt and anger at her body's betrayal taking its place. "Medication? I don't want to take drugs. Can't I just — I don't know — take it easy?"

"It's very safe," the doctor repeats. She is trying to be reassuring, Hannah can see that, but she feels anything but reassured. In fact her heart is racing, the trace on the monitor spiking up and up. She feels again that sickening slide into uncertainty she experienced after April's death — the sensation that events have taken over, and that her life is spiraling out of control. Only this time it's not police officers telling her where to go and what to do and how to feel, it's a doctor with a white coat, but the same pitying, understanding smile that Hannah knows so well.

"No," she says forcefully. "No, this isn't okay. This can't be happening!"

"Your baby is fine," the doctor says again, gently. "This really is just about taking the best care of you both. I understand it's upsetting when things don't go —"

"I'm not upset!" Hannah explodes, though it's so patently untrue that part of her wants to give a sobbing laugh at the irony of that fact. Her throat is tight and she feels like crying. But she cannot. Will not. She takes a deep breath. "I'm sorry. I am, obviously, upset. It's just — it's so unexpected. I feel like things were fine a week ago and now, it's like —"

It's like someone has come in and taken over and everything is out of my hands and moving in a direction I don't want and can't control.

That's what she wants to say. But she won't. Because although it's true, that *is* how she feels, the rational part of her knows that this reaction is only partly about the baby and her blood pressure. A far larger part of it is about April, and Neville, about what happened then, and about what is unfolding now.

And suddenly, with that thought, Hannah knows what she is going to do, and she feels her heart rate slow, and a kind of peace unfold inside her. Because Hannah has had her life ripped away from her by events beyond her control once before. She does not intend to let it happen again.

This time, she will be in charge.

"So, where to?" November asks, as Hannah sinks into the leather-scented interior of the limousine. "Not back to work, clearly?"

Fuck. The shop. Hannah feels like smacking herself in the forehead with the paper bag of pills she is holding.

"I completely forgot about work. I need to phone my colleague. Can you drop me in Stockbridge? I live on Stockbridge Mews, it's near Dean Park Street."

"I have no idea where that is," November says pleasantly, "but assuming Arthur does, then yes."

She leans forward to talk to the driver, while Hannah calls the shop. When Robyn answers, Hannah explains the situation, fielding Robyn's shocked concern and listening to her admonishments to go home, rest up, and on no account to come in next week.

"I'm not going to take it as sick leave,"

Hannah says now, in answer to the last in Robyn's long line of instructions. "I'm not ill — but I've got loads of holiday left, I'm going to ask Cathy if I can take a week as leave."

"Good!" Robyn says sternly. "I don't want to see your face for at least a week. Now go. Rest. Relax. Eat chocolate and *don't worry.*"

She hangs up and Hannah sighs.

I've been sent home, she texts Will. *Everything's okay. Baby's fine. I'm getting a lift. See you shortly. xx*

"Everything all right?" November says, and Hannah nods.

"Yes, work is being really nice, it makes me feel like a complete shit."

"Why?" November asks in surprise. "It's not your fault."

Hannah only shakes her head. It's not because she believes what happened today was her fault. It's because she has no intention of following Robyn's advice. It's not that she doesn't want to — but she *can't.* She was swept along by events ten years ago, and she has spent every year since struggling against that feeling of powerlessness and panic. This time she is not going to sit there while Geraint digs around in her past and lawyers do things behind the scenes. She's going to take control.

"I'm going down to Oxford," she says to November. "I think it's the only way. Since Neville's death I've been going crazy — running over and over my memories of that night, trying to figure out if I was right, if I really did see what I thought. But the more I find out, the more the whole case feels *wrong.* I feel like there was something that I missed, something that's been eluding me all these years."

"What do you mean?" November asks uncertainly. "What kind of thing?"

"I don't know, that's the problem. Maybe if I go back, talk to the other people who were there that night, speak to Dr. Myers . . ." She swallows. "I have a friend in Oxford — Emily. I spoke to her a couple of weeks ago, when Neville died, and she invited me down. I brushed her off at the time — I couldn't think of anything worse than going back. But now . . . now I'm going to say yes."

She looks at November. November's expression is worried.

"What do you think? Do you think I'm crazy? Will does."

"I don't think you're crazy," November says slowly. "I'm just . . . I'm not sure traveling to Oxford alone is such a great idea. It'll be really obvious that you're going down there to poke around, ask questions."

"So what are you saying? I need some kind of alibi?"

"I'm saying . . ." November takes a deep breath. "I'm saying . . . take me."

"Take you?" Hannah tries not to let her face show her surprise. *But we barely know each other,* she thinks, although it's only half-true. She's only known November a few hours — but she's April's sister. A part of Hannah feels like she's known her much longer.

"Look, I've never been there." November is speaking fast now, trying to get her point across. "To Oxford, I mean. I never saw where April lived, and where she died. And honestly — that bothered me. It bothered me then, and it bothers me now. You could bring me down to Oxford and tell Myers the truth — that Neville's death stirred up some ghosts for me, and I want to lay them to rest by seeing where April lived. I don't think the college authorities would refuse that."

"No . . ." Hannah says slowly. "No, I don't suppose they would." The more she thinks about it, the more it feels like a good plan. There's safety in numbers, and November will be able to ask questions that Hannah can't.

"We should make sure he's still there," November is saying. "What's his full name?"

"Horatio." It feels strange on Hannah's tongue, oddly intimate. She remembers April's words, the night of Dr. Myers's party, *Horatio's asked me and a couple of girls to go for a drink in town . . .* It seems scarcely believable now, such a clear crossing of lines.

November taps at her phone, and then holds it out for Hannah to see.

"That's him, right?"

"That's him," Hannah says. It's the Pelham College English faculty page, first entry, Professor Horatio Myers, Senior Dean of Arts. A little older, a little grayer, but surprisingly unchanged — much less so than Neville, the hollowed-out ghost of a man staring out from the BBC website. Myers, by contrast, looks sleek, well-fed, like someone who has lived very comfortably in the intervening years.

"We're just coming up to Stockbridge Mews, Ms. Rain" comes a voice from the front of the car, over the intercom, and Hannah jumps. November presses a button.

"Thank you, Arthur."

She turns to Hannah.

"It was so lovely to meet you, Hannah. This will probably sound stupid, but I feel

— I feel a lot closer to April than I have in years."

Hannah nods. It doesn't sound stupid, because she feels the same way.

"Are you sure?" she says. "About coming to Oxford, I mean? Because you don't have to. If you feel like you have to look after me, then don't. I'll be with Emily. Or I can ask Will."

"I'm coming because I *want* to," November says. The car slides to a halt, and Hannah picks up her bag.

"Well, thank you. And thank you for the lift."

"It was nothing. Take care of yourself, Hannah."

"I will," Hannah says. She climbs out, and watches the car draw away, November's silhouette getting smaller and smaller in the rear window. And for a moment, she looks so like April that it almost breaks Hannah's heart.

AFTER

"You have got to be kidding me." Will's expression, when Hannah tells him over supper what she is planning, is a mixture of frustration, shock, and confusion. "Why on earth are you going back there? And why now? Right when you should be resting up?"

He jerks his head towards the pharmacy bag Hannah left sitting on the arm of the sofa while they ate supper.

"The doctor was really clear — she said there's no need for me to cut down on work or anything," Hannah says again, patiently. They have been through this already — it was the first thing she told Will when she walked through the door and found him pacing the living room, googling *high blood pressure in pregnancy* on his phone. "It's a really low dose; they give it to pregnant women all the time. I specifically asked her if I should reduce my hours and she said no need, this is not a big deal, just to make

474

sure I had a chair and to take plenty of breaks. I mean, this *is* a break. That's the whole point."

"And as for November —" Will says, as if she hasn't spoken. "Does she understand what you went through — does she have any idea what she's asking?"

"She's not asking for anything. It was *my* idea to go to Oxford, not hers. And you'd like her, Will," Hannah says. She takes Will's hand, feeling the tendons and the fine bones, rubbing her fingers across his knuckles. She picks it up and kisses the back. "You really would. She's like —" She stops, trying to think how to put it. "She's like April — but — I don't know. *Kinder,* maybe. And she *does* understand, because she's been through something very similar herself."

"Was she dragged through the courts?" Will says angrily. "Was she doorstepped every day for months?"

"The last one?" Hannah lets Will's hand drop. "Uh, almost certainly yes, Will. She's April's *sister.* Can you imagine what that must have been like? She was eleven when April was killed; she's spent most of her childhood trying to come to terms with that fact, watching her sister get ripped apart in the press and her dad die from the stress of it. I'm pretty sure she gets it."

475

Will has the grace to look slightly ashamed at that.

"I had no idea April's father had died. When did that happen?"

"A couple of years ago, I think."

Will pushes his plate to one side and puts his head in his hands. When he looks up, his expression is drained, almost gaunt, and his hair is ruffled.

"You know I don't want you to go, right?"

"I know," Hannah says gently. "But I need to do this, Will. I've spoken to Emily. I'm traveling down Thursday, and we're going to do a tour of Pelham Friday afternoon. Emily's going to set up a meeting with Dr. Myers."

"On Friday?" Will looks, if anything, even more dismayed. "But I'm working. I won't be able to get the time off at such short notice."

"I didn't think you'd want to come. You said yourself you didn't want to dig all this up."

"I don't, but I don't want *you* down there by yourself, meeting up with strange men —"

"Hardly strange, Will."

"Possibly very, *very* strange, if your suspicions are correct."

"And I won't be by myself, I'll be with

Emily and November in a very public place. I mean, what do you think — he's going to come lurching out of his study with an ax?"

"I have no idea!" Will says. He stands up now, as if his constrained emotions are too great to allow him to continue sitting placidly at the table, and begins to pace the living room. "All I know is, I don't want my pregnant wife going to talk to a potential killer."

"I have to do this!" Hannah stands too. She knows her voice is rising and her face is flushed. "Don't you understand, Will?"

"No!" Will shouts back. "No, I don't understand, I don't understand at all!"

There is a moment's silence as they both stand, glaring at each other, and then into the silence comes a resounding *bang! bang! bang!* that makes them both jump. Their downstairs neighbor is pounding on the ceiling with a broom handle, telling them to keep the noise down.

"I'm sorry," Hannah says, at the same time that Will says, "Oh, Hannah, love," and then somehow she's in his arms, and he's pressing his lips to the top of her head, and she can feel the tightness in her throat and the tears prickling at the backs of her eyes.

"Please," he whispers into her hair. *"Please."*

And she knows what he wants to say. *Please don't go.* She knows him so well, she can hear the words straining at his lips, knows that he wants to fall on his knees and kiss her bump and beg her not to do this.

But instead he says, "Please, be careful, Hannah. I love you so much. If anything happened —"

"It won't," she says. She kisses him, gently, carefully, and then more urgently, feeling that familiar unfurling inside her, that longing for him that is never quite quenched, that ten years of him has not been enough to satisfy. "I love you," she says, and he is saying the words back, speaking them against her cheekbone, her throat, the curve of her neck.

Now he sits, drawing her onto his lap, and she folds into him, thinking that they won't be able to do this much longer, that soon her bump will be too ungainly.

"I love you," she whispers again, and he looks up at her and smiles. And though he is older and his face has lines of weariness, it is the same smile that first caught her heart that day in the hall at Pelham. She wonders how many times she has traced his features in her mind's eye since then — the crinkles at the corners of his mouth, the crooked bump of his long-healed broken nose. A hundred? A thousand? As she lay in bed in New Quad thinking about collections; as she paced the streets of Dodsworth, trying not to think about the upcoming trial; as she tried to sleep in her first rented flat in Edinburgh, reading his letters with her heart aching for everything she had left behind. Now she reaches out and touches his face — running her finger down the ridge of his brow and the crook of his nose.

And she thinks, *You are mine. You were always mine.*

"I'll be careful," she says now. "I swear. But I *have* to do this."

And Will simply nods, defeated.

After

The train journey is long, but she's booked a first-class ticket, which means a free lunch at her seat. It's on the left-hand side of the train, and as they leave Edinburgh, the line runs alongside the coast for a brief, glorious half hour, and there is nothing between her and the water but a thin sheet of glass.

She sits there, her head resting against the windowpane, watching the coastline rise and fall, and the waves beyond, sparkling in the autumn sun, and she thinks back to when Will first came to find her, the September after his degree ended.

She had been living in Edinburgh for just over a year then, but the city was still strange to her, and she had not explored the countryside around it at all. *Let's go for a picnic,* Will had said. *Get out of the city. I hear Tantallon Castle is beautiful.* Will didn't have the bike back then, and they went by train, the same line she is traveling now.

She remembers the way he spread the rug out over the short sheep-cropped turf, the carefully packed sandwiches, the homemade lemon drizzle cake, the silhouette of the castle dark against the pale blue sky. *Are you happy?* he had asked, and her heart had contracted with a love so intense she had been almost afraid of it. Afterwards they had climbed down a narrow rocky path to a deserted beach and swum, just the two of them, in the icy water of the North Sea, and then they had made love on the fine-grained sand in the Scottish sunshine and after, as she lay there in Will's arms, feeling his racing heart slow beneath her cheek, she had thought, *I am happy. For the first time in years, maybe for the first time since April died, I'm happy.*

If only she could hold on to that feeling — to her love of Will, to that brief moment of perfect connection and peace. But as the train picks up speed and the line swings inland, the memory slips through her fingers like the fine white sand, faster and faster the more she tries to hold on to it.

She changes trains in London, and finds a seat on the Oxford service, staring out the window as the train snakes through west London. She had been half expecting a sense of familiarity or déjà vu, but of course

481

the truth is that she only made this journey a handful of times as a student. Once for the open day, a second time for her interview at Pelham, and then again after she came back from Christmas — the time she met Ryan at the station. She doesn't remember staring out the window then, but she must have done, and it's strange to think that the last time she saw these buildings and bushes and fields was one of the last times she was truly carefree. It was before. Before everything changed.

When she arrives in Oxford she waits for everyone else to get off the train so that she can manhandle her suitcase down the steps in peace, but she's surprised when she reaches the carriage door to find a young man waiting there for her, his hand held out.

"Here, let me take your case."

"Oh, no, seriously, I'm fine," Hannah says. She's momentarily confused — why is he acting like she's an old lady? Then she looks down and realizes. He has seen her bump. The knowledge gives her a strange jolt — she is now visibly, undeniably pregnant in a way even strangers can't miss.

"Thanks," she says at last and holds out the handle of her case. "Thank you very much."

He takes it, swings it easily to the ground, and then extends his hand politely to assist her too.

Hannah wants to laugh as she puts one hand on his arm. *How do you think I get up a whole flight to my flat without your assistance?* she wants to ask him, but at the same time she's touched. He's seen something vulnerable in her, and he wants to take care of her, and that's both reassuring and, at the same time, a little unnerving.

The taxi drops her outside an imposing stone building and Hannah walks in, looking around her as she does.

"Can I help you, madam?" a woman behind the check-in desk asks, and Hannah nods.

"Um, yes. I have a room. Hannah de Chastaigne. That's C-H-A-S-T —"

"Ah, yes, I have it," the woman breaks in with a smile. "A suite for two nights, is that correct?"

"A suite?" Hannah says, momentarily taken aback. "I booked a classic double."

"I upgraded you," says a voice from behind her, and she turns to see November grinning at her. "Don't be annoyed!"

"November," Hannah says, exasperated. "I can't — you're only here because I suggested it."

"I'm here," November says severely, "because I asked you to meet with me, and because I rudely inveigled myself onto your trip. And I'm not taking no for an answer. Plus, it's already done. Ask the check-in lady."

"It's true," the woman behind the desk says with a smile, delighted at being a part of this benevolent conspiracy. "It's all paid for."

"November!" Hannah says, but helplessly, with a laugh, and November gives her a droll little wink that is so purely April that Hannah's heart tugs inside her.

"One person, is that right?" the check-in woman says, and Hannah nods, while at the same time wishing Will could have been here. A suite! It might be practically their last chance to live it up before the baby arrives.

Up in the room she stands, taking it all in, while the nice porter shows her how to work the lights and open and close the balcony doors. After he's gone she lies down on the bed for a moment, luxuriating, and then sends Will a series of WhatsApp pictures, with the message *Wish you were here!*

She's just considering what to do next when there's a knock at the door. When

Hannah opens it, November is standing outside, looking, if possible, even more beautiful than earlier.

"Hi," she says with a broad smile. "I thought I'd come up and talk about plans. It's . . ." She glances at her phone. "Almost four. We're meeting Emily for dinner, is that right?"

"That's right." Hannah nods. "Seven p.m. At her flat."

"Then we're going on the Pelham tour tomorrow afternoon?"

"Yes, then tea with Dr. Myers afterwards." November nods. Her face is sober.

"So what —" she starts, but Hannah's phone buzzes in her hand, and glancing at it, she sees it's Will.

Jealous! he's written.

"Sorry," Hannah says. She's trying not to smile. "You were saying?"

"I was just going to ask, what time should we set out? I assume you probably want to slump on the bed for a bit beforehand?"

"I kind of do," Hannah says, surprising herself. She's not normally one for just lying in a hotel room, but she's tired, in spite of having done nothing apart from sit on a train. Her back is aching and there's a twinge deep in her pelvis that feels distinctly odd, probably from sitting in the same position on hard train seats all day.

"Okay, well I'll come and knock about six thirty then? I looked it up on maps, I don't think it'll take us more than half an hour to walk."

"If that," Hannah says. "Oxford's not very big. See you later?"

"See you later," November says, and then, to Hannah's surprise, she leans forward and kisses Hannah gently on the cheek.

"Thank you for this, Hannah."

"Don't be silly," Hannah says awkwardly. "This is hardly fun for either of us."

"I know, but it's not that — it's just — I spent the whole time April was in Oxford begging her to let me stay, and then after she was dead, wondering what her life here had been like. And I never dared to come and find out for myself. I know this can't be easy for you but I just — I'm glad I'm here. I'm glad I'm with one of April's friends. This feels right, do you know what I mean?"

"Yes, I know," Hannah says. Her heart is tight inside her. She wants to take November's hand and squeeze it, but she's not sure if they know each other well enough yet. "I'm glad you're here too. I — I miss April. A lot. And with you here —"

With you here, it's like having a little bit of April with me is what she wants to say, but she isn't sure how November will take it, whether she will bristle at being treated like April's ghost or stand-in. But she *is* like a piece of April — not a shadow or a cheap imitation; November is quite clearly too much her own person for that. But she is also so obviously April's sister that it's impossible not to feel April's presence hovering around them, especially now they are here, back in Oxford after so long.

"I don't know. I feel like she's here too. I hope that doesn't sound strange," she says at last. But November only smiles sadly and shakes her head.

"It doesn't sound strange. I've spent most of my adult life being haunted by April's ghost. It's sort of comforting to know that you have too."

AFTER

"I can't get over it," Emily says again.

They are sitting on Emily's sofa, drinking white wine (lemonade, in Hannah's case) and after half an hour of slightly awkward small talk, the years are beginning to peel back. It must be more than five years since Hannah has seen Emily in person, but she's still the same — sharply impatient, cracking jokes, fiercely ambitious under the self-deprecating veneer (*Oh that? I think only two people read it, and one was me*), and rolling her eyes at this year's intake of students. They've talked about Emily's research, November's work (*What exactly is an influencer?* Emily had asked. *It sounds like a physics experiment*), and Hannah's pregnancy.

Hannah has filled Emily in on Ryan, and Hugh, and told her how much Will hates his job as an accountant. Emily doesn't say it, but there's a very strong current of *he's wasting an Oxford education* in her replies.

Now, though, she sits back, nursing her glass, and looks from Hannah to November, shaking her head.

"Can't get over what?" Hannah asks, laughing.

"I just — the two of you. Side by side on the couch. It's messing with my head — like something out of *The X-Files.* On the one hand you're pushing thirty and *pregnant,* and on the other . . ." She turns to November, half-apologetic. "I mean I guess you get told this a lot, but you *really* look like April."

"I know," November says. "It's one of the reasons I don't go by Clarke-Cliveden professionally."

"Yup, I get that," Emily says. She leans forward, refilling her glass. "I get my fair share of weirdos just from my small role in what happened. I can't imagine what it would be like to be a Clarke-Cliveden. Or you, Han," she adds apologetically. "I can't believe the way the college washed its hands of you. Of all of us, actually, but especially you. They just let you drop out."

"I know, that's what Hugh said," Hannah says, remembering. "He reckoned these days it would be all compulsory post-trauma counseling and CBT, but back then, how did he put it? *Chin up, and we'll go easy on you in the exams.*"

"Ain't that the truth," Emily says dryly. "There's no way I deserved a first, and I'm pretty sure Hugh wouldn't even have passed if it wasn't for April. I mean, I don't want to make it sound like a silver lining, because a cloud that shit doesn't have any kind of lining, but he spent his entire time at Pelham scraping through. I don't honestly think he really belonged there."

"You think?" Hannah is surprised, though perhaps she shouldn't be. She thinks back to Hugh's perpetually worried expression, his frequent complaints about the workload, and the way, the night of April's death, he had confided his worries about the exams and his desperate fear of letting his parents down. At the time she had thought that was just Hugh, and medicine — an anxious high achiever taking a grueling course. Now, though, she wonders. Maybe Hugh *was* struggling. The thought makes her feel disloyal. "They wouldn't have let him in if that were true," she says now. "I mean, what's that exam called, the one they do for medicine? The BMAT. It's supposed to be really hard. Will told me once that Hugh aced it. He was practically guaranteed a place, his marks were so high."

Emily opens her mouth, but before she

can reply, a buzzer goes off in the kitchen.

"Ah, that's the tagine. I've made chickpea tagine, is that okay? I wasn't sure if you were veggie or anything," she says to November, "so I played it safe."

"I actually am vegetarian," November says with a smile. "So that sounds delicious."

As Emily disappears into the little kitchen to check on the food, Hannah rises and looks around the room. It's sparsely decorated — no photos, no mementos of Emily's travels or pictures of her family. Only books and a couple of antique maps on the wall. It's a room that is hard to read — a little like Emily herself. Reserved. Austere. A little severe, perhaps.

"What are you hoping to find?"

The voice comes from behind her and she swings round, to see Emily standing there, hands on hips.

"How do you mean?" Hannah asks. For a minute she's unsure whether Emily means here in Oxford, or here in her house. Was she accusing Hannah of snooping? "What am I hoping to find in Oxford? Or just generally?"

"At Pelham, I suppose I meant. But yes, generally. Are you looking for something specific?"

"Not really," Hannah says. She exchanges

a quick glance with November. They haven't discussed how much to tell Emily. The story they are presenting to Dr. Myers is one they have agreed on — November got in touch with Hannah asking about memories of her sister, and Hannah agreed to show her around Pelham and contact a few friends. But they never spoke about Emily. On the one hand, Hannah has an instinct to hug her agenda to herself. But on the other, Will, Hugh, and Ryan know that she has been digging into the past. Does it really make sense to keep Emily in the dark?

"The truth is . . ." She stops, glances again at November. November says nothing; her expression is supportive, but Hannah can't read anything more from it. She half wishes November would mouth *Go on,* or step in with a cover story.

"The truth is," she begins again, "I've started to wonder. About April's death. Ever since that reporter got in touch."

"Fuck." Emily puts her hand to her forehead. "I knew I shouldn't have told you about him. Was it me set you wondering? Because if it was —"

"No, no, not really," Hannah says. "I mean, you were the first person to tell me about Geraint, but if I'm honest —" She stops, trying to think how to phrase it.

492

"When I met him, after I met him, I realized that a lot of the stuff he was saying — they were doubts I'd been having too. I just hadn't admitted it to myself."

"Wait, so you think he's right?" Emily looks genuinely shocked. "Han — I told you about Geraint to warn you he was sniffing around, not sign you up to his agenda. He's just another conspiracist. These journalists — they all want to believe their pet theory is right so they can write their magnum opus, *April: MY TRUTH,* and get a Netflix true-crime documentary off the back of it. The evidence was there, Neville was convicted. It's not your fault if his defense didn't do their job."

"It's not that," Hannah says, slightly nettled. "But Geraint's come up with genuinely new information. He's told me stuff I had no idea about."

"Like what?" Emily says skeptically.

"Like —" Hannah begins, and then she pauses. *Like the fact that April sent Ryan a positive pregnancy test* was what she had been going to say. But the words feel like a betrayal of Ryan's trust in her. He and Emily may not be together anymore — but this is no small thing she's about to reveal. Does Hannah really have the right to blurt all this out without consulting Ryan?

And yet Emily is her friend too. She has the right to know.

Hannah bites her lip, trying to think how to phrase it. How do you tell someone their boyfriend was cheating on them for a whole year, and may have had a solid motive for murder?

"Yes?" Emily prods. "I'm fascinated to hear this journalist's conspiracy theories, but I'm finding it quite hard to imagine what kind of 'evidence' would counteract an eyewitness."

Maybe it's the audible air quotes she puts around *evidence,* and the implied dig at Hannah for taking Geraint's concerns seriously, but something about Emily's tone prickles at Hannah, in spite of herself. She hears Hugh's voice in her head, reciting April's words: *She said it was Emily's fault for being so stuck up and pleased with her own intellect.*

"Well, for one thing," Hannah says, her voice level, "I had no idea that April played a trick on you right before she was killed."

It wasn't what she'd been intending to say — but it is said now, and there's no taking it back. Emily's mouth has compressed into a thin, grim line, and she folds her arms and stares at Hannah.

"What exactly are you implying?"

494

"Nothing," Hannah says uncomfortably. "I mean — look, none of us were ever suspects, you know that. We had no opportunity. But if she was doing that to you — who else might she have pissed off? It sounds like she was on a tear that last week. She was pranking everyone."

"Everyone except you," Emily says a little coldly. She is surveying Hannah in a way Hannah doesn't quite like. She had forgotten how icily direct Emily could be, the way she ignores the polite woolly conventions that most people use to cushion discomfiting truths. Emily has never shied away from saying something because it was awkward or painful.

"Yes . . ." Hannah says, rather slowly. "Everyone except me."

"The girl making eyes at her boyfriend," Emily says.

"Hang on," November says, but Hannah holds out a hand to say, *No, I can handle this.*

"I beg your pardon?" she says to Emily.

"I'm just saying," Emily says with a shrug. She's recovered herself now, and she gives a little laugh and moves down to the other end of the room, where there are olives and breadsticks laid out on the table. "If we're chucking motives about, it was pretty obvious, those last few weeks. You could practically hear the swelling orchestral chords whenever Will looked at you. And so what, yes, I was pissed off at her. That A-level stunt she pulled was vile, and the planning that she'd put into it — I'm sorry," she says, turning to November. "I know she was your sister, and I don't want to speak ill of the dead. But when you think someone is your friend and then they do something like that, and you realize that the whole time you've been there, supporting them, having coffee with them, sharing drinks, they've been plotting how to fuck you up — it leaves a bad taste in your mouth, do you know what I mean?"

"It's okay," November says. She smiles a little sadly. "I have no illusions about April. I loved her — I still do. But I know the person she was. She could be incredibly kind, but she wasn't always."

"No, she wasn't," Emily says, rather shortly. She puts down her glass a little too hard so that the wine slops, and then disappears again into the kitchen. Hannah makes an *oh my god* gesture to November, putting her head in her hands and miming her own stupidity at putting Emily's back up.

"Should I tell her?" she whispers, under cover of the clank of pots and pans. "About

Dr. Myers?"

"It's up to you," November whispers back. "I mean . . . doesn't she work here now? Would it put her in a difficult situation?"

"I don't think so. Emily works for Balliol. It's a different college. It's not like we'd be making accusations about one of *her* colleagues."

"One of whose colleagues?" Emily says, making Hannah jump and turn around, to where Emily is standing in the kitchen doorway. She is holding a huge casserole filled with steaming chickpeas, plump apricots, and savory spices, and it smells incredible. Hannah and November watch as she maneuvers it onto the mat in the center of the table, and then Emily says again, "You were saying? About someone's colleagues?"

"Well, so, that's the real reason we're down," Hannah says. "I'm sorry I said that about the prank April played on you. That was stupid. But I was thinking about the layout of the staircase — the fact that Neville was convicted because no one could have entered the building between him leaving, and us coming in."

"Right . . ." Emily says slowly. She is dishing out tagine and couscous into three bowls, a furrow between her black brows, unsure where this is going.

"Unless . . . unless they were already in there."

Emily stops. She puts a bowl down in front of November and looks hard at Hannah.

"Hannah, what are you saying? You're saying that someone else on the staircase —"

"I'm saying it's possible. The two guys below — Henry and Philip — they had alibis. They were both together all night in Henry's room, and they gave evidence at the trial about hearing April walking around on the floor above from about ten forty-five and answering the door to someone. And the rooms below *them,* rooms one and two, room one was empty, it was used for some kind of scouts storage. And the girl in room two had her boyfriend over. I know because I knocked on the door on my way down and they came out together. But Dr. Myers . . . he was never questioned at the trial. He didn't come out and see what was going on. Why wouldn't he come out when he heard me screaming like that?"

"Yes. Why wouldn't he . . ." Emily says, very slowly. "Unless he had something to hide . . . Fuck. I can't believe the police didn't rule him out, though?"

"I mean, maybe they did and we just didn't hear about it — but on the other hand, maybe they just never suspected him. What would his motive be?"

"Well, that's a good point," Emily says. "What *would* his motive be?"

Hannah looks down at her plate. She *has* to tell Emily. It isn't fair not to. She takes a deep breath.

"Well . . . we think April may have been pregnant."

She's not sure what she's expecting from Emily. Shock maybe, or a flicker of something indicating that she already knew. Neither comes. Instead a deep, weary sadness spreads over Emily's face.

"Fuck," she says very quietly. "Oh my God, that's awful. Why didn't they bring it up at the trial?"

"According to Geraint, Neville's defense thought it would look bad," November says. "You know — victim-blaming. But if Myers was the father, it wouldn't have gone down well with the college, would it?"

"Or his wife," Emily says. "You know he's married?"

"What?" Hannah is more puzzled than shocked. "When? Recently?"

"No, forever. He was married when we were at Pelham."

"*What?*" Now Hannah really is shocked. "But — but where was his wife then? Had they separated?"

"I don't think so. Fellowship abroad or something? But she came back the following year, after you'd left, and he moved out of Pelham and into a rather nice house in Jericho with her. I think they're still there. She's a professor at Wadham."

"Shit," November says. She looks very sober, in spite of the glass of white wine she's holding. Hannah has a sudden, visceral longing for a glass herself, even though she hasn't drunk since she held her own positive pregnancy test in her hand.

"And this is why you're going to see him tomorrow?" Emily says. She looks rattled now, her cool composure shattered. "To try to — what? Trap him into something? Confront him?"

"Not confront him, no," Hannah says impatiently. She digs her spoon into the tagine, as if the gesture can somehow restore the normality of the situation. "I'm not stupid. We're just — we're going to talk to him. That's all."

"I mean —" Emily stops. She folds her hands in her lap as if she's trying to think how to compose something, and then starts again. "Look, if you think your evidence at the trial could have been based on a mistaken premise, then I can understand you wanting to get to the bottom of that, but — this could be dangerous."

"It won't be dangerous," Hannah says, rather cross now. This is not what she wants. She doesn't want Emily echoing Will's concerns. "As far as Myers is concerned, November and I are just two grieving people remembering April in her last year. He doesn't need to know anything else."

"I really think —"

"I really think this is Hannah's decision," November puts in, and Hannah shoots her a grateful look. *Yes. Thank you.* "If Myers is guilty — which is a pretty big *if* — he'd be absolutely insane to try anything. We'll be together in broad daylight. He's hardly going to gun a pregnant former student down just for coming on a tour of Pelham."

"Ugh," Emily says now, as if frustrated. She runs her hand through her hair, leaving the stiff waves mussed and tousled, and then rubs under the nose-clips of her glasses before resettling them. "I wish I could come with you, but I've got tutorials. Will you *promise* me you'll be careful? And will you report back tomorrow night?"

"Of course we'll be careful," Hannah says firmly. She picks up her spoon again and takes another bite of tagine. "And yes I'll report back tomorrow night. Shall we have dinner somewhere in town?"

"Okay," Emily says reluctantly. "I'll make a reservation and text you."

"Okay," Hannah says. "Good. Now. Let's eat dinner, I'm starving."

AFTER

The next day, as she walks down the High Street towards Pelham College, Hannah thinks she knows what Emily meant the night before, about seeing her and November on the couch together. The sense that she's stepping back in time is overwhelming, almost sickeningly so. Oxford doesn't change — that's part of it. Sure, some of the shops and cafes have different names, but the buildings, the road, the river, the skyline — it's so close to how she remembers it that it gives her a surreal, dreamlike feeling, and a sense of something so strong it's almost nausea washes over her as she crosses Pelham Street and nears the Porters' Lodge. It's not nostalgia — because she has no real wish to be back here. It's something else. A sense . . . a sense almost of the past pressing down on her, suffocating her. And November's presence beside her is part of that. Like a living ghost of April.

"I'm sorry," she says to November as they draw level with the huge wooden gate, the miniature door-within-a-door. "I'm sorry, can we just — I need a second."

"Sure!" November says. She looks concerned, and they stand for a minute, Hannah resting one hand against the golden stone of the outer wall, trying to steady herself. *You can do this, he won't be in there.*

"Okay," she says at last. And she is. Because the picture in her head is not of Neville as he was then — tall and broad and terrifying — but of the man in the article, the frail elderly man in his prison uniform. She feels her breathing steady. "Okay, I'm ready."

"Are you sure?" November asks, a little anxiously now. "Because we really don't have to. We can bow out — send our apologies. I can say I couldn't face it. People will understand."

"No, I'm fine. I want to do this."

"Okay," November says. She puts out a hand towards the big metal handle of the inner door. "Sure?"

"Sure."

As she nods, November pushes on the centuries-old door — and it opens. And together they duck through, and then, for the first time in more than ten years, Hannah is inside Pelham College.

It hasn't changed either. That's the first thing she thinks. It hasn't changed at all. There's the Porters' Lodge to the right, under the arch. There's a kind of sick reflexive lurch in her stomach as she remembers all the times she scurried past, head down, panic choking her in case he was there. But now she forces herself to stop and look, *really* look. Two elderly men are standing behind the counter, white shirts straining over ample stomachs, but Neville is just a ghost in her imagination, and she doesn't know either of them.

November leads the way into the Porters' Lodge and steps up to the counter.

"Hi, we're here for a tour? My name is November Rain, this is Hannah de Chastaigne. We're here to look around the college and then we're meeting with Dr. Myers."

"November Rain?" the older of the two men says thoughtfully, running his finger down what looks like some kind of appointments ledger, then he nods. "Gotcha. I think Dr. Myers wanted to show you around himself. Let me give him a tinkle."

November shoots Hannah a look, and Hannah bites her lip. This isn't what they had discussed. Emily had simply said that the Master was happy for them to have a tour; there had been no discussion of who would be showing them around, and somehow Hannah had imagined someone neutral, unknown to them both, someone who didn't know their history and their connection to Pelham — but of course this makes sense.

The porter is speaking on the phone, nodding and *yes*-ing by turns. Then he puts the receiver down and turns back to them.

"He's coming down. Park yourselves in a corner — or maybe you'd prefer to wait on the bench outside?"

November looks at Hannah with a raised eyebrow, then answers for them both.

"I think we'd rather wait outside. Soak up the last of the sun."

"Right you are," the porter says cheerfully, and they let themselves out.

Outside, November looks even more rattled than Hannah feels.

"Yikes. Is this okay?"

"I think so . . ." Hannah says slowly. "I mean . . . I can't think what difference it makes? It's going to be hard to discuss anything in front of him, but then that would probably have been the case whoever showed us round. We could hardly have stood there going *Oh yes, look, this is where*

Dr. Myers might have done it."

"Yeees . . ." November says. She is beginning to look calmer, less alarmed. "Yes. You're right. Yes, it'll be fine, won't it? It's just a tour."

"It's just a tour."

"Well, well, well."

The voice comes from behind them, and at the sound of it Hannah's adrenaline spikes so hard it feels like a jolt of electricity pulsing through her.

"Hannah Jones."

She shuts her eyes, counts to three. Her heart is pounding. *Think of the baby.* She thinks of the baby. She thinks of April. She thinks of the blood pressure tablet she swallowed this morning with her breakfast orange juice.

She takes a deep breath, opens her eyes, and turns.

He is there. Dr. Horatio Myers. A little older, a little grayer around the temples, but still the same Byronic wind-swept hair, the same slightly self-conscious tweed jacket, like someone playing the part of an academic.

"Dr. Myers," she says.

"How very lovely to see you here, Hannah." His tone is perfect, she realizes, as he takes one of her hands in his, pressing it between his palms. It's welcoming, but also grave, and an acknowledgment that this isn't just any alumnus coming back for auld lang syne, but something rather different, rather more painful. "Although, it is in fact Professor Myers these days," he adds, taking away a little from his air of solicitude.

"Congratulations," Hannah says, unsure what else to say.

"And this must be November," Dr. — Professor — Myers says, turning to her. "You look so like your sister."

"I know," November says, a little acidly, reminding him that this isn't exactly an uncomplicated thing for her. She softens the remark with a smile before Dr. Myers has to fumble to extricate himself. "Thank you for showing us around, it's — well, I won't pretend this is easy, but it felt like something I needed to do. My father died two years ago and he took so many memories of April with him. Ever since then I've felt the need to forge my own."

It's beautifully done. Hannah almost forgets her nerves in admiration of November's performance. If she could, she would applaud. It's so pitch-perfect it's almost . . . April. She doesn't doubt the sincerity for a second — even though she knows that's absolutely not why they're here.

"Well, I am glad to do what little I can to help, my dear," Dr. Myers says. "Now. Where shall we begin? I'm rather partial to the library myself."

Hannah wants to roll her eyes. She can't remember April spending more than five minutes in the library. It sounds more as if they're here for a tour of Dr. Myers's favorite hangouts, not something personal to April at all, but then again — it's Dr. Myers they're here to observe. So perhaps that's to the good.

"The library it is," November is saying with a smile. "Lead on, Macduff."

"Well, my dear," Dr. Myers says as they set off across the Old Quad towards the chapel cut-through, "far be it from me to begin by acting the professor, but considering our destination I cannot allow that to go uncorrected. The quotation is in fact 'Lay on, Macduff,' coming as it does in the context of a sword fight — the reference being, one is invited to infer, an invitation to lay the first blow. And in fact Pelham has one of the very few extant first folios, so I may, if we are *extremely* lucky, be permitted to show you the original line in its very earliest remaining printed form."

His tone is light, conversational, just the slightest touch condescending. The tone of a tutor expounding on his favorite subject to his favorite tutee. And suddenly, it is as if Hannah never left.

It is perhaps an hour later, and they have done the library, the Junior Common Room, the chapel, the Great Hall, and the bar, which means there is only one logical destination left. As they cross Old Quad and pass under the Cherwell Arch, Hannah knows where they are heading, and she feels something inside her tense, preparing herself for what comes next. The baby moves uneasily, as if sensing her nerves.

They cross the lawn of the Fellows' Garden — by right, now, Hannah has to assume, since they are in the company of a fellow — but as they come out of the shadow of the Master's lodgings and into the sunshine of New Quad, Dr. Myers stops.

"Now, as you may know — as Hannah undoubtedly knows — this is New Quad. I assume . . . I don't wish to presume . . . Your sister's room." He looks doubtfully from Hannah to November, as if unsure how to phrase this. "Do you . . . ?"

Do you want to see where your sister was murdered?

Hannah can understand his hesitation. There is no established social formula for asking this question.

"Yes, I'd like to see the set, if that's possible," November says firmly. "But I understand if it's not."

"Well, normally in term time access to student rooms would be difficult, but in point of fact," Dr. Myers says, "in point of fact the room, actually the whole staircase, was turned over to office use in, um, well. In the aftermath of your sister's death."

"Ah," November says, with understanding. It makes sense, Hannah supposes. Staircase 7 must have been notorious among the other students and she can't imagine the parents of any brand-new fresher wanting their daughter to spend their first year at university walking in the footsteps of a murdered student. "Yes. I can understand that. Well, in that case yes, I would like to see it if that's possible. But perhaps Hannah would like a rest." She turns to Hannah, raising one eyebrow. "Hannah? Would you like to sit down here and wait while Professor Myers shows me up to the room?"

Yes, Hannah wants to say. Her feet hurt. Her feelings are churning. The baby is fluttering nervously inside her, responding to her spiking pulse. She knows November is deliberately giving her an out, if she wants it.

"No," she hears herself saying. "I want to come."

She has come this far. She can't turn back now.

As they walk around the edge of the quad, she feels a strange unreality taking over. They are walking — the three of them — to the site of Hannah's worst ever experience, but as they crunch along the gravel it's happier memories that crowd her mind. She remembers herself and Emily, picnicking on the banks of the Cherwell. She recognizes the bench where Ryan carved his name one summer night, and the archway to staircase 3 that some enterprising student taped up for a Rag Week prank. The sun is lowering in the sky, lights are coming on all around the quad. The figures beside her are dim in the gathering dusk. She could have slipped back in time — walking with April and Hugh, back to the set one winter's night.

They follow Dr. Myers under the arch to staircase 7, and Hannah feels the stone beneath her feet, familiar even after ten years. There is the same momentary step into darkness before the lights flicker on up the staircase, the same slight delay. There is the same echo as they move upward. Dr. Myers has stopped his running commentary, as if he is not quite sure what to say.

They pass rooms 1 and 2, where the slips of paper bearing the names of students have been replaced by ones reading stores and admissions 1, and then move up, landing by landing. Some of the doors stand open and inside Hannah can see not beds and students, but desks and administrators — all the myriad back-office functions of a busy college, hard at work.

On the top floor the door to the set is closed, and Dr. Myers pauses on the landing and gives a little *rat-a-tat-tat.*

"Come in," calls a female voice with a slight Yorkshire accent, and Dr. Myers pushes on the door and enters, holding it with his hand so that Hannah and November can see past him. Inside there are two empty desks, a bunch of filing cabinets and box files, and a woman standing by the window putting on her coat.

"Oh, hello, Horatio. Can I help? I was just off."

"Hello, Dawn. Dawn, this a former student of mine, Hannah." He waves a hand at Hannah, and the woman nods politely, seemingly without recognition. "I was giving her a tour and she expressed a desire to see her old room. Are we disturbing you?"

"Not at all, as I say, I was just off. Would you lock up after me?"

"Of course." Dr. Myers takes the keys she holds out and gives a little bow. "I will leave them at the lodge?"

"Ta, that'd be great. Sorry I can't stay, got to pick up the kids from the minders. See you Monday! Nice to meet you ladies."

"Have a good weekend, Dawn."

Hannah stands back to let the woman leave, and then, after she's gone, she steps forwards into the room, feeling the past close around her like a fist.

"You'll find it's rather different, I'm afraid," Dr. Myers is saying, but his voice comes as if from a long way off, hardly breaking into her thoughts. This is where she, April, and the others played strip poker, the very first night they met. That mark on the windowsill was where April burned a hole in the oak with a lit joint. This — her hand touches the ancient wood of the doorway. This was her bedroom.

"Dr. Myers?" Her voice sounds odd in her own ears, too harsh and abrupt, but she can't think of how else to ask. "Dr. Myers, could you — could you give us a moment alone?"

"Well I —" Dr. Myers flashes a look at the unattended laptops and files, and then, almost unwillingly, at the place on the floor where April's body was found. There is a short silence as they all stare at the rug in front of the fire. Hannah wonders what he is thinking. Is he remembering what he did? Somehow here, in his presence, it's harder to believe than ever. Surely there should be a sense of evil coming from a man who killed a young girl in cold blood? A sense of guilt?

But Hannah feels nothing. Nothing but the same immense sadness they all share.

Then, as if making up his mind, he nods.

"Yes. I'm sure I can do that. Take all the time you need."

He backs out of the door, there is a moment's silence as it closes behind him, and then Hannah hears November let out a trembling breath.

"So this is it."

"This is it."

"I — I wasn't expecting to feel so — so, I don't know — *affected.* I thought you might be shaken going back but I thought, I thought for me it would be just another room. But it — it's not."

"No," Hannah says. "No, it's not."

And it isn't. Although it looks like any back office, this is, after all, where April lived and laughed, studied and slept. And it's where she died.

"Which was her room?"

"That one," Hannah says, pointing to the door to the left of the window. She moves across to it, opens the door. She's almost expecting to find it just as April left it, but of course it has been transformed into an office like the others. There's a single desk, a rather bigger one than the two outside; a whiteboard covered with notes; and a lot more files. This room obviously belongs to the boss of the little department. "Her bed was there," she says, pointing. "She had a desk there, and an armchair there — non-regulation. Nothing April had was ever just the standard college stuff, apart from the bed and the wardrobe. And it was a dump — it was always a dump. Clothes every-where. Nail polish. Half-written essays."

Pills, she thinks but doesn't say.

November gives a shaky laugh.

"I can believe that. Her room at home was always awful. Our cleaner used to try to get it into some kind of order once in a while and then April would go raging around the house saying she couldn't find anything. Which was a complete joke because she couldn't find anything anyway — she was always leaving stuff strewn around."

She moves across to the window, looking out at the rooftops of Pelham, past the steeple of the chapel, over the outer wall. In the distance the river is winding its way slowly, glittering in the last failing rays of sun.

"What a beautiful view."

"Isn't it? We were so lucky. And we didn't even know it."

Hannah moves across beside her, rests her hand on her chin.

"You know, one time, I came up the stairs and I heard April screaming in here. I came running into her room —"

"Let me guess," November breaks in, a little dryly. "Another prank?"

"This was before I'd learned to be quite so suspicious. I raced in, and at first I couldn't see April at all. Then I saw it — two pale hands clutching at the windowsill."

"What?" November says with a short laugh, a mix of puzzlement and amusement on her face. "How on earth? We're about four floors up, aren't we?"

"Look down," Hannah says, and November peers over the sill, and then begins to laugh in earnest.

"Okay. I get it. She lowered herself out to stand on that bay window."

"Yup. Except then she couldn't get back in. She wasn't tall enough to get a purchase on the sill, and I wasn't strong enough to pull her up. In the end she had to shinny down the drainpipe."

They both stare out at the rusted drain-pipe that runs down beside the bay window serving the flats below, and November gives a little smile.

"Well, that sounds like April."

There is a moment's silence.

"Do you think —" November starts, and then glances over her shoulder at the closed bedroom door, as if she is looking for someone, worried about being overheard.

"Do I think he did it?" Hannah says. She has lowered her voice, even though it's unlikely Dr. Myers would be able to hear them from outside two thicknesses of wood. And they would have heard him reenter the set.

November nods.

Hannah shrugs.

"I have no idea. Before we came here it felt like the best possibility. But now . . . now I just don't know."

They go out into the main office again and stand there, both looking at the spot where April was found.

"It was there, wasn't it," November says at last. "I recognize it from the photos."

"Yup," Hannah says shortly. Suddenly she very much does not want to be here. The memories are too close, crowding in on her with painful intensity. April, sprawled across the rug, her cheeks still flushed and streaked with the afterglow of the copper makeup.

She sways, steps to try to catch her balance. She feels suddenly as if she might faint.

"Are you okay?" November asks, alarmed at something in her face. "You've gone really pale. Sit down."

Hannah nods and gropes her way to a chair.

There's a knock at the door, and November barks, "Just a minute! Hannah's feeling a bit faint."

"Oh, of course." Dr. Myers's worried voice comes through the wood. "Anything I can do?"

"No, she just needs to sit down for a moment."

"I'm okay," Hannah manages. "I can go."

"He can fuck off," November snarls. "You're sitting here until you feel okay."

That'll be a long time, Hannah wants to say, but she knows what November means. She knows too that it's the truth. She will never really be okay again. Something broke in her the night of April's murder. Something nothing will ever be able to mend — not Will's love or her mother's care, not the baby in her belly. Not the fragile peace she has constructed in Edinburgh.

"I'm okay," she says now, and she stands, carefully, steadying herself on the desk. "There's just — just one more thing."

November watches uneasily as she moves to the other side of the room, to the door to the right of the window, and pushes it open.

Inside it's been transformed into a kind of stationery store, along with boxes of Jiffies, headed paper, envelopes, pens, and branded Pelham maps and leaflets.

She stands, looking, trying to remember. And then a last shaft of evening sun breaks through the autumn clouds and falls through the leaded window, slanting across the old oak boards, and suddenly, there it is — in her old room, with her bed to the right, her old desk across from her. And *she* is there too. Hannah. Not the Hannah of now, but the Hannah of then. The Hannah of before. Young, happy, full of hope and promise, and so unbearably, unutterably innocent of all the horror that life could hold.

She stands for a moment, looking at the shadow of the girl she left behind, bidding her goodbye.

And then she lets the door close, and turns to face the present.

AFTER

"So? How did it go?"

Emily, Hannah remembers with a sigh, is nothing if not direct. They've done the obligatory small talk, ordered and received their food — but now she's getting down to business.

"It went . . . okay, I think?" She turns to November for confirmation, but November is winding ramen around her chopsticks and only shrugs.

"Okay? What does that mean? Did he do it, that's what I'm asking."

Hannah cannot suppress a flinch, and even Emily has the grace to look abashed.

"Sorry. That was a bit brutal. But isn't that why you're here? Did he explain anything? Did he say why he didn't come out to help?"

"He did," November says. She sucks noodles into her mouth, then swallows. "He wasn't there."

"What?"

"That's his story, he wasn't there. That's why he didn't hear anything, why he didn't come out to help, why he was never called to give evidence in court. He was presenting at a conference in Cambridge and stayed the night there. He didn't see or hear anything."

"Is that true?" Emily demands. She looks from November to Hannah, as if they are the ones covering up for Dr. Myers. "I mean, it's a bit too convenient for him, don't you think?"

"I have no idea," Hannah says, a little wearily. "But it's what he said, when November asked him if he could tell us anything about that night. And it would have been pretty easy to check at the time, so if the police accepted it, I would imagine yes, it's true."

"So you're back at square one?" Emily says.

"Maybe," Hannah says.

"So does that mean that maybe you're *not* back at square one? That you found something out?"

"It just means maybe," Hannah says, a little more acidly this time. She is regretting her choice of words now. The truth is that she is not sure if they *are* back at square one. Something has been gnawing at her since her conversation in the set with November, something November made her see with fresh eyes. But she's not sure she wants to share it with Emily. Not yet — not while she's still figuring out the implications.

In the cab back to the hotel, November turns to Hannah.

"Are you . . . okay?"

"How do you mean?" Hannah shifts in her seat. She can't get comfortable. The seat belt is cutting into her bump and her spine aches from the fashionable backless benches in the restaurant. "Is this about me saying I didn't want coffee? I was just tired, that's all."

"I didn't mean that. It was the way you went quiet halfway through the meal. I wondered if something had happened."

"Shit." Hannah bites her lip. "Was it that obvious?"

"It was a bit." November looks awkward. "I mean, Emily started grilling you about Dr. Myers and you . . . you just clammed up. Did I miss something? I mean, that *was* what we went there to find out, wasn't it? It wasn't like she was asking anything we hadn't been thinking."

"No," Hannah says. She rubs her face.

What she said to November about feeling tired was an understatement.

"Are you worrying that Myers's alibi doesn't hold up?" November asks anxiously. "I was thinking about that earlier — I mean, he could have come back. After establishing his alibi at the conference."

Hannah shakes her head.

"I really don't think so. I mean, when? The porters would have seen him coming through the main gates, and if he'd used one of the unmanned ones, he would have had to swipe in, and his Bod card would have been recorded. I mean . . ." Something strikes her for the first time. "I guess . . . there's always the possibility he climbed over that gap in the wall."

"A gap in the wall?" November sounds puzzled, and Hannah realizes that of course she wouldn't know any of this. It's strange, she's so like April, and she clearly knows so much about their friendships and their time at Pelham, that it's hard for Hannah to remember that she was never actually there, that this is all just secondhand information to her.

"Pelham was — is — completely walled," she explains. "And mostly it's pretty secure, but there was this one place behind Cloade's where you could climb over. It was on the route you'd take back from the station. But I can't see Myers doing that. That was something the students did to avoid going the long way round after the gates were locked, not a member of staff on his way back from a conference."

"So . . . what, then?" November says diffidently. She looks uncomfortable — like she is trying not to pry but is genuinely worried about Hannah's silence.

Hannah's phone beeps and she glances down at it in her lap. It's from Will. *How did it go? Can you talk?*

"Hang on," she says to November, "it's Will, I need to take this, he's been worried."

She dials him back, and he picks up on the first ring.

"Hey, are you okay? How was it?"

"I'm fine. I'm in the cab back to the hotel with November so I won't talk for too long, but the meeting was . . . I mean, he was nice. Helpful." She knows it sounds like she's reviewing a hotel receptionist, but she doesn't know how else to put it. "I don't think it was him, Will."

"What do you mean?" Will's voice is uneasy on the other end. "How can you tell?"

"He wasn't there — November asked him outright what he'd seen, and he said he was away that evening, that was why he was never called to give evidence or anything. I'm assuming the police would check up on something like that, so I'm guessing it's true?"

There's a long silence at the other end of the line, as if Will is thinking about something.

"Will?"

There's another silence. Then Will clears his throat.

"I'm sure you're right. If he's got an alibi, he's got an alibi. So . . . you're coming home?"

"Yes."

"Great." The relief in his voice is unmistakable. "I'm glad. I know you wanted to do this, but I'm glad it's over and you've got your worries out of your system."

Now it's Hannah's turn to fall silent. Will waits for her to respond and then says, a little more sharply.

"Hannah? It *is* over, isn't it?"

"I —" Hannah says. She's not sure what she's going to say. She only knows that she can't, *won't* lie to Will. But the truth is, she's not sure it is over. That realization that came to her on the tour is preying more and more on her mind. She just needs some time to *think,* to figure out what it means.

"Hannah . . ." Will says now, and she can hear the note of warning in his voice, and also the frustration. "Love — this is ridiculous. Please, please, *please* just leave it. You've done enough poking around, this is getting stupid. You're not some kind of pregnant Miss Marple."

He probably means the last words for a note of levity, trying to soften his obvious anxious irritation, but it hits a false note — it makes him sound glib, dismissive, and Hannah, already tense, feels her hackles rise.

"I'm glad you find April's death so funny."

She knows the words are unfair as soon as she says them, but they're out, and she can't take them back.

"Hannah, that's *not* what I was saying and you know it," Will says, his voice deliberately even. "Look, I think I've been pretty reasonable —"

It's that tone again. That autocratic, lord-of-the-manor, *I'm the boss here* tone.

"Pretty reasonable?" She strives to keep the sarcasm out of her voice, but it's there. "Pretty *reasonable*? Like, giving me permission to go *poking around,* is that what you mean? How very *reasonable* of you."

"Hannah," he says, and now she can tell his temper is really frayed, and that he's holding on to the threadbare edges as hard as he can, his voice brittle with the effort. "You knew I didn't want you to go. You're six months pregnant for fuck's sake, you shouldn't be digging up some cold case that no one cares about —"

"No one cares?" she cries, so that November and the taxi driver look at her in surprise. "If April's killer is walking free then *I* care, Will, and I can't believe that you don't —"

"How dare you," Will shouts back now, loud enough that she has to hold the phone away from her ear. "How fucking dare you. I care, I care just as much as you, but the fact that I don't want my pregnant wife putting our unborn —"

She hangs up.

Her hands are shaking. Her heart is thumping so hard in her chest that she feels like she might be sick.

Think of the baby. Think of the baby.

"Hannah?" November says tentatively. "Hannah? Are you okay?"

"No. No, I'm not," Hannah says harshly. Her fists are clenched. She has never, *never* been so angry at Will. At *Will.*

This is Will, she reminds herself. Will, who has loved her, waited for her, saved her from herself in so many ways since they were both just teenagers themselves.

And right now she *hates* him.

"What happened?"

"He wants me to pretend there's nothing wrong," she says shortly. "And I can't. I wish I could but —" And then, realizing they are almost at the hotel, she says to the taxi driver, "Sorry, can you stop at that supermarket? I need to grab something."

The driver pulls up outside a Tesco Metro and Hannah gets out. Her pulse is still racing, but she knows it will do her good to stretch her legs for a moment, walk off some of her anger, stretch her aching back. November gets out after her, her face worried.

"Hannah?"

"I just need to get some Gaviscon. I've got heartburn."

"Okay," says November, following her into the almost painful brightness of the little store. "But what did you mean, you can't pretend nothing's wrong?"

"I don't know," Hannah says. She grabs a basket and begins to walk the aisles, scanning for the pharmaceutical section. "I just — it was when we were in April's room. I realized something. Something that made me think that perhaps . . ." She swallows. "Perhaps we'd all been looking at this the wrong way."

"What do you mean?"

"It was when we were leaning out of the window," Hannah says. She's found the Gaviscon now, a box of pills rather than the liquid she's used to, but it will have to do. She checks the label. Suitable for pregnancy. "I'd forgotten that April climbed down one time."

"Yes, you told me," November says, looking puzzled. "But I don't see —"

Then she halts in her tracks, in the middle of the aisle. Her eyes are wide under the fluorescent lights.

"Wait, maybe I do. Are you thinking someone could have —"

She stops, as if she doesn't want to say it.

"Someone could have killed April, and then climbed out the window," Hannah finishes for her. She pays for the Gaviscon at a self-service till and then turns to face November. "We've all been focusing on the fact that no one could have got into the building after Neville left. But that's not the issue. The issue is that no one could have got *out.* Or so we assumed. If Neville's last sighting of April alive was correct, then Hugh and I had the staircase in view the whole time. But what if the killer didn't use the stairs? What if he — or she — climbed out the window?"

530

"Hang on," November says. They are walking to the exit now, and she runs her hands through her short hair, as if trying to cudgel her brains into action. "If someone was already in the set when Neville went up there, he would have seen them."

"Not if whoever it was stayed in April's bedroom. I've been thinking about this all evening — trying to piece it together, and it all fits. By Neville's own account he never went farther than the living room."

"So you're saying —"

"I'm saying someone went up there to see April, probably with the intention of killing her. It wasn't a spur-of-the-moment, crime-of-passion thing, or the students below would have heard an argument. It must have been planned, someone waiting for their chance to surprise her. So whoever it was lulled her into a false sense of security, and then while they were talking, Neville knocked. April went out to talk to him, and the killer stayed in the bedroom. Then they came out and killed her as soon as Neville shut the door."

"But they couldn't have known Neville would come up . . ." November says slowly. Hannah shakes her head.

"No, I don't think that part was planned. I think it was just the killer's good luck that

Neville gave them the perfect alibi."

"The timing would work . . ." They have reached the taxi and November opens the door and slides back inside. Her face, golden in the sulfurous yellow of the street-lamp, is troubled. "It would make sense of Neville's story, and it would explain why you never saw anyone coming out after him. But . . . wait, how would whoever it was know not to take the stairs? They had no way of knowing you were waiting at the bottom."

"I've been thinking about that," Hannah says. She feels more than a little sick, and it has as much to do with what she is about to say as it does with the aftermath of her argument with Will. "And if I'm right, if the killer *did* escape down the drainpipe, then I think what must have happened is this: The killer knew they couldn't afford to be seen coming down the stairs — so they would have waited until Neville was well clear to leave. They wouldn't want to bump into him in the quad if he was still hanging around. So whoever it was, they probably killed April, then hung around by the window to check Neville was gone. By the time Neville came out of the building —"

"By that time, they would have seen you crossing the quad," November finishes. Her face is pale. "Shit. You mean they saw you coming. They *knew* you'd be coming up the stairs, so they had no choice but to escape through the window."

"I think so. The only other possibility is that they heard me coming up the stairs as they were finishing the" — she swallows, the word sticking in her throat — "finishing the job."

"Oh my God." November closes her eyes. The beam of a streetlamp passes over her face as they drive beneath it, illuminating the shape of her skull with ghostly beauty. In the half-light she looks *so* like April that Hannah almost cannot bear it. For a moment it is as if April has come back to haunt her with the specter of the mistakes she made — except that April has never left her. The voice in the crowd. The blond head weaving down a busy street. April has always been here, with her, trying to make her see.

I'm sorry, April, she thinks. *I'm sorry I failed you.*

"So . . . who then?" November whispers. The driver is not looking round at them, but they are both conscious that in spite of the plexiglass screen, he could be listening. *Guess who I had in the back of my cab . . .* "It could have been anyone, then . . . right?"

"Someone with a motive," Hannah says,

ticking the list off on her fingers. "And someone that April trusted." The sick feeling is back. "It must have been someone she knew well. *That's* always been an unanswerable problem with the case against Neville. April hated him. There's no way she would have let him come anywhere near her without a struggle. But a friend? That's different. I mean, not Hugh — because I was with him outside the building. And I'm pretty sure it couldn't have been Ryan. He was still in the bar when we left, although I guess it's theoretically possible that he could have pelted it round the long way and got to New Quad before us. But . . ."

She stops.

"But it could have been Emily," November says with sudden, dawning comprehension. "*That's* why you went so quiet over dinner."

Hannah feels something twist inside her like a knife. Because it's true, and hearing it out loud makes it suddenly and sickeningly real. That *is* what she was thinking. She was sitting there working things out in her head, realizing that Emily's alibi is the shakiest of them all. Yes, she was in the library. But there was absolutely nothing to stop her from slipping through the turnstile without swiping out, climbing the stairs to April's room, sitting there with her, talking, laughing, maybe even poking fun at herself over the A-level prank — and then when Neville came up, providing the perfect fall guy, strangling April before sliding down the drainpipe and returning to her seat in the reading room.

I can't believe it, she wants to protest, and it's true too, except . . . that a little part of her can. Maybe several parts in fact. The part that knows that April had spent all year fucking Emily's boyfriend. The part that recoiled when Hugh told her about the cruel trick with the A-level letter. And most of all, the part of her that remembers walking under the cloisters with Emily and Ryan on a cold November night, and hearing Emily hiss, *If she tries any of that shit with me, I will* end *her.*

The venom in Emily's voice — that was real. It has stayed with Hannah for more than ten years. And even now it makes her shiver.

"It could have been plenty of other people," she says now, trying to persuade herself as much as November. "April had pranked a lot of people. It could have been someone from another college entirely. It could have been —" The idea comes to her, and she clutches at it with a barely concealed desperation. "It could have been whoever was supplying her with the dextroamphetamine. A drug deal gone bad."

This is all true.

But what November said is truer.

It *could* have been Emily. She has always had motive. And now she has opportunity.

"Hannah," November says, and her voice is warning. "Hannah, please, don't do *anything* about this until you've spoken to the police."

"I won't," Hannah says, a little impatiently. "I'm not stupid."

"I mean it — if this is right — if you tell *anyone* —"

"I said, I'm not stupid. I'll phone them up tomorrow, as soon as I'm back in Edinburgh."

"Okay," November says. She looks at Hannah critically, as if she's appraising Hannah's strength, if it came to a fight. She looks worried.

"Why didn't you say anything to Will?" she asks now, and Hannah feels a sudden tightness in her throat.

"Because he won't listen," she says. "I've tried — I've tried over and over to tell him that there's something wrong about that night, something that I'm not seeing, can't remember — but he won't listen, he just wants me to shut up, pretend it's all fine."

She shuts her eyes. It is the worst feeling in the world, to be afraid — and to have the person you love tell you that it's all in your head.

"Look, I don't know him," November says softly, "but . . . I feel like if you love him, he must be a good guy?"

"He is," Hannah says. It feels as if something is lodged at the back of her throat, hurting her.

"He's frightened for you. He lost one person he loved, much too young. I can see why he doesn't want to lose another."

"I know," Hannah whispers. "I know."

She puts her hand up to the corner of her eye and angrily brushes away the moisture prickling there, furious at her body for betraying her. She doesn't want to be that woman — that pregnant woman who bursts into tears at the drop of a hat. She wants to be strong, logical, analytical — but she doesn't feel like any of those right now.

"I could be wrong," she says, forcing the words out as levelly as she can, and November nods, but the concern doesn't leave her face. Hannah *could* be wrong. But if she's not, there is a killer out there. Someone April trusted. Maybe even someone April *loved.*

And that idea makes Hannah very frightened indeed.

AFTER

That night, Hannah can't sleep. Again. It's not just the heartburn, though the Gaviscon pills aren't working as well as the liquid does, and have left a horrible chalky residue on her teeth. It's not just the baby, who seems to have woken up as soon as she lay down and is even now shifting and wriggling and turning like a cat trying to get comfortable on a strange bed.

It's everything.

It's her own fears. It's her argument with Will. It's Emily.

It's Emily.

Oh God, it *can't* be Emily. Can it?

A sickness is churning inside her as she thinks of the dinner they spent together tonight, Emily chatting away, glancing at Hannah with concern as she sat there silently picking at her ramen.

Had she guessed? Does she know what Hannah is thinking? Is she lying awake even now at her house across town trying to figure out what Hannah knows and what has changed since last night?

As Hannah reaches for her phone — 1:47 a.m., the numbers gleam bright in the dim light of the hotel room — she is swamped by an almost overwhelming urge to call Emily, *talk* to her. Because it can't be true. She can't be thinking this about her old friend.

But the alternatives are just as bad. Could Ryan have left the bar after them and run the long way round, around the other side of the chapel? It is *just* possible. He could even have been going up the stairs when Neville was coming down, and ducked into a bathroom to avoid being seen.

Fuck. *Fuck.* Is this really all she has accomplished? She wanted to bring a killer to justice, but instead all she's done is drag two of her oldest friends into this.

Her phone is still in her hand, and now it lights up with a notification. It's an email and she opens it, wondering for a minute if it's Emily, messaging her with some strange telepathy.

It's not. It's someone called Lynn Bishop, subject line *Hello Hannah!*

Hi Hannah, hope you're well! I'm a journalist with the Evening Mail. Following John

Neville's death, we're doing a retrospective on April's case and would love to speak to you about how it feels to have finally laid those demons to —

She doesn't even transfer that one to Requests. She deletes it, feeling sick to her stomach. It's not just the timing — it's everything. The faux chumminess. The exclamation point. And using "April" — like they know her, like she's a mate or a girl they went to school with, when in reality they have no idea what she was really like. "April" — when John Neville gets the dignity of his full name.

As Hannah shuts down her phone and lies staring into the dark she feels a surge of anger so strong it almost scares her. How dare they — the journalists, the public, the vultures who have picked over this case for years like they care, like they have a *right* to the truth just as much as Hannah does. They've stripped April of her identity, of her uniqueness, of everything that made her real and compelling and fascinating — they've reduced her to a cardboard cutout of a girl and a series of Instagram pictures. The perfect victim, in fact.

And as for the rest of the email — "laid those demons to rest"? She would be laughing if she didn't feel so bitter. She has never felt more haunted — by what happened to April, and by what she, Hannah, may have done to an innocent man. And now haunted too by what she's doing to her old friends — to Emily and to Ryan, who have suffered enough already. They've lived through April's murder — is she really going to cast suspicion on them both by speaking up? But if she *doesn't* . . .

She rolls over, faces the wall, fighting the urge to cover her face with her hands. She has a sudden, out-of-character urge for a drink — but that is out of the question.

She turns onto her back, puts her forearm over her eyes, shutting out the light filtering in from the street, trying to count her blessings. At least Hugh is out of it. And Will, far away at his mother's house. Thank God. Thank *God* he was never a suspect. Geraint's words to November whisper treacherously in her ear: *Strangulation typically points to a domestic murder, usually a crime of passion.* Hannah knows what he was trying to say — what that slippery euphemism *domestic* really means. It means a partner. It means that when strangulation is involved, it's usually a man killing his wife or girlfriend.

All the mud Hannah has stirred up would

look very, very bad for Will, if it weren't for his alibi. April was cheating on Will. April was *pregnant,* possibly by another man. If the press wanted motives, she's serving up a plethora, right here on a gilded plate. And they all point to her own husband.

If Will had not been out of college that night, things would have been pretty grim for him when April died, and they would be looking even grimmer right now.

But thank God he was not there.

So why can't she sleep?

She opens her eyes and turns on her phone again. 2:01. She *has* to get some sleep. But the baby twists and turns inside her, and suddenly she wishes, powerfully, painfully, that Will were here. Her anger has evaporated, and now she can't bear the way they left it.

She opens up WhatsApp and finds his last message. *How did it go? Can you talk?*

She feels a sudden rush of guilt. Her words in the taxi come back to her. *I'm glad you find April's death so funny . . . I care, Will, and I can't believe that you don't.*

Not just unfair, but bitterly, vilely so. For Will does care — she has always known that. She has watched him building up his shell of defense around himself, listened to him crying out in the night, dreaming of

April. She has seen his face as the news reports come on, watched him trying to protect the wounds left by what happened, winced as every newspaper article and request for comment reopened them.

He cares, just as much as she does. He loved April, and she knows it. And yes, perhaps he hated her too, but so did Hannah sometimes — she can admit it now, though it took many years.

They were kids. Just kids.

I'm sorry, she types out, knowing that her text might wake him but unable to wait. *I'm sorry I was such a bitch. The things I said — they were awful. I love you. See you tomorrow? xxx*

There is a moment's pause and she sees *Typing . . .* flash up at the top of the message. It shows . . . and then goes away. Then comes up again . . . then disappears. What is he doing? Is he typing the world's longest message? Or is he trying to say something, and deleting it, and then typing it again, and then deleting it again?

Typing . . .
Typing . . .
Pause.
Typing . . .

It goes away again, this time for so long that her screen goes dark and she has to unlock her phone again. And then at last a message comes through.

I'm sorry too. I love you.

And that's it.

Whatever he had been going to say, he has thought better of it.

What was it? *You're right, you were a complete bitch, how dare you say that stuff to me.*

Or, *If you weren't pregnant with my child I would be considering our future.*

Or, *What's wrong with you, Hannah?*

Or maybe none of that? Maybe something completely different. *I'm sorry. It was my fault too. Neville's death has screwed me up.*

She wants to text him back, demand to know what he was thinking of telling her, what he's keeping from her.

Her mind starts running.

There's something I've been hiding.

I've met someone.

I couldn't work out how to tell you.

I want a fresh start.

I don't love you anymore.

No, no, no, no, no! She has to sit up at that, her heart racing in her chest, the baby flip-flopping inside her, jolted awake by her surge of adrenaline.

No, this is completely irrational. It's the paranoia of two-in-the-morning insomnia.

She loves Will. He loves her.

He's not keeping any secrets from her — he probably just couldn't work out how to phrase his apology.

Now she realizes, she forgot to take her bedtime blood pressure pill. She stands and hobbles to the bathroom, a stiffness in her ankles and hips that is increasing ever since she became pregnant — ligaments loosening for the birth, her joints creaking in sympathy.

In the bathroom she turns on the light, blinking at the brightness, and stares at herself in the mirror. Her face is puffy with tiredness, her is hair tousled and wild, and there are dark rings beneath her eyes.

She thinks of Will, of his lips against the top of her head as he was leaving for work. Of his whispered words. *Please. Please.*

She knows what he wanted to say. *Please, Hannah, don't do this.*

She should leave this alone. She knows it. For Will's sake. For the baby's sake.

But for her own sake, and for April's, she cannot. She cannot. She *has* to be sure. If her evidence put an innocent man in jail she *has* to know. She can't live like this.

"I'm sorry," she whispers, to the baby in her belly, to Will's ghost, hanging over her. "I'm so sorry."

She downs the pill with a gulp of water and looks again at her reflection in the mirror. The woman who stares back at her looks exhausted, but also grimly determined. Not the frightened girl of ten years before, terrified and full of an obscure guilt and shame at what had happened, as if it had been as much *her* fault as Neville's.

Now she knows — it was not her fault. And maybe it wasn't even Neville's.

And she is not afraid anymore.

She has stopped running from the monsters. She has turned to face them.

She wants the truth.

AFTER

"Coffee?"

Hannah is staring out the window, thinking, when the question comes, and at first she doesn't hear it.

"Coffee, madam?"

She turns to see a uniformed attendant standing beside her, braced in the narrow aisle, holding out a silver pot. There's a trolley behind her, rocking as the train goes over a crossing.

"Oh, sorry, I was in a dream. No thank you, I've had enough caffeine already today."

"I've got decaf," the woman offers. "It's all complimentary." But Hannah shakes her head. She knows what train coffee will be like — weak instant with powdered milk in little sachets.

"No, thanks, honestly. I'll —" She racks her brains to try to think of a way to accept this kind woman's hospitality. "I'll take a bottle of water, if you have one?"

"Still or sparkling?"

"Still, please."

She is twisting off the cap when her phone rings, and glancing at the screen she sees it's Hugh. The name gives her a slight jolt of surprise. What would Hugh be phoning about?

"Hugh!" It seems rude to open with *Why are you calling,* so she settles for "How are you?"

"Good." Hugh's deep, rather drawling voice comes down the line, instantly distinctive. "How are you? How was Oxford?"

Hannah frowns. Did Will tell him about the visit?

"It was . . . um . . . confusing," she says. She doesn't want to talk about it here, in front of the other passengers, who are mostly attempting to work or sleep. "I'm still trying to figure out how I feel about it all. But . . . I think we can rule Myers out. He wasn't there. He was at a conference."

"He wasn't there? But Will said you and April's sister had an arrangement to see him?"

"No, I mean he wasn't there that night — you know —" She glances over her shoulder. "Back then. When it happened. He was out of college."

"Oh!" Hugh says. He sounds surprised, and a little disappointed. "So . . . back to Neville, then?"

"Maybe. I'm not sure. I realized . . ." She lowers her voice, looks up and down the carriage again. No one is watching her. "I realized something while I was there, Hugh. Someone . . . someone could have been in the room." She is almost whispering now, trying not to use any words that would make her fellow passengers' ears prick up. She doesn't want to say *Pelham* or *April* or *murder.* "While we were coming up the stairs. They could have shinnied down the drainpipe."

"What are you saying?" Hugh's voice is uneasy. Hannah makes up her mind and then stands up.

"Hang on, I'm on a train, I'm going to go out into the corridor. Just a sec."

There is a pause as she maneuvers out of the narrow gap between the seat and the table, makes her way down the aisle, and opens the door into the little foyer between the carriages. It's empty, the window slightly open so that the rushing sound of the air covers their conversation.

"Sorry, I wanted to get out of the carriage. I'm not sure what I'm trying to say. But Hugh, we always assumed that the fact that you and I were watching the bottom of the stairs meant no one else could be involved. What if that's not true?"

There is a long silence. Hannah can almost hear Hugh's brain ticking, realizing what she's saying, realizing what this means. She's not sure what she's expecting him to say, but when he does speak, he sounds . . . she can't quite put her finger on it. Alarmed, almost.

"Who have you told about this?"

"Just April's sister, November. She was there. I — I didn't tell Emily. I couldn't. I —"

She can't bring herself to say the words — *I was too afraid.*

"I'm going to speak to the police when I get back," she finishes at last.

"Hannah, please be really, really careful about this," Hugh says. "I think you should seriously consider —"

There's a silence, as if he's trying to figure out how to say what he wants to say, as if he can't find a way of putting it into words.

"What?" Hannah asks at last. "Are you saying I *shouldn't* go to the police? I think it's the safest thing, don't you? It's better to get this knowledge out in the open, surely?"

"I'm just . . ." Hugh stops. He sounds almost . . . panicked. It's very unlike Hugh, who makes a point of being deliberately urbane and unruffled.

"Hugh, what?" Something in his voice has alarmed Hannah, and now she finds herself speaking more sharply than she had intended. "What is it? Just say it."

"You have to be prepared for what might happen if you keep stirring this. For who might . . . get hurt."

"What do you mean *who*?" Hannah says. She is suddenly uneasy. "You mean me?"

"Not exactly . . . Jesus — oh fuck, this is hard!" He sounds distraught, Hannah realizes. There's a catch in his voice, something out of proportion to any worry about her digging around in the past. What on earth is going on?

"Hugh, do you know something I don't?"

"I don't *know* anything but I just — I just —"

"Hugh, just tell me!" Hannah cries. Then she takes a deep breath. "Look, sorry, I didn't mean to shout, but please, you're scaring me, what are you trying to say?"

There is a long, long silence. So long that Hannah looks at her screen to check that they're still connected, that the train hasn't swept her into a dead spot. But the line is still open. Hugh is still there. And then he speaks.

"I heard something, that morning, when I got back to my room."

"What do you mean you heard something? Someone told you something?"

"No, through the wall. I *heard* something. Some*one.* Moving around."

For a minute a surge of irritation flushes through Hannah. It's like he's speaking in code, beating around the bush, expecting her to understand what he's saying when she has no idea. What does he mean he heard someone? And through what wall?

"You mean you heard someone in the room next to yours?"

"Yes," Hugh says, and his voice is almost vibrating with urgency. It's as if he's begging her to understand what he is saying without forcing him to say it. "At two a.m. Through the *wall.*"

And then she understands. Everything goes cold, a prickling sensation running up and down her spine like ice water. She has to hold on to the grab rail beside the door.

She can hear Hugh saying something on the other end of the phone, but she can't make out the words through the rushing in her ears.

"Hannah?" she hears, as if from very far away. "Hannah, are you all right? Say something?"

"I'm okay," she manages, though her voice is cracked and strangled, and she can barely form the words. Her hand holding the phone feels numb and cold, like a mannequin's, stiff and plastic. "I'm . . . thank you, Hugh. I have to go."

And then she hangs up.

She sits there, staring out the window at the rushing countryside, feeling the chill horror trickling through her veins.

She wants to wail. *No, no, no, no, no.*

But she cannot. She can't say anything. She knows why Hugh didn't want to spell this out. She knows what he wanted to say but couldn't bear to put into words.

She knows why he warned her to be prepared for what might happen.

For that night, the night that April was murdered, when he finally went back to his room in Cloade's at two in the morning, he heard someone through the wall, his neighbor, walking around.

But Hugh was on the end of the block. He only had one neighbor. And that neighbor . . . that neighbor was Will.

After

By the time the train draws into Edinburgh, Hannah has almost convinced herself that Hugh is wrong. Or perhaps she misunderstood him.

It's not possible that Will was in college that night. To begin with, he would have been spotted. The side gates closed at 9:00 p.m., and the main gate was shut at 11:00, so he would have had to knock and be admitted by a porter. And okay, yes, he could have climbed the wall, just as she did so many years ago, but it would have been child's play for the police to break an alibi resting on such a fragile lie.

And second, second, she just can't believe that he could have kept something like this secret for over ten years. Not just from the police but from his family, from the college, from *her*.

Someone would have seen him, at breakfast when he was supposed to be in Somerset. On the train when he was supposed to be at home.

Maybe someone did see him, a little voice whispers in her head. *Or heard him, at least. Maybe that someone was Hugh.*

No, it's not possible. It's *not* possible.

But then she thinks of Will. Of his voice on the phone yesterday, uncertain, hesitant, as if trying to convince himself. *I'm sure you're right. If he's got an alibi, he's got an alibi.*

He was talking about Myers, about the police assumption that the conference put him out of the picture. But now Hannah can't help but wonder what that long pause really meant. Was he trying to find a way to tell her something that he has never been able to confess?

She remembers his endless, halting *Typing . . . Typing . . .* on WhatsApp last night. Was this what Will was trying and failing to find a way to tell her?

She is still turning the matter over and over in her head as the doors open and passengers begin to spill out onto the platform. She's so wrapped up in her thoughts as she exits the barrier and begins dragging her case towards the ramp that she doesn't even hear the voice calling her name at first.

"Hannah . . . *Hannah!*"

Somehow that last one gets through and she stops, looking around to see if it's directed at her, or just someone calling their kid — though the voice is familiar. It sounds like — but no. That's not possible. It sounds like — but no. That's not possible. It sounds like —

She turns. They come face-to-face, almost slamming into each other, and he steadies her with his hands.

"Will!"

"Surprise!" he says, beaming. "Thought I'd pick you up. Though bloody hell, you're a hard woman to stop. You were charging up that ramp like a cricketer going in to bowl. Didn't you hear me bellowing?"

"I'm sorry —" She feels winded, as if they really had collided. "I didn't — I was thinking about something — I — It's nice to see you!"

Nice to see you? She feels like kicking herself. *Nice to see you* is what you say to a colleague you bump into at an art gallery, not your husband after a trip away.

"I missed you," Will says, and he bends and kisses her, his stubble prickling her lips. Hannah feels something twist inside her — not just the baby, but something else, a confusing, contradictory maelstrom of emotions. She wants to return Will's kiss, burrow into his arms — and she wants to pull away until she figures out how she feels about all this. How can both be true? How can she both love this man and be seriously considering that he may have been lying to her for ten years?

She should trust him. He's her *husband.*

She *does* trust him.

So why isn't she telling him about the bay window and the drainpipe?

Meanwhile, Will is talking — asking about her trip, asking about Emily, November, Dr. Myers.

"Sounds like it was something you needed to do for your own peace of mind, but it's all wrapped up now?" he's saying, and her voice is saying *Yes,* while her mind is screaming *Why are you so keen for me to put a lid on this? Is it because you're afraid of what I might find?*

"You're very quiet," he says at last, as she fails to reply to yet another remark. "Are you okay?"

"I'm sorry." Hannah passes a hand over her forehead. "I — I — yes, I'm fine. I'm just *really* tired. I don't know what it is, I feel like I've been hit by a truck the last few days."

"Well, you're, what, nearly twenty-five weeks?" Will says. He kisses the top of her head affectionately. "Six months. Nearly third trimester!"

"Third trimester." Hannah weighs the words in her mouth, momentarily diverted from her round-and-round about April, into a realization that Will's right. "Third trimester, bloody hell. We're nearly there, Will."

"We nearly are." He beams down at her, and as he does, the baby gives a great kick, the strongest she's felt yet, so hard that she stops in her tracks. "What is it? Did you forget something?"

"No, the baby —" She puts her hand to the side of the bump, and to her astonishment, there it is. A long, distinct push against her palm, for all the world as if the baby is trying to force its way out through her skin, like the scene from *Alien.* "Oh my God, Will, quick."

Will looks bewildered, uncomprehending, until she grabs his hand and holds it flat against the side of her distended belly, waiting, waiting — and there it comes again. She feels it at the same time as his face lights up.

"Holy mother of God." Will's voice is awed. "Was that it? Was that *him*?"

"It was. It was *our* baby." She is beaming, the smile so wide it feels like it's splitting her face, she can't help herself. They are standing in the middle of the ramp up from the concourse, people streaming past, banging her case with their suitcases and tutting at the obstacle she and Will are forming, but she doesn't care. She doesn't care about anything in that moment, anything apart from the feel of Will's palm, hot against her taut skin, and the movement of their child inside her.

"Oh my God," Will says again, very slowly, and his expression is a mixture of shock and delight. "Will he do it again?"

"Excuse me," a woman in a business suit says acidly, pushing past with unnecessary force. "Could you move aside?"

"I don't know." Hannah picks up the case, Will drops his palm from where it was pressed against her stomach and takes the handle from her, and the two of them start moving again, up the ramp. "I think he's stopped now. But it's not going to be the last time. I can't believe you felt it!"

"You can't believe it? *I* can't believe it." He's smiling, a great huge smile that crinkles the skin of his cheeks with pure elation. "Our baby. Our baby, Hannah! We're having a baby!"

"I know," she says, grinning back. She puts an arm around him, squeezing him so tight that he almost stumbles, their legs banging against each other, and she feels her heart swell with love for him. And the strangeness, the uncertainty she felt all the way up to Edinburgh is gone, completely gone. How could she have doubted him? How could she have doubted *herself,* her own judgment? This is *Will.* The man she loves — has loved for more than ten years. The man she knows like she knows her own skin.

"I love you," she says, at the same time as he says, "Curry for supper?" and they both laugh, and suddenly everything is all right again. He is her Will. And Oxford is a long way away.

"Curry for supper," she agrees. "And I'll even let you have a beer."

"I'm drinking for three now," he says with a grin, and then he squeezes her back, and she feels her heart overflow.

AFTER

That night Hannah sleeps well — better than she has for ages. She doesn't wake up with the baby pressing on her bladder and then toss and turn for hours with a mixture of leg cramps and heartburn. Instead she goes to bed at ten, falls asleep, and stays that way for eight solid hours.

At 6:00 a.m., something wakes her. She's not sure what — perhaps the central heating coming on. Their boiler is old and often makes strange banging sounds when starting up from cold. Or maybe the milkman in the mews outside, the bottles jingling as his wheels rumble over the cobbles.

Whatever it is, it jolts her fully awake, and she can't get back to sleep.

After a quarter of an hour of lying there, trying to ignore her increasingly pressing need to pee, she gives up and swings her legs out of bed. It's a chilly morning, still dark outside, and she can almost feel the coming of winter in the air as she pads through to the bathroom, her bare feet shrinking from the cold tiles.

After, she makes a cup of tea and brings it back to bed, scootching her cold feet down under the duvet to warm up beside Will's body. He is still asleep, and looking at him now, at his face, unguarded and heartbreakingly vulnerable, she can't believe that she seriously considered Hugh's implication last night. There has got to be some misunderstanding, some innocent explanation. Cloade's was modern, well insulated, not like the old buildings in the rest of the college. A faint, muffled sound, traveling through the concrete . . . what does that prove? It's not like Hugh actually *saw* Will.

And yet . . . Hugh is Will's best friend, and the memory of the anguish in his voice makes Hannah shiver for a moment, in spite of the warmth of the bed. Would he really have said what he did if he wasn't sure?

She needs someone who can back up Will's story, reassure her that he left Somerset when he said he did. But who? Will's sister wasn't there that weekend, as far as she knows; his mother is undergoing chemotherapy for the third time, and his father's memory is increasingly shaky. She can hardly ring up this frail, aging couple and demand to know what time their son left their house one weekend more than a decade ago. Even if one of them remembered, she would never know for sure if they were telling the truth or protecting Will.

The coldness settles around her heart as she realizes — the only person who will ever truly be able to tell her the truth . . . is Will.

For a moment she fantasizes about waking him up and asking him — his voice saying firmly, *This is ridiculous. I came back Sunday afternoon, you know I did.*

November's words come back to her, filled with concern: *Please, don't do* anything *about this until you've spoken to the police.*

But that was what Hugh was trying to tell her. He was trying to warn her that once she spoke to the police, she would be opening a can of worms she'd be unable to shut.

Fuck. *Fuck.*

She puts the cup down on the bedside table, harder than she meant, so that the tea slops over and the wood makes a loud *thunk.*

And beside her, Will stirs.

"What time is it?"

His voice is sleepy, loving, and she feels her muscles instantly uncoil, as if his very presence is all she needed to chase away the doubts. Her fears, so real in the silence of a few minutes ago, disappear, like she's a child turning on the light after a nightmare.

"Six thirty," she whispers, and he groans and slides his arm over what used to be her waist, cradling her bump.

"Six thirty? You're shitting me. On a weekend? Couldn't you sleep?"

"It's good practice," she says, laughing. "For when the baby comes."

She doesn't want to say, *I couldn't sleep. I couldn't sleep because I was spiraling into a stupid, dark fantasy that you were April's killer.* Now, with Will's arm around her, the words seem absurd.

"Well, let's practice something else," he murmurs, his lips warm and soft against the ticklish skin of her side. And Hannah slides down beneath the duvet and somehow the heat, and the comfort, and the reassuring feel of Will's skin against hers succeed in driving out the demons . . . for a while, at least.

Afterwards, Will makes coffee for them both, and Hannah yawns and stretches, working out the kinks the long train journey yesterday left in her spine and hips.

"What do you fancy for breakfast?" Will calls through from the other room.

"What have we got?"

565

She hears the sound of the fridge opening.

"Um . . . nothing, basically."

"I could murder a bacon sandwich," Hannah says. "I had an amazing one at the hotel in Oxford, and ever since then I've had this craving for another."

Will comes into the bedroom, holding her coffee.

"I'll go to the shop."

"You don't have to do that," Hannah says, taking the coffee. "I was only thinking aloud."

"Now you've said it" — he throws himself down beside her, kisses her cheek — "you've got *me* craving one too. I can't rest now."

"It's too early." Hannah looks at her phone on the bedside table. "It's only . . . quarter past seven. The Sainsbury's minimarket doesn't open until eight on Sunday."

"I'll go for a run," Will says. "Get the bacon on my way back. Can you last that long?"

She smiles.

"Yes, I can last that long. See you in an hour or so."

After Will is gone, Hannah opens up her book, but she can't settle. As soon as he left, her doubts began to creep back, like shadows wavering at the edge of a candle's glow, rushing in when the lamp is taken away. Reading doesn't help, her mind is too full, and in the end she gives up and heaves herself out of bed.

As she opens the wardrobe to grab her clothes, she catches sight of herself in the full-length mirror inside. Without her glasses everything has a fuzzy, softened quality, but even so her reflection arrests her and she stands for a moment, side on, just looking at the alien shape of her belly, at the reddish stretch marks creeping around from her hips. The air is chill, in spite of the radiator, and the baby quivers inside her. It's impossible for her child to be cold, but still, Hannah shivers in sympathy and pulls on a T-shirt and sweatpants.

In the kitchen she makes herself another coffee — decaf this time — and sits by the window, looking down at the street, chewing her thumbnail. It's still almost dark, and she imagines Will running alongside the road past the park, the pavement wet and slick with overnight rain, the reflective stripes on his running jacket shining back at the cars as they pass.

At the thought of him, running through the morning darkness to get the bacon that *she* was craving, her heart hurts. How can

she be having these doubts? This is Will —
who wrote to her, month after month, year
after year, even when she was too sad and
broken to reply. Will, who came to find her
in Edinburgh, and in doing so turned the
city from a place of exile into a home. Will,
who she's argued with over flat-pack furniture, and laughed with over bad films, and
shared a thousand candlelit dinners with —
from a single Pot Noodle in their very first
flat to Michelin-starred restaurants on their
honeymoon. This is Will — whose child she
is carrying.

And yet, in the silence of the flat, she cannot stop thinking of Hugh's words.

This is worse than any of her sleepless
nights over Neville, because whichever way
this falls out, she is a terrible person. If Will
has been hiding something from her for all
these years, she is married to a liar and
maybe a murderer. But if he's innocent,
what kind of wife does that make her? One
willing to believe the man she loves might
be a killer just because of a few sounds in
the night?

She *has* to find out one way or another.
But the thought of confronting Will on such
a tiny shred of proof makes her feel sick.
*Were you in Pelham College the night April
died?* She just can't imagine saying the

words — destroying her marriage on the basis of something Hugh may or may not have even heard.

Then it comes to her. Ryan.

Ryan's room was on the other side of Will's. There is a strong chance he would have seen or heard Will arriving. And if Ryan remembers Will turning up at 4 p.m. that Sunday with his rucksack on and his rail card in his pocket, well, that is all the proof she needs that Hugh was mistaken.

Hannah glances at the clock on her phone. 7:35. Early, but not ridiculously so, not for someone with two small kids.

She opens up WhatsApp, sends Ryan a message. *Are you awake? Can you talk? I need to ask you something.*

There's a pause. The minutes tick by. Hannah goes into the bedroom to get dressed, but between every garment she finds herself checking to see if the two ticks have gone blue, showing Ryan's read her message. Ten minutes later she is fully dressed, but they still remain stubbornly gray.

Any time is good she adds, not because it's true, but just to make his phone ping again in the hopes that it will attract his attention. And this time it works. After a couple of seconds the checkmarks go blue, and *Typ-*

ing . . . appears at the top of the screen.

Sure. Is now good? We're heading out to the park in a bit.

Hannah's pulse quickens.

Now is great, she texts back. She glances at the clock: 7:51. Will can't be back before 8:10 at the *absolute* earliest, even if he's queuing at the door at 8:00. *Shall I call you?*

Hang on, Ryan texts back. *Give me two secs, I'll phone you.*

Hannah goes back into the kitchen and waits. Her heart is thumping. Her fingers are numb and cold. Her mouth tastes of metal.

She paces up and down, staring at the screen.

And then at 7:56 her phone rings with a jangle that makes her jump and drop it, clattering to the tiles with a crack that sounds deeply ominous. Swearing, she crouches past her bump and picks it up. There's a long silvery fissure across the screen with a shadow of something dark that seems to be seeping out across the LCD display, but it still works when she presses to accept the call.

"Ryan!" Her voice is breathless.

"Ey up, Hannah Jones." She can hear cartoons in the background, Bella's voice yelling at the girls to finish up their Weetabix. "How's things, pet?"

"Good." She wants to talk, procrastinate, put this off, but she can't afford to. Will could be home very soon. She needs to spit this out. They can chat afterwards — if —

But she can't think about that. Ryan has to give her the answer she's hoping for. He *has* to.

"Listen, Ryan, I — I have a weird question."

"Is it about how wheelchair sex works?"

"What?" She laughs at that, not meaning to, but so nervous that it comes out like a burst of tremulous hysteria.

"Ryan!" she hears Bella shouting from across the room. "I daresay you think you're very funny, but the girls can hear you, you know, and you won't think it's so funny when they're trotting that question out at nursery."

"Sorry," Ryan says, and she can hear the suppressed laughter, the old piss-taking, provoking Ryan in his voice. "Ignore me. Carry on. What was it you wanted to ask?"

"It's about —" She swallows. She feels suddenly sick. Ryan's friendly banter has somehow made this even harder. How can she explain what this means? "It's about that night. When April — when April died."

Ryan says nothing, but she senses rather

than hears his nod down the phone.

"Someone said . . . someone told me . . ."

She hears April's voice in her head, clear as if she were standing next to Hannah, fixing her with that icy blue gaze.

Spit. It. Out.

"Someone told me that Will was in college that night," she says in a rush. "That he wasn't in Somerset. Did you hear him come in?"

"What?" Ryan sounds stunned; whatever he was expecting, it plainly wasn't this. "But . . . but what difference does it make? April was alive when Neville went up the stairs, and dead when she came down them. There's no one else could have done it. *You* were the one who testified to that."

"Ryan —" She's trying to keep her voice calm, but there's an edge of desperation that she knows Ryan must be able to hear. "Look, I don't have time to go into it right now, but all I want to know is, did you see Will come home that night? Did you hear anyone in his room? His alibi for April's death hinges on him not being in Oxford that night. Can you back that up, or can't you?"

"I —" Ryan's voice sounds uncertain. "I . . . I don't know. I'd need to think. I didn't see him come in . . . I guess the first time I saw him was . . . coming out of the shower? Around lunchtime?"

"Lunchtime on Sunday?" She tries to think. How long would it take to get from rural Somerset to Oxford, on a Sunday? Lunchtime is pushing it . . . but just about possible she guesses. "And before that? Did you hear anyone? In his room?"

"The police banged on his door," Ryan says. He sounds bewildered now. "I had to tell them he was away for the weekend."

"But they didn't go in, right? They didn't actually check his room was empty?"

"No, they didn't go in."

"And did you *hear* anything? Anything after you'd gone to bed?"

"I don't know!" Ryan says. He sounds utterly bewildered, his usual joking manner quite gone. "Hannah, what's this all about?"

She closes her eyes. A wave of such faintness and nausea is sweeping over her that she has to hold on to the windowsill.

"I'll call you back," she says. "I — I'm sorry, Ryan. I have to go."

She hangs up. She turns around.

Will is standing in the doorway.

AFTER

"Will."

The voice that says his name sounds strange in her own ears, not her own, strangled, harsh.

"How — how long have you been there?"

"Long enough." His face is expressionless. He's holding his running jacket in one hand and a packet of bacon in the other. Automatically she glances at the clock. It's 7:59.

"You — you're not supposed to be back yet," she manages.

"Ajesh saw me waiting outside. He opened up early."

Oh God. She feels sick. How much did he hear?

"What the fuck is going on?" he says, and his voice is flat and yet somehow colder than she could ever have imagined Will sounding. Will. *Will,* her husband, the man she loves with every fiber of her being.

Even the fibers that phoned Ryan to check

up on his alibi? whispers her subconscious, but she pushes its accusations away. A sob is rising inside her. This cannot be happening.

"Do you think I killed April?" he says now, dangerously calm. She shakes her head. Tears are starting in her eyes.

"No. No!"

"That's not what it sounded like." He puts the bacon on the counter, very, very gently, and takes a step towards her. She starts to shake.

"No, Will, no. I never thought that."

"If that's true, why the fuck didn't you just ask me?" he shouts, and now there is a vein throbbing in his forehead. Hannah wants to throw up.

"Will, please . . ." It comes out like a long whimper of fear and she sees something flash in his eyes, but she cannot read it. Is it anger? Contempt? Hate?

"Ask me," he says, coming closer. She has always loved his height, his lean muscled bulk, the way his body makes her feel safe and cocooned. Now she sees it from the other side. She sees the way he could pick her up with one hand by the throat and pin her against the wall. "Ask me!" he shouts, his spit hitting her face, and she flinches in spite of herself. "Ask me if I killed April!"

Hannah's heart is thumping. Her vision is beginning to crack and fragment, like static spreading across a television screen. She knows she is breathing too fast, and yet she can't stop. *Think of the baby.*

And then something stills inside her. It's as if she has been in a hurricane, and suddenly the eye of the storm is passing over, and that strange illusory calm settles for a moment upon her.

Her vision clears. Her heart slows.

"Did you kill April?" she says, every syllable clear and deliberate.

"What do you think?" he says. And then — he *laughs.*

In that moment, all the blood seems to drain from her body, leaving her numb and chill as stone. She stands there, staring at him, unable to believe what she has just heard. She was so sure — so *certain* that he would say no.

She is still staring, horrified, mesmerized, when her phone rings, making her jump convulsively.

"Who's that, the police?" Will says. His voice is ice-cold, goading, cruel.

November's voice flickers through Hannah's memory again — *Please, don't do* anything *about this until you've spoken to the police.*

Oh God, she has been so stupid.

"Hannah?" Will says. He takes a step towards her. She takes a step back. The phone is still ringing. It's on the counter, within hand's reach. "Aren't you going to answer it?"

Hannah's heart is beating so fast and hard she can feel it in her wrists, in her neck. The baby writhes inside her.

Will is between her and the door.

She has been so, so stupid . . .

She takes another step back towards the window, not breaking eye contact with Will, and with her free hand she gropes blindly for the phone, never losing Will's gaze as she grabs it. He takes a step forwards. She takes another step back. He takes another step forwards.

She is backing into a corner, and she knows it, but if she can just get him to take one more step forwards . . .

She takes one more step back.

He takes one more step forwards.

And Hannah runs.

Will swears, but that last step has put the kitchen table between him and the door, while giving Hannah a clear line.

She runs, barefoot, out of the kitchen, down the hallway and down the stairs, hearing a thumping clatter as Will tries to follow and trips over one of their kitchen chairs. Out in the street the cobbles are bitterly cold under her feet and wet from the night's rain, and she slips, but then rights herself and runs towards the open end of the mews. Behind her she can hear Will's feet pounding down the stairs.

Her heart feels like it's going to burst. She holds her stomach with one hand, as if she can protect her unborn child. She forces herself to run just a little faster down the last few meters of Stockbridge Mews . . . and then she is out, onto the main road, skidding around the corner, the asphalt of the council-owned pavement biting into the soles of her feet. She looks wildly up and down the road. A car passes. Then another. They are going too fast for her to stop, and they don't spare a glance for the wild-eyed pregnant woman running barefoot down the street. Can she flag someone down? Run into a cafe? The nearest one is closed and she draws a shuddering breath and runs on, towards the park.

"Hannah!" she hears from behind her, Will's roar of a kind of fury she has never heard from him before. He has rounded the corner onto the main road and is gaining on her. "Hannah, what are you *doing*?"

She makes her legs work harder — runs

across a junction without looking, and then another and then —

There is a screech of tires and the sound of swearing.

"Jesus Christ! You trying to get yourself killed?"

It's a taxi driver. He's leaning out of the window of his cab, his face red with annoyance.

"You coulda killed yourself — and the bairn!"

Hannah just stands for a moment, panting hopelessly, her hands resting on the bonnet of the car. Will can't do anything in front of a taxi driver, surely? But the man is going to drive away — he's going to leave her — and then she looks up, and she feels a huge, drenching wash of relief.

The yellow light on top of the cab is on. The taxi is for hire.

She doesn't wait. She runs around to the side, wrenches open the door, just as Will comes pounding up to the junction.

"Drive," she says urgently to the cabbie. "That's my husband, he — we just had a row."

A row. The word comes out like a sob, and yet it's so pathetically understated. "A row" barely even starts to cover it. *I have just found out my husband might be a killer.*

And yet she can't say it. She can't bring herself to say the words, to make them real.

Will is a killer.

Will murdered April.

If she keeps repeating the words to herself, perhaps she can make herself believe them.

"Understood, hen," the driver says sympathetically. "Aye, it's a tough one. Where can I take you? Your mammy? Or maybe not, by your accent?"

Hannah thinks of her mother, far away in Dodsworth, several hundred miles south, and tears spring into her eyes. If only she could go back there, fall into her mum's arms, sob out her troubles.

But she can't. It's a good eight hours on the train, more on a Sunday. She has no coat, no shoes. She doesn't even have any money, apart from Google Pay on her phone. She can hardly take a taxi to southern England. Where *can* she go?

And then it comes to her.

Hugh.

Hugh will shelter her. Hugh will loan her money and she can buy herself a jacket and some warm boots and figure out her next move.

"Do you know Great King Street?" she asks the driver, who nods.

"Aye."

"Thanks." She sinks back onto the seat, feeling her heart slow and her numb feet begin to thaw. "Thanks, I'd like to go there."

AFTER

As the taxi draws up outside Hugh's flat, Hannah gets her phone out to pay. To her dismay, the inky shadow inching across the screen has spread. It's now covering almost the whole screen, leaving only a small triangle at the top left.

However, she holds it against the card reader, mentally crosses her fingers, and sighs with relief as it beeps obediently.

"Good luck, hen," the taxi driver says gently. "You need a lift anywhere, you give me a call, ken?" He pushes a business card through the hole in the plexiglass screen, and Hannah takes it, trying to smile. Now that the adrenaline is wearing off she feels almost unbearably shaky; her hands are trembling and cold. "And dinna you be in too much of a hurry to go back tae him. Leave him to stew in his own juices a wee while."

Hannah nods.

"Thank you," she says, and then she takes a deep breath and slides out of the back seat.

Standing in front of Hugh's intimidating brass bell plate, she reflects that she should have called ahead. If Hugh is out, she will be in a fix. But it's . . . She glances at her phone, and then realizes that it's pointless, the clock is no longer visible. It must be before nine, though. It's not likely a single, childless man like Hugh would be up and out so early on a Sunday. Saturday he sometimes does clinics, she knows that. Hugh's wealthy clients don't expect to have to stick to weekdays for their appointments. But not Sundays. Sundays are his days off.

She presses the brass button beside the engraved H. BLAND and waits.

After what feels like an agonizingly long time, her feet getting slowly colder and more numb on the black-and-white tiles of the porch, the intercom crackles and Hugh's very English voice comes over the speaker.

"Hello?"

"Hugh?" Her teeth are chattering now. "It's m-me, Hannah. C-can I c-c-come in?"

"Hannah?" Hugh sounds astonished. "I mean — yes, of course. But what —"

"I'll t-tell you ups-s-stairs," Hannah says. She can hardly get the words out. Somehow the brief interlude of warmth in the taxi has only made the shock of the outside feel worse now that she is stuck here. A chill wind whips down the road, swirling dead leaves in the porch and making her shudder afresh.

"Oh, yes, sure. I mean of course. I'll buzz you in. Fifth floor, yes?"

"I remember," Hannah says. She has her arms wrapped around herself, her teeth clenched to stop the chattering.

There is a drawn-out *bzzzzzzz* and Hannah shoves the door with a force that sends it swinging inwards to bang against a backstop, and hurries into the hallway of Hugh's building.

Inside it's not exactly warm, but it's a hell of a lot warmer than the street, and she presses the button for the tiny old-fashioned lift with its folding screen door, and waits while it clanks down the stairwell. As it rises up to Hugh's flat she has to fight the urge to sink to her knees, cradling her bump, howling with the awfulness of what has just happened — an awfulness she is only now beginning to comprehend. And Hugh — Hugh tried to tell her. That's the worst of it. He tried to warn her what would happen if she kept pushing and digging and refusing to accept the version of events they had all learned to live with. He tried to tell her and she ignored him, and now she is paying the price.

When the lift stops with a clang at the fifth floor, Hugh is standing outside, wearing a paisley silk dressing gown and holding a cup of coffee. He isn't wearing his glasses, which gives his face an oddly unfinished, vulnerable look. But as Hannah pulls back the folding brass grille, his expression changes from one of puzzled welcome to a kind of confused dismay.

"What the — Hannah old bean, what happened? Where are your shoes? And is that . . . is that blood?"

Hannah looks down. It's true. Her feet are bleeding and she hadn't even noticed. She has no idea whether she's picked up a piece of glass or just stubbed her toe on the rough asphalt, but there are smears of red on the checkerboard tiled floor of the lift.

"Oh shit, Hugh, I'm so sorry —"

She bends, trying to reach past her bump in the confined space, but Hugh is shaking his head. He takes her arm firmly, pulling her forcibly upright and propelling her down the corridor towards the open door of his flat with a firm but kindly hand in between her shoulders.

"Absolutely not. You, get yourself inside.

I'll call housekeeping to deal with that."

"But your carpets —" Hannah stops in the entrance to the flat. She had forgotten Hugh's carpets — a pristine cream expanse that runs the length of the enormous hall-way and stairs. Hugh rolls his eyes as if to say *damn the carpets,* but he pauses and opens a cupboard concealed behind panel-ing, bringing out a pair of slippers.

"There you go. Put those on if it's only going to make you fret. Now for God's sake, sit down before you fall down. What on earth happened?"

"It was Will," Hannah finds herself saying, but to her horror, the rest of the words won't come. Instead there are tears crowd-ing at the back of her throat, forcing their way up, prickling out through her eyes and running down the sides of her nose. A great, ugly sob comes out with no warning, and then another, and suddenly she is racked with them — huge, unmanageable, body-convulsing sobs that feel like they are going to tear her apart.

"Oh, Han, no," Hugh says uncomfortably, and then he holds out his arms, awkwardly, and almost in spite of herself Hannah stumbles into them. Hugh is not one of nature's huggers. He is too tall and bony to be comfortable, too physically ungainly. But he is good, and kind, and he is *Hugh.* They stand, locked together in Hugh's hallway, Hannah's bump intruding uncomfortably between them, and she bawls like a child into the embroidered silk lapel of Hugh's dressing gown.

At last her sobs subside into gasps, and then hiccups, and then finally just shuddering breaths, and she gets a hold of herself and pulls away. As she wipes her eyes, and then her glasses, she realizes with a kind of shameful horror that she has slobbered all over what is probably a very expensive dry-clean-only garment.

"I'm sorry," she says. Her voice is croaky. "I didn't mean — oh God, your beautiful dressing gown. I'm so sorry, Hugh." She sniffs and gulps. "Have you got a tissue?"

"Here," Hugh says. She's not sure where it came from, but he's holding out a laundered linen square with HAB on one corner. Hannah looks at it doubtfully. Handkerchiefs in her house are made of paper. But at last she blows her nose and then, unsure what to do with it — she can hardly hand it back to Hugh — she puts it in her pocket, intending to slip it into the laundry hamper when she goes to the bathroom.

"Better?" Hugh says, and she nods. It's both true and untrue. She needed that cry, badly, and she *does* feel better. It was cathartic in a way no talk could ever have been. But in another way, nothing is better. It's just as awful and fucked up and unfix-able as it was when she walked through the door to Hugh's flat.

"Come into the living room, sit down," Hugh says, "and then I'll make you a cup of tea, and you can tell me all about it."

Some half hour later, Hannah is sitting on Hugh's white velvet couch, with her slippered feet tucked under her and a blanket around her legs, and Hugh has his head in his hands.

"So he admitted it?" he asks now, as if he can't believe it. "He actually *said* he killed April?"

"Not in so many words," Hannah says. The sentences feel unreal in her mouth. "But I asked him, and he said —" She stops, gulps, and forces herself on. "He said *'What do you think?'* And then he laughed."

"Oh my God," Hugh says wretchedly. He looks up at Hannah, his face utterly bleak.

"I wish — God, I almost wish I'd never told you about the noises."

Hannah shakes her head.

"Hugh, no. God, no. If it's true —" But she stops at that. She can't bring herself to

588

say it. "Hugh," she asks instead, knowing she is clutching at straws, "Hugh, was it *definitely* him? It couldn't have been a scout or sound traveling through the walls or something?"

But Hugh shakes his head. He looks ten years older, as if he is still coming to terms with what he set in motion.

"No," he whispers now. "It — it was *him,* Hannah. I heard him, through the wall, speaking to someone. It was Will."

Hannah feels her last shred of hope snap. She feels as if she has been hanging on to a fraying rope for dear life, and that last fiber has just been severed.

He was there. He was *really* there. And he has lied about it for more than ten years — for the entirety of their relationship.

"Why didn't you *say* anything before?" she manages. "Why didn't you *tell* anyone?" She doesn't mean it to sound as accusing as it comes out, but Hugh only shakes his head wretchedly, as if accepting any blame she wants to throw at him.

"Because he was my friend, Hannah." He sounds broken. "And because I didn't think it *mattered.* It was Neville — you saw him coming out of the staircase, we both did. There was no way anyone could have got up there between Neville leaving and us arriving — so did it really matter if Will arrived a few hours before he said he did? And besides, no one asked. They never said, *Did you hear your best friend coming home at a time that totally breaks his alibi?* I would never have lied outright, Hannah, never. But to go to the police with that — when we all thought Neville was guilty . . ."

He stops, takes off his glasses, covers his face. It must, Hannah reflects dazedly, be almost as much of a shock for him as it is for her. She has lost her husband. Hugh has lost his best friend.

She feels the tears welling up again, and grits her teeth. She can't keep bursting into sobs. She *has* to get a grip.

They have to figure out what to do.

"He didn't try to stop you leaving?" Hugh asks.

"He did," Hannah says. She almost can't believe it herself. "He — he ran after me. But he tripped over the table. I don't know what would have happened if he'd caught up with me."

A picture comes to her. Will's lean, strong hands wrapped around April's throat —

The image washes over her with a physical shock like ice water, making her cheeks flare and her breath quicken.

She pushes the thought away. She can't

think about that right now. About the reality of what this means. All she can do is put one foot in front of the other.

"Okay," Hugh says now. He stands and paces to the end of the living room, to the beautiful floor-to-ceiling windows overlooking the street. He runs his hand through his hair. "Okay. Let's think. Let's think about what to do. Did Will know you were coming here?"

Hannah shakes her head.

"No."

"And what about your phone — is there any way he could be tracking you? You should turn off location services."

"I can't." Hannah digs in her pocket and draws out her cracked and broken phone. The screen is completely dark now, ink-black and unreadable. "I broke it this morning. It's completely dead. But I don't think it's a problem anyway. Will had no —" She swallows, takes a breath, tries again. "He had no reason to —"

She stops again. It's extraordinarily hard to say what she means: her husband had no reason to spy on her until today.

She cannot believe she and Hugh are having this conversation.

All she wants is to hear Will's voice, hear his incredulous laugh as he says *What? Are you crazy? Of course I didn't kill April.* But instead what she hears is that cold, brutal *What do you think?*

She puts her head in her hands. November was right. She can't handle this herself anymore. It has gone too far, become much too dangerous. Whatever the truth, she *has* to hand her fears over to the authorities. And although the thought of sharing her suspicions makes her feel sick, there's a kind of relief too, in the idea of passing on this burden to someone else. For more than ten years she has been pushing away these doubts, pushing away the certainty that there was something *wrong* in what she saw that night. It's time to confess.

"I think . . . I think I have to go to the police," she says. "Can I use your phone, Hugh?"

"Of course," Hugh says, though he looks as sick as she feels at the thought. "I'll speak to them too if you want. But, look — if you phone them, they'll probably want you to come down to the station, make a statement. Do you want to get cleaned up first? You look absolutely all in."

Hannah looks down at herself — at her crumpled sweats and her bloody feet in Hugh's borrowed slippers. She wants to phone the police — get this over with. But at the same time she can see that Hugh is right. Once she has started the ball rolling, she can hardly say *I'll be down in a few hours, once I've had a shower.*

"Okay," she says now. "Good idea."

Her stomach growls audibly, and she realizes suddenly that she is almost faint with hunger.

"Actually, before I do that, could I — could I have some toast, Hugh?"

Hugh nods.

"Of course. Come through to the kitchen and I'll get you set up."

It's maybe half an hour later that Hannah walks into Hugh's palatial marble bathroom to see a steaming bubble bath awaiting her, already run.

The sight makes her do a double take. She had been intending a quick shower and then straight down to speak to the police — it must be already getting on for 10 a.m. But it seems pointless to drain the water in an already-run bath.

Setting the cup of tea to the side, she strips off her sweatpants, T-shirt, and underwear, steps out of Hugh's borrowed slippers, and climbs gingerly into the warm water.

It's unbelievably good. The foam is

scented with some kind of spicy citrus-smelling perfume; the bubbles are rich and foamy. Even the painful stinging of her feet can't take away from the fact that this is, undeniably, exactly what she needs. She closes her eyes and feels the tears she has been keeping at bay for the last hour prickle behind her lids. But she cannot — she can't give way to this. She has to be strong — she has to get to the police and say what she knows, for April and November, who deserve justice after all this time, and for Neville, Ryan, Emily, everyone who has lived with this pall of potential guilt hanging over them.

She will be angry soon. She can feel it underneath, the searing, white-hot rage that will envelop her when this is done. *How could you.* She wants to shake Will, spit at him, slap him around the face.

And maybe that is what will save her from the despair.

As she lies in the bath she can picture it so clearly.

Will, coming back early from the weekend — climbing the wall behind Cloade's to avoid having to go around the long way, through the main gate. And then, maybe preplanned, maybe just on a whim, he didn't go back to his own room, but up to April's.

Maybe it was open. She thinks she locked it on her way down to the bar, but a decade on, she can't be sure. Or maybe April was already back, maybe she welcomed Will inside. *See, I came back for you — you* are *more important to me than my mother.*

And then . . . what? An argument? No, not an argument, or the boys below would have heard it. A hissed disagreement, maybe.

Or perhaps if Will was already in the room before April came back from the bar, he saw something. Another pregnancy test. A note from Ryan.

Perhaps he opened the door, smiling, pulled her in for a hug. *Let me take off my makeup,* she would have said. And so he let her wipe off the terra-cotta foundation. Perhaps it was then, as she bent over her dressing table, cotton wool in hand, that he came towards her, hands outstretched —

And then there was a knock on the door.

April would have known nothing, suspected nothing.

She would have pecked Will on the cheek and then gone to answer it.

From inside April's room, Will would have heard the conversation. Neville handing over the parcel, April trying to hurry him away, Neville's footsteps as he retreated down the stairs.

And then April, coming back into her room, all smiles.

"Got rid of him."

And Will would have walked towards her, arms outstretched, but instead of cradling her face in his hands, as he has done so often to Hannah — and her heart cracks a little further as she thinks of it — he would have slid his hands down to her neck, and squeezed . . .

No, no, no! The revulsion is so strong that she has to sit up, holding on to the sides of the bath as the water sloshes back and forth. It doesn't make *sense,* Will is not that person!

But then she thinks of all the articles she has read over the years, all of the *it's always the partner* pieces, all of the statistics about women killed by the person they're sleeping with. She thinks of Geraint's euphemistic hints about a *domestic murder,* all the whispers she's ignored for more than a decade. *I never liked the boyfriend . . . They said she was sleeping around . . . He was never even a suspect.* She has always ignored them, always clung to what she *knows* to be true — that Will is not that person.

596

But now, with the knowledge that he has spent their entire marriage lying to her about that night, she is not so sure.

The sudden movement of sitting up has made her head swim; there are little flashes of light, like paparazzi bulbs, flickering at the edges of her vision, the flashes the midwife warned her about. Was the bath too hot?

Don't faint, don't faint, don't faint . . .

She is whispering the words aloud, and then the moment has passed, and she is okay.

Except she's not. Her legs are weak as jelly, and when she tries to stand, she's not sure if they will hold her.

Fuck. *Fuck. Don't do this,* she wants to beg her body. *Not now . . . please not now.*

She holds her bump, feeling the baby move. It's reassuring. However much her body is letting her down, it's taking care of their child.

Their child. The word strikes to her heart. Because if this is true, *if* this is true, this baby will no longer be born to a father and a mother. It will be the child of a murderer. With a father in prison.

The faintness comes again, and this time it's accompanied by a wash of nausea. She crouches, naked in the bath. Is it going to be okay?

And then suddenly it's not, and she needs to get to the toilet *right now.* Trembling, she hauls herself out of the bath, wet and dripping, her legs shaking, and scrambles over the side, slipping on the wet tiles, to fall to her knees in front of the toilet, shivering with a mix of cold and shock.

She heaves, but nothing comes up.

For a few minutes she kneels there, shaking and dripping foamy water onto the beautiful geometric tiles, and then slowly, very slowly, she gets up and gropes her way to the towel rail. She has to hold on to the sink as she goes. She cannot slip and fall, not now. She is all this baby has.

She wraps herself in a towel and then slides down to the floor, her back to the heated rail, her gaze unfixed in front of her, waiting for the shivering to subside.

But it never does.

It's maybe an hour later that Hugh taps on the door.

"Hannah, are you okay? It's gone very quiet."

She doesn't answer. Her teeth are chattering too much.

"Hannah?" Hugh is starting to sound alarmed. "Can you say something?"

He waits, then knocks again, and then says, "Hannah, I'm coming in. Is that all right?"

She wants to speak. She wants to tell him she's okay, but it's not true.

The door creaks slowly open, and Hugh's head comes cautiously through the gap. He is wearing his glasses now, and has changed into herringbone trousers with a sharp crease ironed down the front.

His expression changes as he sees her huddled against the towel rail, white and speechless and shivering.

"Jesus, Hannah, you're in shock. Let me help you up."

She tries to stand, but her legs are weak as rubber, and Hugh has to help her, holding the towel around her to try to protect her nakedness, averting his eyes as it slips to expose her bump.

"I'm s-s-sorry —" she keeps trying to say, and he keeps saying "Don't worry, don't worry — Han, I'm a doctor, I've seen this all before, it's okay, you're in delayed shock. It's completely natural, the news about Will — it would have shaken anyone up. Come through here. I'll get you something hot and sugary. Come on, you're okay. You're okay."

Together they make their hobbling way down the corridor to Hugh's guest bedroom, and Hugh pulls back the covers and helps her slip underneath.

"Don't go to sleep, okay?" Hugh says sternly. "I'm coming back with something for the shock."

The shivering is subsiding, and she is hugely, unbelievably tired, but she tries to obey, dragging her lids open. Hugh returns in a matter of moments with a hot water bottle and a cup of tea so sweet it makes her want to retch as she drinks it, but he forces her to have at least a few sips.

"Let me sleep," she begs at last. She can't think of the police, not now, not like this, while she's white and trembling. In an hour, maybe. Right now she is suddenly crushingly exhausted — tired in a way she can't remember ever being before. Hugh looks at her for a long moment and then nods.

"All right. You look absolutely done in. I'm just going to take your blood pressure, okay?"

She nods, and he leaves, and then comes back a few seconds later with an electric monitor. He sits there, listening to the clicks and whirs as it takes a reading, then pulls off the cuff and pauses for a moment with his finger on her pulse, counting.

"Is it . . . okay?" The words are hard to

form. She's so unbelievably tired. Hugh nods.

"It's fine. *You're* fine. Don't worry. Are you cold?"

She shakes her head. Her hands and feet still feel numb, but the trembling is subsiding, and she can feel the warmth from the hot water bottle seeping through her.

"Go to sleep," Hugh says gently. "I'll wake you in a few hours. Okay?"

". . . kay," she manages. And then she lets her eyes close, and slips into a merciful darkness.

AFTER

"Hannah." The voice is gentle, insistent . . . and not Will's.

"Haaa-nah. It's time to wake up."

"What?" She struggles to sit up, blinking, wondering where she is — and then she remembers. She is in Hugh's flat. And she is — oh God, she is naked. And somehow it's dark.

She pulls the covers up over her breasts, and the memories come back. The bath. The flight to Hugh's flat. *Will.*

The pain is like a knife to her side. Unbearable.

Hugh is standing over her, looking worried. His fringe is in his eyes and he blows it off with that habitual gesture, and her heart aches.

"What time is it?" she croaks, putting a hand up to her throbbing head. She feels . . . the word comes to her like a surprise. She feels *hungover.* Like she spent a night on the tiles. It's so far from the truth that for a second she wants to laugh. Is this what shock feels like?

Hugh looks at his watch.

"Nearly four. We're due at the police station at four thirty. Are you feeling okay?"

"Nearly *four*?" Hannah sits up fully at that, shock running through her. "Are you kidding? I've been asleep all day?"

"You went out like a light. You still don't look quite right."

She puts her hand to her head. *Not quite right* is an understatement — she feels completely groggy and disoriented, and there is a vile taste in her mouth, bitter and chemical. Then what Hugh just said sinks in.

"Sorry, did you say the police?"

"Yes, but listen —" Hugh holds up a hand. "I didn't tell them *anything,* I figured that wasn't my place. I just said that I had a friend who had important information and could we come in and make a statement. And they said how was half four. You can still back out if you want."

"No." Her hands are cold, and her cheeks feel pale, but she knows she wants to do this. She knows she *has* to do this.

The bottom line is, someone *could* have been in April's room that night. They could have killed her after Neville left. And that person — she can't hide from the possibility any longer — could have been Will.

She has to tell them that.

"No, I'm — I'm ready."

"Your clothes are on the end of the bed." Hugh waves a hand at the foot of the bed where her clothes are draped, along with a jacket that's clearly one of Hugh's. On top of the pile are her glasses. On the floor is a pair of flip-flops. Hugh sees her looking at them and makes a face.

"Sorry. Best I could do, I didn't want to leave you alone in the flat. We can pick up some trainers en route if you're bothered."

But she shakes her head. It doesn't matter. None of it matters now.

Hugh leaves, tactfully, and Hannah gets slowly back into her clothes. Finally, she reaches for her phone, tapping the power button to check on the time — and then she remembers: it's dead.

Still, she shoves it in the pocket of Hugh's coat, and then leaves the room.

"Ready?" Hugh asks, and she nods, even though it's very far from the truth. He's holding car keys, and she frowns.

"Are we driving?"

"I thought so, they said they'd give us parking and I don't really want you standing in the rain for a bus. You still don't look great."

She nods dully. It doesn't matter. Nothing matters now — except the baby. She has to keep it together for the baby.

Oh God, is she really going to do this . . .

The faintness rises up inside her again and Hugh takes her arm, looking alarmed.

"Hannah? Hannah old bean?"

"I'm fine," she says, her teeth gritted. It's not true, but she will be, once she has spoken to the police. For whatever the truth, whatever happens now, November was right. This is the only way she can make herself safe, the only way she can protect herself.

In the car she lets her head loll against the window. She is not just tired but exhausted, the exhaustion of grief and fear and shock. There's a strange familiarity to it now — it's the same sensation she remembers from last time, the same numb, sick horror as she sat, wired and sleepless, through interview after interview, surviving off bad tea and worse coffee, as the police prodded her for inconsistencies or anything she might have forgotten.

The thought of going through it all again leaves her with a kind of light-headed nausea. And perhaps that's it — perhaps this is why it feels so much worse the second time around. Because she has done this all before — and for what? So that an innocent man could die in prison.

And now she is going to do the same thing again, but this time to incriminate the father of her unborn baby.

A picture comes into her head, of Will's lips pressed against her hair, of his low, soft voice rumbling in his chest, *I love you.*

She thinks she may throw up.

"Are you okay?" Hugh asks, and she shakes her head. "Do you want some water? You're probably dehydrated."

He gestures to a bottle in the door, and Hannah nods. There is a horrible hungover taste in her mouth. Maybe the water will make her feel less sick. But it doesn't. When she takes a long gulp, it has the same flat chemical taste as everything else, and she screws the lid back on and replaces it in the door.

Instead she shuts her eyes, hoping for darkness, for oblivion, and Hugh starts the engine. It purrs for a moment, and then he slips the car into gear, and they slide away into the darkness.

It's some time later that Hannah opens her

eyes. She hasn't been asleep exactly, just drowsing, trying to throw off this weird groggy feeling before they reach the police station. But the noise of the traffic has faded away, and they seem to have been driving for a long time, longer than she would have thought.

It takes a while for her to focus on the road ahead and make sense of what she is seeing — because they are not in Edinburgh anymore, but on a country road, quite a narrow one. There are no streetlamps, only the powerful beams of Hugh's headlamps lighting up the low hedges on either side of the track. It's not a route she recognizes, but from the dark shapes of the hills she thinks they may be heading west, towards Berwick.

"Hugh?" She sits up, pushes her glasses up her nose, looks around, trying to figure out where they are. The chemical taste is still in her mouth, and her throat feels dry, her voice croaky. "Hugh, what's going on?"

Hugh makes a rueful face.

"Sorry, only just outside Edinburgh, but I must have put the postcode into the satnav wrong. It took me all round the houses before I realized what I'd done. We're heading back now. Sorry, incredibly stupid of me. I'm just trying to find a route round, I don't want to pull a U-turn in such a narrow road."

Hannah sinks back in her seat and they drive for a while in the darkness. They pass a farm track, then another, and beneath the fog of tiredness she begins to feel uneasy.

"Hugh? Should you turn around? This road only seems to be leading us farther away. Look, there's a house coming up." She points, but Hugh doesn't slow, and it flashes past.

"Don't worry," he says, his voice calm, "I've got another route planned out."

But when Hannah glances across at the satnav on his dashboard, it's turned off.

Her fingers close around the phone in her pocket, before she remembers, and a kind of sick shiver runs through her.

"How long until we get to the police station?" she says.

"Oh, not long," Hugh says. "Twenty minutes maybe?"

Hannah flicks a look at the clock on the dashboard. For a moment her vision is too blurred to read it, but she blinks, concentrates. The screen says 4:41. They have been driving for more than half an hour.

"We're late," she says.

"They sounded quite relaxed about the time," Hugh says, "but you could call them if you're worried. Give them a heads-up."

"I can't," Hannah says. She tries to keep her voice level. "My phone's broken, re-member?"

"Oh, of course," Hugh says breezily. "Well, never mind. We won't be long now."

She falls silent and they sit in the dark-ness, Hannah listening to Hugh's breathing and hearing her own pulse in her ears. The countryside is becoming more and more deserted. The clock on the dashboard ticks down the minutes: 4:47, 4:49, 4:50. A sick feeling is starting to roil in Hannah's stom-ach. What is going on? Does Hugh not want her to go to the police?

"Hugh," she says again, and this time she can hear the tension in her own voice. "Hugh, turn around."

"Relax," Hugh says. His voice is smooth, urbane, reassuring. She imagines it's the voice he uses on his patients. "We'll be there shortly."

She looks at his profile in the dim light of the dashboard. She feels strange, sluggish, slow-witted, as if she has not properly woken up, as if this is all one long night-mare. Why, *why* is she so tired? Is it pos-sible . . . She glances down at the water bottle in the door, remembering its strange chemical taste, the same taste that was in her mouth after that horrible sweet tea, and a prickle of fear runs through her.

Something is wrong.

Something is wrong.

The minutes tick on. 4:52. 4:57. 5:00.

And with a kind of slow, mounting sickness, Hannah realizes the truth. Hugh is not driving her to the police. Hugh hasn't called the police.

Instead he drugged her, and he is driving her to an unknown destination, far from Edinburgh.

She just doesn't know why.

Because Hugh cannot be April's killer. He *can't* be. He was with Hannah from the moment April left the bar until the moment they discovered her body. He is the one person she has always known she could trust, absolutely.

So what is he doing? And why?

She thinks of November's words again. Of her urgent voice, *Please, don't do* anything *about this until you've spoken to the police.*

But Hugh was safe, she wants to wail. *Hugh was the one person I could rely on. Hugh was* there.

And then suddenly, Hannah knows.

She sees the whole picture, clearly, spread out in front of her with an awful crystalline clarity, the picture she has struggled to see, to remember, for so many years.

She sees the open door.

She sees April, sprawled across the rug, her skin still blotched with terra-cotta makeup.

She hears her own screams, hears Hugh's feet on the stairs, watches as he runs to April, presses his fingers to her pulse.

She sees him, crouched over April, desperately administering heart compressions. *Go,* she hears him gasp. *Hannah, for God's sake go and find someone.*

She has been so, so stupid.

And now she is locked in a car with a killer, her unborn child in her belly, and a broken phone.

But she is not going to die.

Turning her head as if to look out the window, Hannah glances casually at the passenger-side lock. It's down. She could try the handle anyway, but somehow she doubts Hugh will have overlooked that, and if she tries it, and it doesn't work, Hugh will know. Her best bet, she thinks, is to play along. Lull Hugh into a false sense of security until . . .

But she can't think about that. There has to be an opening, an opportunity, *something* she can take advantage of. She is not going to die here, and she is not going to let her child die with her. *Think, Hannah,* think.

What does she have on her that she could defend herself with, if it came to it? Not even her keys, she realizes with a kind of nausea at her own stupidity. Nothing. She has no bag, no purse. She's not even wearing proper shoes to run for it — even if she, six months pregnant, could outrun Hugh's long, lean cricketer's legs.

She has nothing but a broken mobile phone.

The thought snags, catching at some memory at the back of her mind. It's a memory of Hugh asking casually, *And what about your phone — is there any way he could be tracking you?*

She thought he was protecting her from Will, but now she realizes — he was protecting himself. Even then, he was thinking ahead, to this moment in the darkness as he drives her to an unknown destination, making sure that her phone could not be tracked. He has turned off his own, and the satnav.

She had shown him her broken phone, and Hugh — Hugh had nodded and accepted it. But it wasn't quite true. Her phone *screen* is broken, but the phone itself is not — it functioned fine when she tried to pay the taxi driver. And Hugh doesn't know this, which is a tiny, tiny advantage in her favor. It's the one piece of information she has that Hugh does not. But how can she use it without a working screen, and more to the point, how can she do so without alerting Hugh?

Her hand goes into the pocket of the borrowed jacket, tracing the hard, familiar shape of it, running her fingers over the buttons, feeling the shattered glass.

Some phones have a way of calling the police from the lock screen, she knows that. She saw a video on Twitter once, a woman showing you how to activate it on an iPhone. You had to press the side button and one of the volume buttons. Or was it the power button? Whichever one it was, the phone autodialed the emergency services without the user having to do anything else. But in the video, the phone let out a loud siren as it called the police. Hannah could turn down the volume, but she has no way of knowing whether the siren overrides the volume setting. If it's some kind of deliberate safety feature, a warning to the user that they've dialed 999, then it would make sense to have it sound no matter what.

Should she risk it?

She glances over at Hugh. He's staring at the road ahead, not showing any uneasiness.

If she calls the police and her phone lets out a siren call, Hugh will know she has a working phone, and he will find some way to dispose of it, she's sure of that now.

No, she can't use that feature.

Oh God, if only Hugh had been right. If only Will *were* tracking her. She shuts her eyes, imagining Will roaring up behind the car on his motorbike, forcing Hugh to a stop, and a lump forms in her throat, almost choking her. But she cannot cry — if she does, she will never stop, and Will isn't coming; she is going to have to rescue herself from this.

But Will . . . Will *is* the one person she could call.

A sudden shiver runs through her.

"Are you cold?" Hugh asks conversationally.

She shakes her head.

"No, it was nothing, just a goose on my grave."

But it wasn't nothing. It was hope.

She is going to have to be very, very careful now. This is going to take timing, and dexterity, and she is going to have to be very inventive about what she says to Hugh and how she phrases it.

The phone is hard and reassuring in her

hand. She lets her finger rest on the side button.

"Hugh," she says.

"Mm?" Hugh doesn't look away from the road. They are a long way out of Edinburgh now. She can hear the sound of the sea, she thinks, and rain is beginning to spatter against the windscreen.

"When we get home, after I've spoken to the police, do you think I should" — her shaking finger presses the side button on the phone, the button that activates voice commands, and then she raises her voice as loud as she dares — "call Will?"

She hears the faintest, almost imperceptible chime of a ringtone starting up through the phone's internal speaker, and she gives a loud yawn to cover it, her fingers diving for the volume button, pressing *down, down, down* as hard as she can. The ring dies away, her heart thumping in time with its fading rhythm. With the speaker muted, she has no way of knowing whether Will has answered. *Please, please,* she finds herself thinking. Hugh is speaking, but she can't concentrate on his words, all she can think of is whether Will has picked up, or if he's grunted furiously and sent her call to voicemail. *Oh God, oh Will, please, I'm sorry — I'm so sorry — if you ever loved me —*

615

Maybe he's not even there. Maybe the ringer is switched off. Maybe he's drowning his sorrows in a pub, and can't hear her call, and it's already gone to voicemail.

Please, please, please. I'm sorry, Will, I'm sorry I doubted you.

". . . what you're going to say to him?" Hugh is asking. He's frowning.

"I guess you're right," Hannah says. Her heart is thudding so hard her belly is shaking with it. It feels like a miracle that Hugh can't hear it, can't see how scared she is, but his eyes are on the road. "I just wish — oh God, I just wish we hadn't left it that way. He must be frantic — wondering where I am, whether I'm safe." *Oh God, please don't hang up, Will. Please hear what I'm trying to tell you, please stay on the line.* She shifts in her seat, feeling the baby pressing against her pelvis.

"I know," Hugh says, and his voice cracks with what sounds almost like realistic emotion. "I know, Hannah. God, I mean, I know it's not the same, but — he's my best friend, you know? Was." There is a long silence.

Please don't hang up.

"How long, do you think?" Hannah says at last. "Until we get to the police? We seem to have been driving for ages. I feel like we must be halfway to Berwick." *Are you listen-*

616

ing, Will?

"Oh, nowhere near there," Hugh says with a laugh, but he sounds a little uneasy. He taps his fingers on the steering wheel. The wipers swish back and forth with hypnotic rhythm. "Why don't you have a nap? I can wake you when we get to the station."

Hannah nods. But if she hadn't been sure before, those words would have made her so. Because no one could possibly think she was tired — she's done nothing *but* sleep since she drank that tea. Another surge of fear runs through her. She rests her arm against the window and stares out into the night, looking, desperately, for something, anything to give Will a clue about her whereabouts.

And then it comes. A pub, looming out of the darkness.

She blinks, strains her eyes. She cannot afford to miss the sign, but the writing is small, the rain is so hard, and the sign isn't illuminated . . . and then it flashes past and she has caught it.

"The Silver Star . . ." she says shakily, trying to make it sound as if she is just thinking aloud. "What a pretty name for a pub . . ."

She yawns, hoping it sounds convincing. The groggy stupor from earlier is wearing off, the adrenaline of fear pumping through her body, pulling her forcibly out of that pit of exhaustion, but she has to pretend to Hugh that she is more tired than she is. He cannot know.

Did you hear that, Will? Are you even there?

A sob rises inside her because after all, maybe this whole thing is hopeless. There's every chance Will's phone went to voicemail, her call timed out, and she's talking to no one at all. And then she realizes something: The phone in her hand is growing warm, and not just from her touch. It is hot, the kind of heat that builds up when she's on a long call.

Will is there. He is listening.

And maybe he is coming.

AFTER

It is the third pothole that does it, jolting Hannah so hard that her head cracks painfully against the car window and, with a sinking feeling, she realizes this is it. It is time to stop pretending. She can no longer feign sleep or ignorance because no one, not even Hugh, could believe that Hannah would trust this track.

"Where are we, Hugh?" She is, oddly, a little proud that her voice comes out steadily, without shaking, in spite of how afraid she is.

"What do you mean?" Hugh says, and then he looks across at her, and sees something in her face, palely lit by the dashboard display and the headlights reflecting off the rain, and he sighs. "Oh dear. I suppose it was too much to hope . . ."

He trails off, and Hannah finishes the sentence for him.

"Too much to hope that even someone as

stupid as me would believe this was the route to the police station?"

"Hannah," Hugh chides her gently. "That's unfair. I never thought you stupid."

"Oh really." Her voice is bitter. "Not even when I went to court and gave evidence against an innocent man?"

"The evidence was pretty compelling, to be fair . . ."

"Not even when I came to you sobbing, believing that my own husband was a murderer?"

"Well, you had cause . . ."

"I had cause because *you* gave it to me, Hugh! Why? Why Will of all people? How could you? He's your *best friend*."

"Because he was the only person I thought you might care about enough to protect," Hugh snaps suddenly. "You were clearly happy to throw anyone else to the wolves." The car jolts through another pothole, making Hannah's teeth crack together so hard that her skull hurts. The baby inside her kicks violently, as if in protest at the jolt, and she shifts uneasily in her seat, trying to take the pressure off her bump. The rain has slowed to a drizzle, but she can see nothing at all outside the car, no lights, no houses. No Will. They are very far down a long farm track; even if he's heard all her messages, even if he's followed the trail of clues she's tried to leave him, the chances of him picking this tiny obscure road out of all the others is so impossibly remote . . .

"Where are we?" she says again, her teeth gritted. "Where *are* we, Hugh? You owe me that — you owe me the truth about one thing at least."

Hugh laughs.

"Don't you recognize it? Some wife you are."

"What?" She frowns, puzzled. And then she realizes.

It's the beach. It's the beach where Will took her, that first week he came to Edinburgh. The beach where they swam and lay together on the sand, and where Hannah finally admitted to herself that she was going to love this man for the rest of her life.

The phone in her pocket is so hot now that she can no longer grip it. She can feel it burning her thigh through the thin layers of material. It's almost painful, but she doesn't move it away, because the heat is the one thing she has to hold on to. The one scrap of hope that tells her Will is there. He is listening. And perhaps, if she can keep Hugh talking for long enough, he is coming. If only she can manage to tell him.

"It's our beach," she manages now. "The

one where we — near Tantallon Castle. But how —" she tries, and then swallows and tries again. "How did you know?"

"Because he asked me where to take you," Hugh says. He looks . . . he looks *weary,* Hannah thinks. And perhaps he is. He has been carrying his secrets for more than ten years. It must, in a strange way, be a relief to set that burden down at last. "I'd just finished a summer work experience placement here, do you remember? He said he wanted to take you out somewhere, but it needed to be cheap; a cheap, romantic place that you could get to by train."

"And why —" Hannah swallows again. She puts her hand on her bump, where the baby is quivering nervously, as though it can feel her unease. "Why here? Why now?"

Hugh's face twists with some very strong emotion. Hannah can't tell what it is. Disgust? Remorse? Pity? Maybe all three.

"Because it felt right," he says at last. The car has stopped. Its lights are shining out over the headland. Far below, Hannah can hear the crash of waves beating against the rocks. It is high tide.

Right for what? she wants to ask, but in her heart she knows. And it *is* right. Because Hugh knows her almost as well as Will does, almost as well as she knows herself.

It is where she would come if she were going to kill herself.

The thought — the realization — should make her panic, but instead it is as if the opposite happens. Her pulse seems to slow down. Her head feels clearer than at any time since she drank that fucking tea — clearer than it has for weeks, in fact. Everything seems to shiver into focus, like a hand turning the dial on a microscope infinitely slowly, until suddenly the picture is crisp and unforgiving.

Hugh is going to kill her. He is going to make it look like suicide. And it makes a certain horrible sense — Hannah, running out of the house, distraught, after accusing her husband of killing her best friend. She jumps into a taxi. She takes off — to where? No one knows. She didn't tell Will. She didn't tell her mother. She could be anywhere.

The phone burns in her pocket, hotter than hot, but she knows she doesn't have much time now. She has to stall Hugh for as long as she can — but if Will can't find her, if Will can't make it in time . . .

"Take off your shoes," Hugh says gently, and she knows why. She can't wear anything that would tie her to him. She nods and bends down, past her bump, wriggling her feet out of the borrowed shoes. There is no point in resisting. She is better off trying to delay for as long as possible.

"Isn't it going to look strange?" she says as she inches one foot out of the plastic. "A corpse with no shoes? Will they really believe I came all this way on the train, with no shoes on?"

Hugh shakes his head.

"I'm hoping there won't be a corpse." He nods to the cliff, and Hannah hears again the pounding, sucking roar of the waves. "The currents around here . . ." He trails off. Hannah knows what he means. Every year people go missing — swimmers, fishermen, probable suicides. Only a few bodies are ever found. "But if there is," he says, "who's going to think anything of a missing shoe?"

Hannah nods. She knows she should be scared. But this is Hugh. Kind, gentle Hugh, with his surgeon's hands and his flopping fringe. It feels like they are discussing a play, or a book. She has a sense of total unreality. The only thing that anchors her is the phone in her pocket, burning, burning against her leg.

"Aren't you going to ask me how?" he says now, and Hannah looks up at him, frowning.

"What do you mean? April?"

"Yes. Don't you want to know how I did it? How I was in two places at once?"

And suddenly Hannah almost wants to laugh, because this is *so* Hugh. It's the Hugh who proudly took her out for a drive in his brand-new BMW two years out of med school. *Isn't she a beauty?* It's the Hugh who drops his Damien Hirst into conversation, the Hugh who wears his old school tie in spite of the fact that only a tiny number of people care or even know what that means, the Hugh who signs his personal emails *MD, FRCS, EBOPRAS,* and all the other myriad letters he is entitled to, just because he can.

He wants to show off.

Hannah grits her teeth. It's against every instinct she's got to indulge him — he *killed April.* He shouldn't get to crow about that — even if he's spent ten years waiting to be able to do it. But her best chance of buying time is making Hugh talk. So she takes a deep breath.

"I know how. I just don't know why."

"You know how?" Hugh sounds slightly annoyed. His expression is skeptical. Hannah nods.

"Yes. I know — I know I spent months, years barking up the wrong tree. But I'm pretty sure I know now."

She thinks back to that moment in the car, the dial of the microscope inching round, the picture suddenly clicking into focus . . . She's not pretty sure. She's certain.

She sees the room again, April sprawled across the rug, her cheeks flushed, her arms flung out — like something in an oil painting, she had thought, even at the time. A set in a stage play. The beautiful girl, the tragic scene. Romeo and Juliet. Othello and Desdemona.

"You do," Hugh says. He folds his arms. Smiles. "Go on, then."

"I was half-right, in a way," she says. "The fact that no one came out of the staircase between John Neville leaving and us arriving, that was a red herring."

"And yet," Hugh says gently, "I didn't shinny down the drainpipe, Hannah. Or have I got it the wrong way around, did I somehow shinny *up*?"

"No," she says. Her pulse is steady, her blood pumping inside her. She is suddenly conscious of her whole body doing its best to keep her and her baby alive. She wants to *live*. "No, I was the one who had it the wrong way round. Because April wasn't dead, was she, Hugh?"

"What do you mean?" Hugh says, but he's parrying, she can see it in his eyes. She has scored a hit, and they both know it. "You saw her dead body yourself."

"But I didn't, did I? I saw April lying on the floor, *playing* dead. Just as you and she had devised."

There is a long, long silence, and then the stillness in the car is broken by a single clap that makes the baby jump inside Hannah's belly, and then another, and another. Hugh is applauding.

"Bravo, Hannah Jones. So. You finally figured it out. I knew you would eventually."

Yes. He had known she would get there eventually, if she kept digging and digging. And he had tried to warn her off, persuade her not to keep asking questions, and then when that failed, divert her attention to Will, the one person, as he put it, that she might have unbent from her dogged search for the truth to protect. But she had not. She had refused to turn aside, even for Will. The thought makes her heart hurt.

"It's been bothering me," Hannah says, almost to herself, "Why did April never do anything to *me* that last week? She was punishing everyone. Will for leaving her. Ryan for refusing to dump Emily. Emily for having the temerity to hold on to Ryan. But she never did anything to me. And that made no sense. At first I thought it was because she didn't know about me and Will — I mean, there was nothing *to* know, really. We weren't doing anything behind her back." *Except that kiss,* her heart says, but she ignores it and pushes on. "But people *had* noticed. You said it yourself — you didn't need to be Freud to see how Will and I felt about each other, and April was very, very good at reading people. She knew. She absolutely knew. So why did she punish everyone but me? And then I realized."

"Yes?" Hugh says, with his gentle, old-world curiosity and politeness. "Do go on."

"I realized she did punish me — and that was it. That last night, the night I found her dead in our room, *that* was my punishment. That was showing me what a bitch I was being. *You'll be sorry when I'm gone* — it's such a teenage reaction, and the people who say it never mean it, least of all April. She would never have killed herself. She valued herself and her life far too much for that. But she wanted me to know what it felt like. She wanted me to feel, even if just for half an hour, twenty minutes, that tearing, unbearable knowledge of what I'd done, and what it had cost me."

The phone in her pocket is red-hot now. She will have a mark against her leg tomorrow — if she survives tonight. *Will, where are you?*

"So," Hugh says. He folds his hands together, for all the world like a tutor, leading her through an argument, testing her case for weaknesses. "So, she waited for you to come up to the room, and played dead. What next?"

"You were in on it," Hannah says. "You had to be — because she knew that if I got too close I'd be able to tell she wasn't dead. So she enlisted your help. That was your role, to come rushing up the stairs when I opened the door, then fall to your knees beside her 'corpse' and tell me, with all the authority of a first-year medical student, that April was dead. Then send me running out to make a fool of myself by summoning the authorities, at which point April would sit up and claim to have been asleep or something, and I'd look a drunk, hysterical idiot."

"Very good," Hugh says. He pushes his spectacles up his nose and blows his fringe out of his eyes. "I'm impressed."

"But of course what really happened was that as soon as I left the room, you killed her, probably before she could even sit up.

Under the cover of the noise I was making, banging on doors, screaming in the stairwell, you strangled her. But a body that's been strangled doesn't look like someone lying there playing dead. You had to keep me out of the room when I came back up the stairs with the authorities. I remember you standing there at the top of the stairs, barring the door, saying *Nobody must go in, no one should disturb the body,* and you know what" — she gives a bitter, hollow laugh — "you know what, I remember being impressed at your forethought, at the way you knew what to do. But it was bullshit. You just didn't want me seeing the body of my friend, her face swollen and her arms bruised from you kneeling on them, bruises that weren't there a few minutes ago. The police surgeons didn't know — how could they? By the time they came to examine the body, they couldn't possibly tell if she was murdered at 10:59 or 11:05. And with you and I insisting that we both found April dead at 11:03 . . ."

She swallows.

"Poor John Neville. He never had a chance. I made sure of that."

"Neville was a pest," Hugh says briskly. He turns off the engine, and Hannah feels a rush of fear. Oh God, oh God, where is Will?

630

And then, with a horrible lurch, she realizes the phone in her pocket is no longer burning her leg. In fact, it's cooling rapidly.

Either Will has hung up or — and the realization comes to her with a sickening certainty, as she remembers the battery bar hovering at the 50 percent mark before she dropped the phone — the battery has died. She is screwed. She staked everything on Will getting here in time, and she has lost, and now she cannot even dial 999.

Just in case, hoping against hope, she presses the power button and the side button together, bracing herself for the siren, but it doesn't come. She tries the side button and the volume button. Nothing again.

So. This is it. She is alone. It's just her and Hugh.

But then the baby inside her kicks, and she realizes she is not alone.

And she is not going to die.

"It's time," Hugh says.

"But what about why," Hannah parries desperately. "I told you I knew how, but why, Hugh? Why April?"

But Hugh only turns and looks at her, and then he shakes his head, as if he's pitying her foolishness.

"I'm not going to tell you that, Hannah. This isn't a James Bond movie. I'm not going to lecture you for forty-five minutes about my motives. They're none of your business. Get out of the car."

"Hugh, no." She puts her hands over her stomach. "Please. You don't have to do this. I'm pregnant, doesn't that mean anything to you? It's not just me, it's my baby. You'd be killing my baby, *Will's* baby."

"Hannah," he says, very slowly, as if he's talking to someone very stupid, "get out of the car, or I will kick you in the stomach until your baby dies. Do you understand me?"

She goes completely cold.

Hugh is smiling at her pleasantly, and then he pushes his Stephen Hawking glasses up his nose.

"Please," she whispers. "Hugh please, I wouldn't tell anyone. I would never do that to you. You're my *friend.*"

"Oh please," Hugh says, and he sounds . . . amused, and a little sad at the same time. "We both know that's not true, Hannah. You wouldn't even turn aside when you thought it was Will you were protecting. Do you seriously expect me to believe you'd do it for me?"

"No," she says, and her throat is dry. "Not for you, no. But for my baby, I would. For my baby, I would keep this secret. If you let me go, Hugh, I swear — I swear on my baby's life —"

But he is shaking his head.

"I'm sorry, Hannah, it's too late."

He puts his hand in his pocket, and when he takes it out, Hannah goes completely still. He is holding a gun.

"You can't —" she manages, but her mouth seems to be too numb to speak. "You can't shoot me here — think of all the evidence — all the blood on your car. It won't look like a suicide."

Hugh sighs.

"I am aware of that, thank you. Get out of the car, Hannah."

She shakes her head. If she gets out, that's it, and she knows it. He cannot afford to kill her in his car; the evidence will be impossible to remove. Her only hope is to stay here as long as she can. But then, suddenly and without warning, he leans across the gap between them and slams the butt of the gun hard into her bump.

The shock is electric — a jolting pain that seems to run right through her body, making her scream, and the baby inside her flails like a fish, and Hugh shouts full into her face, "Get out of the fucking car, Hannah!"

It's the first time she's ever heard him swear, and she knows this is it — she can't prevaricate any longer — and half bent over, cradling her throbbing bump, she fumbles for the door handle and stumbles out into the drizzling rain.

"Walk over to the cliff," Hugh says. He is standing on the other side of the car, rain running down his face.

Stumbling, shivering, Hannah does as she's told. Hugh's jacket is still wrapped around her, and she has a sudden, piercing flashback to that night, so long ago, when they ran across the Fellows' Garden together, Hannah wrapped in Hugh's jacket. That was how it ended for April. And this is how it ends for her.

She is right on the edge of the cliff now. Behind her there is nothing but empty space and the pounding roar of the waves against the jagged rocks, ready to take her body and smash it into an unrecognizable pulp — a raw bloated mess that will cover up any bruises, wash away any DNA. And for Hugh, what's the worst that could happen? The taxi driver remembers taking her to his house? She has his DNA under her nails? All he needs to say is that she left early that morning, told him she was taking a train. Or a taxi. Yes, she seemed depressed, Officer. No, he doesn't know where she went.

Oh God, this is it.

"Throw me the jacket," Hugh says, and, shivering even harder, she pulls her arms out of the jacket and tosses it towards him. It lands in a crumpled heap at his feet. He takes it, and then nods at the cliff edge. "Now, jump."

Hannah looks behind her, over her shoulder, and shakes her head helplessly, hopelessly. She cannot do it. Not even if the alternative is Hugh shooting her, she can't bring herself to do it, to throw herself and her unborn child into that sea. She can't do it.

Hugh raises the gun.

And then Hannah's heart seems to stop in her chest, and start beating again with a quickening hope. Because above the roar of the sea, she hears a different kind of roar. The roar of an engine, coming closer. And a light, twisting and turning along the narrow lane. It's a motorbike, and it's coming fast, faster than is really safe on the rutted, unfinished road.

It's Will.

Hugh turns, distracted, shading his eyes against the glare as the light comes closer. And then he says something under his breath, something Hannah can't hear, and he turns to face the track as the rider skids around the last bend and bumps into the clearing.

Will roars to a halt, just a few feet away from them both, and scrambles off without even killing the engine, pulling off his helmet. His eyes are black with fear, but Hannah can tell he is trying to seem calm.

"Hugh," he says, holding out his hands. "Hugh — listen to me — you don't have to do this."

But Hugh — Hugh's shoulders are shaking.

For a minute Hannah doesn't understand. She looks from Will, hands outstretched, pleading, and then back to Hugh. Is he crying? He shakes his head helplessly, and then she sees — he is not crying but *laughing.*

"Hugh?" she manages. She takes a step forward, away from the cliff. The movement seems to tear at the muscles of her womb and a fresh wash of pain ripples across her stomach, radiating out from where Hugh hit her.

"You absolute imbecile," Hugh says now. He wipes what could be tears of laughter from beneath his glasses, but might be rain, or just plain tears. "You *idiot,* Will. You could have lived, don't you realize that? And instead, you've solved everything."

"What the fuck do you mean?" Will says. He takes a step closer and Hugh turns swiftly, pointing the gun at Hannah's stomach.

"Don't come any closer unless you want to see your baby *right now,*" he says, and his voice is suddenly cold.

"Okay, okay," Will says, and he puts up his hands. Hannah is trembling. Her eyes meet Will's. *I'm so sorry,* she tries to say. Will closes his eyes, shakes his head very slightly. *It doesn't matter, it's okay.*

Then he turns back to Hugh.

"What do you mean? Solved everything?" He's trying to sound calm, hopeful, but there's a tremor in his voice. But Hugh is shaking his head.

"It doesn't have to be a suicide anymore," Hugh says wearily. "Don't you get it? I mean I could have just shot her, but if the body washed up, a gunshot would have been hard to explain. But this — this is much better. You killed your first girlfriend, and then when your wife got suspicious . . ." He shrugs. "You shot her, and then you killed yourself. It's almost too perfect."

He raises the gun. Now it is pointing at Hannah's chest.

"Hugh, no," Will says. His voice is full of an agony so raw it makes Hannah's heart hurt. "Hugh, you were my *friend.*"

"I'm sorry," Hugh says. "But you just

made it too easy." He clicks off the safety.

Hannah closes her eyes. For a fleeting minute she wonders if dying this way will hurt, and how quickly her baby will die too.

And then she hears Will's anguished roar as he tackles Hugh. The gun goes off, a bullet whipping past Hannah's shoulder, and she ducks instinctively, even though the bullet is long gone, splashing into the sea.

Hugh and Will are rolling on the muddy ground, grappling each other, the gun sandwiched somewhere between them, Hugh's finger still on the trigger.

"Will!" she screams, as the two men wrestle wordlessly in the rainy darkness. She has no idea what to do. She wants to run to help Will, pull Hugh off him, but she can't risk another blow to her stomach. The side of her bump where Hugh hit her is throbbing now with a dull red heat and she is feeling an ominous tightening deep in her pelvis. "Will!" she screams again, his name tearing at her throat.

Hugh is below, and then on top, and then suddenly she sees the gun — he has dropped the gun, or Will has forced him to drop it, she's not sure. It is lying on the wet grass as the two men roll away from it towards the cliff edge.

Hannah knows what she has to do.

She runs for it, her bare feet slipping in the slick muddy grass, her belly griping with every unwary movement. But Hugh has realized what has happened, and he scrambles for it too, reaching it, grabbing it — the gun comes up, pointing towards Hannah. Will tackles him again, with the desperate strength of a man with nothing left to lose, throwing himself between Hugh and Hannah with a terrible reckless abandon — and then she hears it — the second gunshot, and then a third. Far louder this time, two tearing bangs that leave her ears screaming with shock.

Will goes limp.

And the blood begins to pool.

THE END

In the car, on the way to the crematorium, it starts raining. Hannah is glad. She sits there, staring out the window at the weeping world, and feels the tears slide down her own cheeks, soaking into the collar of her black coat.

"Are you okay?" Emily whispers from the seat beside her, and then shakes her head. "I'm sorry. Stupid question. How could you be okay?"

The driver of the funeral car says nothing. He is used to people weeping in the back of his limousine. The box of tissues between the seats is testament to that. Hannah isn't sure what he's been told — but he must know something about the circumstances of what's brought them here. The fact that this isn't a normal funeral — someone weary from old age, or taken early by cancer or heart disease or a thousand and one other inevitabilities of life.

No, this is a tragedy, nothing more, nothing less. And suddenly the unfairness of it all washes over her — the fact that Will should be *here,* with her, holding her hand, but he's not — and she has to go through this alone. And all because of Hugh, and her own unbearable, inexcusable stupidity.

It's like a bolt of anger tearing through her, and as the car draws up outside the crematorium, it's that more than anything that gives her the strength to stand up and make her unsteady, top-heavy way across the gravel to where the others are waiting — Ryan in his wheelchair, Bella with a sympathetic hug.

She can get through this. She *will* get through this.

And then the baby inside her gives a long slow kick, more of a press, pushing outwards against the wall of her womb so that she can actually see the tight-stretched black fabric ripple and move against the pressure, and she corrects herself.

They will get through this. Together.

"Are you ready?" Emily says, and Hannah nods.

"As I'll ever be."

"We've got you," Ryan says. And she nods again, and even manages a smile.

"His parents are already inside," Bella

says. "We should head in. Are you ready, Ry?"

Ryan nods, clicks the controller on his wheelchair, and they begin to move slowly up the ramp, towards the chapel of the crematorium.

Hannah is not sure what to expect when they enter the chapel. There are only two other people there in the cool dark, heads bowed, and they are the two people she has been dreading seeing. Because what can she say? What *is* there to say when the worst thing that can happen to a parent has happened to them?

But in the end, she doesn't need to say anything.

His mother simply comes to her and holds her in a wordless hug. And they stand there, the two of them, bathed in the light from the memorial window, the stained glass surrounding them both with a sea of blue and green. And then the organ music starts, Hannah wipes her eyes, and they turn to face the front, as the vicar intones, "We are here to commemorate the passing of Hugh Anthony Bland."

And Hannah knows it is really over.

THE BEGINNING

"Maternity's the other way!" the lady at the desk calls to Hannah as she passes through the front entrance and walks up the corridor towards the lift.

"Oh, I know," she shouts back over her shoulder. "I'm not here for me, I'm visiting my husband."

In the lift she stands, feeling the slow heave and shift of the baby inside her. Its movements have changed over the last week or so — *not* slowed down, as the midwives keep stressing. But instead of the frantic flurrying activity she has become used to, the movements are becoming more deliberate. Her child is growing into its limbs, and growing out of space to shift and turn. *It's flipped head down,* the midwife said at their last appointment. *I can't promise it'll stay like that, but . . . fingers crossed.*

She puts her hand on the hard round bump jutting out just below her ribs. Its buttocks, the midwife had said, tracing the long rounded curve of her belly. And there's its spine.

The lift pings and she heaves herself into action, out of the doors and up the corridor to the right, where Will's ward is situated.

He is sitting up in bed, talking to a doctor, nodding.

Hannah hangs back for a moment, unsure whether to interrupt, but Will sees her and his face lights up.

"Han, come and sit down. Dr. James, this is my wife, Hannah."

"Ah, so you're the lucky woman," the doctor says. "Fingers crossed we can have him up and about for the big day." He nods at her stomach.

"Dr. James was just saying I could probably get a discharge tomorrow," Will says, grinning.

"With conditions," the doctor says firmly. "And sign-off from occupational therapy. Because obviously your wife isn't going to be doing any lifting. You need to be able to maneuver yourself on and off the commode and so on."

Will makes a face and nods, but Hannah can tell he's taking it as read, and he puts out his hand and squeezes hers as hard as he can.

Afterwards, when the doctor has said his goodbyes and left, Will turns to her and pats the pillow beside him.

"Come on up."

"Will, are you nuts?" Hannah looks at the narrow sliver of bed, and then down at her own ample width. "There is no way I'll fit on there."

"Come on." He shifts himself across, wincing as he does. "You'll fit. I'll hold you in."

Gingerly, trying not to disturb the dressing on his side, Hannah climbs up and slides into the narrow space beside Will on the bed. She leans back against his arm, feeling him grip her shoulder with a surprising strength. She remembers that long, nightmarish wait for the ambulance in the darkness of the beach, Will's hand holding hers, slippery with his own blood, his grip faltering as he flickered in and out of consciousness, and her own heart stopping every time his grip slackened, imagining that this time, *this* time Will was slipping away from her, into the darkness, as Hugh had already done.

She shuts her eyes for a second, giving herself one long moment to acknowledge the horror of that night, and then opens them, firmly pushing the image away.

"Is that okay?" she asks, trying to keep her voice brisk and matter-of-fact. "I'm not hurting you?"

"You're not hurting me," he says. He brushes the hair off her face with his free hand, stroking her cheek with such tenderness that her heart clenches with love. "Now, tell me how it went this morning. Was it bad?"

"Oh, Will." She puts her hand over her face. "It was awful. His poor parents. The vicar was amazing, but what could he say? How can you celebrate a life like that, knowing what everyone knows?"

"I'm still kind of amazed they let you all come," Will says. "His parents, I mean. In their shoes . . . I don't know. I think I would have said no mourners."

Hannah nods slowly. She had been thinking the same thing in the limousine to the crematorium, wondering why Hugh's parents had said it was okay, but when she felt Hugh's mother's arms come around her, she thought she understood.

"I know. Me too, but in a way . . ." She stops, looking out the window across the Edinburgh rooftops. "In a way, I think they knew we needed to say goodbye too . . . Do you know what I mean? Like, it was closure or something. And maybe . . ." She gropes for the words she's seeking. "Maybe they needed to see me too. See that the baby and I were both okay, in spite of what he did."

"Yeah, I get that," Will says. He shifts, with a little grimace of pain, and Hannah tries to lean away from him, thinking she is hurting him, but then she realizes — he is reaching for his mobile. "Did you see," he says as he slides it towards himself with his fingertips across the bedside locker, "the police made a statement about Neville?"

Hannah shakes her head.

"No, I've not been online much. What did they say?"

"Just . . . Hang on . . . let me find it." He opens up his phone and begins scrolling down Twitter, awkwardly left-handed, because his right arm is holding her, then he stops. "Here it is." He reads aloud from the linked article: "Thames Valley Police announced today that in light of compelling new evidence recently uncovered, they would be asking the Court of Appeal to begin the process of quashing the conviction of John Neville, sentenced in 2012 for the killing of Pelham College student April Clarke-Cliveden. Mr. Neville died in prison earlier this year, having protested his innocence to the end. His solicitor, Clive Merritt, commented, 'It is a profound tragedy that John Neville did not live to see his exoneration, but died in prison for a crime which he did not commit. However, his friends and family will take comfort from the fact that his name will finally be cleared of this heinous crime.' Geraint Williams, spokesperson for the Clarke-Cliveden family, said, 'The Clarke-Clivedens extend their heartfelt sympathy to the Neville family over this grave miscarriage of justice. There is no joy, but some measure of relief, in the knowledge that justice will finally be done in this matter, allowing the friends and families of both April and Mr. Neville a peace they have been cruelly denied.' A Thames Valley Police spokesperson expressed their profound regret and condolences to Mr. Neville's friends and family. It is understood that no further persons are being sought in relation to the crime."

They sit in silence for a moment, Hannah trying to come to terms with all of this. She imagines November, huddled in a cafe with Geraint, trying to put into words feelings for which there *are* no words, feelings which she herself has spent almost every waking hour since Hugh's confession trying to figure out.

Because how do you come to terms with such a thing? How can Will live with such a betrayal by his best friend? And how can she live her life knowing that she condemned John Neville to a lonely, ignominious death?

"Hey." She hears Will's voice, feels his lips on her hair before she understands what is happening, realizes that there are tears running down her face. "Hey, Hannah, no. Listen to me. No more crying — do you understand? This wasn't your fault. It *wasn't* your fault."

"It was," she says. "It *was,* Will. I condemned him for being old, and weird and awkward — and that's on me, don't you understand? That will forever be on me."

"It wasn't your *fault,*" Will says, more urgently. "Hugh fooled you — but not just you, he fooled all of us. You, me, the police, the college authorities. Even April. Everyone. He was —" His voice cracks, and she remembers again his helpless crying in the days and weeks after the shooting. "He was my *best friend,* for Christ's sake. I loved him. And *I* introduced him to you, to April. Doesn't that make me just as culpable?"

Hannah lies back on Will's pillows, and she takes a deep breath, trying to quell her own tears. She knows Will is right. This is on Hugh — and only Hugh. And yet, she is right too. They all believed Hugh not because of what he was, but because of what he seemed — charming, gentle, harmless, handsome. All the things that John Neville was not. And that is on them. And it will be, forever. She will have to learn to live with that knowledge — for the rest of her life.

"I tell you what ticks me off," Will is saying now, bitterly. He wipes his eyes with an angry swipe of his free hand. "It's that line *evidence recently uncovered,* like Thames Valley Police were the ones who dug all this up. *Evidence handed to us on a fucking plate by a bunch of civilians at risk to their lives* would be nearer the mark."

Hannah nods. She and Will have talked about this — about that nightmarish night, about Will's long, terrified motorbike journey through the darkness with Hannah's voice whispering in his ear beneath his helmet as she drew Hugh inexorably through his confession. He has told her how it felt, that growing sick certainty as he sped around bend after bend, raced through tunnels, bumped over cattle grids, and he realized not just that Hannah was in trouble, but how and why.

It was his recording of that conversation that clinched everything with the police, and even now Hannah goes cold with a mixture of relief and fear when she thinks of that split-second choice, of what might have happened if Will hadn't made the decision to record her call. She could have ended up in jail herself — or Will could have. Because when the police had finally arrived, to find Hannah hysterical, Hugh dead, and Will shot through the side and bleeding out into the sandy soil of the clifftop, they had been inclined to treat Hannah as the potential killer, cuffing her and bundling her into a separate ambulance as Will was blue-lighted away into the distance.

Her story, after all, was almost too fanciful to be believable — a decade-old murder, her own growing doubts, and Hugh's actions — the kidnapping, the struggle, the shooting, first Will, and then himself, through the heart. Had his gun simply gone off as he and Will struggled back and forth with the barrel between them? Or maybe . . . Hannah thinks of his weariness in the car, the weight that seemed to be pressing down upon him as they drove deeper into the night. Maybe he had finally grown sick of the toll, of everything he had sacrificed to protect his own secret.

They will never know the truth about those final moments. Not even Will knows — the dark nightmarish struggle is as unclear to him as it is to Hannah, and all he remembers is his own pain, the shocking realization that he had been shot and was bleeding out, great gouts of spreading warmth. But it was Will's phone in Hannah's hand, sticky and red, the phone she had passed across to police, unlocked with shaking bloodied fingers, that spelled out everything else, Hugh backing up Hannah's story in his own words. *Bravo, Hannah Jones. So. You finally figured it out. I knew you would eventually.*

But she hasn't figured it out. Or not completely.

Because she still doesn't know why he did it. No one does.

In the taxi on the way back from the hospital she calls November on her new replacement phone, fills her in on the funeral, on how Will is doing.

"He might be out tomorrow," she says, and just saying the words sets up a little thrill inside her — the thought of having Will back home. Battered and bruised, to be sure, with a hole in his side the size of a fist, and black and yellow hemorrhaging that's spread across most of his torso, but *home.* It has been lonely these last couple of weeks, just her and the baby. Lonely, waking in the night gasping from nightmares that she is still there, still in that car driving to an unknown destination, with a man she knows to be a killer. Lonely, knowing that if something happens, if she goes into early labor or begins to bleed, it will be just her in the cab to the hospital, waiting for the doctors, trying to plead her case. The bruise where Hugh hit her has gone from blue-black to a sickly yellow-green, but she can still feel it sometimes in the night when she turns awkwardly, her whale-like belly dragging the blankets with her. It twinges, the torn muscles aching deep inside.

Her mother came up to stay for the first week, making her comfort food dinners like spaghetti and meatballs and big stodgy lasagnas. But after seven days, Hannah told her, gently, that she needed to go home. That she, Hannah, needed to get used to this, to managing by herself. And besides, she might need her mother here even more if Will wasn't out before she gave birth.

"Come and stay with me," her mother urged. "Just until Will's well again."

But Hannah shook her head. She couldn't leave Edinburgh, not with Will so sick, not even in the early days when all she could do was sit by his bed and watch his eyes flickering restlessly beneath closed lids. Still less once he woke up enough to miss her presence.

"And how were Hugh's parents?" November asks now, dragging her back to the present and Hugh's funeral. "Was it weird?"

"Oh God, November, it was *so* weird. I just . . ." Her throat fills with tears at the memory of Hugh's mother's fragile bewilderment, his father's stiff, brittle courage. "I had no idea what to say. He was their only child, their *everything*. What *can* you say?"

"And they didn't . . . they didn't throw any light on . . . why?" November asks.

"No," Hannah says sadly. "I mean . . . I didn't ask them. But they clearly loved him so much. I keep thinking about that last conversation I had with him at Pelham, before April died. When Hugh walked me back across the quad and talked about his father, and how proud he was of getting in to study medicine in his dad's footsteps . . . it just . . . it kind of breaks my heart a little."

"April always said he didn't belong at Pelham," November says. She sighs. "She told me once . . . how did she put it? Something about giving him a leg up, but it wouldn't do him any good in the end if he couldn't keep up."

"Giving him a leg up?" Hannah is puzzled. "But April didn't study medicine, how could she possibly have helped Hugh?"

"I don't know," November says. "I think a friend of hers helped people with their exams or something? Some kind of tutor maybe?"

Hannah's breath seems to stick in her throat. April's voice comes to her, as clearly as if she's on the other end of the line, with November. *Oh, that! I had an ex at Carne who made a pretty good living taking people's BMAT for them.*

And suddenly she knows.

It's like the last few boxes of a sudoku, with almost every grid completed so that the remaining numbers simply slot in, as easily as one, two, three.

One. Hugh's desperation to follow in his GP father's footsteps.

Two. April's *leg up.*

Three. The way Hugh had never quite felt up to the work at Pelham.

What was it Hugh had said? *Chin up, and we'll go easy on you in the exams.* And Emily's dry retort, just a few weeks ago but it feels like a lifetime now: *Ain't that the truth. There's no way I deserved a first, and I'm pretty sure Hugh wouldn't even have passed if it wasn't for April.*

So many small things made sense now. Hugh's shocked horror that first night, at finding April in the dining hall. The way April ordered him around, made him fetch and carry, forced him to come to her play, even the night before his most important exam. Why did Hugh keep saying yes? Hannah had never understood that. But now it made sense. Hugh literally could not afford to say no.

And finally . . . the pills. The innocent little capsules on April's bedside table, half-colored, half-clear. They had never figured out where April was getting those — it was before anyone knew about Silk Road and all the other darknet market sites. Back then, you had to know someone with access to a prescription pad. *NoDoz for grown-ups,* but not NoDoz at all. Stronger. Much stronger. Just as April had said to Hugh, that night at the theater. *Sod flowers. You should have brought something stronger than that, Hugh . . . Just what the doctor ordered, am I right?*

"Hannah?" November is saying now, on the other end of the phone. "Hannah? Are you still there?"

"Yes," she says. Her throat is dry, and she swallows against the obstruction. "Yes, yes, I'm still here. I think I know. I think I know what happened. Hang on." The taxi is pulling up to the mews, juddering over the cobbles, and she leans forward and pays the driver with her new, uncracked phone, and slides out to stand in the drizzling rain as the car drives off.

She feels a coldness sink over her as November says, "Hannah?"

"I'm still here," Hannah says. The rain is running down the back of her neck. "November, I think I know why Hugh killed April."

"Wait, what, you know? But just a second ago you were saying —"

"Yes, I know, but it was what you just said — about April giving him a leg up. She told me once, she told me that she had a friend, an ex-boyfriend, who took people's BMATs for them."

"What's a BMAT?" November sounds more bewildered, rather than less.

"It's the exam you have to take to get into Oxford to do medicine. It's really important — Hugh told me once that if you do well in the BMAT, that basically overrides your interview, it probably even overrides your A-levels to an extent. And Hugh did well. He did *really* well. He got one of the highest marks in his year. It was what made me so puzzled, when he was so anxious about his prelims — because he'd aced the BMAT, so why was he worried about some crappy little first-year exam? Except maybe . . . maybe he *didn't* ace the BMAT. Maybe someone else did."

"But — but how could he do that?" November's voice is shocked, uncomprehending. "April's ex, I mean. How could he pretend to be Hugh? Or anyone, for that matter?"

"I don't know," Hannah says. She is desperately casting her mind back, trying to remember. "If it was like the entry test I took for English, it wasn't like regular exams, you had to go to a testing center — and I don't remember anyone asking for ID. I mean, why would they — what are the odds that someone roughly the right age and sex is going to turn up claiming to be Hugh Bland just to take an exam in his place?"

"Unless . . ." November says slowly, "unless you were someone who'd been paid to do exactly that. But how would Hugh have paid this guy? It doesn't sound like he had much spare cash."

"He didn't," Hannah says. "But he had a father who was a GP, and probably access to his prescription pad. It wasn't digitized in those days — most GPs were still handwriting their prescriptions. How hard do you think it would be for a bright kid like

Hugh to steal a few scripts and write them out for lucrative prescription-only drugs?"

"Drugs like dextroamphetamine," November says, with a sudden, flat understanding. "Oh God. You even said it could have been a drug deal gone bad."

"I think it was *many* drug deals gone bad," Hannah says now. She feels an awful, desperate certainty. "April never did know when to stop, when she was pushing people too far. I remember her offering me the pills, the way she said *there's plenty more where those came from.* I mean, she'd been taking them for ages, hadn't she? Long before she came to Pelham. I think she must have been milking Hugh for drugs for months, ever since he took the test in fact. When she discovered he was at Pelham, she looked so pleased — like the cat that got the cream — and I couldn't understand it, even at the time, because they were never particular friends. But I think this must have been why. Her little drug supplier — not just there in Oxford, but right at the same college as her. And she held it over him all year — until he finally snapped. But what could he do? He had no hold over April, *she* wasn't the one who had taken the BMAT for him. She was just an innocent bystander. But April had a hold over him.

And she was going to keep using it. Maybe forever."

"But he didn't say anything," November whispers now. "He just told her sure, he could get her more drugs. And he probably even sympathized with her about you and Will, told her that she was quite right to be angry about Will fooling around."

"He must have helped her plan that last prank," Hannah says. "He probably suggested it, in fact. He must have convinced her to play dead, told her that he could persuade me there was no pulse, set me up to look an idiot in front of the Master and the rest of the college. And then, he leaned over her, pretending to be doing CPR . . ."

"And as soon as you left the room, he strangled her," November finishes. Her voice is flat. There is a silence. Hannah stands in front of the door and feels as if a strange weight is both lifting from her and pressing her down.

Oh, Hugh.

"I have to go," she says to November. Her voice cracks. "Will you be okay?"

"Yes, I'll be okay," November says sadly. "Bye, Hannah."

They hang up.

Hannah puts her key in the lock and climbs the stairs to the flat slowly, step-by-step. She is out of breath by the time she gets to the top, her lungs made shallow by the child pressing up from beneath.

Inside she goes and sits in the kitchen, by the window, staring out into the street.

She should be phoning Will for the latest news on his discharge, contacting occupational therapy, booking taxis, arranging grab handles, setting all the thousand and one things up for his return home. But she doesn't, even though she is longing for him with a force that is an almost physical ache inside her.

Instead she wakes her phone, goes to Google, and types something into the search bar — five words she hasn't had the courage to search for in almost ten years. *John Neville April Clarke-Cliveden.*

And then she presses search.

The pictures flicker up, one by one, and each one gives her a little reflexive jolt, a shock of muscle memory from the time when every news item made her flinch, every headline was like a punch to the gut.

'PELHAM STRANGLER' CONVICTION TO BE QUASHED, SAYS THAMES POLICE

JOHN NEVILLE INNOCENT. HOW DID THE POLICE GET IT SO WRONG?

She clicks through to one at random, and there they are. Neville, glowering out of the page from his college ID picture, April in a photograph taken from her Instagram page, glancing flirtatiously over her shoulder in an emerald-green handkerchief dress.

Hannah looks at them both — and for the first time in ten years, she finds she can meet their eyes, even though her own are swimming with tears.

She reaches out and touches their faces — John's, April's — as though they can feel it through the glass, through ten years, through death.

"I'm sorry," she whispers. "I'm so sorry, I let you both down."

She doesn't know how long she sits there, staring into their faces: April's laughing, full of secrets; John's dour and filled with resentment. But then her phone vibrates with the warning of a new email, and a little alert pops up. It's from Geraint Williams. The subject line is *How are you doing?*

She clicks through.

Hi Hannah, Geraint here. Hope you're doing okay, and the baby too. And I hope Will is feeling better. I spoke to November about your ordeal with Hugh; I'm so sorry, that sounds completely terrifying. I can't believe what a nice bloke he seemed. I guess he fooled all of us.

Listen, I thought twice about sending this, because I'm sure you've got enough on your plate with Will's injury and the baby being due in a few weeks, and you may not be ready to talk (plus I'm not sure how much you can say until the police are finished doing their bit). But, well, I'm working on the podcast again. It's a bit different from what I imagined, obviously. Neville's innocence isn't in dispute anymore, and most of the ten questions I posed in my original article are answered. So this one is going to be more about April and her life — and about the ripple effect of a crime like this. How the media treated her, her family, that kind of thing. I'm calling it THE IT GIRL. November's agreed to act as executive producer and I'm pretty pleased with how it's going. And what I wanted to say is, if you ever wanted to talk — put your side of the story. Well, I'd be honoured, that's all. Your choice, and no hard feelings if you don't or aren't ready just yet.

I'm so glad we managed to get some kind of justice for Neville, in the end. He was obviously quite a troubled man, but he didn't deserve that, no one does. I'll always be grateful to you for making that happen.

Anyway, don't answer straightaway. Take your time to think it over. But I'm here when you're ready to talk — whether that's six weeks, or six months, or even longer.

Geraint

P.S. The first episode isn't finished yet, but if you want to hear a rough cut of the opening, here's a link. Password is November.

Almost before she has had time to think better of it, Hannah clicks the link.

There is a short pause, and then a voice breaks the silence — not the one she was expecting, Geraint's. Instead it's a voice that's eerily familiar, one that raises the hairs on her arms. It is high and reedy, in a way that once made her shiver just to imagine it. It is John Neville. But he doesn't sound exactly like she remembers. He doesn't sound belligerent and self-important. He sounds . . . sad.

"April Clarke-Cliveden was one of the most beautiful girls I've ever seen," he says, the little sound bars rising and falling on her screen as he speaks. "They used to call her It Girl, because she had everything — looks, money, brains, I suppose, or she wouldn't have been at Pelham. Everybody knew her, or knew about her. But someone took that all away from her. And I will never stop being angry about that. I want that someone to pay."

Hannah reaches out and pushes the pause button on her phone, and for a long moment she just sits there, her hands pressed to her face, fighting tears. The baby turns inside her.

She thinks about Neville, about the truth, about how his voice has been silenced. She thinks about April. She thinks about the rest of her life, stretching out before her — a life that neither of them will ever have.

Her breathing steadies.

Then she crosses to her laptop and opens it up, bringing up Geraint's email. She wants to reply before she can change her mind.

Dear Geraint,

Nice to hear from you. I saw your name in the news as the CC spokesperson. I'm glad November's got you to support her with handling the press. As for me, I'm doing okay, thanks. So is Will — at least, he's not out of hospital yet, but they say he may be discharged soon.

I know you said not to reply straightaway, but I'm going to — I'm going to give you my answer now, and please know that it's not going to change.

I am ready. But not to talk. In some ways, I feel as if I've done nothing but talk. I've told my version again and again: to the police, to the courts, to you and November and Will. I've been telling it for more than ten years.

I've said everything. And now it's time for me to shut up — and move on.

I listened to the opening of your podcast, and I hope it's a huge hit. You know the truth, and you'll tell it well. And April's life deserves to be celebrated, just as Neville's voice deserves to be heard.

But I've said enough. I've given enough of my life to April's death.

Be safe. Stay well. Take care of November. She needs someone like you.

Love,
Hannah

She hovers for a moment, with her mouse over the paper airplane button, and then, very firmly, she presses it and the email whooshes away, leaving her staring at her inbox, and the line of folders ranked next to her unread emails. *Bills. House. Personal. Receipts.* And then finally, *Requests.*

Slowly, very slowly, she opens up the folder, and for the first time in years, maybe even the first time ever, she scans down the list of emails.

Hannah, urgent we talk! Fee available.

Message for Hannah Jones re Pelham Strangler case.

Important update on the Clarke-Cliveden case!!! Time sensitive!!!

ITV News request for comment re April update.

Interview request for Mail — please pass to Ms. Jones

There are dozens of them. Hundreds. Thousands, going back years, and years, and years. Slowly, very slowly, she checks the box marked "all." A dialogue box pops up: *All 50 messages on this page are selected. Select all 2,758 messages in Requests?*

She clicks to select all 2,758. Then she

moves over and presses the delete button.

This action will affect all 2,758 messages in Requests, her computer prompts. *Are you sure that you want to continue?*

She clicks okay.

The page hangs for a moment, as if giving her the chance to change her mind . . . and then the screen goes blank. *There are no messages with this label* it says.

Her email pings again, and she glances at it. It's from a reporter she doesn't know, someone called Paul Dylon. The subject line is *Urgent request for comment re quashing of Neville conviction, for 6 o'clock news.*

Hannah presses delete and watches as the message swirls away into the ether. She closes down her laptop, stands, and stretches long and hard, feeling the baby inside her shift luxuriantly, as if reveling in the extra space. The bones in her hips and spine click, and she releases a long breath.

Then she walks over to the cupboard in the corner of the living room, the one where they keep the screwdrivers and the Allen keys and the spare fuses. She pulls out the toolbox and takes it across to the window, clearing a wide space on the rug.

It's time. She has a crib to build.

ACKNOWLEDGMENTS

Beginning any novel is daunting (have I forgotten how to do it, will the plot come good), but writing about Oxford is a particular kind of challenge — it's been novelized so frequently and so well that it feels slightly hubristic to add to the pile of books about the college experience. It's particularly daunting when, like me, you didn't actually go to Oxford yourself, so huge thanks therefore to the friends who helped with my questions and queries about the minutiae of college life, entrance exams, and what exactly I could get away with in the name of artistic license — in particular Kate Bell and Chris Moore, Rosie Wellesley, Joe Moshenska, and Beth and Amanda Jennings. Thanks also to Fiona Nixon who answered my questions about studying medicine. Needless to say any stretches of the imagination are mine, as are any flat-out mistakes — and it probably doesn't need saying, but Pelham College is an entirely fictional entity, and its pastoral failings certainly aren't based on any real Oxford colleges.

Thank you to Sam Gordon for his advice on elimination DNA and crime scene processes, to AA Dhand for his pharmaceutical knowledge, and to Colin Scott for invaluable help with aspects of the court case (as well as countless other things).

A big thank-you to the two readers who supported the charity Young Lives vs. Cancer, also known as CLIC Sargent, by bidding to have their names included in the novel. Robyn Grant and Rubye Raye; your generous donations mean more than I can say, and I hope you like your characters.

Huge and heartfelt thanks to my fabulous agent, Eve, and her brilliant assistants Ludo and Steven, and many, many individual thank-yous to the small army of people who have supported this book behind the scenes at Simon & Schuster in the UK, US, and Canada, and at my publishers in other languages and abroad. To Alison, Jen, Suzanne, and Nita, I am thankful every day for your joint editorial brilliance and the faith you've shown in me and my characters. And to Ian, Jessica, Sydney, Sabah, Katherine, Taylor, Adria, Maeve, Felicia, Kevin,

Mackenzie, Gill, Dom, Nicholas, Hayley, Sarah, Harriet, Matt, Francesca, Jennifer, Aimee, Sally, Abby, Anabel, Caroline, Jaime, John Paul, Brigid, and Lisa — I owe each and every one of you a huge debt of gratitude for helping to shepherd this book out into the world, and for introducing it to readers. It is infinitely better (not to mention far prettier) than it was when I first typed "the end," and I will never stop being grateful for the care and attention you lavish on my imaginary creations.

Love and kisses to my family — you had nothing to do with this book apart from giving me the space to write it — but you make the nonwriting parts of my day so much more fun than they would be otherwise.

Finally, to my readers — and in particular *you,* the person reading these words right now — this book literally exists because of you, and I thank each and every one of you.

ABOUT THE AUTHOR

Ruth Ware worked as a waitress, a bookseller, a teacher of English as a foreign language, and a press officer before settling down as a full-time writer. She now lives with her family in Sussex, on the south coast of England. She is the #1 *New York Times* and *Globe and Mail* (Toronto) bestselling author of *In a Dark, Dark Wood; The Woman in Cabin 10; The Lying Game; The Death of Mrs. Westaway; The Turn of the Key;* and *One by One.* Visit her at RuthWare.com or follow her on Twitter @RuthWareWriter.